Under the Fig Tree

a novel by
Linda Harper

Copyright © 2023 Linda Harper

All rights reserved.

No part of this publication may be reproduced, distributed, or transmitted in any form or by any means, including photocopying, recording, or other electronic or mechanical methods, without the prior written permission of the publisher, except in the case of brief quotations embodied in critical reviews and certain other noncommercial uses permitted by copyright law.

Acknowledgment

Many thanks to Miss Nannie, an elderly lady who lived two doors down from my family when I was a child. She fired my ten-year-old imagination when she knocked on our door asking to "borry a cat." Her reason was simpler than Miss Millie's, she wanted to rid her house of mice. Maven, our cat who chose our lawn as a birthing place for her six babies and won our hearts, has taught me everything I know about cats. I'm grateful. My mother and my sister, Ann, now both deceased, fed my love of fiction with frequent visits to the library, a favorite place of my childhood. Books were honored treasures in my home. And, dear Vicky! Thank you for insisting that I publish the manuscript after it had rested comfortably on my desk for far too many years. My Spiritual Director, Jennie, helped me name, then push against, my resistance in pursuing publication. I'm indebted to all who read my manuscript over the years and offered excellent critique and encouragement, especially Tim, Steve, and Mike, brave men who gave their time to read a book such as this. Finally, and most of all, Phillip, I'm forever grateful for the time you've given to this project. It wouldn't have happened without you. You are forever my First Reader.

Dedication

For Phillip

Table of Contents

Nathanael asked, "Where did you get to know me?"

Jesus answered him, "I saw you under the fig tree."

John 1:48

Prologue

She slipped from her bed in the early morning darkness and padded down the hallway. The bathroom door hinges squeaked as she pushed it open, halting her movement momentarily. She held her breath, listened, and then breathed again. The noise hadn't awakened either of them. She closed the door, holding the round porcelain doorknob to the open position, releasing it slowly so there wouldn't be a telltale click, another opportunity to awaken her sleepers. She took three steps toward the commode, closed the lid, and sat, wrapping her arms tightly around herself. She stared at the beige tile wall an arm's length in front of her, her mood matched by the early morning darkness. For as long as she could remember, she'd thought of this time of day as Blue Time.

In the safety of the small enclosed space, she allowed the sadness to envelop her. All thoughts of what lay on the other side of the door—a loving husband, a beautiful baby boy, a promising life— weren't allowed to invade this private space of sorrow. She gave herself over to it. Post-partum, some called it. Not her, but some. The pain had been inside her for as long as she could remember, accompanied by a helpless feeling that life was going on around her as she watched. What should have been the happiest time of her life had instead increased this unnamed, unwelcome feeling to the point of being almost unbearable. The only time she allowed herself to indulge completely in wallowing in her grief was in the early morning hours when she slipped out of bed, fed the baby, rocked him back to sleep, then entered her little beige cocoon.

She laid her head on the cool porcelain of the sink. Shifting slightly, she slid her right arm underneath her head for a cushion. Her left hand curled into a fist, a fortification, a determination that she wouldn't give in to this *aloneness*.

Warm tears slid down her cool cheeks—a weakness, she knew, but one she gave herself over to. The tears dropped to the thin fabric of her nightgown, the moistness against her skin startling her for a moment. The leakages of childbirth were new to her, and for a moment, she attributed the damp feeling to that. The darkened spots on the front of her light blue nightgown seemed to shake something loose inside her, and, covering her face with both hands, she gave way to deep sobs. She was careful to keep them quiet; the home she shared with her new baby boy and only slightly less new husband was small. For a few short moments, she allowed herself the luxury of cleansing tears and sobs.

Abruptly she stopped. She stood, breathed deeply several times, soaked a washcloth with cold water, and held it against her throbbing face. When she looked, the mirror reflected a pretty oval face, puffy from her tears. Brown hair, recently cut in a short, easy-care boy-style haircut, was tousled from a night of tossing, turning, and frequent checking to see if the baby, snug in the bassinet beside her bed, was breathing. Her brown eyes, her best feature, were now framed with painful, swollen lids. She stared defiantly at her image. "This is your life," she said. "Be thankful for it. Forget the dreams..." Just in case her husband was awake, she flushed the toilet—lid still closed—straightened her shoulders, and opened the door to her life.

CHAPTER 1

"Main Street Groceries." Elizabeth Manley answered the phone and smiled as she watched Jackson, the younger of two amazing men in her life, shoulder his way into the store, his bulging backpack sliding towards the floor as he strode toward her, momentarily distracting her from her caller. "Miss Millie! I've already collected your order. Jackson just walked in, and as soon as he has a little snack, he'll be right over."

A sound, much like a cold, unused car engine coming to life, sputtered on the other end of the line. "I'm grateful I caught him then," Millicent Stich answered. "I need some additional items. Would you add two cans of tuna to the list? It doesn't have to be the best. Grated rather than chunk style will do just fine."

Liz felt a rush of sadness for the old woman. At three o'clock in the afternoon, she was probably hearing the only words spoken aloud by Miss Millie since their early morning phone conversation in which she had ordered groceries. As far as Liz knew, she was Miss Millie's only real link to the outside world. "You're eating an awful lot of tuna these days, Miss Millie. We have a nice ham salad in the deli, made fresh today. How about some of that?" By Liz's quick calculations, these two newest additions brought the total to ten cans of tuna in as many days.

"No, thank you, dear. Tuna serves my purposes very well. And, one more thing. Do you have a cat that I might borrow for a few days?"

"A cat? No, ma'am, I don't." Liz raised her eyebrows, held the phone out, and stared at it as if somehow these actions would make sense out of this nonsensical conversation.

"Well, then, just the tuna. And, of course, the rest of the items on the list I gave you this morning. I did mention that I need a litter box and cat litter, did I not?"

"Oh, you mean you want to *try* keeping a cat for a pet? Why, I think that's a great idea, Miss Millie. A cat will brighten up your life."

"Indeed! A cat will *complete* my life."

Liz hung up. That makes a little more sense, she thought. But why in the world is she buying food and other essentials when she has no cat? And apparently no prospects for getting one since she just asked to borrow one from me.

"Hey, Mom," Jackson's long legs stretched across the three steps to the elevated open corner office in one quick movement. He reached across her desk and gently ruffled her hair. At seventeen, he preferred to initiate the few displays of affection between the two of them. And while it tweaked her heart, she knew it was best. If he— and Richard—didn't hold her back, she would still tuck him in at night.

Jackson stuffed the last of a ham salad sandwich into his mouth and tugged the aluminum foil cap from a pint of orange juice. A package of cheese crackers peeked from the pocket of his shirt.

"Man!" he exclaimed. "No baseball practice, no track practice! Two weeks to do just what I want. Fish with grandpa, hang out with…"

"Deliver groceries," Liz interjected. "As in, right now. I just hung up from Miss Millie's three o'clock update. Her reminder call just in case we've forgotten her. You also have the Boyds, Mr. Frank, and fresh bread and milk for the nursing home."

"Slave driver," he teased. "Did you know they have laws against child labor?"

"You're seventeen," she reminded. "They don't apply to you."

Both mother and son liked the easy banter they exchanged. Not that they had ever been asked, but if they had, they—and Richard—would have answered that there was very little they would change about their family dynamics. Liz often questioned herself about the nagging unrest she felt, but never to the point of addressing it head-on. Her life, to those who observed—and to herself and her family as well—seemed almost perfect. A husband who loved her, a talented, good-looking son headed for his senior year and academic scholarships, and a thriving family grocery business in a solid community of two thousand people. She really couldn't ask for anything more. But in her secret heart, she did.

"Go to Miss Millie's first," she instructed, knowing as she said the words that he didn't need to be told.

"Mom, something strange is going on with her," Jackson said.

"I know, something about a cat. She wants a cat. It'll be good for her."

"Mom! She's trying to *catch* a cat. When I was there on Monday, there was this big yellow and white cat in her backyard. She wanted me to take a bowl of that tuna she keeps buyin' and try to get it to come inside. That old cat just ran off, like I knew it would, and I just hoped nobody saw me. Do you think she might have that old timers disease?"

"Alzheimer's, Jackson. And no, her mind is as sharp as mine. I think she's just lonely and wants a cat for a companion."

"But you can't go takin' somebody else's cat," Jackson argued. "That's the same as stealin'. Cats don't always stay in their own yards."

Jackson left muttering to himself about that "crazy old lady."

"Be nice, Jackson. You'll be old yourself someday," she called after him.

***

Jackson parked the 1995 red two-door Honda Accord he'd inherited from his mother on his sixteenth birthday on the street in front of Miss Millie's. He efficiently popped the trunk lid open and the last cheese cracker into his mouth at the same time. He checked his hair in the mirror, noting as he did the similarity of his haircut to his mother's, thanks to Loretta, who had cut both his and his mother's hair for as long as he could remember. "I've got to find somebody else to cut my hair," he muttered. Unlike his mother, who loved hearing that her son looked just like her, he cringed at the thought. Both mother and son had cropped brown-black hair, dancing brown eyes, and complexions that turned a deep golden brown well before June each year.

Miss Millie was standing on her front porch waiting for him, dollar bill in hand. He'd long ago given up explaining to her that she didn't need to tip. "It's part of our service" (words from his father), he'd said to her so many times before.

"But, my dear, I'm tipping your *smile,* not your service," she'd reply each time.

"Thank you, Miss Millie," he said as she gently tucked the folded dollar bill into his shirt pocket and opened the screen door on the left side of the porch. Always the left, never the twin door to the right of the long front porch. The house reminded Jackson of his first lessons in symmetry from second grade when his teacher instructed the class to fold a piece of paper, draw a simple design starting and finishing at the fold line, and then cut it out. Liz had kept a supply of recycled papers in the grocery store office from which he created an entire colony of symmetrical "outer space monsters."

"Right through here," Miss Millie directed. As if he didn't know. As if he hadn't carried bags of groceries through these same musty rooms at least twice a week since the beginning of time. Well, at least since he had been driving. Living room, dining room, kitchen. "Here we are. Just right over there on the table." She pointed to the exact spot on the table every time.

The table, as with all the furniture in the house, had not been updated in years. The said table, white Formica top with an inch-wide red border at its edge, sported shiny chrome legs and trim. It was pushed to the window behind it, and three matching chairs, red plastic with a white plastic V running down the center of the backs, were pushed against it. All in perfect condition. On the table sat a clear glass sugar bowl with matching salt and pepper shakers. A stack of folded white cloth napkins rested in a small wooden bowl. Standing behind the cluster of necessities accented by the white of sheer curtains in the background was a carved Madonna and child, a beautiful silver and pearl rosary draped around her neck. Single square-inch alternating black and white tile rectangles gave both the kitchen floor and countertops the appearance of giant checkerboards.

"I have just one small favor to ask of you, Son."

"What is it, Miss Millie?" Jackson asked, peering through the open screen door into the backyard. No cat.

"I've attempted—and failed, I might add—to prop this screen door open. I think if I set a tuna trap for that old cat, a small dollop on the stoop with a larger serving inside the door, she just might take the bait. Then, instead of eating my tuna and running off for further exploration, I'd have her right here inside with me. What do you think?"

"I think it'd be a whole lot easier to go to the animal shelter over in Batesville and pick up a kitten nobody wants."

"Oh, no, my dear! I don't want to *own* a cat. I fully intend for the owners to have this one back. I just need it for a short time."

Mom's wrong on this one, Jackson thought. She really has gone looney-tunes. He decided against asking *why* she wanted to use a cat and then return it.

"What do you need me to do, Ma'am?" Jackson asked.

"Well, what I've attempted to do—and, as I've told you, failed— is to get this broom to hold the door open. Just enough to allow the cat to squeeze through, mind you, and not wedged in so tightly that I can't grab it quickly when the cat enters. Do you think you might help me?"

Jackson made several unsuccessful attempts to prop the door open before he hit on a plan. He set a chair behind the wooden door, braced it against the wall, removed the detachable broom from the broomstick, and wedged the stick between the screen and the main door.

"Perfect," Miss Millie declared after she had removed it and replaced it herself. "What a brilliant mind you have, Jackson. You make your parents proud."

"I'll let myself out, Miss Millie. You have a good day now."

"One more thing, dear, before you go. Is there a food for cats that doesn't require refrigeration? One that can be left out for several days at a time."

"Yes, Ma'am, we carry two or three different kinds of dry cat food at the store."

"Then I'll need some of that eventually. Would you be so kind as to ask your mother to have that ready for my next order?"

I'm asking Mom to switch her over to morning delivery, Jackson thought as he continued on his route. Darren can play cat catcher for a while. Miss Millie had gotten a loose screw and a loose tongue all at the same time. Never before had there been more than two or three pleasant exchanges between them during a grocery delivery.

***

Richard Manley was scraping the last of the ham salad into a large plastic container when Jackson slid around the display case.

"What's next, Dad? Do you want me to start with stocking?"

"Hey, Jacks. I didn't expect to see you this early. Don't you have some kind of practice you need to see to? Baseball? Trumpet?"

"You forgot, no baseball. We're finished with school ball for the season, and summer ball doesn't start for two whole weeks. Man! Two whole weeks with nothin' but school and work. It's like a vacation."

Richard's pride in his son erupted into a smile on his face. What a kid! He had his mother's easygoing personality and Richard's own penchant for work.

"Soon as I finish cleaning out the deli case, I need you to deliver this leftover food to the nursing home." Rather than toss out prepared food left over from the noon offerings of the grocery store's popular deli, Richard always sent any significant leftovers—an infrequent occurrence—for the staff to share for supper. Not only did it prevent food waste, something he abhorred, but it gave the workers something to look forward to. His food creations were wildly popular in Roslyn, Mississippi.

Richard had begun three years ago by offering cold-cut sandwiches loaded with fresh lettuce and tomatoes on his own home-baked bread. Slowly, he had added to the menu: homemade soup, vegetable and pasta salads, and saucer-sized fresh-baked cookies. He was constantly experimenting with different sandwich spreads. The little deli had become so popular that he had hired Cora Lee Wilhelm to work an additional check-out station just to cover the noon rush. Also an excellent cook, she often helped Richard with the cooking, especially baked goods and pastries. Richard loved the grocery store, but his passion was preparing good food.

"Cora Lee had to leave early today. We didn't have time to get this ready for her to drop off. When you come back, you can take over stocking shelves. Edward'll need to get on home. His mama expects him by 5:15, and she'll walk clear to the store if we don't get him home on time. We don't want her having a heat stroke or a heart attack walking all that distance." Edward Myatt, a middle-aged man who'd never found the courage to leave home, lived with his elderly mother. She often began walking towards the grocery store to meet him as he returned from work, walking him back home as one would a small child.

"Can I leave by 7:00?" Jackson asked. "I was go'n pick up ..."

"Yeah, yeah. I know. Lainie. Sure. Just be home by 9:00. You may be on *vacation*, but you still have school tomorrow."

Richard tucked his worries away. He had to keep in mind just who his son was. If he didn't, Liz's obsessive concerns about the amount of time Jackson and Lainie spent together would eat away at his own peace of mind. Lately, they seemed inseparable.

CHAPTER 2

Liz infrequently manned a check-out lane at the grocery store, and when that happened, she enjoyed the mindless movement of items across the conveyor belt. She liked picking up her customer's chosen items and scanning them as they chatted with ease. The talk was usually about the weather, school and church events, or how the fish were biting. It was a welcome relief from the tedious and endless ordering and balancing of books, which occupied most of her time in the store.

When Grace Carlson showed up in her line for check-out, Liz reminded herself that she would have to endure the badgering for, oh, say, three minutes. Then, she would be on her way. Liz was sure Gracie's mother would have found another name had she known how Grace-less her daughter would become. Or maybe she had taken one look at her tiny infant and sensed that the child would need a constant reminder that grace was forever available in this world. Perhaps the childish name *Gracie* stuck early because Grace was too big for her to live up to. It seemed to Liz, however, that the old woman didn't give any signs of familiarity with the concept of grace.

"Yes, Miss Gracie, these kidney beans were three for a dollar. I charged you 34 cents because you bought one. Here, let me take a penny off this can of biscuits. There, it all works out."

Liz glanced at her watch: 3:15. She was due at church at 4:00 to put the finishing touches on Wednesday night dinner and to get the serving line started. No time to run home and freshen up. The way Miss Gracie questions every price, I probably won't make it on time anyway, she thought. "Yes, Miss Gracie, that banana *is* slightly bruised. Let me finish checking you out, and I'll go pick a better one for you." Better to soothe and placate than to confront and argue.

"Mom, you have a phone call." Liz glanced up, relief showing on her face, glad that her son had arrived in time to take over the register and allow her enough time to brush her hair and teeth in the bathroom in the back before showing up for duty at church.

"Take a message. I'll call as soon as I get Miss Gracie taken care of."

Jackson edged in behind her. "Let me finish up with her. It's Miz Clark, and she says it's an emergency. She needs to talk to you right now."

Liz wondered what kind of emergency Mrs. Clark, an acquaintance who drove to Batesville for her groceries rather than shop locally, could possibly have that involved her. She picked up the waiting phone. "Yes, Mrs. Clark? How can I help you?"

"Elizabeth, my boy Jacob just got in from school. He and his friend Mike—you know, Hester's grandson? —anyway, they were all a fluster. They said they stopped by Miss Millie Stich's house to check on the cat. You know Miss Millie took on Mike's cat a few days ago? They knocked on the back door, and nobody came. They peeked in the little slit in the curtains and saw Miss Mille laying there on the floor, that little gray cat sitting right beside her like she was guarding her or something."

Liz's mind raced. The cat ... when had she last talked to Miss Millie? Last Monday? Jackson had been there and helped her prop the door open with the broomstick. She had called on Thursday and ordered dry cat food—"the best you have, with no harmful additives"—another litter box and litter. At the time, Liz had wondered about the necessity of two litter boxes for one cat, especially since Miss Millie's house was rather small and there was no second floor. She dismissed the thought with an "Oh well, stranger things have happened with Miss Millie and the cat adventure."

Dear God in Heaven! She hadn't talked to Miss Millie on Monday. How on earth had she let that slip by? Today was Wednesday ... how long had she been on the floor?

"Elizabeth, are you there?" Nell Clark's voice brought her back to the present.

"I'm here, Mrs. Clark. Did you call an ambulance?"

"I did. They've already been there and taken her. They took her up to the hospital in Senatobia. Wouldn't tell me a thing about her condition. I couldn't tell if she was breathing or not when they took her out, and she didn't make a sound. She must have still been alive though because they didn't cover ..."

"Thank you for calling me, Mrs. Clark." Liz knew that if she didn't interrupt and hang up, the woman would have continued talking until sundown. In Roslyn, people, especially women, had to make their own drama, and years of experience produced some very creative players. Mrs. Clark was one of several.

Liz grabbed her purse and hurried to the register that Jackson had taken over from her, only to be met with another mini-emergency.

"Miss Gracie, the sign says *Buy one pound, get one free.* You just have one pound."

"I know how many grapes I have, young man. I don't need *two* pounds of grapes. There's just one of me. What you can do is let me pay for half a pound and give me half a pound free."

"But, Miss Gracie ..."

"Take them, Grace." Liz had never spoken to the woman in such a short tone. "Consider them a gift." She turned to her son. "Put them in her bag, Jackson. We need to talk."

***

Liz left Jackson with instructions to call the church and let them know that something had come up. Fretfully, she had made the decision. It was almost impossible for her to fail to meet a commitment, but she knew there was someone who could fill in for her, and, as far as she knew, there was no one who could see to Millie Stich. She reached Interstate 55 and headed to Senatobia, a larger town some fifteen miles north of Roslyn. Glancing at her watch, she realized that only ten minutes had passed since her conversation with Nell Clark. At least the woman had made the right call about the hospital. How Mrs. Clark knew that the old woman's doctors were in Senatobia and not in Oxford, Liz didn't have a clue, although she suspected it was the product of Roslyn's active gossip mill. Whatever the source, Liz was grateful for this small blessing.

For the past three years, Liz had taken on the role of medical taxi for Miss Millie. One of the grocery delivery boys had reported that the woman's car was sporting a "For Sale" sign. When Liz questioned her about her reason for selling it in one of their telephone grocery-ordering conversations, the explanation was that she was too old to contend with the heavy volume of traffic. Besides, Miss Millie had explained, the only place she really needed to go any longer was to Senatobia for her medical visits. Further questioning led to the understanding that a taxi would be her choice of transportation. "A trip to my doctors' offices, a brief stop at Walgreens for prescriptions and necessities of the drugstore variety, that's all I need, my dear. It's not worth taking the chance of allowing an old woman like me amid all that traffic. I'm a danger to the safety of others."

"But, Miss Millie, we don't have a taxi service in Roslyn," Liz had explained.

"That's of no consequence, my dear. I've already checked it out. There's a taxi service in Senatobia. I plan my trips to the doctor well in advance so all of that can be arranged beforehand."

Liz couldn't imagine what the cost might be, and she had no idea what her elderly friend's economic situation was. What she couldn't accept, however, was the image of this proper old woman, seemingly alone in the world, sitting on the back seat of a taxicab. She imagined a variety of sordid episodes that could have occurred there. While taxicabs were a necessity in New York City or Chicago, they served an altogether different purpose in small towns, especially in an area like theirs that was populated with college students and lake vacationers. The town of Roslyn had miraculously held on to its small-town values and was largely unaffected by the tourism of the lakes area, the college population of Oxford, and the proximity of Memphis, Tennessee, a mere hour away. In Roslyn, people took care of people. If one needed a ride to the doctor, one simply asked a neighbor. "I'll take you to your doctors' appointments," Liz had blurted. Even as she said the words, she wondered how she would find the time to squeeze yet another activity into her busy life.

After much discussion—Miss Millie insisted on paying her, and Liz refused—they agreed on a solution that worked for both of them. Liz had long supported St. Jude's in Memphis and suggested that, instead of giving her money that she really didn't need, Miss Millie send a donation there, whatever amount she thought she could spare. Two days after the first trip to the doctor, Liz received a note from Miss Millie. *My Dear Liz, I insist on paying for the gas required to make the trip and the wear and tear on your vehicle.* Tucked inside was a twenty-dollar bill. On subsequent trips, Liz pretended not to notice as the folded bill was tucked in her console. She knew she couldn't win the argument.

Liz parked her car near the emergency room entrance to North Oak Memorial Health Center and checked in with the receptionist.

"Are you family?" the woman asked.

"No, a friend," Liz replied. "As far as I know, Millie Stich has no family in the area. I'm not absolutely sure, but I don't know of anyone she depends on more than me."

"Well …," the receptionist shuffled through papers on her desk and wheeled her chair to a desk away from the office window. Liz watched as she talked to a young girl wearing a blue smock sprinkled with brightly patterned butterflies, some on flowers resting with folded wings, others in flight. Details. She was always distracted by details. It seemed apparent to Liz that, in spite of her whimsical attire, the young woman had more clout than the woman seated in the desk chair. The pretty blond nurse—Liz had decided she must be a nurse—glanced her way. Liz knew that she was getting a three-second assessment and met the professional's eyes with a calm expression on her face.

Concerned as she was for Miss Millie's condition, she really didn't feel any emotional attachment or distress over the situation. Trips to the doctor had increased in frequency in recent months, but their relationship had remained static. Conversation centered on the weather, Jackson's activities, and recent events discussed in the newspaper and on television. Neither shared anything personal.

The young nurse stepped to the window. Liz had apparently passed the test. "Miss …?"

"I'm Liz Manley," she said. "My husband and I own the grocery store in Roslyn and … well, I guess I've kind of inherited Miss Millie because we deliver groceries to her. I bring her here to Senatobia for her doctors' appointments …"

"Could you tell me the names of her doctors?" the nurse interrupted. "By the way, I'm Michelle Orb. I'm assisting with your friend's care. Dr. Stevens is with her now."

"Her internist is Dr. Thomas, but she's been seeing a Dr. Radcliffe for the past year. He's a heart specialist?" Liz felt slightly embarrassed to claim friendship with Miss Millie and know so little about her. "Really, I'm not much more than an acquaintance. I bring her for her doctors' appointments because she …"

"You're very kind, Mrs. Manley. And this helps us. We don't have much to go on since your friend is still unconscious. We're in the process of admitting her; she'll be in the ICU, so your contact with her will be limited. Would you like to come back with me and see her now? Maybe hold her hand and let her hear your voice?"

Liz followed the trim young nurse, who looked no older than Jackson but had the professional manner of someone much older, down the hallway to a small, curtained cubicle. She looked down at the frail old woman. Everything was white: sheets, hair, face. There was no movement except for the tiny flutter of heartbeat in Miss Millie's neck. The only sound in the room was the hiss of oxygen and the beep of the IV machine. For the first time, she felt real compassion for the woman, and her eyes pooled with tears. She's a real person, Liz thought, and I've never treated her as such. Whom did she love, and who loved her? What did she *do* during her life? She felt a sudden yearning to know the answers to these questions. Liz took the small hand in hers and looked closely at the perfectly manicured and buffed nails on the bent, bony fingers. She'd observed Miss Millie's hands in the past as they'd gone to appointments and had wondered then about the careful grooming. She wondered again, "Who is this woman?"

The nurse touched Liz's elbow. "Would you like someone to show you to the ICU waiting room? We should have Mrs. Stich settled there in about half an hour, and you could see her before you leave. The nurses will take your contact information in case ... once you're ..." The young woman was also touched by the situation: a human being, probably at the end of her life, utterly alone.

"I'll ask the receptionist for directions," Liz said. "Thank you for all you've done."

***

In the waiting room, Liz picked up an old copy of *Better Homes and Gardens,* dated June 1998. The magazine was floppy from use; its pages ruffled at the edges. She fanned through the pages and absently stopped at a feature about building your own greenhouse. A memory came to her as clearly as if she had experienced it last week. Her *greenhouses.* That's what she'd called them. She didn't even know what a greenhouse was, but she had given her creations that name. In her 5-year-old way of thinking, they were houses, and there was lots of green. Moss, to be exact. Green moss.

It occurred to Liz now, waiting in the little ICU alcove, that her favorite tree to play under had been next to Miss Millie's front yard. She hadn't thought of it in years, but now she realized that there *was* a connection between the two of them: an old lady and a child. If they had ever exchanged a word, she couldn't remember it. She remembered, however, looking up from her play more than once and seeing Miss Millie—that's how her parents had always referred to her—gazing out the window. They would make brief eye contact before Liz returned to her gardens. Once, the woman—she seemed old to Liz even then—had stepped outside on the porch from the door on the right and sat quietly watching Liz. Liz had looked up at her for a moment and returned to her work. She thought now of the … *encouragement*? she had felt coming from the woman.

"Mrs. Manley?"

Liz looked up to see a rotund, balding man in a white coat approaching.

"I'm Dr. Stevens from the emergency room. We have Mrs. Stich settled now. She's still unconscious but stable. We've contacted both her doctors and will turn her care over to them. Do you have any idea what happened?"

"I'm sorry, but I don't," Liz apologized. "Like I told the nurse, I really don't know her all that well. We've lived in the same small town, Roslyn, and I've known *of* her all my life but have only recently become a part of her life. And really not a part; we deliver groceries to her twice a week, and I bring her here for her doctors' appointments, but I don't ..."

Liz saw the slightly impatient look in Dr. Steven's eyes and realized she was babbling on without really answering his question.

"No," she said simply. "I don't know what happened. Do you?"

"We thought perhaps a stroke but have ruled that out. I'm pretty sure she didn't have a heart attack, although we've detected a rather serious heart condition. She had a pretty good lump on her head, but, of course, she had fallen. We just don't know what made her fall. She owned a cat?"

Liz paused. How do you answer *that* question? "Well, maybe."

His facial expression—just the hint of a raised eyebrow and the slightest uplift of his head—cautioned Liz to choose her words carefully. Clearly, the doctor already thought he was in over his head with Miss Millie and her and was counting the minutes until he could turn the case over to her regular doctors.

"I know that she wanted a cat and was ordering supplies from us so that she would be prepared in case she got one." That was the truth, simply spoken.

"One of the ambulance attendants reported a gray cat running out the door when he went in the house to see your friend. We're surmising at this point that perhaps she tripped over the cat. She seems to have lain there for at least a couple of days. She's severely dehydrated, so we're administering fluids intravenously. The next 24 hours will be crucial, but as I said, she will be in the hands of Dr. Thomas and Dr. Radcliffe now."

Liz thanked him and shook hands before following him back to the Intensive Care Unit. She gave her phone numbers and work schedule to the attending nurse and walked over to her friend's bed. Again, she was struck by the whiteness of everything. Only occasional stainless-steel connectors, clear tubing, or mysterious wires offered relief. It was a picture void of color except for the pale blue hospital gown that covered Miss Millie's chest, a blue that added to the icy cold feeling of the scene, a wintry study in black and white. Is this what humans are reduced to in the end, Liz wondered?

"I'm here again, Miss Millie. It's Liz Manley. They're taking excellent care of you here in the hospital, and your doctors know you're here. I have to go home now, but I'll be back tomorrow." She paused, tears again forming in her eyes. "You're not alone, you know. We'll help you get better, whatever it takes." In her heart, she said a prayer. Please, God, don't let her die. Give me a chance to get to know her. No one should die without being known.

CHAPTER 3

The clock on the dash showed 8:02. It had only been four hours since Liz left the grocery store, but she had the same feeling one often experiences on returning home from a long trip. It seemed that the hospital clung to her, that in the few short hours she spent there, she had lost touch with the rest of the world. Liz decided she had been either exceptionally lucky or healthy—possibly both. Except for the few days when Jackson was born and the occasional visits to friends or family members who were hospitalized for brief illnesses or births, she had spent virtually no time in hospitals. Her mother had died quietly at home, and her dad ...? She had given little thought as to where her father had actually died.

Liz had found her mother lying in a pool of sunshine on the sun porch. She had looked peaceful and relaxed on the daybed with its faded pink and green floral cover. She appeared as though she had stretched out for a nap and had drifted off, which was probably exactly what had happened. An open copy of *Reader's Digest* still rested on her chest, clutched in her hand. Her mother had died just the way she had lived, without complaint, without notice. Her heart simply quit beating. Liz was grateful that her mother hadn't lingered in a hospital bed connected to machines with tubes and wires. She only wished there had been time for talk. So many questions left unanswered. So much silence.

Tears sprang to her eyes, and she reached up to brush them away. Interstate driving was not her favorite thing to do, especially at night. It certainly wasn't the time to relive the painful past. She turned the radio on to be blasted by Mariah Carey's "Always Be My Baby" and quickly turned the volume down and changed the station. Jackson. She'd sent him to fill her car with gas when he'd come in from school earlier. She pushed buttons until she found a news station. McCain had endorsed his up-to-now arch-enemy, George

W. Bush. Turning the radio off, she declared to the darkness, "Always a hot news story. At least we've survived the doomsday mentality of Y2K and moved on to something else."

She intentionally turned her thoughts to the present. Graduation was next week, and while it would be an entire year before Jackson walked down that aisle, as an active PTA member, she was very involved in helping with the plans for this year's graduating class. Each year, First Baptist and First Methodist took turns hosting the baccalaureate service, and this year, it was up to First Baptist, her church. As usual, her role involved food. She was in charge of arranging the reception—really a small luncheon—for graduates and their parents after the service. Next year, as luck would have it, First Methodist would host, leaving her free to enjoy the time with Richard and Jackson.

There is so much to do next school year: visit colleges, complete applications. It seemed like yesterday that she was doing the same things for herself. *By* herself. And to what end? Well, for starters, an end to her menstrual cycle and, as time went on, an end to her dream of a Master's in Fine Arts at Mississippi Southern. But she had Richard. And Jackson. She had a second chance through her son; he would be able to do all the things she had dreamed of for herself. Not writing, Jackson wasn't a writer, but he would be able to get away from this small town that she'd allowed to trap her. He could see the world and then *choose* where he settled in. Her musings about Jackson's future accompanied her to the driveway of her perfect home, her refuge from the confining world that surrounded her.

Lights shone from every window on the lower floor of the house. They're home, she thought; my boys are home. The sight of her lighted haven made her heart jump. She and Richard had built this house five years ago. They had designed it themselves and, with the help of family members and friends, had also decorated and furnished it. It helped to have generous, talented people in the family. Liz had once lamented to Richard, "How did I end up the only one with no talent?"

"You? No talent?" he'd said. "How can you say that about yourself?"

"Look at the people in this family," she'd responded. "There are contractors, interior designers, floral designers, hair stylists, landscapers ... I could go on, you know. Then there's me. I balance the books at the grocery store." Even as she spoke the words, she remembered the little notebooks of scribbled phrases in the drawer of her bedside table. Scribbles she shared with no one, not even Richard.

"Hey boys, I'm home," she called now as she entered.

"In here, Mom," Jackson called. "Lainie 'n me are in the kitchen."

Jackson and Lainie sat at the big trestle table with books and empty bowls scattered about. Liz dropped her purse in a chair and slid coasters under sweating glasses of soda. "Looks like you're hitting the books pretty hard there, kids," she said.

"Oops, sorry, Miz Manley," Lainie apologized as she adjusted the coaster. "I have a chemistry final tomorrow, and Jackson's helping me get ready. I don't know what I'd do without him."

Liz couldn't keep the thought from forming in her head: *In just one year, you'll find out.* Liz didn't dislike Lainie; in fact, just the opposite. She liked her a lot, but she also saw her as an obstacle to Jackson leaving this town behind. Their friendship had begun way back when Jackson was in fourth grade. Lainie, a third grader, had moved to Roslyn during the summer from the Mississippi coast.

They'd had their share of disagreements, but those never lasted long. Their "official" first date had been last summer when Lainie turned sixteen, and it seemed to Liz that, even at their young age, they had a strong commitment to each other. Liz looked forward to the separation that would be forced by Jackson going away to college.

"Where's your dad? Did he make dinner? I'm starved." As she spoke the words, Liz realized how hungry she really was.

"He's in the study. Yeah, he brought home some new recipes he made to serve in the deli tomorrow. It's some kind of chowder, he says. Tastes pretty good. What is chowder anyway?"

Liz left the explanation to Lainie and found Richard sprawled in his old leather chair, sock-clad feet crossed on the footstool in front of him. On the TV screen, two men and a woman all talked at once about the significance of John McCain endorsing George Bush for president. All three seemed to have differing opinions and were intent on expressing them at the same time.

"How do they know what the other one is saying?" Liz asked. She walked over and planted a kiss from behind on top of Richard's head. "Hi, Hon."

Richard laughed. "That's the idea. If they stopped and listened to somebody else, they might need to rethink their own position. They're not about to do that." Grabbing the remote, Richard switched channels. "I meant to put that new show on, the one with Regis Philbin ... something about being a millionaire?"

"'Who Wants to Be a Millionaire?'" Liz said. "And it's not new; it's been around for months now. Shows how little time we have to watch TV in this house. At least they take turns talking; questions, then answers, one at a time."

"You look beat. What's going on? Jackson said something about that little old lady he delivers groceries to. Miss Millie?"

"Millicent Stich, to be accurate. She's in the hospital, and as far as I can tell, there is a total of zero relatives around here. Not even any real friends. Can you imagine being in that situation?"

Richard shook his head. "I can't." Then he grinned, "Not to say there aren't times I'd *like* to be in that position. I could use a little quiet time every now and then. Just me and my boat—my daddy's boat—out on the big blue lake.

"Have you eaten? I waited for you. Soup's in the fridge. The kids said it's pretty good, but you can be the final judge."

Liz shook her head in response to his question. "Jackson said you'd tried a new recipe for the deli tomorrow. I'm famished. If you don't mind, I'm going to take a quick shower and change while you get it ready."

She was speaking to his back as he made his way to the kitchen. She smiled to herself and wondered, "How did I get so lucky?" How many 18-year-olds have the wisdom to make good decisions, especially about a lifetime commitment like marriage? Even as she allowed the thought to form, Liz recognized that it wasn't wisdom— or luck—that had brought them together permanently almost 18 years ago. Serendipity? Providence? But not wisdom. If she were forced to name what had brought them to this place in their lives, she could only say Divine Providence. She knew that at a time in her life when she couldn't make a sound decision, God had looked out for her. No matter what other mistakes she had made, Liz had never regretted her decision to marry Richard Manley.

***

"I see you got comfortable," Richard said as she walked into the kitchen wearing an old t-shirt and worn sweats cut off just above the knees. "Just in time, too, for a feast."

Not only did Richard know how to make delicious food, he also knew how to serve it. He had insisted when they moved into their house that Liz choose new dishes she truly liked, never mind the cost, and that they use those dishes daily. She had always loved the combination of blue, white, and yellow with a dash of rainbow colors sprinkled in. She had chosen a combination of compatible solids and patterns, a mish-mash to some perhaps, but pretty to her. They had begun a collection of wooden trays years ago, and Richard had chosen her favorite on which to serve their meal tonight, a golden-toned oblong tray. He'd filled two blue-glazed pottery bowls with his yellow chowder and placed four already-buttered rolls in a small basket covered with a blue-and-yellow striped napkin. Two glasses of ice water in ruby red glasses completed the meal.

"Hey, Jackson," he called as he headed down the hall with the loaded tray towards the study. "I left the rest of the rolls on the counter. You can heat your own." To Liz, he said, "At the rate we're eating these, I'll need to do more baking before Sunday."

Sunday afternoon was baking time for Richard. He baked enough bread and rolls for their extended family as well as for his specialty sandwiches in the grocery deli. He enjoyed spending time in the great country kitchen they'd designed to be the heart of their home. Richard had insisted on not one, but two, large ovens and a freezer in the garage whose sole purpose was to store his home-baked bread.

"Let us know when you leave to take Lainie home," Liz reminded her son. "We'll be in the study. Don't be too late, Jackson."

"We're almost done, Miz Manley," Lainie said to Liz's retreating back. "I have to be home by 9:15. Thanks for the soup, Mr. Manley," she called. "It was delish!"

When they were settled in the study, the TV turned to mute, Liz said, "Tell me about your day first. I just want to eat and listen."

"Not much to tell about my day. Mr. Donnelly stopped by. Oh, but you knew that already. He has a couple of new prospects for restaurants; one seems doable, and the other is a remote possibility. He's doing the market analysis on the lakes area. Thinks that because of easy access from the interstate, we can pull from a wide area for a high-end gourmet-type restaurant somewhere near Sardis Lake. He left some recipes he wants me to experiment with. Get ready to eat French."

"What's the other possibility, the remote one?" Liz asked. She felt the need to indulge in a little dreaming.

"Oh, it's way down in south Mississippi, south of Hattiesburg. A lake setting again, but he thinks the market is right there, too, for a high-end restaurant."

"Whoa!" Liz exclaimed. "You could do your gourmet chef thing, and I could go to the university! How's that for a dream?" She smiled. "Does your Mr. Donnelly know how much he's torturing you? This restaurant entrepreneur who just *happened* to wander in from I-55? Just *happened* to stroll into our grocery store at lunch time and head on back to the deli? And you'd just *happened* to make that yummy shrimp soupy concoction that day?"

"I don't know why I keep talking to him, Liz. Except that dreaming is fun. I've told him there's no way I can get out from under the grocery store. It's a family business, for goodness sake, and it has to stay in the family. There's no way Dad will give up his retirement, and Jackson…"

"Leave Jackson out of this," Liz spoke sharper than she had intended. "I'm sorry," she said. "But you know what I mean. I want Jackson to have choices."

"I know, Babe. I don't know why we're even talking about this, Liz. We have a good life. There are millions of people who would trade places with us in a minute. Where's our gratitude?"

"The bumper sticker says 'Choose Life,' not 'Let It Happen to You,' Richard. We just let it happen. Remember all those plans we made back in high school?"

"You're mixing your metaphorical bumper stickers, Lizzie girl. But dreams are what it's about when you're young and in love. That's what your boy and his girl are doing now, under the guise of studying for a chemistry test. They're laying big plans."

"Mom!" As if on cue, Jackson called from the hallway. "We're leavin' now."

"Do me a favor, please?" Liz called as she hurried towards Jackson's retreating voice. "Would you go by Miss Millie's house and make sure everything is closed up? There may be a key in the door. If there is, lock up and make sure the lights are turned off. If not, just close things up."

"Got it, Mom. Be back in about half an hour."

"Tell me about Miss Millie, Liz. What happened to her?" Richard felt relief at the interruption. Unlike Liz, he could live in a dream world for only so long before feeling the need to return to reality.

"Oh, Miss Millie. I don't know, Richard. I don't know what happened to her. They don't think she had a heart attack or a stroke, but something made her fall. She's in pretty bad shape, and I think she's going to be mine to take care of to some degree. Seeing her in that hospital bed with all those tubes attached to her broke my heart. I guess I never thought of her as a real person until tonight. Now, I can't get her out of my head. I have no idea what to do about her."

"You will, my Liz. You always know what to do. And then you do it. That's one of the many things I love about you."

CHAPTER 4

Instead of getting up when the alarm sounded the next morning, Liz hit snooze and fell asleep again. On reawakening, she jumped out of bed, threw on her robe, and hurried downstairs to find an empty kitchen. She went to the stairs that descended into the basement, Jackson's quarters, and seeing that lights were still on and hearing the sound of the shower, she understood that he, too, was running late. She returned to the kitchen to a cold coffee maker. It appeared that the entire household was running late, including Richard, who had apparently decided to wait and have his coffee at the store. She measured coffee, poured water into the container, and sat down to consider her day.

Liz heard a faint scratching sound coming from the direction of the laundry room. Puzzled, she got up from the table and followed the sound through the mudroom and into the laundry room. She stopped just inside the door and stared at a blue plastic animal-carrying case on the folding table. The case was big enough to house a small dog. Moving closer, she stared down at a yellow and white tabby. The cat, obviously aware that its hope for exit was through the metal gate, was scratching furiously at the plastic beside it.

She quickly processed the events of last evening. No, there hadn't been a cat in her laundry room when she went to bed. Yes, Jackson had come in after ...

"Jackson!" Liz called as she headed for the stairs. "Where did this cat come from?"

"Just a minute, Ma. I'm comin' up."

Liz returned to the kitchen. The cat, either agitated or encouraged by Liz's appearance, had begun to meow loudly as if calling her to return and release it, an act she had no intention of committing inside her home. She had visions of what such an animated creature could do to her draperies and furniture, not to mention to her own person. This cat was clearly accustomed to freedom and was loudly demanding to be released from *his? her?* prison.

"We didn't know what to do, Lainie and me. He was at Miss Millie's, curled up on her bed, when we went in to check on things. You know she was looking for a cat. Looks like she found one."

Unless her memory was playing tricks on her, Liz recalled a gray cat. "The doctor said a gray cat was seen running out the door. This cat is not gray ... look for yourself."

"Ma, I *know* it's not gray, but I'm tellin' you, this cat was in Miss Millie's house last night when we went in. He jumped off the bed and went under it, but we didn't think we should just leave it there. We went to Lainie's house and got her dog carrier. She couldn't come back with me, so I found a can of Miss Millie's tuna and used it to trick the cat into the carrier. It took about half-an-hour, but it worked. I felt like Miss Millie sittin' there in the dark, waitin' to trap a cat. Crazy!"

As Jackson told his story, he and Liz had returned to the laundry room. Jackson picked up a discarded dryer sheet, twisted and knotted it, and stuck it inside the cage, just out of reach of the cat. The cat batted at it, then retreated to a corner and sat quietly watching.

"He must be an outside cat. He still has claws," Jackson said.

"She. It's a girl cat, Jackson—probably soon to be a mama cat. Look at her." The distended belly, which could have been from over-indulgence in tuna, did indeed look like that of a cat about to give birth. "But that will be somebody else's problem. This cat goes home today, wherever home might be."

"Whatever," Jackson replied. "Are you mad?"

"You did what you thought you needed to do ... of course I'm not mad. Just ... frustrated. Something else to take care of."

"Sorry, Mom. Has Dad already left?"

"He has, and he left oatmeal on the stove for you. Fixings, too, on the counter. Get moving, or you'll be late for school. When was the last time we *all* overslept?"

"Yeah, and I'm pickin' Lainie up today. She wanted to go over her chemistry notes one more time before her final." Jackson emptied the remaining oatmeal into a bowl and put it in the microwave.

Liz sat at the table with a notepad and pencil. Her mind had returned to all the jobs that must be accomplished today. Now a new one was to be added: *Return cat to home.* She loved the alone time she had in her home most mornings. Richard left first, then Jackson, after which Liz had a half-hour of solitude before Rose, on the days she worked, arrived. It was her time to plan the day, to make a list of tasks that she must accomplish before she could, once more, retreat behind the closed doors of her home and simply be. Her half-hour in the morning never seemed to be enough.

She watched as Jackson opened the microwave and reached in to pull out the steamy bowl of oatmeal. "Ouch!" he yelled.

It was as if she could feel the burn in her fingertips. "Get a tea towel."

"I know, Mom. I know!" He gingerly moved the steaming dish from the microwave to the island and began heaping brown sugar and dried cranberries on top.

"There's cream in the ..." Liz began.

"Mom! I know!" he silenced her.

Why do I do this, she wondered. Still, she plunged ahead. "Aren't you and Lainie spending an awful lot of time together? What about your other friends?"

"She's my *best* friend, Ma, and I do spend time with my other friends." Jackson had started to join her at the table but instead returned to the counter and began to thrust large spoonfuls of barely cooled oatmeal into his mouth.

Liz's first thought was to remind him to be careful not to burn his mouth; her second was to correct his manners. Something in Jackson's tone and posture warned her to do neither. Uncharacteristically, she paid attention to her son's signals and to her wiser self and kept quiet.

Jackson put his empty bowl in the sink and ran water in it. "Is Rosie coming today?" he asked, obviously changing the subject.

"Is today Thursday?"

The sound of the door opening and closing gave an affirmative to both questions. Followed by, "Law me! Where dis animal done come from?"

"I'm outta here." Jackson grinned and crooked an arm around his mother's neck, kissing her on top of her head. "You get to deal with The Rose. Hey, Rose. Bye, Rose," he greeted as he brushed past her.

Rose Walker had come to help the Manley family 'temporarily' after Jackson's birth. Temporary turned into short-term, which turned into 'just-a-few-more-weeks,' before settling into permanent. Her role was hard to define: nanny, housekeeper, cook, grandmother, confidante. She was all of those to the young family.

She stood now in the doorway, looking ominously at Liz. "I done tol' you, I can't take on nothin' else. Four legs or two, no matter. This somethin' Jackson bring home?"

"I'm with you, Rose, all the way. I can't take on anything else, either. And, yes, to answer your question, this is something Jackson brought home. Last night. And I can promise you it will be out of here today. Give me a few hours. On second thought, hand me the phone, please. Oh, never mind, I'll do this myself." Liz got up, picked up the phone and the phone directory, and thumbed through till she found Nell Clark's number.

"Mrs. Clark. Hi, this is Liz Manley. Thank you for calling the ambulance and me yesterday. Yes, she was still unconscious last night when I left. She's at North Oak." Liz listened.

"No, I don't know of any family. Was there anybody in the neighborhood that she was especially close to? Hmm ... I was afraid of that.

"Yes, I'll keep you posted. But, Mrs. Clark, the reason I'm calling is about the cat. Can you tell me again who owned the cat Miss Millie 'borrowed'? By some strange turn of events, it's ended up here at my house in an animal carrier. Too long a story to go into, but ..."

"What? That can't be. It was in Miss Millie's house last night when Jackson ..." Liz listened again before finally ending the conversation with, "Well, thank you. If you hear of anybody else missing a cat, would you call me? It's a yellow and white tabby. Pregnant, I think."

She hung up, and for a moment, she and Rose stared at each other.

"Well?" the black woman broke the silence. "This don't sound like 'outta-here-today' to me. What's goin' on?"

"I wish I knew. Give me a minute to try to figure this out for myself."

Liz realized that Rose didn't know anything about Miss Millie's hospitalization and didn't, in fact, know much about Miss Millie at all. As briefly as she could, she explained to Rose what had happened over the past few days, ending with her unexpected visit to the hospital in Senatobia yesterday.

"So, they saw this cat in her house? This gray cat? And it run out? And it come back after everybody's gone and turn itself into a gonna-be-mama cat that's yellow and white?"

Leave it to Rose to succinctly put into words what seemed to have happened. Liz knew there had to be a logical explanation, but for the life of her, she couldn't figure out what it was. The problem at hand, however, was to find another place for the cat.

"I'll put signs up in the store as soon as I get there. Somebody will know where this cat belongs; we're not that large of a town."

***

As she left for the store, Liz took the key that Jackson had found in Miss Millie's back door the night before. She wanted to see for herself that everything was in order in the older woman's home and hoped to find some clue as to the mystery of the cat that now resided on her laundry room folding table.

She didn't know what she expected to find. She had never been inside Miss Millie's home. No matter what the weather, she had always pulled up in front of the house, and the woman had appeared on her porch, always dressed in weather-appropriate, obviously expensive, classic attire.

Liz felt like she was entering a well-preserved kitchen from the late fifties. Except for the dinette chairs scattered about the room and the stench of an uncared-for litter box behind the door, everything was immaculate. How pretty! Liz thought. This wasn't what she had expected at all. The kitchen had been planned with as much thought and care as she and Richard had devoted to their own some thirty years or so after this one had been designed.

Now that she was here, she was reluctant to invade the older woman's privacy.

Miss Millie Stich had made her wishes known over the years by her consistent behavior. She really didn't want people inside her house, even people like Liz, on whom she relied. Rather than empty the litter box, Liz picked it up and set it outdoors. She came back inside and walked through a short hallway connected to a room next to the kitchen. The hallway was tastefully designed with bookshelves lining each side. They were filled with small sculptures, sketches, photographs, and books. At the other end was a bedroom and, from its comfortable, dated appearance, the room in which Miss Millie lived. The floor was carpeted in a muted floral pattern. Four long windows were treated with floor-length cream-colored sheers; the shades behind them pulled three-quarters of the way down, the distance appearing to have been precisely measured. An antique sleigh bed was covered with a dusty rose spread that coordinated perfectly with a subtly striped upholstered rocking chair. "This woman has impeccable taste," Liz murmured to the empty room.

Except for another barely used litter box tucked behind the chair, everything seemed to be in order. Clearly, the cat had favored the kitchen litter box, but why had there been two? Did she have two cats? A gray one *and* a yellow and white one? Had she become a crazy cat lady in her final days? The untended litter box didn't quite fit with the otherwise immaculate rooms. Liz carried the box out and set it near the other one, returning to the kitchen for one last look.

She was about to leave when she noticed the envelope with her name on it: *Elizabeth Manley.* No mistaking who it was meant for. Beside the envelope were several sheets of stationary with the simple monogram *MSL* at the top. One sheet, seemingly having been written on, was turned upside down. Another, with several lines in no-nonsense cursive writing, topped the other sheets. An uncapped fountain pen lay on the table beside the papers. Liz wondered momentarily what the *L* stood for. More importantly, she wondered if the unfinished note was intended for her. Her curiosity was strong, and emboldened by the envelope with her name on it, she picked up the paper that lay face down. The note, dated four days earlier, began, *Dear Elizabeth.*

CHAPTER 5

Liz looked around at the porch of the home where she had lived the first eighteen years of her life. The wrap-around porch had been completely restored: no missing rungs in the railing, no sections of floor to avoid. Comfortable chairs, tables, and spring décor looking to have been randomly placed—but had been, in fact, carefully arranged—made the porch look exactly like what it was: an invitation to sit and relax. In two short years, Luann, Liz's older sister, had turned their old home into a showplace.

Luann, her husband, Rob, and two young daughters had moved to Roslyn from Atlanta. Rob had left a large veterinarian's practice there, a practice that required almost a year to close down. He was in the process of building another equally vibrant clinic in the lake's area. Luann had lobbied for years to relocate their family to a small town where life moved at a slower pace. After her mother's death, she easily solved the problem of what to do with the property by buying Liz's portion and moving her family to Roslyn. She was happy to precede Rob in their move, settle the girls in school, and dive into renovating her childhood home.

Liz pulled the cord on the antique doorbell, opened the screen door, and called, "Lu, it's me. Are you in there?" Hearing no reply, she stepped inside. The most likely place to find her sister at this time of day was in the back, tending her garden. The girls, Maria and Madison, would have been dropped off at school, and her sister would have begun her project for the day. Liz looked around the entry hall flanked on one side by a large living area and on the other by a dining room, all with the same comfortable, lived-in look of the front porch while appearing to have been designed by *Southern Living*. How does she get away with using color so extravagantly, Liz wondered. The space was a burst of bright colors: green, yellow, purple, blue, orange. Had her sister left out any of the colors featured in the eight-count box of Crayola crayons?

Hearing noises coming from the back of the house, Liz called again, "Lu, are you back there?" They met in the kitchen. Her sister dirt-smudged from her hands to her feet, held a colander filled with tiny spinach leaves. "You don't have spinach this fresh in *Main Street Groceries*," she greeted.

"I do in my own backyard, though," Liz retorted. "So does everybody else in Roslyn, which is why you'll find very little spinach in the vegetable section this time of year. We know our market."

"You do, little sister, you do. Speaking of ... I need the biggest and bestest brisket Richard can find for our Fourth of July celebration. Maybe more than one. I'm in charge of meat this year." Luann, always on top of everything, was planning for an event more than six weeks away.

"Remind me when it's closer to time," Liz said. "I have far more pressing things on my mind today. Do you need a sec to clean up? If you can spare a minute or two, I need your advice on something." Liz eyed her sister's grimy hands and dirt-stained knees.

She sat down at the glass-topped antique wicker table in the sunroom to wait. The room, transformed, was still achingly familiar. It was filled with things, such as the table, from their childhood. The same daybed, upholstered now to serve as a sofa, still remained, as did the old wicker rocker her mother had sat in to read her endless novels and magazines. Liz grew sadder as she sat waiting and looking out at the canopy of trees surrounding the closed-in porch: pecans, redbuds, mimosas, at one time her refuge, still familiar, yet somehow different.

Luann interrupted her reverie by appearing with a tray loaded with steaming coffee mugs, cream and sugar, and scones. "Sorry, the scones aren't warm; leftovers from breakfast," she apologized.

"Whatcha got?" she asked after they were settled.

"You know about Miss Millie?" Liz asked.

"Yeah, the girls and I were just getting home from school yesterday when the ambulance came. It's all the neighborhood talk, how they found her unconscious on her kitchen floor."

"Well ... read this," Liz said as she unfolded the letter and pushed it across the table to her sister."

Her sister picked it up and read, as Liz had just minutes earlier:

Dear Elizabeth,

I hope this gruesome discovery has not proved too taxing for you. I knew I could count on you to check on me when you didn't hear from me on grocery-ordering day. If all goes as planned, I will no longer be on this earth or will be so weakened in my body that there will be no return to health. Simply stated, I wish to die. Or rather, I wish to expedite my death, which, according to my physician, is imminent.

You are, my dear, a true friend. You only gave, never asking for anything in return. Not even information, though there were times I knew that your curiosity about me was overwhelming. I am (was) a strange one, according to your Southern customs. Just suffice it to say, I came from a different place, a different time, and one can't change who and what they are.

I make no attempt to explain what has happened here except to say I gave the plan much forethought and not a little effort. My life is complete, and I simply have no wish to continue it. I want to repay you for your considerable trouble and, while I recognize that friendship cannot be purchased, show you how valued you are to me. Please contact my attorney. His card is enclosed. He has instructions as to how you are to be rewarded for your generosity to me in life ... and in my death.

Sincerely,

Millicent Stich

P.S. The matter of the Cat. He belongs to a nice young man by the name of...

Luann looked up from the unfinished note, "Who does the cat belong to?"

"Lu! How could that be the first thing out of your mouth?" The humor of the situation hit both sisters at the same time, and they began laughing, at first trying to hold it in, then giving way to it. Liz, still giggling, said, "This is not funny. On so many levels."

"Funny, no ... bizarre, yes. How do you get yourself into these things, Liz?"

"You have no idea how many times I ask myself that very question. My life seems to have a mind of its own and goes off in directions that I really don't want to go. But here I am. What should I do?"

"Well, for starters, and I'm serious here ... what about the cat?" Luann began giggling again.

"Lu! Stop it. Although that is a mystery ... and a problem. Right now, at this very moment, there's a yellow and white, probably pregnant cat in a carrier in my laundry room. I had Jackson stop by to make sure Miss Millie's house was okay last night, and he brought a cat home with him. It was in her house. The poor thing must have been starving because he lured it into the carrier with one of Miss Millie's cans of tuna that she's been ordering by the truckload.

"I knew she wanted a cat from phone conversations we've had, but it appears that she just wanted to borrow a cat. I can't imagine why, especially when she was obviously planning to off herself. Did she plan to trip over a cat and kill herself? That makes no sense whatsoever, but that's what the ambulance driver on the scene thinks happened: she tripped over something, and the cat is the most likely culprit. She wasn't used to having an animal in her house. Listen to this. A grey cat ran out the door when the paramedics entered. A grey cat. Nell Clark's son had something to do with this, and when I called Nell this morning, she said the grey cat was safe at home. So where did this yellow and white cat come from?"

"Take a breath, little sister. You're talkin' way too fast. And, as you say, the cat isn't your biggest problem. What are you going to do about this letter?"

"Yeah." Liz picked up the letter and read out loud, "'Please contact my attorney. His card is enclosed.' There wasn't a card," she said. "I searched the table, and there was no card."

"Was there a desk? Maybe it was in her purse. Maybe she got up to get the attorney's card and tripped," Luann said.

"Well, it means I have to go back," Liz said. "Would you go with me? I don't mean right now; I have to get to the store—I'm late already—but maybe this afternoon before you pick the girls up from school?"

"Sure, I can do that. I've always wanted to see inside that house anyway. I'll bet she hasn't changed anything in 30 years. And I'll bet it's just full of good stuff."

"Lu, we're not snooping. You haven't been inside that house for a reason. She didn't want anybody in there. And now ..." Liz's voice trailed off. "It's so sad. She's lived in this town forever and kept all of us out. I wonder why?"

"We know about that, don't we, Little Sis? We lived with our share of secrecy, too."

Both women were taken aback by this turn in the conversation. Liz felt rather than saw a quick stiffening in Luann's posture, and a sudden moistness formed in her eyes. They had never discussed their childhood, and with the events of the past twelve or so hours, the mere mention of their shared painful past was too much. Liz, almost imperceptibly, shook her head.

"Liz, I'm sorry. I didn't mean to open that can of worms just now."

Luann reached for her hand, but Liz pushed her chair back and stood. "See you around 2:00?" she asked.

Luann followed her sister to the front porch and watched as she walked down the sidewalk to her car, head down, shoulders bent, looking like a motherless child. Luann resisted a sudden impulse to run after her and hug her. She knew it wouldn't be received well, if at all. They had never been hugging sisters. It had only been in the last two years since Luann and Rob had moved to Roslyn from Atlanta that they had been sisterly at all.

Luann stood on the porch long after Liz had turned the corner. She thought of the young girl she'd left behind all those years ago. How old had Liz been? Fourteen to her eighteen? Yes, her little sister had been so young, so different from her. On occasion, Luann had tried to encourage the girl to get out there and be with her friends. The span of years separating them made it impossible for them to run in the same circles.

Looking back, Lu realized that she'd been so caught up in her own need to escape from the sadness that permeated their home that she'd not had much to offer her little sister. As she recalled the sadness that had enveloped her family, she spoke her new commitment out loud. "Little Sister, we have a lot of our past to recover. I promise not to abandon you again."

***

Luann was waiting on the porch when Liz stopped by to pick her up that afternoon. She lived so close to Miss Millie's house that walking would have been easier, but since they hadn't clearly stated their plans, she waited to see if Liz would show up. They drove the short distance to the house in silence, but after Liz had parked, Luann reached over and touched her arm.

"Don't say anything, but just hear me out. I'm not going to force this now; you have too much going on. But we're going to talk soon, and I mean talk. This is your big sister speaking, and you have to believe me when I say I need to talk about what went on all those years ago as much as you do. There are ghosts in that house where I've brought my family to live. Don't get me wrong; I love that house, but I don't want the unhappy spirits of Mama and Daddy hanging around my girls. I made a promise to myself when you left the house today. I'm not going to abandon you again. Promise me, Liz, that we'll do what we have needed to do for a long time: talk about what happened in our family. For yourself, for me, for Jackson, for Maria and Madison, for all of us. Please?"

Liz sat for a moment, thinking. *When I start talking, where do I stop?* Luann had been gone, in one way or another, for so much that had happened. Finally, looking straight ahead, she replied, "Someday. Maybe."

"Well, that'll have to do for now," Luann said. "Let's go pillage those antiques."

Luann's reaction to the kitchen was much the same as Liz's had been earlier in the day. "Oh, my goodness, Liz! This is amazing. Just look at this stove! It's a Wolf. Was Miss Millie a gourmet cook or something? Who would ever have guessed that the inside of this house would be like this? And we've only seen the kitchen! Oh my! That table and chairs are the real deal."

"Lu! We're not here to take an inventory of an old woman's belongings. We're here to find something important and then leave." Liz wondered if it had been such a good idea to bring her sister here after all. "Help me look for the business card. Her room is just through this little hallway," Liz said, leading her excited sister through the little passageway into the bedroom.

Luann immediately began opening drawers, first in the large chest, then in the nightstand.

"What are you doing?" Liz snapped at her.

"I'm doing what you asked me to do. You wanted to find the attorney's card, didn't you? You don't think it's going to jump out of its hiding place into our hands, do you? You asked me to help you look, and that's what I'm doing, for goodness' sake!"

Liz's exasperation increased with every word she heard from her sister and accelerated rapidly when Luann let out an excited yelp.

"Liz! I found it. Not the card, but look! This was her plan," she said, holding up a bottle of pills. "Sleeping pills," she announced, "but look at the date on this prescription. 1992. They're almost ten years old, but I'll bet they would have still done the trick. There are enough in here to kill a horse. All she's missing is a glass of water to chug them down."

Liz's mind closed at the thought of finding Miss Millie dead from an overdose of pills, and her sister's irreverent description of the scene caused a flash of anger. The real evidence that her friend had a viable plan shook her. "Put those down, Lu. You don't know anything about what she had in mind."

Luann set the bottle of pills back on the nightstand and moved toward the closet with a shrug of her shoulders. "Ooookay," she said in a placating voice. "Where do you think she might keep her purse? The closet, maybe?" She opened the door and peered inside. "Look at these clothes," she exclaimed. "Not a thing in here less than ten years old, but touch this fabric." Luann pulled a suit jacket out to examine it. "I've never even heard of these labels, but this fabric just screams dollar bills. Our Miss Millie has some bucks."

Liz couldn't watch. She knew there was no stopping her sister, but she couldn't bear to invade her friend's privacy. She perched on the edge of the upholstered chair and surveyed the room. She spotted a thin black leather book under the phone on the nightstand, walked across the room, picked it up, and began to thumb through it. "Here it is," she announced. "This has to be her attorney. Jamerson, Johnson, and Brimmer, Attorneys-at-Law," she read. "They're in Memphis." She picked up the book and walked across the room, still thumbing through it. "And here's a ... what's Fr. an abbreviation for?" she asked. "Luann! What are you doing?"

Her sister had opened the door and was walking into another hallway, a space very similar to the connection between the kitchen and Miss Millie's bedroom. Liz followed her sister into the adjoining room. "It's a boy's room," her sister said. "Look at the blue walls, the rock collection on the bookshelf, the maple furniture. I remember now they had a son, much older than us. I remember because he used to visit every summer and always drove an expensive car. Probably a Corvette? Porsche? You didn't see many of either of those in Roslyn back then."

Luann was already opening the next door, which again led to a small hallway, this one obviously used as a butler's pantry. The door at the end of the hall led to the dining room. "Haviland," she announced after opening the glass door of the China cabinet and inspecting it.

"Wait," Luann said, turning back to the butler's pantry and retreating into the boy's room. "Bathrooms? Where are the bathrooms?" She looked for the answer to her question by opening doors, both in the boy's room and in Miss Millie's room. There they were, back-to-back—or more like end-to-end—two bathrooms also arranged train-like in the center of the house.

"Luann, we really shouldn't be here," Liz protested, mildly. She wanted to see the home as badly as her sister but felt disloyal to her friend. In spite of the feeling, she continued the unescorted tour of the home.

The dining room was separated from the formal living area with double French doors, both open. "Look, here's the outside door and another door to the adjacent room," Luann pointed out as she opened said door. "This house is perfectly symmetrical," she said. "Now I get it. You know how there are two front doors, one at either end of the front porch? You can enter either one and go straight back to the other end of the house, or you could have at one time." Luann continued through the requisite hallway as she spoke. "I'll bet there was a door between the boy's bedroom and this ..." Luann turned the knob on the door to the final room, opened it, and stepped inside.

"Liz, look." She moved aside so that her sister could enter the room. "Look at this! Your Miss Millie has a studio. She's an artist!"

The room, smelling faintly of turpentine and paint, had not been used for a very long time. Everything was orderly and neat. Painted canvases were stacked against the wall in several places, the visible ones all showing children. A covered easel stood in the corner of the room between two heavily curtained windows. Luann lifted the drape on the canvas and gasped. "This is incredible," she said. "I've seen her work in Atlanta. I know it's the same. I can't remember the name, but it starts with an L. La-something. LaSalle ... something like that. She paints children mostly. Look at this, Liz. It's beautiful."

But Liz had already seen it. As if sleepwalking, she walked to the window facing the front and pulled the drapes open. There, near the tilting public sidewalk, where she had spent many hours escaping into her greenhouses, stood the old oak. She could see the uneven sidewalk, raised and broken by the roots of the tree. Her favorite tree.

She turned back to the painting on the easel. "That's me, Lu. Miss Millie painted me while I played under her tree. It's as if she really knew me, even when I was a little girl."

CHAPTER 6

Liz sat in the office of the grocery store, staring at the screensaver on her computer. Various-sized bubbles skittered across the screen, bursting into other brightly-colored bubbles. Endlessly. Repeatedly. Just like my life, she thought. From the time she was a little girl, she had believed that if she could just *be* there or *do* something, she could be in control of a given situation. She had spent her entire life trying to keep things under control, thinking she was handling the events in her life like a master juggler.

In truth, the balls in the air probably resembled those floating aimlessly across the screen. Even as she had struggled to keep all the balls in the air, she could feel life going on without her and knew that she was waiting behind for her real life to begin. How did she end up being responsible for a little old lady? What gave her sister the right to stir up the long-dead past of their childhood? And why did she have this increasing feeling of dread that she was losing control of her son, the one thing in the world that was truly hers?

The sound of raised voices interrupted her mental meandering. Grace Carlson again.

"You're just going to take it to those old people over at that home. I'm an old person. Why can't you give it to me?"

Reluctantly, Liz walked over to the register. "Take a break, Maggie," she said. "I'll finish up with Miss Gracie."

The relief on the face of the check-out attendant was evident. "Thank you," she mouthed.

She slid behind Liz and away from the wrath of Grace Carlson.

The conversation that followed had been well-rehearsed between Grace and Liz. Every so often, she would come into the store, order the special from the deli, refuse to pay Cora or whoever the cashier in the back might be on the pretext that she needed to "pick up a few grocery items and would just pay for everything up front." Whereupon she would attempt to wheedle a free sandwich or soup, sometimes both, from the cashier who rang up her order.

The conversations would go thus:

"It's two o'clock—Elizabeth, Maggie, Chuck—the lunch hour is long past."

*"But we're a business, Miss Gracie. We don't have a deli giveaway at two o'clock. But I'll tell you what. We'll do it just this once. You can pay for soup (or the sandwich, or half-price—*the offered deal varied) *and have the sandwich for free."*

Liz knew it wasn't 'just this once.' Grace would wait a few weeks and try the same thing again. She made a point of looking for new, inexperienced check-out people and tried to make them believe that her "free deli food" was standard practice. Poor Maggie had made the mistake of standing up to the cheap, conniving old woman.

"I hear you got yourself mixed up with that snooty Millie Stich," Grace said. "You been to see her?"

This was a part of the recent drama that Liz had allowed to slip into the back of her mind: the hot telephone wires. The town gossips, Grace Carlson leading the pack, were telling their stories about Miss Millie. The fact that Millicent Stich had never connected with any of the social opportunities of Roslyn, Mississippi, made her life far more interesting to them than it would have otherwise been. Most of the women who were of Grace's generation remembered when the Stiches had moved to Roslyn as a young family and how all the attempts made by the townspeople to initiate them into their social life had been rebuffed. Gracious though the refusals to participate were, in small-town life, they were considered a slap in the face.

"I have," Liz replied.

"Well? Will she make it?" Grace was on an information-gathering expedition. She wanted to score points with her sharp-tongued friends by getting the scoop.

"I really don't know much, Miss Gracie," Liz said. "I just saw her for a short time last night after she was admitted." Over the years, Liz had learned to give Grace Carlson as little information as possible. Any details she gleaned could be exploded into full-blown lies.

"Hmpff!" the old lady grunted. "You must think you're extra special hobnobbing with The Lady Astor of the Holy Catholic Church."

"Excuse me? Lady Astor?" The generational gap in name-calling escaped Liz. Experience had taught her that engaging in an extended conversation with Grace Carlson was a mistake, but she was so angered by the woman's attempt to make something ugly of her relationship with Miss Millie that she took the bait.

"The Queen of New York, or as your friend thought, the Queen of Roslyn," the old woman clarified.

"Miss Millie didn't think of herself as the *Queen* of anything, Grace." In her anger, Liz had dropped the small-town title of respect given to the woman. "She was a kind, generous woman who needed a little help. But, unlike some people, she was willing to pay for whatever she received."

Dear God, Liz thought, what have I done? I've lived my entire adult life walking on eggshells around this woman, knowing how vicious she's capable of being, and now, in one fell swoop, I've unleashed her anger. She continued to look straight into the other woman's eyes, hoping to convey that she wasn't at all afraid of her. But her fast pulse and inability to control her breathing told her the depths of her own fear.

"Well, now. Maybe Millicent Stich isn't the only Lady Astor we have in Roslyn. Maybe some other people are a little too uppity for their upbringing after marrying into the right family. Did somebody forget she's the daughter of one of our town drunks?"

***

"She's not finished with me," Liz said to Luann. "She'll think of every vile thing imaginable and then add to it. She and her little gang of town gossips."

Liz had asked Luann to accompany her to Senatobia to check on Miss Millie, then on to Memphis to meet with the lawyers. She had been surprised when she called the attorney's office the day before and identified herself as Millicent Stich's friend. The secretary had put her right through to Mr. Jamerson, and he had personally scheduled a meeting with her for 1:00 the following day.

It seemed to Liz that in forty-eight short hours, her life had begun to unravel right in front of her. She felt the need for additional moral support, someone other than Richard or Rose, her current confidantes. She didn't consider either of them likely candidates to whom she could divulge her deepest hurts from the past. For the first time in her adult life, she saw her sister as someone she might confide in. Maybe.

Yesterday, as she had left Lu standing on her front porch, Liz had felt the strong urge to run back up the sidewalk and tell her sister everything she had kept bottled up inside for what seemed forever. She didn't, of course. Loneliness, once shared, became something alive. If one person saw it, acknowledged it, or examined it, then there was no stopping it. It would consume her if it ever saw daylight. For survival's sake, she had to keep it contained.

"Liz," her sister said now, "what Grace Carlson says or doesn't say has nothing to do with what's real. Did you know there are places where people live, Atlanta being one, where people neither care nor talk about what other people do?"

"I don't live in Atlanta. I live in Roslyn, where everybody can tell you who everybody's great-great-grandparents were, what they planted in their gardens, what they did in the dead of night. They can even tell you what a family had for supper on a given Saturday night. And if they don't know, there are plenty who will make it up."

"Remember, I grew up here, too," Luann reminded her. "I also chose to come back here after 'getting away.' It's a good place to live, Liz, with more good people than bad. You just have to know who you are and not let the gossip get the best of you. How do you think Miss Millie survived here all these years? You think she didn't know that people made up stories about her?"

Liz was silent as she thought about her friendship—that's how she had come to think of the relationship in the past hours—with Miss Millie. She thought of their short phone conversations, groceries being the only topic they discussed, the trips to Senatobia to the doctor, usually spent in quiet travel both ways but still characterized by an air of peace. She felt accepted and cared for, as she did with Richard, only in a different way. Miss Millie demanded nothing of her. She *needed* Liz, but it wasn't an expectant need.

"There *is* something different about her," Liz finally answered. "I wish I could be more like her; then, maybe I wouldn't feel the need to be so involved in everything. Sometimes I feel like a big cake sporting a placard: 'Take a piece of Liz, please.'"

Luann laughed. "I prefer pie, thank you very much. But I think you're on to something, Little Sis. You *do* advertise. The question is, why? My little sister, who loved to lose herself in a book, wrote in journals from the time she could scribble. The girl who could sit in the grass for hours searching for four-leaf clovers. How did you get so busy?"

They sat in the parking lot of the hospital, neither woman willing to end the conversation. Liz opened the windows of the car and turned to her sister. "You were never there," she said. "You were always with your friends, on a date or cheering the Roslyn Bulldogs to victory, then left for Auburn. I couldn't leave. Mama and Daddy were so sad, and then Daddy was gone. When I did leave home, I pulled the rug out from under everybody, including myself, by getting pregnant with Jackson. I have to stay busy to keep from remembering."

CHAPTER 7

An empty ICU waiting room greeted Liz and Lu when they arrived shortly after 9:00 the next morning. Liz wondered about the vacant chairs. Where were family members of the critically ill patients lying behind closed doors? Were they already standing beside their beds? Had they given up and made a choice to go about their business of the day while leaving their loved ones in the hands of professionals and fate? Where was everyone, she wondered impatiently. Luann found a magazine and a chair while Liz looked around for someone who could give her permission to see her friend. She called to a nurse who hurried through the swinging entry doors to the unit, "May I come back with you to see my friend, Millicent Stitch?"

On hearing the name, the obviously overworked nurse slowed her movements and turned to Liz with a smile. "You'll be pleasantly surprised," she said, "your friend came around this morning, just at shift change. She's still very weak, not talking at all yet, but she has a look on her face that says she's glad to be among the living.

"You won't want to ask her any questions. She needs all the energy she can gather just to let her body heal. My guess is that she would be easily confused by talk at this point."

Liz followed the nurse to Miss Millie's bed. Again, she was struck by the pallor of the tiny woman, the way she seemed to almost disappear in the bed. Liz looked for a place to touch, but it seemed that every part of the old woman's body was connected to some kind of hissing, clicking mechanical device. She finally settled for the shoulder, and the coming together of hand and near-fleshless bone brought a tightness to Liz's throat.

"Miss Millie," she said softly, "you're back with us! The last time I saw you, you were sound asleep. You've given us quite a scare."

The woman's lips parted slightly.

"No, no," Liz cautioned. "Let me do the talking. They'll throw me out of here if they hear you say a word. I promised I wouldn't let you use your energy by talking."

With her mouth still open, Miss Millie inhaled a shallow breath. Liz was surprised to see white, even teeth in the septuagenarian's mouth. She would have guessed that Miss Millie had "removable" teeth at her age. She'd thought of her elderly friend for so long as "Poor Miss Millie" that she had allowed this characterization to cover every aspect of the woman's life. Yesterday's discovery of the beautiful paintings was clear evidence that, in spite of how the woman lived now, she was certainly not "Poor Miss Anything." She had a rich, vibrant past. There was much to discover about her.

Liz patted the tiny shoulder. "I'm going to take care of you, Miss Millie. I have an appointment at one o'clock this afternoon with Mr. Jamerson. My sister, Luann, is with me, and between the two of us, we'll make sure that you are well taken care of.

"Shhh ... don't try to talk now. We'll stop by later today on our way home from Memphis. You work on getting strong again."

"She's a tough little bird," the nurse told Liz when she had finished her visit. "I don't know how she survived this. She must have lain unconscious on that floor for at least two days. She was severely dehydrated. From the bruises on her body, she took quite a tumble. It's almost unbelievable that she didn't have a broken bone anywhere. Dr. Radcliffe was in yesterday and brought us up to speed on her heart medication. Like us, he couldn't believe she was still among the living. You'll stay in touch?"

"Oh, I'll stop back by this evening," Liz told the chatty nurse, who appeared to have found an oasis of time in her busy morning, "but let me give you my cell phone number."

The nurse pulled a sticky note off the ledge in the nurse's station and handed it to Liz along with a pen. Printed at the top were the words: *Contact for Millicent Stich*, and below were Liz's phone numbers. She added the other number and handed the slip of paper back to the nurse. "Thank you for keeping me informed about her. I feel awful that I haven't been back since she was admitted, but I've been busy taking care of things for her at home. I have a meeting this afternoon with her attorney in Memphis. Hopefully, he'll have some information that will give me a legal right to be here. If not, then I'm sure he'll know who to contact about her."

"Don't worry about that. It won't always be this easy, the way the government is getting involved in every little detail of hospital business, but for now, we can accept your word that you're the only person in charge of her care. Anyway, just between the two of us, I still believe that human kindness should trump bureaucratic rules." The nurse's final utterance was spoken in *sotto voce*. Liz understood immediately that she was speaking for herself alone, not the hospital higher-ups.

"Thank you," Liz said and really felt gratitude toward the woman—and God—for the nurse's kind and honest words. "Miss Millie is in good hands here."

***

"Lunch?" Liz asked as she and Luann left the hospital parking lot. "We have plenty of time for a sit-down meal. Or would you rather grab fast food and keep driving?"

"Let's head on to Memphis," Luann suggested. "I know a great little place downtown just a couple of blocks from your lawyer's office. We can be there shortly after 11:00, beat the lunch traffic, and be within walking distance."

"How do you know all these things, Lu? You've been away from this part of the country for ... how many years? You're back in Roslyn for a couple of years, and you know more about what's going on than I do."

"You've gotta get out more, kid. There's an entire world out there that you've been turning your back on."

"Some of us like staying close to home," was Liz's final retort. She lapsed into silence as she merged into traffic on the interstate.

Luann matched her sister's quiet mood, and each became occupied with their own thoughts. Liz thought about the woman she had left behind in the hospital bed. It seemed to her that they were somehow cosmically intertwined. She had given the woman little or no thought in childhood or her teen years. There had been a few times when, as a small child lost in creative play in her favorite spot under the giant oak tree, she had looked up and realized that the woman was sitting and watching her intently in one of the white wicker chairs on her front porch. Liz had never acknowledged the woman's presence but had gone back to her greenhouse construction.

Now, Liz tried to remember exactly what had prompted her to take Miss Millie under her wing. She could only think of one thing: need. Miss Millie had needed help; Liz had become aware of her need and had offered her assistance. *Am I one of those pitiful people who need to be needed?* She thought of Sarah Windham, one of their customers who was forever taking someone's empty grocery cart and returning it to the corner at the front of the store. Invariably, another customer would show up minutes later, complaining, "Somebody took my cart. I went down the aisle to pick up a six-pack of Coca-Cola, came back, and it was gone." Every employee in the store had tried to convince Sarah not to move empty grocery carts, only to be met with the reply, "Oh, I'm so sorry. I was just trying to help!"

Liz recognized that she was deeply involved in several of the town networks: school, church, and civic. Richard, Rose, and sometimes even Jackson were quick to point out her busy days, which often extended well into the night. So why had she felt compelled to add Millicent Stich to her responsibilities? And why, now, was Miss Millie's well-being uppermost in her mind? A mental picture of the woman lying unconscious in her hospital bed flashed into Liz's head and, with it, the rush of feeling that had overcome her two nights ago. That, she recognized now, was an honest feeling. Perhaps *love* was too strong a word, but ...

"Liz! Where you goin'? Nashville? You missed our exit!" Her sister's voice brought her back to the present.

***

The law offices of Jamerson, Johnson, and Brimmer occupied the ninth and tenth floors of the Alton Building, a 20-story structure with mirrored panels reflecting blue sky and sunlight. The sisters stood across the street from the imposing building, Luann with her head thrown back and her hand cupped above her eyes as a makeshift visor. Liz looked around for a place to sit so she could check her teeth and face once more.

"I thought you did that in the restaurant," Luann said, still gawking at the building in front of her.

"I did," Liz said, "but the light's brighter out here. Just want to be sure I don't have lettuce stuck in my teeth. I knew I should have brought a toothbrush. The dressing on that salad had garlic in it. I smell like a fire-breathing dragon. Do you have any gum?"

"What? You want to go in some high-class lawyer's office smacking gum? Here, take a breath mint." Luann held out the plastic box of mints and frowned at her sister. "Since when are you so fussy about the way you look and smell?"

"Luann, it's not every day—really, it's not *ever*—that I'm in some rich lawyer's office. Do I look okay?"

Luann took a few steps back and looked at her, eyes moving from Liz's stylish cropped hair to the low-heeled pumps on her sister's feet. "Well, I think you could stand to gain a couple of pounds just to make the rest of us feel better. But, other than that ..."

"Lu, I'm serious!" Liz said and turned to cross the street to the office building.

"I was sayin', other than that, you look like you just stepped out of a J. Jill catalog. You *look* perfect, Liz. Now, if you can stop worrying about impressing some lawyer who's no smarter than you or me, you'll be just fine. Stop *fidgeting* with yourself. Be yourself, and if you get really nervous, just superimpose Grace Carlson's face on his. You know how to deal with her." Her sister laughed merrily.

The elevator opened to a quiet, carpeted reception area. It was empty except for a young woman seated behind an elegantly simple counter in one corner. Liz stepped in front of her and waited until the receptionist acknowledged her with a friendly, "Hello, may I help you?"

"I'm Liz Manley," she said. "I'm here to see Mr. Jamerson about..."

The woman was already pushing buttons and adjusting her headset. "You're here about Millicent Stich," she finished. "I'll let Mr. Jamerson know you're here. Would you and your friend like a cup of coffee? Tea?"

No sooner had Liz declined than the young lady stood and said, "Mr. Jamerson can see you now. If you'll follow me on back?"

"Is it okay if my sister comes with me? Luann ...?" She turned to her sister.

"Of course, just follow me. I'm Lucinda," she said. Formalities aside, they walked together to the end of the wide corridor. Polished double doors stopped them. The small, inconspicuous silver plate on the wall read, *Donald Jamerson II, Attorney-at-Law*. Lucinda tapped on the door with one hand and opened it with the other.

"Mr. Jamerson," she said as she led the sisters into the impressive space. "Liz Manley and Luann ...?" She paused and looked at Luann.

"Luann Latham," she finished and extended her hand to the handsome middle-aged man who walked towards them. "I'm Liz's sister."

Taking her cue from her confident sister, Liz extended her hand.

"I apologize for my appearance," he said, noting the open-collared shirt and knife-creased jeans he was wearing. "I usually follow Lucinda's lead and ignore the 'dress-down-Friday' tradition, but we're going to some barbecue over near Corinth tonight. Something my wife got us into. Forgive me if you would."

His easy manner did exactly what it was intended to do: it put Liz at ease. She liked him immediately. "You have a beautiful view," she said, looking out at the pyramid-shaped civic center perched near the Mississippi River.

"You should see a sunset from here," he answered. "Something I frequently do!"

Whether he intended it to be or not, Liz took this as a reminder that the attorney's time was valuable and turned the conversation to Millicent Stich.

"Thank you for seeing me so soon," she said after they were seated. She opened her purse and drew out the unfinished letter. "This is probably a good place to start."

"Oh, please accept my thanks," he countered." Miss Em is a special client. She and my father enjoyed not only a professional relationship but a personal one as well. In fact, I was one of her first painted children." He laughed. "Anyone who was painted by Miss Em is proud to be called a 'painted child.' There are many of us in Memphis, St. Louis, Chicago, D. C ..."

"Miss Em?" Liz asked. "You called her Miss Em?"

"Left over from childhood days. That's what she asked us to call her. Before she began a portrait—when she painted only portraits— she spent hours getting to know her subject. For me, she recognized my love of animals. I think I got maybe—three? four? —trips to the zoo out of her before she started painting me. Then she had the sittings in the zoo. My mother later told me that Miss Em said I was truly myself in that setting." He gave way to his infectious laugh. "Maybe she thought I *belonged* in the zoo.

"But that's not what you're here to discuss," he said in an apparent attempt to bring them back to the reason for their visit.

"What you're telling me is fascinating," Liz said. "The truth is, I don't really know Miss Millie—Miss Em—at all. I had never been inside her house till yesterday. My son has, but only in certain parts. He delivered groceries to her from our store. When I picked her up for her doctor's visits, she was either on her front porch or must have been watching from inside. She always came right out to the car."

"Since my dad passed, I'm afraid I've been negligent in seeing to her personally. In fact, my guess is she's lost touch with almost every one of her group of friends here in Memphis. But I'm not surprised to hear you say those things about her. If there's one word that could sum her up, it's *independent*. As warm a person as she is capable of being, her privacy is of extreme importance to her. I think she was always afraid she'd lose herself to public life if she didn't guard herself very carefully."

Up to this point in the conversation, Luann had sat quietly, taking in all the new information. She spoke now, "She's lived down the street from us ever since we were born, and I didn't know until yesterday when I saw that room full of paintings that she was a well-known painter. Millicent Labelle. Who would have ever guessed that we've had a famous painter living right there among us in Roslyn, Mississippi?"

"A roomful of paintings?" Mr. Jamerson seemed to have latched onto those four words. "There are paintings in her house?"

"Oh, several dozen," Luann said. "They're stacked against the walls in one of her front rooms. The one she painted of Liz ..."

Donald Jamerson stood. "Ladies," he addressed them, and they could hear the rising excitement in his voice. "You have uncovered a gold mine. Our first order of business is to get those paintings to a safe place."

CHAPTER 8

The sequence of events that began with a flood of emotion in Liz on the night she stood by Miss Millie's bedside in the ICU of North Oak Memorial culminated late in June when an ambulance pulled into the driveway of the Manley home, its purpose being to deliver Miss Millie to her new home.

The strong emotional connection Liz had felt when she saw the painting of herself under the big oak planted the seed in her head, a seed which germinated into a fully grown plant. During the month Miss Millie spent in rehab, Liz spent many hours thinking of how she could care for her friend after she was released. After she'd become fully convinced in her mind that she could take care of the woman in her home, she talked to Richard. When she presented her plan to him, he'd shaken his head repeatedly before uttering a word. He knew it was going to happen; he'd learned over the years that once Liz thought something through, his best approach was to simply rubber-stamp her idea and stay out of the way. "I don't know about this," he said, "but if you're sure, then go ahead." He, too, had been captivated by the woman when he'd accompanied Liz to the rehab center in Senatobia. Jackson and Lainie had gone with Liz on two occasions and were equally taken with her.

Donald Jamerson was elated when she took the idea to him. "You're like family to her," he'd said, "her only family. I'll support you in any way possible. Would you like me to present the idea to Em?"

"No, I'd rather do that," Liz said, believing that Miss Millie (she had yet to think of the woman as *Em*) would put up a stronger argument against the idea than anyone else. Her fears were confirmed, but she saw a ray of hope when she said, "You'll enrich our lives, Miss Millie. If you don't let us do this, we'll miss out on one of the best things that could happen to our family." After Liz spoke those words, she knew by the look on the woman's face that, with a little help from Donald Jamerson, she could make her plan happen.

Miss Millie didn't, as Liz had thought, present the strongest opposition. That came from the least likely source: Rose.

"It's not enough that you plop that big ole' mama cat under my feet where she curls herself up in my clean laundry. It's not enough that she spit out four little babies with all their mewings and flea bites. Who did all that alcoholic swabbing of those ears and combing of those fleas? Rose. Who put out the food and clean the nasties from the litter box?   Rose. Who ...?"

"Rose, you know you loved every minute of that. And you didn't do it by yourself. I combed fleas. Jackson and Lainie combed fleas. And once you taught Latisha how to clean their little ears with cotton swabs, she made you promise to keep that job for her till Jackson picked her up from day camp every afternoon."

And it was true. Latisha, Rose's prodigy grandchild, had taken on the care of Miss Liberty's babies with a vengeance. Rose had attached the name Miss Liberty to the yellow and white stray early on because "she take liberties with everything around here." Latisha, Maddie, Maria, Lainie, and Jackson had named and renamed each kitten at least three times. Maddie and Latisha, bodies sprawled on the floor, pencils of every color scattered around them, painstakingly drew each cat on separate pages of their sketchbooks. When a new name was offered, they added it to the list: Muffintop, Princess, Delilah—from Jackson. What had begun as a mystery (still was) and a misery had turned into a full-blown summer project for the kids. Even Rose, who won approval from all on her choice of name for the mama cat, joined in the naming competition.

Liz continued her argument. "And what about your days off? Who do you think took care of them on Wednesdays, Saturdays, and Sundays? I know you think we can't do anything for ourselves, Rose, but we manage to survive when you're not here." Liz had learned early in their relationship that Rose not only expected this kind of talk from her, but she *enjoyed* the argumentative tone their banter often took. This had begun early in their relationship, soon after Jackson's birth, when Rose had discovered that she could break through Liz's post-partum depression by taunting her: *"Look in the mirror, girl. You got enough grease in yo' hair to change the oil in my car. White girls don't want grease. Get up outta that bed and go wash yo' hair."* One of the first signs that Liz's depression was lifting was that she began arguing back: *"Leave me alone, Rose. Maybe I've hung around you so long that I* like *grease in my hair."* To an outsider, these exchanges might seem harsh or disrespectful; to Rose and Liz, they were evidence of the deep love and respect each held for the other.

Their mutual trust was the reason Liz included Rose in the decision about whether to bring Miss Millie to live with them. She was surprised to find real resistance.

As was their usual custom when a disagreement arose between them, the two women dropped the tough talk. Liz poured both of them a cup of coffee, and they sat at the kitchen table. "What's your objection, Rose?" Liz asked.

"The truth is ..." Uncharacteristically, her eyes filled with tears.

"Time out," Liz said. She left the room and returned with a box of tissues, pulled one out, and set the box on the table near Rose. "This may be the first time I've ever handed you a tissue, Rose, but I owe you a few. *I'm* the one who sheds tears."

Several tissues later, after she'd wiped her eyes, blown her nose, and walked to the trash can to discard her used tissues, Rose stood for a moment with her back to Liz and said, "I can't take this death thing. You know 'bout my mama. She won't be with us long. And my daddy ... I don't know what he's gon' do without her."

"Oh, Rose," Liz said as she walked over and put her arms around her. "I'm so sorry. And I didn't even think about your mama having anything to do with this. She's finished with her treatments, isn't she?" For the past several months, Rose had accompanied her mother and father to Senatobia for chemo treatments in hopes of stopping the progression of cancer.

"She's finished," Rose declared now and broke into tears as the reality of the double entendre hit her. "They can't do no more for her. She's taken to her bed now for most of the day. Daddy helps her up and out to the porch when she feels like it, but she only feels like it ever' now and then. Hospice people comin' to our house too, just like you say they'll be comin' here for your Miss Millie."

Liz had shared all the details about Miss Millie's condition with Rose as she had learned them without thinking of the parallel of the two older women's timeframe. Everyone involved with the decision knew that part of the arrangements would include eventual Hospice visits.

Miss Millie's heart condition had progressed to the point of terminal. Six months, at most, the doctors had predicted. The only other option available for her care was a nursing home facility, and although she had the means to afford the best, Liz had been adamant about caring for her at home. It didn't hurt that Donald Jamerson had been the first to warm to the idea. His fond childhood memories of "Miss Em" were strong, and while he hadn't maintained connections with her that would warrant inviting her to live in his own home in her last days, he had jumped at the idea of moving her into Liz's home when she presented the idea to him.

They had approached Miss Millie together and after several conversations in which the details of visiting nurses, extra paid help, hospice, changes in the guest room, and adjoining bathroom—all to be made at Miss Millie's expense—the agreement was made. Millicent Stich would spend her remaining days on earth in the Manley home.

The painful conversation between Liz and Rose cleared the air between the women about the changes in their household. Liz accepted Rose's reluctance to get involved with Miss Millie and assured her that she would in no way be responsible for her friend and that any extra work required would be picked up by other people. "You don't have to be involved at all, Rose. You have enough on your plate already. And you know that I'm willing to help out with your mama any way I can."

"I'm not so sure about not bein' involved," Rose said. "We all see what happened with them cats." After allowing Liz to see the sadness she carried around with her on a daily basis, it was essential for Rose to recover her equilibrium with tough talk.

***

The careful arrangements Liz had made to have Miss Millie delivered to a quiet house early on a Friday afternoon unraveled slowly. Pick-up time from the rehab center for Miss Millie was set for 1:00, and everyone—including Rose—had been instructed to be away from the house when Miss Millie arrived at around 2:00. A glitch in planning at North Oak Care Center caused a delay in the plans; the ambulance was late for pick-up. Liz spent the afternoon pacing the floor, watching out the front windows of her house, and calling to check on the status of the planned arrival. By four o'clock, Liz's nerves had gotten the best of her.

She watched, puzzled, at the sight of Lainie, Latisha, and Jackson tumbling out of Jackson's red Honda and running to the side door. Even as the question, "What are they doing here?" formed in her mind, she knew what had happened. They'd forgotten that Rose had taken the afternoon off so that she could pick Latisha up from day camp and take her straight home. The three burst into the kitchen as though it were a normal June day, only to meet Liz shooing them out. "You're not supposed to be here," she shouted louder than she intended.

"But, Ma, I live here!" Jackson began, only to be interrupted by Lainie.

"Oh, Miz Manley, we completely forgot! Remember, Jackson?" she said, tugging on his arm. "Rose was going to pick up Latisha today. Oh, Miz Manley, I'm so, so sorry. We forgot that you wanted a quiet house to bring Miss Millie home to. Let's go, Jackson."

"No, Lainie," Liz said, calmer now, "wait. Let me think for a minute." She stood head down, fingers nervously drumming her upper thigh. "Okay," she said seconds later, "we'll call the day camp and ask them to let Rose know what happened. She can wait there, and you two can drive Latisha back over ..."

She was interrupted by the sound of an opening door and Rose's voice. "Them kids got all mixed up ..."

Only to be interrupted by Latisha wailing, "Miz Liz! Creampuff and Whiney are missing! No, Miss Liberty, put him down! Put him down!" The last put-him-down was yelled as she chased Miss Liberty through the kitchen with Jocko clutched firmly in her jaws. The teenagers joined in the chase.

"What's she doin'?" Jackson yelled as the entire entourage trailed after the determined mama cat.

"She's hiding her babies from us," Lainie explained. "Mama cats don't like us people interfering with their babies. Look! She's hiding them in the closet."

Five people watched in awed silence as Miss Liberty disappeared through a slightly open closet door in an unused bedroom. Their silence was interrupted by the untimely ringing of the doorbell.

"Do you want me to answer the door or settle these chilluns and wild animals down?" Rose asked.

"I'll get the door. Get them out of here!" Liz groaned. "Put those kittens back in the laundry room," she instructed. "Please," she amended. "All we need is for somebody to trip and fall on a *cat* again!"

"This ain't what I call a quiet afternoon," Rose muttered, walking down the hall. "What you kids thinkin'?" she scolded. She opened the closet door, picked up the mother cat in one swoop, and ordered the youngsters to "get them babies put away." In a matter of minutes, she had restored order, sent Lainie and Jackson on their way, and settled Latisha in a chair with a book.

Rose puttered in the kitchen. Her movements were accompanied by the whir of wheels rolling down the wood floor of the hallway and the gentle murmurings of the two attendants as they assisted the older woman out of the wheelchair and into one of the upholstered chairs in her bedroom. The front door closed, and a car motor started. Finally, the silence that Liz had hoped for earlier descended on the house.

Liz walked down the hall towards the kitchen just as Rose picked up the tray she had prepared—her favorite, the natural wood with faded blue flowers surrounded by green stems and leaves bordering the edge—and turned to carry it down the hall. The women met in the doorway.

"Rose, I'm so sorry ... what have you got? Oh, Rose, you were coming to meet Miss Millie!" Liz exclaimed.

"She seems like the kind of lady who takes tea," Rose said. "I made a pot a' that Earl Grey you had in the cupboard. Can't see how anybody drinks hot tea on a June day, but it just seemed right. She bein' an artist and a lady and all that."

"Rose, you're the artist. Look at that tray. You picked the perfect cups and the prettiest napkins. When did you make those sugar cookies?" Liz was thrilled to see the effort extended by Rose.

"Who says *I* made them?" she asked. "Other people in this house cook beside me."

"You're the only one who makes them so perfectly round *and* sprinkles them with sugar. Come on, let's go meet Miss Millie. But first, set that tray down, and let's put another cup on it. You didn't give yourself one. I think we're going to establish a tradition this afternoon. High tea in the Manley Mansion!"

CHAPTER 9

The tradition of afternoon tea was to become a regular happening in the Manley household during the summer of Miss Millie's residence there. The only question was who might be in attendance. Most frequently the group was made up of Rose, Millie, and Liz, but Luann, once invited, made sure she showed up whenever possible. She'd often call Rose and ask permission to pick up Latisha early from day camp, sometimes getting her before lunch and going back to her house so that her girls and Latisha could have playtime before they all headed to Liz's house mid-afternoon. Madison and Latisha, both due to be third graders in the fall, and Maria, a soon-to-be fifth grader, got along beautifully. Maria, with a personality much like her Aunt Liz, would drift away from the younger two when they gave in to more giggles than she could tolerate.

"We're home!" Latisha called as they opened the door to the mudroom. "I'm getting the kittens out!"

"You stop right there, Little Missie," her grandmother ordered, meeting her in the hallway to the laundry room. "Ain't no kittens coming into this kitchen while there's food on the table."

"Hey there, Miss Lu. Looks like you got your hands full. These girls been behavin' theirselves?"

"Rose. They *always* behave. They don't behave, they answer to me. Right, girls?"

"Yes, ma'am!" The girls saluted, then collapsed into giggles.

"Law, me! I don't know how you stand them, all three together." Rose, in spite of her groaning, was pleased that Latisha spent so much time with Luann and her children. Raising a grandchild was no easy task, especially considering the time she spent working and taking care of her own aging parents. LaMont, Rose's son and Latisha's father, returned home so infrequently that the child hardly knew she had a father. And her mother? Only the good Lord knew where she was!

Rose's church friends often chided her for spending so much time with "those white folks," but Rose just listened without comment, a behavior very uncharacteristic of her. She knew, whether her friends understood or not, that Liz and Richard Manley would always be there, not just for her, but for her family as well.

Now, she herded the children to the big table, where she'd already laid out plates, apple slices, and peanut butter cookies. "Which you want? Milk or fruit juice?"

Maria reached over and touched one of the cookies. "Ooo, they're still warm. I want milk, warm cookies, and milk."

"Me too!" the younger girls chorused. "Jinx, you owe me a Coke," they chimed in unison, then fell to the floor in giggles.

"Could I take mine to the deck?" Maria asked, looking at the two younger children and shaking her head in adult fashion.

"Good idea, 'Rie," her mother said. "But no kittens outside. When you finish your snack, come back in and supervise the kitten party.

"And before you ask, no, you can't take one home with us today. They're still not old enough. They need another month or so with their mother and with each other. Remember what Dad told us; they learn to be gentle by playing with each other and by being taught by their mother when enough is enough. Just like you two—three," she corrected herself. "The more time they spend together supervised by their mother, the better pets they'll be. Just like you girls."

"Mom, we're not pets," Maria said indignantly.

"How 'bout we trade kittens for girls?" Rose asked Luann as she handed her the tea tray. "You take four kittens to your house, and we keep two girls here?"

"You might want to think about that awhile, Rose," Luann said. "At least you can keep the kittens in a cage."

"I'd get me a big ole' cage," Rose said as she poured three glasses of milk into large blue glasses and set them on the table in front of the children. "One that could hold three little girls."

Luann lifted the delicate antique teapot from the perfectly laid tray and filled it with steaming water from the kettle. "I'll take this on back if you'll finish getting the kids situated," she said.

"Don't forget this fancy table cover," Rose said, draping a small white cloth embroidered with delicate purple violets over Luann's arm.

"I'll be there soon," Rose called as Luann disappeared down the hallway. "Just get myself a Co'Cola. Can't drink that nasty old hot tea on a summer afternoon."

Miss Millie was sitting in her favorite chair by the large window in her bedroom. Luann set the tray on the long window seat, pulled a folding table out of the closet, and set it up in front of the frail woman. "Okay, Lady Millie, time to preside over the teapot," Luann said. While she was still too weak to pour tea—High Tea, they jokingly called this time of day—Miss Millie was still considered to be in charge. While Luann poured hot water over Earl Grey teabags and placed cookies on napkins for everyone, Liz finished rearranging the comforter on the old sleigh bed they had moved from Miss Millie's home. Tea time followed rest time for Miss Millie.

"After just one week, I'm already spoiled," Liz said as she perched in the window seat beside Rose. "I may never go back to the grocery store again. And all this time, I thought I *liked* working there. How did I ever find the time?"

"Lucky for you, Denise wanted to go to work," Luann said. "How did Richard pull that off, anyway?"

Richard's older sister, Denise, had never worked outside the home. After earning a business degree from Ole Miss, she'd returned to Roslyn with her husband Carl, who had set up his dental practice in Batesville. Denise promptly given birth to three children, one right after the other. Her youngest, Cal, was to be a sophomore at Ole Miss in the fall. With an empty nest, she'd jumped at the chance to step in and take Liz's place in the store. In just one short week, Liz had shown her the ropes and turned everything over to her with a cautionary warning: "Don't let Grace Carlson bully you!"

"Poor Richard. It's either his wife or his older sister—who, by the way, has been known to call him Richie-Poo—looking over his shoulder. He likes it, though. Actually, he's the one who thought of asking her," Liz said.

"He says that Miss Gracie don't pull her chain near so often as she pull yours," Rose said. "Why you think that is?"

"Don't start on me, Rose," Liz warned. "I don't want to be reminded of that old woman. Sorry, Miss Millie. I didn't mean any disrespect to old people. But Grace Carlson is in a category of people all by herself, old or not."

"No offense taken, my dear. Don't forget, I know Grace Carlson, too. She didn't take too kindly to my appearance in Roslyn when we moved here."

"Really?" asked Luann. "Why was that?"

"I was an outsider," Miss Millie said simply, "and I chose to stay an outsider." She laughed. "Not that I really had any choice in the matter. Perhaps you understand this—but, then again, perhaps you don't since you've been born and reared here—but when one comes from outside, especially from a city, to a small southern town, one is never truly accepted. This is most true if one originates, as did I, from a *northern* city."

Liz couldn't decide which story she wanted to pursue: how Grace Carlson had treated Miss Millie or how Miss Millie had ended up in Roslyn. Rose chose for her.

"Where was it you 'riginated from?" Rose asked.

"I grew up in Chicago," Miss Millie said. "That's where I met and married my Rudolph. We had happy years there."

"I always wanted to go to Chicago," Rose said. "My mama's brother went off up there way back in the fifties. Ain't seen nothin' of him since. You still got family there?"

"No, Rose, I do not. After my mother's passing, neither Rudolph nor I had any ties to Chicago, so we rarely went back. Prior to my marriage to him, it had only been my mother and me. Alone in the world, so to speak," Miss Millie said with a sad smile.

The room was silent as each woman absorbed the information. Rose, never at a loss for words but not knowing how to respond, finally broke the silence. "This tea gone cold on you, ma'am," she exclaimed as she reached for Miss Millie's cup.

The elderly woman reached for her hand, holding it gently. "Thank you, Dear, but I've had plenty." Liz looked at the work-worn brown hand, much larger than Miss Millie's delicate blue-veined one, and a pleasant feeling engulfed her. Peace? Contentment? *Love*, she realized. These two women that she loved—one of them for years, the other just a few short weeks—were expressing in the simplest of ways the love they had for each other. And just by witnessing the gesture, she, too, was included. Still holding Rose's hand in hers, Miss Millie looked at Liz first, then Luann. The soft murmuring of the children could be heard from down the hall.

"You're my friends," she said. "May I indulge myself with stories of my past? I've been my only audience for these memories for too many years. There are periods of time when I doubt the truth of them. Perhaps talking to my friends will renew my faith."

"You'd honor us." Luann was uncharacteristically solemn, her eyes bright with tears. "Start at the beginning, too. After just a few short tea times, I feel like I've known you forever. I just don't know your *history*."

"My beginning," Miss Millie said and laughed. "In the beginning ... Not quite that long ago! I was born in 1924 in the month of April. To save you the mathematical trouble, that makes me 76-plus years of age. I'm afraid my recently passed birthday was the turning point that involved all of you in my life because that's when I decided I didn't want to be on this earth any longer. But, as you already know, the cat interfered with my plans." Her eyes twinkled.

"The cat came close to completing your plans," Liz said. "But that's another story. Tell us about your childhood."

"I had a very subdued childhood," she replied. "I was only six when my father disappeared. My mother talked little about it, but from the few things she said, he left Chicago for Alaska to find his fortune. I think she knew when he left that she'd never see him again, but she kept up the pretense for years. He was to come back for us at some point, either to live in luxury in Chicago with the wealth he'd earned or to take us back to Alaska with him. Neither of those things happened. My mother was never bitter. I don't recall in the few years I had them both that they ever spoke a harsh word to each other or to me. Perhaps that's what my father missed—excitement. I'll never really know.

"My mother was an excellent seamstress. She had made all our clothing from the time I could remember, and after my father left, she used that skill to support us. I remember going with her to the beautiful Marshall Fields & Company store in downtown Chicago to look for work. I couldn't walk for looking upward at the colorful Tiffany dome, which was the crowning glory of the department store. She somehow convinced them to allow her to do alterations for them in our home. She made the same arrangement later with Goldblatt's. I have vivid memories of falling asleep to the sound of her sewing machine whirring away. I slept on a little daybed in her sewing room until I was a teenager and needed the privacy of my own bedroom."

Miss Millie spoke as though to herself. When she paused for breath, no one spoke. No one was willing to break the mood. After several seconds, she made a small pleasant sound, like laughter, and resumed talking.

"It was her sewing skills that landed Rudolph for me." She laughed out loud. "I still see him in the little Five and Dime where I worked to help with my expenses in art school. I attended the Art Institute after graduation from high school," she interjected.

"The Art Institute of Chicago. Wow!" Luann exclaimed. "You learned from the best. Like I didn't already know that," she said. "Look at your work.

"Oh, sorry, Miss Millie, you were talking about landing Rudolph," Luann apologized for her interruption.

"Oh, yes. I can still see that handsome young man wandering the aisles of the Five and Dime, looking for the Notions Department. He couldn't tell a spool of thread from a skein of yarn, and he was planning to repair a giant rip in the underarm of his suit coat. He wouldn't move his left arm at all for fear of exposing the rip. When he explained to me what he needed and what he intended to do, I was so overcome with pity for him that I offered him my address and my mother's services. Completely out of character for me!" she exclaimed and clapped her hands together.

"You was already in love, Sweet Lady!" Rose said. "Love at first sight."

"Perhaps you're right. Maybe I was in love with him from the very first minute I laid eyes on him. It's a certainty that he was the only man I ever loved. My one true love."

"So, how long before you were married?" Liz asked.

"We were very patient, my dear. Even then, Rudy was working for the railroad and was gone for long periods of time. My art was very important to me, in spite of being deeply in love. We didn't get married until June of 1948, three years after we met. The truth is I think he loved my mother as much as he loved me. We had some wonderful times together, the three of us. Later, after we were married, Rudy Junior was born, and we began to plan our move to Memphis; Rudolph did everything he could to convince her to move with us. To no avail."

Screams from the other end of the house brought Luann, Liz, and Rose to their feet all at once. Luann was the first one out the door and down the hall. She'd taken only a few steps when Maria met her, yelling, "Those *children* have let Miss Liberty and all *four* of her babies go outside!"

***

Later, after the cats were corralled, Rose had cleaned up from teatime, taken Latisha home, and Luann and the girls had left. Liz sat with her elbows on the big trestle table in the kitchen, chin in her hands. Miss Millie's words echoed in her head: "We were very patient, my dear." Where, she wondered, had Miss Millie gotten her patience? Yes, Miss Millie had been older, but not that much older. No, Liz thought, age wasn't a factor. Richard had asked for a few weeks to focus on his finals at Ole Miss and to think about their relationship. A few weeks. As much as she loved him, she couldn't give him that. She was afraid he wouldn't come back to her. She'd said, "No. Let's end it right here." Out of anger and loneliness, she'd turned immediately to Steven Parker. She had shown the exact opposite of patience; she'd acted impulsively. And, though she had no regrets about Jackson, she knew she'd spend the rest of her life regretting her impulsive behavior.

CHAPTER 10

Liz Breedlove and Richard Manley fell in love in 1978 in the halls of Roslyn High School, just a few paces down from her locker. She remembered fighting unsuccessfully with the combination of her lock between algebra and civics classes. Three minutes to hurry to her locker, change out her books, and get to class without a tardy. And she couldn't get the lock to work.

"Need some help?" She was embarrassed to see the face that went with the voice when she turned and saw Richard standing there. Embarrassed to have a sophomore watch a lowly freshman fumble with her combination lock.

They had known each other forever, it seemed. But they had never run in the same circles. The truth was, Liz didn't run in any circles at all. She had friends at school. She ate lunch with a group of girls and would occasionally meet up with them at a ball game. In fact, she was well-liked, but Liz rarely went to any place other than school or church. Her one sport was bowling, but she did that only on the rare occasions when the youth from her church went as a group for an evening of recreation; otherwise, she rarely participated in any physical activity. Luann, a senior when Liz was a freshman, participated in everything.

"What's your combo?" Richard asked.

"Combo?" She blushed a deeper red as the word hung there between them, irretrievable. "Oh, you mean my combination. It's ... uh ..." She fumbled in her pocket, pulled out a crumpled piece of paper, smoothed it as best she could, and handed it to him.

Richard spoke the numbers out loud as he turned the knob on the locker, opened the door, and stood back. She grabbed her civics book, plopped it on top of her algebra book, and turned away to hurry down the hall.

"Hey!" he called after her. "Didn't you forget something?"

She turned to thank him and plowed right into a scrub bucket and mop that had been left at the side of the hallway, upending the entire thing and falling right in the middle of the puddle of dirty water. Richard was there in a second, taking her books—she'd clasped them to her desperately out of fear of ruining them—and helping her to her feet.

What happened next caused her to fall hopelessly in love. "Come on," he'd said. "You can't go to class looking like that. I'll take you home, and you can be changed and back to class by the next hour."

"I can't leave," she said. "I'll be suspended."

"Go," he told her. "My truck's in the parking lot. You know, it's that red Chevy. I'll go by the office and get permission for us."

Richard had just turned 16 and inherited his dad's red Chevrolet truck, so he'd assumed everyone in town knew about it. Liz, barely able to distinguish a Ford from a Chevy, figured there couldn't be too many red trucks in the parking lot. What she should have questioned but never did was how he could so easily gain permission to leave the school grounds. Much later in her life, she realized that, even at his young age, Richard was already regarded as a young man of strong principles. He'd been granted permission for such an unusual request, just as he knew he would be, on the strength of his character.

Much later, after they'd dated more than a year, they were discussing the merits of living in a small town like Roslyn versus a place like, say, Memphis. "People who live in big cities don't know what they're missing," Richard said. He went on to explain his position. He said that with so many people in big cities, it was hard to know whom to trust, so people just ended up not trusting anybody. He continued by talking about his family and generations of families who chose to live in the area. It wasn't just him that people knew, he told her; his reputation came in part from his family's known character. He was lucky to have that history and didn't ever intend to do anything to damage it.

After the locker and upturned mop bucket incident, the two were inseparable, as much as an almost 15-year-old and barely turned 16-year-old could be inseparable. They ate lunch together, met at youth group every Sunday and Wednesday night, and Liz discovered a sudden love for basketball. She attended every home game to cheer for the handsome guard. Every Sunday after church, Liz went home with the Manley family for lunch and, within a few short weeks, had been taken into the family as one of their own. She loved it.

After washing the dinner dishes and putting the leftovers away, Richard and Liz picked apples in the orchard, walked to the stream in the nearby woods, or fished for perch in the pond. Later, the family would pull the leftovers out for a light supper before Liz and Richard headed back into town for their Sunday evening youth group meeting, after which Richard would drop Liz off at her silent home.

Even after Richard graduated from high school, leaving her behind for her senior year, they still had weekends together. Nothing changed until the spring of Richard's college freshman year.

Those early days of their courtship played over and over in Liz's mind. Afternoon tea time proved to be a double-edged sword for Liz: she loved the conversation with the women in her home at the time, but on later reflection, she found that the talks stirred up memories that she hoped she'd laid to rest permanently.

Lying beside Richard late at night after Miss Millie had told about meeting and falling in love with her Rudolph, Liz, unable to fall asleep, had snuggled up close to him. She shook him gently by his upper arm and called softly, "Richard!" It took several attempts before she awakened him.

"Hmm? What?" he murmured.

"Nothing, really. I just have a question for you."

"A question at ..." he raised himself up and looked at the clock before continuing, "... at 12:43 in the morning? Could it wait till 6:00?"

"I can't sleep," she said. "Just tell me one thing, and then I'll let you go back to sleep. Why was it you really wanted time apart?"

"Time apart from what?" he asked sleepily.

"From us," she said.

"Hon, I don't have any idea what you're talking about. When did I want time away from us?"

"When you were a freshman in college and I was a senior in high school," she said.

"Liz, that was in another life. Why are you asking such a question? And why have you picked such a strange time to relive our youthful mistakes?"

"I was just thinking."

"For how long have you been thinking? You gotta get back to work, girl. You've got too much time on your hands."

"Maybe you're right. This is the first time I've spent this much time at home since ..."

"Since Jackson was born," Richard finished for her.

"And that didn't really count. I wouldn't call hunkering down in bed with the covers over my head 'spending time at home.' More like retreating from the world."

Richard was wide awake now, and both of them lay quietly. Liz, to some degree, regretted waking him. But she also felt compelled to talk, a rare thing for her.

Richard finally spoke. "Liz, there's no reason to go back over all that. I know having Miss Millie here has you all stirred up emotionally, but *our* family is good. We always have been."

"Hey, you still there?" he asked after a moment.

"It's not just that," she finally answered. "It's Jackson and Lainie, it's Luann, it's that awful Grace Carlson!"

"Whoa there, kid. That's an awful lot to take on at once. How do they have anything to do with what happened to us all those years ago?" Richard had given up trying to put an end to the conversation. Now, he was truly concerned. It wasn't like Liz to express multiple concerns in a single sentence.

He turned on the tiny lamp on his nightstand. "What's going on, Liz?" he asked.

"It's just this feeling of impending doom I carry around. I imagine all the old biddies in town talking about everything I've ever done. Just the other day, Grace Carlson reminded me that I was the daughter of one of our town drunks. Don't people ever forget anything in this town? Who am I trying to kid? I know the answer to that.

"I worry, sometimes, Richard, that Jackson will find out. That *everyone* will find out. I don't think I could live here anymore if that happened. And even that wouldn't make things better because if Jackson ever knew ..."

"Stop it, Elizabeth." There was exasperation—a hint of anger even—in Richard's voice. "You and I are the only people in the world who know about our son. I'm certainly not going to tell him. Are you?

"And I'm confused," he continued. "What does Luann have to do with this conversation? I thought things between you two were better than they'd ever been before. Looks to me like you two are finally having some fun together."

"We are, and that's part of the problem. We're getting close for the first time in our lives, and she wants to bring up old stuff that happened with Mama and Daddy when we were kids. Stuff that Grace-less Carlson thinks she knows all about. Luann's tried to make me promise that we'll talk about those days soon. About Daddy's drinking and Mama's ..."

She couldn't make herself say the word.

"Liz, your mother did *not* have an affair. This whole town would have known if your mother had an affair. Maybe she was attracted to that guy for a time, and maybe he'd have liked to move in on her, but I promise you: There. Was. No. Affair."

After a moment, Richard said, "You need to talk about it, Liz, but not to me. This is like a big wad of fishing lines all tangled up together. You need to take one thing at a time. I think Lu's right;

you two need to talk about your childhood. Maybe you'll find out it wasn't quite as bad as you've always thought. She was older, so she'll have a different perspective on things." He reached over, turned off the light, and pulled her to him.

"Things always seem worse at night," he told her. "Let's get some sleep and untangle that fishing line tomorrow."

***

Richard was right. In spite of having a rip-roaring headache the next morning, Liz's attack of "doomsday dread" had settled back to its normal low-grade discontent. None of the issues had disappeared, but with daylight came her familiar feeling of being able to control what was in front of her. She decided that Richard was right; she needed to take Lu's advice and talk about their childhood. It wasn't fair, she realized, to dump all this on her husband. He was her "Steady Eddie," but even he had his limits.

Liz's fist was raised to knock on Miss Millie's door when it opened. Charla, one of the visiting nurses, was leaving after having attended to her morning routine. Miss Millie was able to do most things for herself now and had even ventured several times to the large kitchen to be with the family. Still, she tired easily and needed early morning assistance with her shower and attire. Even in her weakened condition, she still dressed for the day, complete with nylons on her legs and perfectly coiffed hair. No expense was spared in keeping up her appearance, in doing for her things that she no longer had the strength to do for herself.

"Come in, dear," she greeted. "You look especially tired this morning, Elizabeth. We can't let my presence be a strain on you. Remember our agreement."

Miss Millie had been insistent from the start that any extra work involving her would be paid for by her. She had given a generous increase in pay to Rose, in spite of protests, because in her words, "One extra person in a household increases the workload, whether you have any direct responsibilities to that person or not, and that demands an increase in pay." And, as in most things, once Miss Millie issued a decree, one could consider the matter closed.

"You're not a strain, Miss Em." Liz now called her friend *Miss Em*, adopting the pet name she was called by Donald Jamerson, the attorney who handled her estate. In fact, the two names, *Miss Em* and *Miss Millie,* were now used interchangeably by everyone in the woman's new circle of friends. Liz thought of *Em* as the letter *M*; to her way of thinking, it was a matter of being economical with syllables.

She continued, "You are now and always will be a bright spot in my life."

"Perhaps it's sadness I see in your eyes rather than tiredness. Why are you so sad, dear? If you don't have immediate plans, would you sit down with me for a few moments and talk?"

The lift and fall of Liz's shoulders, accompanied by an extended sigh, confirmed Miss Millie's observation. She turned to the wide window that looked out over a large, unmown field, alive with color and activity. Summer wildflowers were in full bloom; Queen Anne's lace mixed with wild daisies, purple coneflower, and orange butterfly weed attracted bees, butterflies, and hummingbirds.

Still standing with her back to her friend, Liz began. "I feel like an over-stuffed file cabinet, one that's been used for years to hide unfinished business and dark secrets. If someone opened any of the drawers and began to pull files, they'd be shocked and disgusted with the contents. Leaving the grocery store and spending time at home has made me slow down for the first time in my married life. I think I've survived by staying busy so I don't have to think about anything except what's right in front of me."

Miss Millie was quiet. After several minutes, Liz sighed heavily again, then turned and sat in the window seat. She leaned against one end so she could face her friend, pulled her feet up, and stretched them out in front of her. "I really don't know *what* this feeling is."

"It sounds like shame, my dear. Unwarranted, undeserved shame. Whatever those "dark secrets" are that you carry around with you, they do not define you. You'd do much better to allow those of us who know and love you to mirror back to you what we see when we look at you. Ask any one of us: Luann, Rose, any of the children, Richard ... Shall I go on?"

When Liz didn't answer, Miss Millie continued. "I'm not one to advise talking things over with someone. And you might not want to take advice from one who spent several years retreating from humankind and then attempting to put a permanent end to life."

"Why did you retreat, Miss Em? Why did you come to Roslyn in the first place? And why did you quit painting so suddenly?"

"Those are two different stories, my dear. One of them full of joy and anticipation, the other full of sorrow. Which would you like to hear first?"

Liz considered the question for a moment before answering, "I don't think I can take another dose of sadness. I think I'd rather hear something happy."

"It was a very happy time in our lives that brought us to Roslyn. Yes, I think I'd rather tell that story."

Miss Millie launched into the story of how she, Rudolph, and little Rudy came to Roslyn all those years ago. After they'd settled in Memphis and she'd gained a reputation as a painter, a reputation that put her more in the public eye than either of them felt comfortable with, they'd begun by going on excursions around Memphis, one of which had brought them to Roslyn.

"We drove around the sleepy little town just minutes from the highway and fell in love with it. Not just the town, but the house too. Rudolph had a love affair with both trains and symmetry, and the house reminded him of both: long and symmetrical. There was a *For Sale* sign in the yard, and once we walked inside and saw the way the house was arranged and the possibilities it offered, we knew it was ours."

She explained how the close proximity to all they needed to continue their lives as they were, hers as an artist and Rudolph's as an engineer on the train, sealed the deal.

"The one downside," she said with a sad smile, "was our lack of knowledge about the religious prejudice against Catholicism here. We hadn't considered changing the location of the place where we practiced our faith—it was worth the drive to Memphis to stay in our parish—so we didn't explore the possibility of a priest here in Roslyn. After some months of living here and being bombarded"— this said with a smile— "with invitations to all the churches and civic or social groups, we began to understand that there were no Catholics in Roslyn. Rather than offend, we decided to be the best neighbors we knew how to be while keeping our private lives private. In hindsight, perhaps that wasn't the best plan, especially in light of how things turned out later in our lives.

"But that's another story for another day." She clasped her hands together and turned to Liz with a sad smile on her face.

"There's irony here, you know. Perhaps this is a case of it-takes-one-to-know-one. I'm feeling a certain amount of shame myself these days. Had not God intervened in the form of that gray cat, I would have most likely succeeded in my plan to end my life."

"Were you really going to do that?" Liz asked. "End your life, I mean?"

"I was, my dear. I was so ... alone. That is, I *felt* so alone. And I knew that my life wasn't going to last much longer anyway, no matter what I did. I had just decided to hurry-up the process. I was so tired I didn't even consider the right or wrong of the act. In my church, you know, suicide is a mortal sin. However, I had convinced myself that God would understand and forgive me. Instead, He understood and stopped me."

"There's something I've wondered about, Miss Em. How did the cat—maybe I should say cats—figure in your plans?"

As if on cue, Miss Liberty strolled into the room, jumped up on the window seat, and curled up at Liz's feet. "She's looking for relief," Liz said. "Her babies are so playful they wear her out, so she has to take a break."

"Yes, she's coming in here more and more frequently. I think, too, she remembers me. Perhaps she's looking for more of that tuna I so generously offered."

"Okay. Would you please explain to me—and this is a two-part question—why did you want a cat at all when you were planning to die? And how were there two cats involved in this? The ambulance attendants insist that a gray cat ran from your house on the night of your accident. When Jackson went back to lock your house that night, Miss Liberty was there."

"It does seem quite a mystery, doesn't it," she answered. "The answer to the first question is very simple. I didn't want to die alone. I'd never owned an animal, but I knew them to be a great comfort to many people. I knew that cats were very independent creatures and that one could live unattended—with plenty of food and water, of course—for days. Obtaining one was far more difficult than I thought. It meant that I had to involve people."

Miss Em explained in detail how she had borrowed the gray cat from neighborhood boys after giving up on trapping Miss Liberty, whom she dubbed a "consummate escape artist."

"Boys being boys, they never thought to ask why I needed to 'borrow' the cat. They, as well as I, were reassured of its return because of a collar with a tag around its neck offering an identifying phone number."

"We can only guess about Miss Liberty," Liz said.

At the mention of her name, the cat stood up, stretched, and jumped down to curl up at Miss Em's feet.

"She probably wandered in while the door was propped open during the chaos. Looking for more tuna, no doubt."

As the two women laughed, it occurred to Liz how easy it was to forget herself when she talked to her friend. It was as if she became a different person in Miss Millie's presence, as if what happened between them at any given moment was the most important thing that *could* happen at that moment.

She tried to think of a way to express her thoughts to the elderly woman but failed. She slipped from her comfortable seat to kiss her friend gently on her forehead. "Thank you," she said.

"Look in the mirrors, Elizabeth," Miss Millie said. "They're all around you. Unburden yourself of shame."

CHAPTER 11

"Where this summer gone?" Rose lamented as she peeled potatoes for the salad to be consumed at the Labor Day picnic scheduled for later in the day. A screened canopy, intended to protect the mountains of food from flies, had been set up in the Manley's backyard; tables with red checkered vinyl tablecloths dotted the grass. Richard had prepared the smoker early that morning, and the aroma of ribs and roasting chicken was thick in the air. The last count of attendees was 56, but everyone knew that was just an estimate; family members often issued last-minute invitations to whomever they happened to run into on the street.

"I hope this doesn't turn out like our Fourth of July picnic," Liz said. "Remember, Rose, nobody brought paper products, and we were ready to eat before anyone realized it. Good thing the family is in the grocery business, *and* good thing we had hot dogs in buns to start the kids on. They were so hungry we'd probably have had a mutiny on our hands. Can you think of anything we've forgotten?"

"Like you say, anything you forget, you just jump in your car and run to the grocery. Stop frettin', Lizbet. Just 'cause this picnic is at your house don't mean you got to do everything. Other people got their part to do. You've already gone above and beyond. Just the meat and drink! That's all you're s'posed to provide."

Rose was right. The Manley clan loved celebrations and had hit on a system years ago by which the work and expense were shared. They rotated hosting duties and shared in contributions to the meal. The rotation included Richard's parents, his sister, both of his aunts and uncles, Liz and Richard, and, since their return to Roslyn, Luann's family. Their main events were Labor Day, Thanksgiving, Christmas, New Year's Day, Easter, and the Fourth of July. However, a celebration could arise out of so small an occurrence as the senior Manley's freezer being full of Richard Senior's catch from Sardis Lake. More than once, Liz had picked up the phone to hear Richard's mom say, "Liz, honey, call your sister, and all ya'll come on out Friday night for supper. Richard came home with a boatload of fish today, and I don't have anywhere to put 'em unless I clean out the freezer. I swear that man needs to go back to work! Anyway, I've called everybody else. Just bring something to go with the fish if you have time to make it. If you don't come on out anyway. There'll be plenty."

No one bothered with reciprocation. If you felt like cooking for a crowd, you did. If you didn't, nobody noticed or cared. If you wanted to bring two or three extra people along, so much the better. Food was plentiful. Maybe the crowd needed to eat in shifts, and maybe the plates needed to be washed and rewashed, but no one minded. The kids ate quickly and organized games of hide and seek or touch football; the adults talked about hunting, fishing, craft shows, or politics.

Liz had grown to love these occasions early on. Richard's family took her in as one of them, and for a girl who had grown up in a home where silence reigned, the constant chatter and activity were as welcome as a gentle rain after a long, dry spell.

She'd never become as comfortable in her hostess role as the rest of the family, and this time was no exception. Rose kept her in check by alternately chiding and comforting her, depending on Liz's degree of neediness.

"You bought enough potatoes to feed the whole town of Roslyn," she told Liz. "We don't even have a pan big enough to cook 'em in." She grumbled as she rattled the pots and pans and finally came up with two large ones. "Looks like we gonna have *two* bowls of potato salad 'stead of one. I hope they come hungry!

"Hey there, Miss Em. Sit right down over here, and let me make you a cup of tea. Maybe you can put some calm into Lizbet's mind." Rose welcomed the distraction, knowing that the presence of the older woman in the room had a calming effect on Liz.

With the help of a walker, Miss Millie now moved about the house freely. Liz pulled a chair out and helped the woman to the table. Rose, well-acquainted with her tea habits, began preparations for the tea.

"Let me get these potatoes cooking, and I think I'll sit right down with you," Rose said. "Lizbet, quit your fussin' and come sit with us."

"Yes, Elizabeth, come join us. There's something I want to talk over with the two of you," Miss Millie agreed. "Now is as good a time as ever." Rose and Miss Em worked like a tag team with Liz. Without any private discussion, both women recognized the below-the-surface struggle that was ongoing in their young friend. As the summer progressed, Liz had become increasingly tense, holding off any attempts by Richard, Luann, Rose, or Miss Em to get her, in her own words, to open up "those overfilled file drawers" and deal with the hidden secrets stored there.

"There's something I want to do," Miss Millie said. "I want to paint again."

Liz and Rose, seated across the table, stared at her.

"Yes, I want to paint again," she repeated. "Your ears do not deceive you."

"You want to paint?" Liz asked.

"My dear, I want to paint," she repeated patiently.

"But ... how?" Liz asked.

"*How* is not nearly as important as *whom*," the woman responded. "I want to paint children again, starting with Latisha. She'll be my first. Then I'd like to paint the other girls, Maria and Madison. Then, if there's time, on to Jackson and Lainie. It'll be very simple, in reality. Simple for me, that is. If you, my strong friends, can collect my easel, brushes, and paints, then everything else will be easy. I know these children, you see. I already see the paintings in my head; it's just a matter of putting them on canvas. We'll start with Latisha sitting in the window seat with her book. She reads, I paint. I can capture her essence completely."

"You sure you're up to this?" Rose asked, finally finding her voice.

"Dear Rose, I'm not only, as you say, 'up to this,' I'm looking forward to it. I'm *anticipating* this venture. Not to introduce a morbid note, but this is the first thing I've truly looked forward to since I planned my own demise."

"And we all know how that turned out!" Rose exclaimed. "Miss Em, you sure come up with strange notions."

Miss Millie laughed, and the sound of her laughter caused Liz and Rose to join in.

"There are preparations to be made, preparations which will require a field trip to my house. Not an easy thing, as I haven't been inside my home since my unfortunate—or perhaps, in reality, fortunate—accident. Do you suppose we could impose on Luann to join us?"

"Luann salivates at the very mention of your home," Liz said. "She'd pay to get in there and run her hands over your antiques again, Miss Em. But we have a picnic to prepare for right now. What about tomorrow afternoon? Rose, does that work for you?"

Rose, lost in a cloud of steam from the potatoes she poured into a strainer, didn't reply.

"Rose?" Liz asked.

The woman turned, her dark face dripping with moisture. Had it not been for her quavering voice, one might have missed the fact that some of the wetness was from her eyes. "She wants to paint my girl. I'll walk to Jackson and back for them paints and brushes. My child's been called *colored* lotsa times. Ain't never been a *painted child,* though. Miss Millie, I thank you."

***

Liz and Luann were arranging and rearranging food on the tables as the crowd gathered for the Labor Day picnic when Liz brought up the subject of Miss Millie resuming her painting.

As Liz had predicted, Luann was elated at the chance to return to Miss Millie's home, but as Liz and Rose had been earlier, she was also concerned about taking the frail woman there. "She hasn't been *anywhere* since you brought her here, Liz. How do you know she has the stamina? And have you thought about how we're going to get her in the house? Besides, how do you think being there with all those memories is going to affect her? I don't think it's a good idea for her to go back there."

"I'm not sure she's thought it through," Liz said. "Wouldn't her brushes be stiff from disuse and paints dried out after all this time? According to Miss Em, it's been years since she's painted. Maybe we need to have her make a list of supplies and start fresh."

"Tomorrow is soon enough for that problem," she continued, moving bowls of assorted salads and vegetables closer together on the serving table. "We've got our own little issues to take care of right here. Like, how are we going to get all this food on the tables?"

"Where do you want me to put these ribs?" Richard asked, approaching the laden tables of side dishes. Answering his own question, he called to Jackson, "Come on over here, Jacks. Bring out another of those folding tables in the garage and set it up for the meat."

"And don't even think about leaving as soon as we eat," Liz called to her approaching son.

"Aw, Ma, give it up," Jackson replied. "Just 'cause Gramps and I went fishing after the Fourth of July picnic doesn't mean I do that all the time. You were just sore because somebody invited Grace Carlson, and Gramps wasn't there to keep her entertained."

Jackson, had he known the extent of misery a simple reminder of Grace Carlson could bring his mother, would not have brought up that disastrous day at Denise's house earlier in the summer. Miss Gracie had simply appeared around noon on the day of the Fourth of July picnic, stating she'd need a ride home before dark.

"Who invited *her*?" Liz had asked Denise.

"I didn't invite her," Denise replied. "You can try to run that down if you want to, Liz, but you know as well as I do that Miss Gracie never gets invited anywhere. Heck, her own children don't invite her to anything; they don't even come to see her. She has her own standing self-issued invitation to any event in town that she hears about. Let it go, honey; don't let that old sourpuss spoil your day."

But it was already spoiled. Since her last encounter with Grace Carlson, she'd been thrilled that she didn't have to face her in the grocery store several times a week. While she hadn't been completely successful at putting the ugly words spoken by the woman out of her mind, she'd at least kept busy enough not to be tormented by them. She'd managed to pull herself together enough after her midnight breakdown with Richard and subsequent talk with Miss Millie to at least give the appearance that nothing was bothering her. Or so she thought.

She'd done her best to avoid Miss Gracie that Fourth of July afternoon, all the time knowing that her efforts would be in vain. Grace Carlson *would* find an opportunity to wave a red flag in front of her. Liz knew that was a given. Still, she wasn't prepared for the venom sprayed on her by the old woman.

Long before darkness had fallen, Liz was entertaining the children on the driveway by handing them lighted sparklers, one at a time. Each child drew a simple "air picture" with the lighted wand as the others watched and tried to guess what it was. Shouts of "a tree," "a house," and "a dinosaur" filled the early evening air. Liz was having as much fun as the children and didn't notice the woman as she approached her from behind.

"Guess you learned that little trick from your artist friend," Miss Gracie said.

Liz's first thought was to ignore her, simply to pretend she wasn't there. She considered ending the game and walking away. But she knew neither of those options would have silenced the old bat for long. She would have sought her out again. Get it over with, she thought.

"Not really," she said and shrugged. "Just thought it up on the spur of the moment."

"Like you did when you took the hoity toity Millicent Stich in? Seems to me that even you would know better than to take an atheist into your home. Course, all that money she has hidden away spoke loud and clear, I'd imagine."

The buzzing in Liz's ears drowned out other sounds. She barely had the presence of mind to end the game and send the children on to a game of hide and seek before she turned her attention, and fury, on the woman.

"Atheist? That would be a compliment coming from you. I'll take that to mean that Miss Millie denies the god that you know, Grace. And that would be to her credit. If your small-minded, conniving, petty ways are an indication of your god, then I'm an atheist too. I much prefer the God that Miss Millie knows to the one you pretend to know."

"Well, Missie, I'm glad to hear you admit it. That Catholic God is not the same as ours. I wonder what Brother Collison will think of you now when he hears about this. You rejectin' your Bible teaching and lining up with the Catholics! Now that beats all!"

In the weeks that had passed between that early July evening and now, Liz had done her best to forget that ugly exchange of words. In reasonable moments, she realized that Grace Carlson wasn't the real source of her anxiety. True, the woman brought out her worst fears of being "outed." While she knew that the Grace Carlson version of her life wasn't the true one, that interpretation hung over her head like a weakened tree branch that could fall at any moment and crush her life. Even as she held those who loved her—Miss Em, Luann, Rose, Richard—at arm's length, she remembered and took comfort in Miss Em's words from that June morning: "Look in the mirrors, Elizabeth."

Liz looked up at Jackson. At six feet, he now towered above her. She reached up and put a hand on each cheek, bringing his face close to her own. "Just remember, if you see Grace Carlson approaching, tackle her, grab a rack of ribs, put her in your car, and take her home. This is my home, and she's not welcome here.

"And, no sneaking off with your grandpa to Sardis Lake."

CHAPTER 12

Liz had given the key to Miss Millie's house to Luann on Monday night after the cookout. They'd agreed that Wednesday would be the best day to take care of the supplies after Miss Millie approved their plan to start with new paints and brushes. She made two lists: one of things to be gathered from her home and the other of things to be purchased. Luann suggested that she walk to the artist's home early Wednesday morning and meet Liz there to collect blank canvases, an easel, and other supplies. They would then drive to Memphis to purchase oil paints and other necessities. Just as Liz had suspected, when she arrived at Miss Millie's house, Luann was already there and had apparently been for some time. She was in the dining room admiring the chandelier that hung over the table.

"Who would have ever guessed the quality of furnishings and accessories in this old house?" Luann questioned. "You really need to talk to Mr. Jamerson about plans for the remaining furniture here. It's worth a ton of money."

"Disposing of Miss Millie's belongings isn't my business, Lu," Liz replied. "I'm not the one in charge here."

"Oh, but you are, dear sister, whether you recognize it or not. When was the last time Miss Em's Memphis connections were in her home? None of them, including Mr. Jamerson, have a clue what's here unless you've told them. *She* certainly hasn't! Material things hold no claim on our dear new friend."

"But the paintings ..." Liz began.

"The attorneys sent an art curator to supervise that move. Yeah, they wanted to get those paintings to a temperature-controlled, safe place in a museum. Compared to Miss Millie's art, this furniture is peanuts, but still."

"Okay!" Liz, exasperated by Luann's insistence that she take on yet another project, was uncharacteristically short with her big sister. "But that's not why we're here today. Let's load up those easels and canvases. I parked out front."

Changing the subject seemed a good idea. "I don't know about you, but I, for one, am glad the kids are back in school. I am more than ready to turn in my resignation as Chairman of Summer Recreation," Luann said.

"Do you realize that you're talking to the mother of a graduating senior?" Liz asked as she gazed at the huge oak tree outside Miss Millie's studio. "My baby is getting ready to leave us."

"What a way to put it!" Luann exclaimed. "For one thing, he's not *your baby*. For another, how far is he going to go, for goodness sake? By the way, what colleges has he applied to?"

"A sum total of none," Liz said. "There's already a stack of letters from universities, but every time I mention replying, Jackson suddenly has something very important to take care of. He acted the same way this summer when I asked if he was set to take the ACT again. I finally threatened to take care of it all myself, including driving him to the testing center. Can you believe after all that resistance, he scored a 29, up from a previous 27? I know I sound like a proud mama, but then, I am."

"I know I'm a long way off from those concerns about Maddie and Maria, so I'm probably not the one to say this, but maybe you should back off just a smidge, Liz? Jackson has never given you any reason to worry about where he's headed. If he doesn't get into the college of *your* choice, he has the option of several junior colleges within driving distance."

"That's just what I don't want to happen," Liz said. "I'd like to get him away from Lainie. In my opinion, they're way too serious."

"Too serious for what?" Luann asked. "And, by the way, I thought you were in a big hurry to get this stuff packed up. Could you step away from the window and help me?"

Luann picked up a stack of blank canvases and headed out the door. Liz continued to stare out the window. Her mind drifted back to the many times she'd played under this tree, and she wondered how many times Miss Millie had stood or sat in this very spot and watched her. The painting of the child under the tree—it was difficult still to think of the child as herself—rested on an easel in her living room, but she rarely looked at it. How could this spot give her so much comfort when the painting itself seemed almost unreal? A vague thought played at the edges of her mind. Something about a mirror. She remembered now Miss Millie's words about looking into a mirror. That's exactly how she felt as she stood here. In this spot, she could look at her long ago self as Miss Millie must have looked at her.

Liz became aware that Luann had returned and was standing behind her, resting her hands lightly on her shoulders.

"Hey, little sis," Lu said softly as she began gently massaging Liz's neck and shoulders, "I understand. I really do. You're afraid that Jacks is going to make the same choice you made and never experience life away from Roslyn."

Liz breathed deeply. She had found this to be the only effective defense against the tears that seemed ever-present just behind her eyeballs. It seemed to her that she vacillated between angry retorts and clamming up when those she loved touched on a raw nerve. Everyday routine and mundane tasks seemed to be what kept her going. There were too many things just below the surface or too many overfilled file drawers that she dared not open.

"Whoa, you have some tight muscles there. Ever think about seeing a massage therapist?"

Liz gratefully grabbed this diversion from her feelings. "And just when do you think I'd find time for that?" she asked as she shrugged Luann's hands from her tense neck. "Maybe squeeze it between our trip to Senatobia and getting back to church to make sure Elaine and Maria followed through on the ham dinner for Wednesday night supper? Or, let's see, I could make time tomorrow after the visiting nurse leaves but *before* the committee meeting to plan for the senior trip next spring? Or maybe ...?

"Sit down, Liz," Luann commanded, pointing to a chair she'd seemingly pulled out of thin air. "Sit," she said again.

Surprised at the directness of her sister, Liz did as she was commanded. Luann perched on the low ledge of the window sill.

"I don't pretend to know all that you're dealing with," she began, "but I do see that you're trying to do far more than one human can handle. How did you get to this point, Liz? How did you change from that dreamy little girl who loved to chase lightning bugs and look for four-leaf clovers? The little sister who could lie on her back for hours and watch puffy clouds float by? What happened to you?"

Liz sat silently, her lower lip firmly clasped between her teeth, staring at a point just to the left of Luann's head.

"Talk to me, Liz," her sister urged softly. "I want to help. I really do."

They sat in silence for what seemed to be minutes, but in reality, it was only seconds. Finally, Liz asked, "Do you remember ... before?"

"Before? Before what?" Luann asked

"Before, when our family was happy. Before, when Mama touched us. When we sat at the table after we'd all finished eating our supper, and Daddy asked us what had happened at school. When, after supper, Mama and Daddy went to his workshop in the backyard to refinish a table or a chest she'd found at an auction, and we played outside till dark?

"It's crazy. I know there was a *before,* but all I can remember is the *after.* I remember how quiet the house was, how ... *polite* Daddy was—when he was there, which was like almost never. I remember how you got me ready for church instead of Mama and how Daddy dropped us off, and the Grishams always took us home. I hated going back home on Sunday after church, eating a tuna fish sandwich or macaroni and cheese that was barely warm instead of fried chicken and mashed potatoes and gravy while Mama pretended to clean up in the kitchen, and Daddy went off to who knows where." She paused before asking, "What do you remember, Lu?"

It was Luann's turn to sit quietly. Finally, she spoke. "I'm so sorry, Liz. I really haven't been a very good big sister, have I? Somehow, I managed to convince myself that you were okay with all of that. That you were so young when it happened that it didn't affect you. Yeah, I had moments of guilt about leaving you when I went away to Auburn for college, but I figured you'd get in the swing of things in high school and be okay without me. You were such a quiet kid and didn't ask for much, so I took that as a sign that you didn't need much. And Mom always managed to provide the basics, even if she wasn't the same warm, fuzzy Mama we had, as you say, before.

"There were really two *befores,* you know: before the Big Silence and before Daddy died in the car accident. Where do you want to start?"

"That's the thing, Lu, I don't know if I really do want to start. Sometimes, I think it's better if I just keep on doing what I'm doing."

"Yeah," Lu said. "The unexamined life and all that ... look where that's gotten you. You're so tightly wound I'm afraid to touch you for fear your mainspring might break, and you'll splatter all over the walls. Liz, I know we had trauma in our childhood, and I know you think Miss Gracie tightly grips the key to your happiness in that regard, but in spite of what you think, most people in Roslyn really care about us. Cared about Mama and Daddy, too. Sure, there were gossips who wanted to create drama, but I always say if you spot 'em, drop 'em. And they're easy to spot. Looks to me like you're living your life based on what other people think of you, and not the best people either."

Her sister's words resonated with Liz and reminded her of what Miss Em had said days earlier: *Look in the mirrors around you.* Maybe she had been looking in the wrong mirrors.

"So, what do you know, Lu, that I don't know?" she asked.

Again, Luann hesitated, seeming to consider where to take the conversation.

"Don't get mad, Liz. I know you were the one who stayed at home and made sure Mama was cared for, and I never came back after college. But remember the summer before Mama died when she came and spent a month with us? After Maddie was born? She talked to me about what happened. I'm not sure why. Maybe she wanted to warn me about what could happen when married couples drift apart and don't work to get connected again. Maybe she just needed to get it off her chest. I do know—because she told me this—that she didn't want to burden you with the details because, in her words, you had to face the same people she faced every day of your life, and she didn't want you carrying her burden. In spite of how she chose to live her life, she knew us very well, Liz, and she loved us fiercely. She loved Daddy, too, and she never recovered from the guilt she carried about the imagined "affair" that supposedly turned him to drinking. She blamed herself, you know, for the accident."

Liz stood and gazed out the window. Her tree. Her comfort. She thought of the nights many years ago when she'd slip out of bed after all the downstairs lights were turned off, all except a dim lamp in the entry hall, and keep her silent vigil at the top of the stairs. She waited till she heard the click of the closing door to her parent's bedroom, her signal that her mother was in bed for the night, before she settled in to watch for the faint beam of headlights as her daddy returned home from his nightly escape. This was the first sign that he'd returned; the next was his soft shuffle on the front steps, the sound of his key in the lock—sometimes, on hearing the repeated sounds of metal on metal, she fought the urge to go down and let him in. He always entered quietly, turned off the light in the hallway, and opened the door to the room he still shared with her mother. Only then could Liz slip back to the warmth of her bed. Often, she fell asleep on the hard floor, waking up cold and stiff. Her signal that all was well was the light in the hallway. If it was off, she'd go to bed; if she saw the soft glow of lamplight, she stayed on watch. Her magical thinking told her that as long as she followed this routine, her daddy would always come home. Except one night when she was twelve years old, he didn't. She lost her magic touch.

"Me, too," she said.

"You, too, what?" Lu asked.

"I always blamed myself," Liz said. "I know in my mind it doesn't make any sense, but I was twelve, Lu. Twelve years old. I kept thinking things would change back to the way they were. I thought if I could wish on the right star, find the right four-leaf clover, and be the perfect child, they would love each other again. That we'd become a family again. That you'd stay home and not spend every night you could away from home with a friend."

Liz was crying now, her words increasingly difficult to understand. Lu stood, grasped both of Liz's hands in her own, and pulled her to her feet. She wrapped her arms around her little sister. Together, they sobbed and began to release their shared anguish. It occurred to Liz that they'd never done this before, even in the tragedy of their father's death. Even when they lost their mother, they'd both stoically taken what was handed them. The loss was a way of life, and the difference in their ages and their temperaments had convinced both of them that they had very little in the way of comfort to offer each other.

Their sobbing subsided and was replaced with sniffles, then silence. Still, they stood with their arms wrapped around each other, Liz's head resting on her sister's shoulder. It felt good. Liz somehow felt cleansed. Not that anything had changed, but then, something had. In letting go, she'd gained something. She could neither name it nor describe it; she simply felt it.

Lu, in customary fashion, took the edge off the sadness. "We're a fine-looking pair to face the shopping world," she said as she fished in the pocket of her jeans for a tissue. Finding none, she pulled the tail of her shirt to her nose and blew noisily.

"Yuck!" Liz exclaimed. "Can't you ask? I have tissues in my purse. You're disgusting."

"But I know how to reduce puffy tear-soaked eyes," she said. "Come on, let's get this easel loaded and stop by my house. We can't go paint shopping looking like this."

Luann chose to walk the short distance between her house and Miss Millie's home while Liz locked up and drove her car there. She was in the kitchen putting ice cubes in a glass when Liz arrived. Liz watched as she filled the glass with tap water and took four spoons from her silverware drawer. Her curiosity increased as Luann put the spoons in the glass of ice water.

"We have to wait about 5 minutes so the spoons get really cold," Lu said. "Are you wearing eye shadow or mascara?" Lu looked closely at her sister. "I see from the smudges that you were before the crying started. Come on to my bathroom; let's get this stuff off our eyes before we shrink our puffy eyelids."

Liz followed her sister and accepted a cotton pad drenched with eye make-up remover.

"Okay, I'll bite," Liz said. "What are we doing with the spoons in the ice water?"

"It's either that or cold cucumber slices, and since my cucumbers are long gone, we're left with this alternative," Lu answered. "Cold reduces swelling, and what's colder than a cold spoon? Besides, it's the perfect eye socket shape."

"Where do you learn these things?" Liz asked.

"I am, after all, your smarter older sister," Luann said, picking up the glass of water and moving to the sun porch. "We'd just as well make ourselves comfortable and take a little rest while the spoons do their magic. In answer to your question, I read this little hint in some magazine, can't remember which one."

Luann directed her sister to the daybed-turned-sofa in the bright sunroom. Once Liz was stretched out, Luann placed the cold spoons on her eyes, drawing a loud "Ooooo" from her sister.

"Actually, it feels pretty good," Liz said. Hearing no response, she called. "Lu?"

"I'll be right back," Luann called from somewhere in the house. And then, a flash. Liz jumped up, the spoons clanging on the tile floor.

"What on earth are you doing?" she asked.

"I couldn't miss this photo op," her sister said, giggling. "You looked too cute, like some alien creature with antennae protruding from your eyes."

It felt good to laugh. Liz had never known what it was like to cry with someone one minute and laugh with them the next. Except with Rose, but Rose wasn't her peer and wasn't in her age range. She wasn't her sister.

Their eyes closed, ice-cold spoons causing temporary blindness; the sisters lay quietly, Liz on the daybed, Luann stretched out nearby on the floor. Her sister's voice was gentle in the darkness. "Liz, there's lots to tell you about Mom and Dad. It wasn't all bad, you know. I think when you hear what Mom told me, you'll understand, maybe even be proud of her. There's something else," she added. "There's someone we both need to talk to. Remember Brother Paul, our pastor when all of that started? He was still here when Daddy died. He's retired now and lives in Oxford. Mom told me she talked with him several times after you left home. He knows the whole story. I think we should go talk to him together. I'll call and see if we can visit him.

"But for today, no more talk about this. I'll fill you in on what I know, but not today. Today, we're going to lighten the mood. Let's get going, little sister. We've got to put ourselves back together and get on the road. You're driving, but I'm in charge of entertainment. I've had enough of this heavy stuff for one day."

CHAPTER 13

Liz tucked the soft blanket around Miss Em's legs and leaned over to give her a quick kiss on the forehead. "See you this evening. I hate missing our Thursday tea time, but this senior trip meeting was scheduled back in the spring. Since I'm chairman ..."

Miss Em chuckled. "Chairman-of-Everything you are, my dear. Have you considered resigning any chairmanships?"

"You sound like my sister," Liz said. "And, yes. Yes, to both of you. I've considered resigning, but then, what would I do?"

"What do you *want* to do?" Miss Em asked. "If you could spend your time doing anything you wanted to do, what would it be?"

"I'm not sure," Liz replied. "I haven't given it much thought since high school. What's the use in thinking about things that aren't possible?"

"They're called dreams, my dear, and it's with dreams that things begin. What are your dreams, Elizabeth?"

Liz thought about the question as she drove across town. *What would I do with my time if I didn't stay so busy with committee meetings and community projects?* She loved scribbling down notes in her journals: conversations she'd overheard, quick observations of animal behavior, descriptions of unique appearances of people or places. Someday, she always told herself, she'd have enough time to make something worthwhile out of her assorted notes. Something that made sense to another person who might enjoy reading her scribbles. *Who am I kidding?* she thought now. *What do I have to say that anybody would want to read?* What was that Lu had asked her yesterday? *How did you change from being that dreamy kid?*

I could put my life into a pie chart, Liz thought. The first eight years were innocent childhood years—truly dreamy years, years that now were virtually lost to her memory. She did recall snippets of happy occurrences: walking in the front door after school to the smell of cookies baking, knowing that her mother would drop whatever she was doing to give her a hug, a glass of milk, and a fresh-baked cookie, the toot-toot-toot of her dad's Buick horn as he pulled in the driveway after being on the road for days; the anticipation of an evening, her parents sitting in the swing,— invariably she pictured Luann down the street playing and herself lying on the smooth painted floor of the porch—intermittent comfortable silences mixed with laughter and talk. But the memories were only snippets. She longed to recall those years because, deep within her, she knew they were the best years of her life. Yellow, she'd color those years yellow.

The next four years would definitely be gray, she concluded, the *after* years. The years when her daddy only came into the house to sleep, eat, or pack his clothes for a trip. His remaining time was spent in the workshop in the back—alone, no more joint refinishing projects—or driving off in his Buick to who-knew-where. Instead of coming home to the aroma of baking cookies, she and Luann came home to a grocery list and a mama sitting quietly at her sewing machine. After-school snacks consisted of a candy bar or a handful of chips. Her once-active mother rarely left the house, even to buy groceries or go to church.

When she was twelve and was forced to give up hope forever of her father returning to the family, the world turned black for a period of time before returning to the dull, unbroken gray. For Liz, until she met Richard just before she was 15, those years were hazy, fog-like, with no bursts of color. Lu, the only person in their house who clung to real life, left for college and took any hope of happiness in the family with her. Brighter colors periodically defined her life after she met Richard and was taken into his family, so those years, she would color gray with swirls of color drifting throughout. Those times were marred when she impetuously tossed Richard aside and later discovered she'd become pregnant after a lapse in judgment. No bright color in her life during that bleak period. As she struggled to come up with a color for that period of her pie graph, she realized she was putting the car in park and turning the key in the ignition. She had arrived at the school, and it was a good thing. Her wool-gathering was getting her nowhere except to her meeting with a headache.

Liz breathed in the school smell—books, teenage smell, stale food odors—as she walked down the hall to the library. She remembered the huge stack of books she'd hauled around all morning just so she could use her time between classes to see Richard instead of going to her locker. The smile that unknowingly had come to her lips from those memories greeted the rest of the senior class trip committee members as she walked into the small room in the corner of the library.

"We were waiting for you," Karen said. "Just about ready to call and see if you'd forgotten."

"Forget a chance to plan the most exciting trip of a lifetime?" Liz laughed. "At least if you're a senior at Roslyn High. What could be more fun than traveling five hours on a bus with sixty teenagers and then spending three days in a big city like St. Louis with them? I'd guess that no more than twenty percent of them have been any farther than Memphis. Have we all lost our minds? Sixty teenagers in Busch Stadium! Are we really up for this?"

"So long as we have a minimum of one-to-four ratio of chaperones. Hopefully, mature, responsible adults who can keep up with 18-year-olds. That's our biggest hurdle. Especially since we're asking them to pay their own way," Karen responded.

John Graves pushed himself away from the table and walked over to close the door to the small room. "Well, that could be our out with Miss Gracie," he said in his slow drawl. "Mature, responsible... maybe she can squeak by those requirements. Hmmm," he slowly shook his head and rubbed his bristly chin. "Pay her own way and keep up with 18-year-olds? I think we've got her on those two."

"She's already paid her deposit," Karen said. "A check for $100. She stopped me in Commer's Drugs last week while I was picking up a prescription for Emma's strep throat. I was so exhausted from being up with a sick kid the night before I couldn't think of any gracious way to refuse her. Here it is." She dangled the mint green rectangle in front of them, holding it gingerly between her index finger and thumb.

"There is no gracious way to tell Grace Carlson *no*," Liz laughed ruefully. "Now there's a sentence for some deep analysis." She reached across the table and picked the piece of paper from Karen's fingers, using the same digits as her friend. The action, intended to suggest contamination, brought laughter. "I'll give it back to her along with a definite refusal of her offer to chaperone. She's no more interested in chaperoning than I am in walking barefoot across hot coals. She sees this as her one and only opportunity to go to a Cardinals game. Did you know she came to our Fourth of July picnic wearing a Cardinals' jacket? It was 99 degrees in the shade, and she wore that thing the entire day!"

"I don't think she could pay the rest of the cost, and really, she's not capable of chaperoning," Karen began. "The only way we could let her go ..."

Liz stopped her with a raised open palm. "She's not going," she declared. "I'll take care of it."

Joe Howard, whose graduating son Micah was a late-in-life surprise, spoke up. "You might be surprised about her being able to pay for the trip. Her old man, Roger, believed in saving every dime he earned. How do you think Miss Gracie got in the habit of begging and manipulating people for every last thing she needed or wanted? That old woman has money in the bank. I guarantee you."

"I don't care if she could buy the entire Cardinals' team," Liz said. "She's not going on the senior trip. And I have heard enough about Grace Carlson for one day. Karen, do we have confirmation on the hotel?"

With the discussion of Grace Carlson closed (*How could she dominate so many conversations?),* the rest of the meeting went smoothly.

"Thanks, John, for being in my corner about Grace Carlson," Liz said as the two of them walked to the parking lot. "We can't allow her to bully us, and besides that, we'd need an extra chaperone just to watch out for her. She'd walk right out in the middle of traffic and expect cars to stop for her!"

"No worries, Liz. I've got your back on that one. I'd be happy to return her check if you want me to."

"And rob me of my pleasure?" Liz retorted.

She opened her car door but continued talking. "By the way, somebody told me—probably Lainie, since she lives on the same street—that the old Fitzgerald house finally sold. They were asking a huge price for that. Must be somebody with money. Do you know who bought it?"

"Heard it was somebody from out of state. California, maybe? Somewhere out west. Yeah ... somebody who used to live here back in the eighties. Coming back here to retire, I hear. I forget the name."

****

Late afternoons were quiet times in the Manley household. Before she left for the day, Rose made sure Miss Em was situated following her afternoon nap, usually with soft music playing and a variety of books and magazines within easy reach. The visiting nurse arrived soon after to help the woman with her late afternoon routine. Liz timed her return home from the meeting with the expectation that she would enter a quiet house since Jackson went straight to the grocery store to help with stocking shelves and deliveries. He and Richard usually arrived home within a half hour of each other, somewhere around seven o'clock. The portrait painting sessions were scheduled to begin the following week. Latisha would sit with Miss Millie three afternoons a week after school and for an extended time—with breaks—on Saturdays and then again on Sunday afternoons.

For now, Liz relished the thought of a quiet Thursday early evening with no interruptions. She tiptoed up the stairs to her and Richard's bedroom. They had planned it as a sanctuary to escape to when Jackson filled the house with young friends but seldom used it as such. They realized that being close at hand when a crowd gathered was important, not only to Jackson but to them as well. They enjoyed being around noisy teenagers, and Jackson and his friends welcomed them in small doses. Rather than retreat to their bedroom, Liz and Richard hung out in the cozy family room down the hall from the kitchen. Close, but not too close.

Liz stood in front of the large window that looked out on the same view Miss Millie had below. The open field of tall grass spread over the wide distance that ended with the wooded space to the east. Sprinkled randomly in the field were subtle hues of autumn wildflowers: yellows, dull oranges, and golds. Where had the bright, vivid blues and reds of summer gone? It seemed just weeks ago that she had made the renovations below for Miss Millie's arrival. She felt sadness wash over her as she acknowledged the quick passage of time. How much longer? Miss Em seemed to thrive with the care and attention she was receiving, and while the doctors were pleased with her progress and had even extended the time they'd initially estimated for her, Liz knew that appearances were deceiving. She'd seen the test results, talked with the doctors, and understood the prognosis: no more than a year. As the quick disappearance of summer reminded her, a year was a short period of time.

Liz turned from the window; the scene spread out in front of her too reminiscent of death. She loved the subtle changes of fall, the reminder that winter was near, but she also was saddened by those same changes. Given her mood, Liz almost changed her mind, but typically, since she'd given herself a task to do, she wouldn't leave until it was done. She pulled out the bottom drawer of her dresser and removed the worn brown album. She walked across the room, folded back the soft yellow comforter, and lay crossways on the bed on her stomach. She opened the musty album and began to turn pages. She was looking for a particular picture that had popped into her mind earlier in the afternoon. Her mother wore a pale blue sleeveless blouse and a full print skirt, a huge smile on her face. She stood on the front porch, her foot poised in mid-air above the first of the two steps that led to the sidewalk. Her blond hair, chin-length, perfectly framed her face. Her left hand was raised, lifted towards her face as though to brush the hair from her eyes. Looking at the photograph, Liz remembered the gesture, her mother's lifelong habit of brushing her hair back from her face; in anyone except her mother, it was a gesture that might seem flirtatious. To Liz, it seemed to ask a question: am I pretty enough, am *I* enough?

As she studied the picture, Liz realized why it had captured her attention. It didn't fit with the rest of the photographs in the album.

Most of the others were of Luann, then Liz and Luann together, a few of the girls separately in their Easter dresses or opening Christmas presents. There were shots of a perfectly set table and centerpieces for Thanksgiving, Christmas, Easter, or whatever the holiday being celebrated might have demanded. Still, others showed her mother standing by a before-and-after picture of a piece of furniture that had been refinished. Some were of the entire family (*who took those?*) dressed up for church. All were either posed or random shots that had to do with a holiday. In none of the pictures did her mother look so young and, yes, Liz recognized, happy.

Liz slipped the picture out of the album and turned it over. *Come away with me.* The short note was signed *W.* Nothing more. Liz drew a deep breath. What did that mean? Who was W? A sliver of memory shot through her. She shook her head. No. That couldn't be it.

W. Wallace. Mr. Wallace, she and Luann had called him. But Wallace wasn't his entire name. His given name was Wallace. Wallace *something*? *Something* Wallace? Mr. Wallace? That's what Brother Paul and the rest of ... Rest of who? Liz struggled to remember. It had something to do with the church and the new church building. She had a vague recollection of spending many hours in a room with Luann while her mother, Mr. Wallace, Brother Paul, and several other people met across the hall. She remembered one late evening in particular. The meeting was over; she and Luann were in the car. Luann was in the front seat, sighing loudly every few minutes and saying, "Can we go now?" to her mother's back as she stood with the car door open and talked to Mr. Wallace.

Liz picked up the phone and punched in Luann's number, glancing at the clock as she did so. Please don't let the girls be inside, she pleaded, as the phone rang repeatedly. Please let Lu be at home.

"Hello!" Clearly interrupted and out of breath, her sister's agitation showed through.

"It's me, Lu. Got a minute?"

"Hold on," she said, calmer now.

Liz listened as she yelled out to the girls. "You two go ahead. I'll be back in a few minutes. Maria, remember that you can't throw the ball as hard to Maddie as you throw to me."

"What's up?" she asked, coming back to the phone.

"Sorry to interrupt you, but I have a question for you. I was looking through one of Mom's old picture albums and came across a picture that made me curious. Who is W?"

"Well, there's George W., there's the W Hotel, there's ... can't think of any other W's, Sis. Tell me more."

"Does the name Wallace mean anything to you?" Liz asked.

"Ye ... ah." Luann drew the word out. "How does Wallace have anything to do with Mom's picture album?"

Liz described the picture and read the inscription on the back.

The line was quiet. Finally, Luann spoke. "He's the guy, Liz. He's the one Mom supposedly had an affair with. But this is what I know, and you have to trust me here: It didn't happen. Mom said it didn't happen, and I believe her. She confessed that she was attracted to him, liked his company, and had great respect for him. But she didn't give in to temptation. She was faithful to Dad, Liz. She *loved* Dad! Whatever anybody in this town may think they know, that's one thing I *do* know. She was faithful to Dad. I just wish he'd been able to accept that."

"I want the whole story, Lu. Everything you know. I have a right to know as much as you do. That argument of having to look the same people in the eye is lost now. You live here, too."

"Slow down, Liz. I agree with you, and I'll tell you everything I know. I'll tell you what I remember. After all, I was twelve when all that happened, and I was present for most of it. So were you. Present, I mean, not twelve. What I'm trying to tell you is she didn't hide anything. I'll tell you all that she told me as well. But not right now, Liz. I have two kids in our backyard—*our* backyard, did you hear me?—who are waiting for their mother to come out and play."

"I can wait," she said. "I've waited a couple of decades. When?"

"I talked to Brother Paul this morning. Had meant to call you and tell you, so I'm glad you reminded me. He can see us next week. Does Monday work for you? I'll fill you in on what I know between Roslyn and Oxford next Monday."

CHAPTER 14

All those involved in Miss Em's painting project—Latisha, Rose, Liz, Luann, and the artist herself—were eager for her to begin. Since Rose didn't work weekends, the women had prearranged that Liz would drive out to Rose's place (in reality, Rose's parents' place) to pick up the little girl and bring her back to the Manley home for the morning. The nurse, approving the idea of Miss Em resuming her painting, cautioned everyone to move slowly. Her exact words were spoken in the language of a nurse. "Take this in small doses," she'd cautioned.

"I'd begin on a day, a Saturday, perhaps, when both our acclaimed, reclaimed artist and the child can relax at frequent intervals. Miss Millie won't be able to paint for long periods of time, but she can have short sessions over several hours," the hospice nurse advised.

Liz turned off the main road to a narrow dirt lane lined on both sides by tall grasses that led to the home of Retha and Willa Walker, Rose's parents. Liz had known Mr. Retha and Miss Willa long before she met Rose, their daughter. As a little girl entering kindergarten, she'd been entranced by the stooped old (to her eyes) man who pushed a bucket on wheels and sprinkled pink dust on the classroom floors when one of her classmates threw up their lunch or breakfast. He seemed to be as much a part of the school as the little tables and chairs where she did her work. In fact, until she was in third grade, she thought the building where she attended classes belonged to him. It was only after Jake Simpson, a fellow third-grader, went to Mrs. Wilkes, their teacher, to settle their argument about who owned the building that the matter was cleared up for her. Nor did she connect Mr. Walker with the tall, queenly brown woman who joined him at the end of the school day to sweep the classrooms and hallways till she was much older. It wasn't until her junior high years that she had the courage to open a conversation with Miss Willa. In conversations that followed, Liz learned that Mr. Retha and Miss Willa were husband and wife and that they had a daughter named Rose and a grandson named LaMont.

In one of their afternoon tea times, Rose had lamented all those lost years with her parents. "I didn't know what I had," she'd said, speaking of her loving, supportive parents. "I was just so mad at them. Always cleaning up after the white kids and talking 'bout different ones like they was special. All the time, I'm going to the colored school over yonder on that old clay hill. I'm glad my Civil Rights didn't catch up with me till my schooling years was over. How you think it would feel to come to school every day and see your mama and your daddy cleaning up other people's messes? I do have my regrets about ending my schooling years too soon. I couldn't wait to get outta this town. First chance I got, I was on my way to Memphis."

She had paused to reflect, and the rest of the women waited in silence. All recognized the courage it took for this special woman to talk about those difficult years.

When she resumed, her voice was shaky. "Fifteen years old and pregnant," she said, shaking her head. "One thing I know is: there are good people everywhere, even in big cities like Memphis."

"Of course, there are, my dear," Miss Millie interjected.

"I met some of them, good people like my Mama and Daddy, who knew right from wrong. It's a good thing, 'cause that boy who took me there didn't have no more sense than me. We'd have starved to death if I hadn't heard my Mama and Daddy's voice in my head tellin' me to find a good church. Those people found me a place to live, found me a good job, and helped me with my little LaMont. They just waited till I had the good sense to say, 'I'm goin' back home where I belong.' It was my little LaMont did it for me. Five years old he was, and staying from here to there while I tried to earn enough money to keep body and soul together. Ain't no way for a child to live."

"And your Mama and Daddy were tickled pink when you came back home. It's funny, Rose, but I knew your parents and LaMont before I ever met you," Liz said.

Liz turned to Miss Millie to explain. "LaMont was two years behind me in school, and one of the things I liked about him was how proud he was of his grandpa. By then, Miss Willa had retired, but LaMont checked on Mr. Retha before football practice to see if he needed anything lifted or moved. The school board had hired additional custodians, but Mr. Retha was still in charge."

"He's a good boy," Rose agreed. "Just wish he could be a good daddy to Latisha. He hardly never comes home from those oil rigs in the Gulf."

"He knows she's in good hands, Rose," Miss Millie comforted. "And if you think of it in another way, it's his loss, too. He doesn't have the pleasure of watching his kind, intelligent little girl grow up. He's doing the best he can."

Liz stepped out of the car and looked around at the immaculate property. Small but carefully tended. Field rock clearly marked the dirt driveway and turnaround space in the side yard. Monkey grass lined the sidewalk that led to the wide front porch. Flower beds, kept in their boundaries by old brick lined up end to end, hugged the foundation of the house. To the rear of the house was a large garden enclosed in a tall wire fence, most of it plowed under now, waiting for spring planting.

Liz wondered if the old man would have the strength and health to plant another garden. The odds were definitely against Miss Willa surviving the winter. It was a toss-up as to who would go first, Miss Willa or Miss Millie. Too sad to consider now.

The front door flew open, and Latisha burst out and down the steps on her way to the car.

"Hey, wait up, kid. I want to go in and say hi to your grandma and your Gigi," Liz called after her.

The child stopped and pointedly turned her back to Liz. She folded her arms, lifted her shoulders, and then dropped them in an exaggerated motion.

"No pouting allowed. This is a pouting-free day, my friend. You can wait in the car or come back inside while I talk to your family. I won't stay long."

And Liz couldn't stay long. Seeing Miss Willa lying in the old iron bed, a brightly colored patchwork quilt covering her frail body, was overwhelmingly depressing. "Oh, Rose, I'm so sad," she said to her friend as they talked on the front porch. "I had no idea things were this bad. What does her hospice nurse say?"

"Maybe the end of the year, maybe sooner. Daddy says he's strong enough to take care of her, but I don't know. Maybe ..."

Liz anticipated where Rose was going with the conversation. "We'll work something out," she said. "You have to promise me that you'll let me know when you're needed here full time. Your parents are your first obligation, Rose."

"They've been through thick and thin together. Fifty-five years this November. They've always been each others' best friend in the whole world. I don't know what Daddy's gone do without her."

"Fifty-five years. A lifetime. You and Richard are lucky, Rose, to have parents so committed to each other. *Thick and thin* is a good way to put it."

***

The painting—or sketching as it turned out to be on this particular day—energized Miss Em rather than tired her. She and Latisha spent the entire morning together, Liz showing up periodically with hot chocolate, hot tea, or a short conversation. At one point, she found Miss Em snoozing in her chair, and Latisha curled up in the window seat with a book. As she turned to leave the room, Miss Em called after her, "I'm not sleeping, dear, just considering."

Liz turned back with a smile on her face. "Is that something like collecting buffalo fur?" she asked with a glance at Latisha.

The child looked up from her book with a sheepish grin on her face.

"Tell Miss Em about collecting buffalo fur," she encouraged the child.

"You tell her," said Latisha. "I forgot."

Latisha put her hands over her face as Liz began the story but couldn't entirely hide her grin. Once, when Rose had been in a hurry to leave, Liz had found Latisha flat on her back, staring at the ceiling, her eyes wide open. She'd tried to help Rose out by moving the child along and had said, "Latisha! Stop your wool-gathering and get your shoes on."

As the girl walked out the door with her grandmother, she turned to Liz and said, "What did you mean when you told me to stop *collecting buffalo fur*?"

"Just as I thought," Miss Em said as Liz concluded her story. "The child really *sees*. Words open up an entire world to you, don't they, Latisha? You, too, are an artist."

As they'd agreed, all work stopped at noon. Rather than return Latisha to her home, Liz called her sister to check on the possibility of the little girl spending a couple of hours with Maria and Maddie before returning home. After seeing for herself the condition of Miss Willa, Liz had decided that Latisha needed a more upbeat environment on the weekends.

"And I thought summer was bad," Luann moaned. "One would think they'd be content to hang around home and do nothing on a Saturday, but I've already heard 'I'm bored' a jillion times this morning. By all means, bring her on. Maddie will be thrilled, and Maria will have someone to impress with her older-sister knowledge. On second thought, never mind about bringing her; we'll come pick her up, grab McDonald's, and have a picnic lunch in the park."

***

Miss Em woke from her nap refreshed. "I feel like an afternoon drive," she told Liz. "Will you return Latisha to her home this afternoon? If so, then I'd like to come along."

"Are you sure, Miss Em? You haven't been for a drive since ..."

"Since I arrived here in June," Miss Em finished for her. "And now it's late September. Don't you think it's time I viewed the world from outside rather than inside? I've become quite an expert at navigating the hallway and various spaces inside your home with my faithful friend here." She patted the state-of-the-art walker, complete with bicycle horn—Jackson's idea for emergencies—attached to the frame.

As usual, when Miss Em explained why something should or should not occur, Liz saw the logic in the situation. The up-to-now little used wheelchair served its purpose in transporting the little woman down the ramp and to the waiting car in the driveway. Liz offered minimal help to her as she situated herself in the passenger's seat, and they set off to pick up Latisha. Miss Em waited in the car while Liz went inside to collect the little girl, who repeated her pouting act from earlier in the day.

"You don't want Miss Em to see that pouty little face, now do you? She's waiting for us in the car," she chided Latisha.

"Miss Em?!" she squealed. "Miss Em is in the car?" She was out the door in record time, Maddie following close behind.

Latisha jumped in the backseat while Maddie hung on the passenger side door. "Can I go, too?" she quizzed her mother, who'd joined the entourage to witness Miss Em's first outing.

"Not this time," Luann answered. "Miss Em wants a peaceful drive in the country, and two nattering nine-year-olds won't contribute to that at all."

"I'm not nine," Maddie began but was halted in mid-sentence by a stern look from her mother.

Latisha kept up a steady stream of conversation as they drove her home. The women listened as she gave a monologue about everything that had happened during the afternoon, and Liz silently patted herself on the back and thanked her sister for cooperating in keeping the child entertained. Rose heard the car approaching and met them in the driveway. "Law me! Is 'at Miss Millie I see in the passenger's seat? Who woulda thought? You be drivin' the car next time I see you!" she chortled.

Miss Em's reluctance to return home matched Latisha's. "Let's drive around and view the countryside," she suggested. "That was one of our favorite things to do when Rudolph was home for an extended time. He loved driving almost as much as he loved the rails, and I loved being with him."

"What about Rudy?" Liz asked. "Did he enjoy your drives?"

Miss Em laughed. "Not unless it included a stop at country stores along the way for a cold drink and a candy bar with the promise of a stop at the ice cream shop when our drive was complete. No, we didn't enjoy our drives nearly as much when Rudy was with us. Rudy grew accustomed to a more active pace in his life very quickly. Because Rudolph and I had, out of necessity, been required to make our own way, we decided to give Rudy every opportunity to succeed. Perhaps I'd have chosen differently today, but I have no regrets about the way we brought him up.

"We had two places of residence: a wonderful apartment in Memphis in which we conducted our social life and our lovely home in Roslyn, where we lived privately. As Rudy grew towards adolescence, he naturally preferred the active life of a large city. We had wonderful friends with whom we would have trusted our lives, friends who had children with whom Rudy was friends, friends who took him into their homes as though he was one of their own. To Rudolph and me, our house in Roslyn was our true home; to Rudy, it became a place to visit. We had weekends and many entire weeks together in the apartment, but when school was in session, he rarely came here."

"So, he never went to school in Roslyn?" Liz asked.

"Oh, yes, my dear. He had a lovely elementary education in the Roslyn Schools. He was quite happy with that arrangement. It was only later in his junior high years that we made the change. And then, of course, there was Christian Brothers."

"That's a high school, isn't it?" Liz asked.

"And a college as well," Miss Millie continued. "But Rudy chose Yale."

"How could you allow him to go so far from home?" Liz asked. "Jackson will probably go no farther than Ole Miss if he goes anywhere at all, and I'm struggling with that."

"Stop the car, my dear. Let's find a place to pull off the road and park. I'd love to open the car doors and feel the air move around this old body. In the old days, one spoke of going for a walk as going out for an airing. I need a good airing."

Liz knew the perfect place. They were near the home of Richard's parents, the place where she had spent so many happy Sunday afternoons with Richard and his family in her teen years. She turned down the lane that led to the pond where she and Richard had paddled around in the old john boat. The late afternoon sun reflected itself in the water. Pine trees edged the far side, and in the distance, Liz saw the comfortable old farmhouse where Richard had grown up and where his parents still lived. Like Liz, he'd lived in the same house his entire life until they were married. The view was peaceful and comforting.

"Beautiful," affirmed Miss Em. Liz opened the doors of the car, and for a few minutes, the two women watched and listened. The soft swish of the pine trees created a soothing background to the put-putting of a tractor somewhere in the distance. Miss Em laughed with delight when an exuberant grasshopper landed on her lap; the grass seemed alive with their frantic movement.

"They seem to not know that it's time to prepare," she said. "Winter is coming, and what are they doing? Jumping around and enjoying life, short though their time."

"Reminds me of Jackson," Liz said. "He keeps putting me off about college applications. I think he'd be content to live at home and go to junior college in Senatobia."

"And is that a problem if that's what he chooses?"

"Is that a problem!" Liz exploded. "Didn't you just tell me that Rudy chose Yale?"

"The key word, my dear, is *chose*. Rudy *chose* Yale. We didn't choose it for him. We would have been quite content had he chosen to stay in Memphis, but that's not what he wanted to do. Have you asked Jackson what he wants to do?"

"Oh, I know what he wants to do. What he wants to do and needs to do are two entirely different things. He *wants* to skip college completely, but that won't happen. So—this is his latest concession—he can commute to the university or to a junior college and help his dad in the grocery store. Naturally, he'd prefer the junior college because that would be easier to walk away from in two years. What he really wants is to eventually run the store. Fourth generation, he says. I think Richard is secretly encouraging him rather than trying to talk him out of it. He thinks they can have some kind of arrangement: a combo grocery store/ restaurant."

"Four generations faithful to the same business. That's impressive," Miss Em said. "And the business is improving, no doubt, with each generation. As an outsider, my dear, keeping the family business alive and thriving seems a laudable goal."

"And what happens when everybody goes to Walmart because it's cheaper and easier to get everything in one place? Running a grocery store is not a high-profit business, Miss Em. Neither is running a restaurant."

"Perhaps not highly profitable, dear, but obviously highly rewarding. At least to some. Are you willing to listen to Jackson as he talks of his plans, Elizabeth? Very few people, particularly sensitive, intelligent people, care to have their hopes and dreams trampled upon, even by those who love them. *Especially* by those who love them. My Rudolph was particularly wise in that regard. It wasn't easy to allow our son to live away from us at his young age. Perhaps, had I insisted that he stay close by, the course of his life would have changed, and he'd still be on this earth. Perhaps. But— and there's no perhaps with this part—he wouldn't have been the same person he became before his death. He wouldn't have known the wonderful career he pursued, the lovely wife he chose, or the many friends who enriched his life. Rudy chose his path, Elizabeth, and even though I lost him much earlier than I'd anticipated, he loved his life, and he was grateful to his father and me for allowing him to choose."

Miss Em stopped talking. Something in her silence alerted Liz to keep silent, too. They sat together and allowed the breeze to surround them until Miss Em spoke again.

"I've never spoken of Rudy's death to you, nor, for that matter, have I spoken to you of Rudolph's death. My husband's death was devastating but survivable. We'd had many good years together; we lived life fully. His passing was quick—a heart attack that took him immediately, no lingering as my condition dictates. He would have chosen that, was prepared for it. Every detail, even to the selection of flowers for his casket. He was a detail person." She stopped and turned to Liz with a sad smile before turning her head to gaze again at the field surrounding them. Again, the silence descended, and again, Liz waited. She sensed that Miss Em was drawing deeply from her inner strength to continue her story.

"I've never shared this story with another living person," she began. "It's difficult to talk about the loss of a child, the *permanent* loss of a child," she clarified. "Rudy was thirty-four when we lost him and his beautiful wife, Joanna. I believe I told you that they made their home in Atlanta. Have I not? Well, yes, they lived in Atlanta. Rudy practiced law there quite successfully, I might add. Joanna was an attorney as well but chose to practice almost for free. She had a big heart, did that girl! She represented clients who couldn't afford their rent, much less an attorney's fee."

"I can see why you were proud of them, Miss Em," Liz offered. She felt the need to give a break in the seemingly endless flow of words from her friend.

"Oh, yes, my dear! They were people to make one proud."

"They were en route to the airport when they were struck from behind as they attempted to merge with traffic. As far as the accident went, that's all I ever learned. I spared myself the gruesome details by intentionally ignoring them. Their deaths were instant, and for that I'm grateful."

"Miss Em!" Liz reached across the seat and grasped her friend's hand. Miss Em continued to stare out the window.

"They were on their way to Roslyn," she continued, "to share their good news with me. A baby. My first grandchild."

Tears coursed down Liz's cheeks. She wiped them with the backs of her hands, then rested her head on the steering wheel. Miss Em's earlier words whirled in her head: *Hopes. Dreams. Choose.* Liz knew about hopes and dreams. Choosing? Not so much. Life happened, and she went with it. And, in the end, what difference did it make? Rudy had made choices, good choices, and in the end ...

"There's a chapter in Ecclesiastes. The third one, I believe. It talks about seasons of life and, to my way of thinking, choices." Miss Em's voice broke through Liz's thoughts. "To everything, there is a season," she quoted. "In the space of two months, I lost my husband, my son, my daughter-in-law, and my unborn grandchild. My season of grief lasted eleven long years, years in which I gave up everything I had loved: faith, friends, painting. I sealed myself off with my sadness, and—you know the rest," she finished.

"Don't be so sad, my dear," she said as she reached over and laid a hand on Liz's leg. "We can't *control* what happens in our lives, but we can still make choices." Liz was shocked to hear a small chuckle coming from the woman who'd just told a story of immeasurable sadness. "I seem to have misjudged a season of my own life when I made the decision to leave it all behind. I wrongly assumed that it was time to kill, as the verse says, when, in reality, it was time to heal. Desperation leads us to mistakes, Elizabeth. Recognizing God's involvement in our own lives rather than attempting to direct the life of another is a much better avenue to follow. Allow your Jackson to make his own choices, mistakes and all. Just be there to help him up when he asks you to. Listen to him. Wait for him to come to you with questions. Give him guidance. But most of all, have faith in him. You and Richard have done your job well. He's a good boy with good goals."

Liz felt consumed with selfishness. Miss Em had shared with her—the first person ever—her story of the loss of her husband, her son, his wife, and her unborn grandchild. And rather than Liz comforting her, she was comforting Liz. In spite of this recognition, Liz couldn't seem to hold the words back.

"If only he could get away from this town!" she blurted out.

"Like Rudy? There are trade-offs, my dear. I'm grateful for the time I've been given here at the end to reflect on my life, including my losses. You've given me a second chance to experience giving and receiving love, Elizabeth. And that's what life is all about."

CHAPTER 15

"I've never known anyone quite like Miss Em," Liz said to Luann. She had picked up her sister just after noon, and they were headed to Oxford to talk with Brother Paul, as promised. "She makes me think about things in a different way. How does a person get so wise?"

"Guess that's proof there aren't many wise ones among us," quipped LuAnn. "The part about you not ever knowing anybody quite like Miss Em? I know what you mean. She *is* a wise woman. But why on earth did she try to off herself if she is so wise?"

"I know the answer to that," Liz said. "Desperation. Desperation, sadness, and extreme loneliness. She talked to me about that this past weekend." Liz told her sister the tragic story of the loss of their friend's family eleven years ago. Luann reacted much the same way Liz had when she heard of the deaths of Rudy, his wife, and their unborn child.

"Miss Em says desperation and loneliness can cause a person to do dumb things—my word, not hers. I don't think the word *dumb* is in Miss Em's vocabulary," Liz said.

"It makes me wonder about Grace Carlson. Could that be the reason for her obnoxious behavior? She's made a dumb lifestyle, crashing everybody's family gatherings, spreading gossip nonstop, demanding special treatment. I could go on, you know. Is all of that bad behavior caused by desperation and loneliness?" Liz was talking more to herself than to Luann and was a little startled to hear her sister reply.

"So, are you signing up to be her friend?"

"No! Emphatically no. But you might consider taking that on," she joked. "With two kids, you have all kinds of experience in arbitration and mediation. And with the girls in school, you need something to fill your time."

The sisters continued their easy conversation till they parked in front of Brother Paul's tiny house. They had driven down a narrow gravel road situated between two fields of winter hay. It appeared to lead to nowhere until they rounded a curve and entered a pine grove. Nestled among the trees was a white frame house, small sections of green roof barely discernible among the brown pine needles covering it. The surrounding lawn was covered with the same brown carpeting.

Luann, always on charm patrol, breathed out a "Wow!" as the women walked up the steps to the small porch. Hanging on the green-painted front door was a sign carved on a pine plank: *Please Come In,* its invitation read. Luann and Liz looked at each other, frowning slightly. Liz shrugged, opened the door and called, "Brother Paul?"

"Liz! Luann! My dears, you're here," they heard from somewhere in the rear of the house. "Come in, please. And look at the two of you," the old man beamed as all three of them entered the small living area. "Two of my very favorite ladies."

It was as though the years fell away; Liz and Luann were transported to their youth as the vibes of comfort and acceptance from Brother Paul washed over them. *Ladies,* he would call them when they were children, making them giggle. "We're *girls,* not *ladies,*" one or the other would invariably say.

"Ladies-in-the-making," Brother Paul always responded.

"Just look at you," he said now. "My prophetic words revealed. And beautiful ladies to boot! I'm delighted to have you in my little castle in the woods."

"I love it, Brother Paul," Luann said. "What a perfect home! But don't you get lonely out here all by yourself? And isn't it a little unsafe to leave your door unlocked and invite people to just walk in?"

"Bosh!" he exclaimed. "What would anyone want with an old man like me? And, besides, they'd have to contend with the Master here. "Master!" he called, "come greet our guests."

The scritchy-scratch of toenails on a hard floor sounded from what Luann and Liz guessed to be the kitchen area, and a lanky German shepherd appeared in the doorway. He stood and gazed at them sleepily, then plopped down in the doorway, resting his chin on his paws. His gentle eyes peered up at them.

"Now I'm comforted," Luann laughed. "We can rest in the knowledge that Master would stare an intruder down."

Later, after the formalities of offering coffee and small talk, the three friends settled down for a serious talk. "I moved out here the year after May died. Was that '93? I loved the active retired life we had in Oxford, but after May was gone, it wasn't the same. I realized that solitude was what I craved. Just the birds, the trees, and me. It's how I experience God's vast love for me now. I call this my little hermitage."

"Do you ever see people?" Liz asked.

He gave a gentle laugh. "Well, my dear, I'm seeing you, aren't I? Yes, I have frequent visitors, and I infrequently go into town, even going on out-of-state or out-of-country trips when the need arises. But it's on my terms—and God's—that I interact with people."

"You remind me, in a way, of Miss Em," Liz said.

"Miss Em?" Brother Paul questioned.

The sisters gave him a shortened version of the events that led up to Miss Em being a permanent house guest with the Manley family.

"Sounds like she and I have a lot in common," Brother Paul said. "With one exception: she's had much tragedy in her life. My life, though I've experienced loss and sadness, has been a gentle one. Who can explain the human condition?

"But enough of this. You ladies are on a quest for answers. Ask your questions, and I'll see if I can be of any help."

Now that they were here, neither Liz nor Luann knew how to begin the conversation. With a glance at Liz and a nod of her head, Luann silently instructed her sister to begin. Liz ignored her and picked up her coffee mug. She stared into it before taking a sip and placing it back on the table in front of her. She absently repositioned the mug and, after each repositioning, rubbed invisible stains from the mat on which it sat.

Brother Paul broke the silence. "Let me begin with a story," he said gently. "I had a twin, a brother named Mark. Our mother desperately wanted at least one of us—preferably both of us—to be a preacher, and she thought the odds were increased if she gave us Biblical names. It became apparent quite early in our lives that Mark had no interest in being a minister. He excelled in school and received scholarships to several large universities. He chose one in California, intent on getting as far away from home—and our mother's directives—as possible.

"I held deep resentment in my heart towards Mark because I really didn't want to go to seminary. Simultaneously, I felt obligated to carry out my mother's wishes, so I packed my bags, buried my resentment deep in my heart, and set off on a path to the ministry. I found early on that it suited me. Had I not felt forced into it, chances are I would have entered that path anyway, without the resentment. Buried deep inside me, that resentment grew to include my brother. He was a highly successful businessman earning vast amounts of money. My resentment grew as his family grew. You see, May and I were not able to have children, something we desperately wanted to happen."

"I never knew that," Luann said. "I'm so sorry. That's why you..."

"You couldn't know," Brother Paul said. "Nor could you ever know the empty spot you children filled in my heart in the days when I was your pastor.

"Another thing you would never know is that I held deep judgment and resentment in my heart for my brother. I planned my visits home so that they wouldn't coincide with his. I'm ashamed to say I never visited his home until his death, an early death, by the way. I assumed that because he had wealth, he lived a life very different from mine. The reality was quite the opposite: he raised his family in a very modest home and taught his children good values. But I only learned this after his death. I still correspond with and occasionally visit Nell, his widow. She's a wonderful woman. And I have a rewarding relationship with my niece and nephews. But before that could happen, I had to recognize that I was extremely judgmental and let go of my resentment towards him. I regret that this happened after his death, but I'm grateful that it finally did happen. Forgiveness is more for the person who needs to forgive than for the person who is to be forgiven. It's best if it can happen between two living persons, but the results are the same in either case: release."

"Now you really sound like Miss Em," Liz said. "Are you telling me that I still have unforgiveness towards my parents?"

"Only you can know that," Brother Paul said. "Do you? And if so, what do you need to forgive them for?"

Liz picked up the tray and began collecting coffee mugs. "I need a refill." She left the room, taking her time to fill all three cups. She looked around the simple kitchen equipped with only the basic necessities for cooking. A perfect hide-away. But from Brother Paul's description, it wasn't a hideaway to him at all; it was a sanctuary. Was there a difference between a sanctuary and a hideaway? And if there was a difference, what was it? Could the difference be in a person's attitude?

She re-entered a quiet room. Luann was in a reflective mood; Brother Paul seemed to be recollecting, waiting. Liz handed filled coffee mugs to each, offered cream and sugar to Brother Paul, and sat down.

"I want to know," she said, "what you know about our parents. Why did they both stop going to church? What happened to cause Daddy to start drinking? I didn't know that's what was happening at the time, but that came pretty clear to me after the fact. Did our mother have an affair with that Wallace person? Wallace, the man who helped with the remodel of the church?" There! She'd said it all.

"Liz, I can't give you all the answers to all your questions," he said quietly. "But I can tell you who I knew your parents to be. They were both fine people. You had a mother and father you can be proud of. Remember that.

"Your mother was one of the most talented people I ever met. She could see the big picture, *and* she could take care of the details as well. That's a rare combination. Most people can do one or the other, but not both. Did you know she was the first woman ever in the First Baptist Church of Roslyn to be on the building committee? And she could handle those men with ease. I daresay every idea she had about our remodeling was included. And she didn't force the issues; she just finessed them. We had a plush remodeling fund, thanks in part to my brother Mark. Another thing that I held resentment about. I told myself he was trying to buy good graces with me and with God when the exorbitant checks arrived every six months. That money allowed us to hire one of the best architects in Memphis, Wallace Banks. He worked with us from the beginning, and I could see right away his attraction to your mother. Again, she handled him with the same finesse as the others but in a different way. I don't know what she felt in her heart—she obviously enjoyed his presence; he was a remarkable man as well as an excellent architect—but I never witnessed her behaving in a way that was unseemly."

"But you know about him coming to our house, at least that one time, the time he brought the roses? Did you know about that?"

"Yes, I knew. And I knew about the devastation it caused in your parent's marriage. I talked with both of them on several occasions, usually individually, but on at least two occasions, I spoke with them together. Luann, Liz, your mother was a victim of town gossip; your father gave in to his broken heart and wounded pride. I did all I could to help them repair the damage, but I'm afraid I couldn't overcome those two obstacles."

"But what about our wounded pride and broken hearts?" Liz asked. "Do you know what it feels like to know that people are talking about your daddy's drinking? To live with the fact that your daddy died on one of his nightly excursions, probably from drinking and driving?"

"My dear, you probably know more about those nightly excursions than I do," Brother Paul said. "But on the night your father died, he'd spent the better part of it with me, and he was stone-cold sober." The wise man paused briefly to let that simple fact hit home, then continued. "He was ready for change, and we spent the evening talking about forgiveness, just as we have here. The story about veering to miss a deer that the sheriff gave your family is, from what I know, a true story. It wasn't made up to protect your family. Again, town gossip. People like drama, my dear, and many people have such dreary lives that they create drama in other people's lives to prevent themselves from dying of boredom."

"Daddy was with you?" Liz's voice was almost too faint to be heard. "Why didn't we know this?"

"You were a child, Liz. In hindsight, you probably should have been told the full story early on, but adults don't always consider the deep needs of children in situations like that. They are too busy trying to hold themselves together."

"And Mama felt so guilty," Luann added. "She just couldn't bring herself to talk about any of it."

"What about Mama?" Liz asked. "You haven't really answered that question. Did she and Wallace Banks have an affair?"

"They did not. If Mr. Banks could have had his way, they would have. He was a confirmed bachelor who had his choice of many young socialites in Memphis, but your mother—quite unintentionally, I must add—charmed him. I regret deeply that you ladies didn't know your mother for who she was, but then, again, I believe you did. What you remember of her from your childhood is more than many people receive in a lifetime."

"But that's the problem, Brother Paul. I don't remember very much," Liz said from behind hands cupped over her face. She removed her hands and looked at the kind minister. "I only remember being so terribly lonely and scared."

"Forgiveness, my dear. Let go of the bad memories, forgive both your mother and father and the good memories will begin to come. You're clogging the channel, blocking the true light."

Absorbed as they were in conversation, both Liz and Luann had failed to notice that Master had ambled over to *his* master. He was gently nudging the elderly man's ankle. Brother Paul laughed and stood, affectionately rubbing the large dog's head. "That's my signal," he said. "We've talked well into this old boy's relief time. He needs an outdoor stroll."

Luann gathered the coffee mugs and walked towards the kitchen. Liz followed her, and in silence, they rinsed the mugs, returned the sugar and creamer to their respective places, and joined Brother Paul and Master outdoors. The sun had dropped behind the pines, and a slight chill was in the air. Master, having accomplished his task, curled up on the small porch. The three of them walked towards Liz's car. Liz stopped and turned to Brother Paul.

"Can I give you a hug?" she asked.

"I wouldn't let you leave without one," he said with a twinkle in his eye. "That and a promise from you that I'll see you again soon. I want to hear 'the rest of the story,' as Paul Harvey says. You must check in with me again, my dear ladies."

"Why has it taken so long, Brother Paul?" Liz asked.

"To everything, there is a season," he replied. "That's from the Bible, you know."

"What I know is that you and Miss Em are conspiring against me. That's exactly what she quotes to me!"

CHAPTER 16

"Five full weekends between Thanksgiving and Christmas," Richard moaned. "Do you know how many hours of stocking shelves that means?"

"Aw, Dad, Justin and Andy can keep up. You're worryin' about nothin'," Jackson said.

Jackson, freed from any sports in the winter months, had taken a more active role in the store. Liz was pleased that most of his free time was spent there and had attempted on several occasions to subtly approach the subject of the infrequency of his time with Lainie. On that topic, he was evasive, seeming to sense that his mother's delicate prying was to reassure herself that things between the two of them were cooling off. His replies to her were vague and offhand. Several times, he'd responded that Lainie was involved in helping her new neighbors get settled. According to Jackson, they were an older couple from Arizona who had lived in Roslyn years ago. "She loves strays, Mom, stray cats, stray dogs, stray people."

The three of them—Richard, Liz, and Jackson—were enjoying a rare Friday morning breakfast together on the day after Thanksgiving. Miss Em was exhausted after the full day of activities hosted yesterday at Luann's house and had chosen to have a simple breakfast of tea and toast in her room. Rose had finally taken Liz up on the offer of taking time off to be with her mother in her final days. To her amazement, Liz was enjoying caring for her home, family, and a live-in guest all on her own.

"Don't remind me that Christmas is coming. Let me enjoy the peace and quiet of Thanksgiving just for this weekend," she said.

"I know what you mean," Richard replied. "Everybody has full stomachs and plans for hunting or Black Friday shopping today. That gives us a little relief in the grocery store. But just a little. They'll be out in hordes by Monday, stocking up on brown sugar and little green cherries for fruit cakes. You sure those two boys will be enough, Jacks?"

Liz couldn't help but notice the easy way her husband and son discussed the business at hand. She longed for the same ease of conversation with Jackson that was so evident between father and son and knew deep within herself that it was she, not Jackson, who kept this intimacy from happening. With Brother Paul's soft voice in the background of her thoughts, she breathed a prayer of thanksgiving for this simple revelation. But what was she to do with a revelation?

"What's on your agenda for today, Liz?" Richard asked.

"Not much. The nurse should be here this morning by 10:30 to sit with Miss Em. I'll get her situated so she can put the finishing touches on Latisha's painting and then run a few errands. My main goal for today is to return Grace Carlson's down payment on her trip to St. Louis with the senior class."

"What? No way! Grace Carlson on our trip?" Jackson was incensed.

"Settle down, Jackson. I said I'm returning her money. No, she's not going. She doesn't know that, but she's soon to find out. I intend to make it clear to her that she will not be on the bus."

"Don't envy you that task," Richard said. "You sure you're up to that? The wrath of Miss Gracie?"

"I think I am," Liz replied. "Grace Carlson is nothing more than a lonely, desperate old woman."

"And don't forget, mean and nasty and crazy ..."

"Jackson! Those may all be true, but just think that; don't say it out loud. I'm trying to turn over a new leaf here." Liz had given much thought to Brother Paul's and Miss Em's words about desperation and had decided to think about the bitter old woman in those terms instead of applying her usual unpleasant adjectives to her.

"Hope you're ready for her to stomp on your new leaf, Mom. She's all those things and more. Do you know what she said?"

"Don't want to know, Jacks. It probably wasn't true anyway," Richard interrupted. "She really is what your mom said. It's best not to repeat what comes out of Miss Gracie's mouth."

Liz shot him a grateful look. Later, as she dressed for the day, she realized how she missed those early morning times with her family that had been replaced with her attention to Miss Em's needs. She didn't resent the change but simply acknowledged that it was different. A season for all things, she thought. It's really true.

***

By the time Liz had finished her errands and pulled up in front of Grace Carlson's home, darkness had fallen. She sat in her car and looked at the once proud home that now appeared almost abandoned. Grass that should have been mown before the frost turned it to a brittle brown crept from the lawn into once-tended flower beds that surrounded the house and lined the sidewalk that led to the front porch. Perennials, never dead-headed, displayed sad flower heads that disappeared into the weeds that engulfed them.

Liz tripped and almost fell over chunks of concrete that had dislodged from the sidewalk as she made her way to the porch. Attached to the wall beside the front door was a porch lamp with cracked glass panels; inside it, a single lightbulb burned. The light fixture was so coated with dirt and filled with dead bugs that it was virtually useless. It gave just enough light to attract a swarm of moths and other fall-hardy insects. Liz pulled on the sagging storm door and knocked on the peeling, faded red door. As she waited, she was overtaken by a wave of sadness. How, she wondered, can a person go home to this every night? A house crumbling around them, no one—human or animal—to welcome them. She knocked again, this time peering inside the tiny viewer in the door meant for observation from the inside out rather than the outside in. She was so intent on peering inside that she failed to hear the key turn in the lock and was startled when the door fell away from her face. Not a good start for her mission.

The old woman, glasses removed and gray hair pointing in all directions, reminded Liz of old crones described in fairy tales. "Hansel and Gretel" came immediately to mind, and Liz had a sudden ridiculous fear that she would be dragged inside and stuffed in the old woman's oven.

She breathed deeply and began. "Miss Gracie. I'm so sorry to interrupt your evening, but ..."

"What are you doing here?" the old woman spat out. Liz noticed a spot of red—spaghetti sauce?—staining the worn blue terry cloth robe.

"I'm sorry, did I interrupt your supper?" Liz asked.

"Yes, you did, Miss. And for what? Why are you here? You're letting cold air in."

Liz weighed her options. Ask to come in? She could barely stand to be on the porch where she at least could enjoy fresh air. She didn't want to imagine how depressing the inside of the neglected home might be. No, she'd get it over with quickly and be on her way.

"I've come to return your down payment check for the senior trip to St. Louis," she said firmly. "We already have enough chaperones." Inwardly, Liz winced at the small lie. They were still short three chaperones.

"Are you a committee of one?" the old woman asked. "My money is as good as anybody's, young lady."

"It was a decision of the entire committee, Miss Gracie. We're taking young, energetic teenagers, and they require a great deal of..."

"Are you saying I'm too old? Are you discriminating against me because I'm not a spring chicken? That would be like you. Or is it because I'm not fancy enough to be seen ...?"

Liz decided that if interrupting mid-sentence was good for Grace, it was equally good for her. "It has nothing to do with that, Miss Gracie, but this trip is about the seniors, and we have to make the best possible plans for their supervision."

"So, I'm not good enough!? You're just a chip off the old block, Elizabeth. Just like your mother. Always planning and finagling to make things come out the way you want. She got her comeuppance just like you'll get yours someday. Thought she had your daddy wrapped around her little finger, always going off on those weekend trips here and yonder. Off up to see the Cardinals play while the rest of us had to listen on the radio. What do two little girls care about a trip like that?"

The accusations were hurled so quickly that Liz barely had time to absorb the words. Weekend trips? Cardinals? Two little girls?

Then suddenly, like a flash, Liz saw the blue 1969 Buick trunk lid open, her mother standing there in the early morning light with a picnic basket covered with a blue cloth calling to her. "Liz, make sure you go to the bathroom before you get in the car. Your pillow and blanket are waiting for you on the backseat."

"Here, Miss Gracie." She thrust the folded check towards the surprised woman, not caring if she took it or not. "And thank you. You'll never know how much I thank you." She turned and ran to her car, not looking back. As she started the ignition, she became cognizant of laughter—her own—and tears flowing down her cheeks. She'd never experienced such extreme emotion in her life. Memories washed over her like a warm shower: Her daddy tucking her into bed, full of excitement; waking up to the sound of her parents' voices, the front screen door slapping its frame as one more travel essential was loaded into the car; her sister calling, "Get up, Lazy Bones, or we'll leave you at home."

Liz drove to the Roslyn Burger Shack, backed into a parking space, and ordered a cup of coffee from the gum-smacking teenager who appeared at her window. She was oblivious to the comings and goings of customers eager for a burger or hot dog after gorging on Thanksgiving turkey for the past two or three meals. She leaned back in her seat, sipped her coffee, and let the memories envelop her.

One trip? Two? Multiple? She now experienced them as a movie, with fade-ins, fade-outs, fragments, and feelings. All good. Pimento cheese sandwich and an ice-cold root beer. Gazing up at the Gateway Arch as she ate, wondering how they got it to stand up (She wondered about that still!), a little concerned that it might topple over on her family as they sat in the grass by the big river and had their picnic lunch before the ballgame. Later in the day, a hot dog bought from a man carrying them around in a big box hanging around his neck. Sleeping in a strange room in the same bed with Lu, her mother and her father right there in the room with them. Laughing at the sound of the strange word: motel. She said it to herself now, "Motel." She'd always loved the sound of that word, choppy and meaningless, and now she knew why. How had she forgotten those good times with her family?

They were buried under unforgiveness and bad memories, Brother Paul would tell her. Had she really been that unforgiving of her parents? Had she forgiven them now? Was that why the memory of the family trip (trips?) to St. Louis was so vivid now? Could that really happen to a person? From absolutely nowhere, a flood of memory? Yes, she answered herself. It could because it did. She had no doubts in her mind about the reality of those experiences she'd had as a child. It didn't matter if it was one trip or multiple trips. It was the feeling of family; that was the reality that buoyed her.

And what about the roses? Was there a memory somewhere inside her that could open a floodgate of sadness brought on by a beautiful bouquet of roses given from someone who loved to someone who wasn't allowed to love in return? Might have loved, but couldn't because of a deeper love? A love for family? A tear trickled down Liz's cheek. A tear for her mother and, possibly, for Mr. Wallace. Then, a child, but now a grown woman, Liz could recognize the pain that had been a reality for the two of them. Yes, she could forgive both of them. For what? For being human? In her mother's case, for having feelings that she put aside for something better. For Mr. Wallace, for his loneliness and recognition of a spark of light when he saw it in her mother. For his attempt to capture that spark but instead experience rejection. Yes, she could forgive that.

Liz broke from her ruminations as a car pulled into the stall next to her. An older gentleman in his 70's, maybe his 80's, was driving.

In the passenger's seat, a woman sat, probably his wife. Yes, definitely his wife. She betrayed her wifely role by licking her finger, reaching over and gently wiping something from the man's cheek, then giving him a loving pat in the same location. Liz watched as he rubbed the same spot, looked at the woman, and said something that brought a chuckle from his now-decided-by-Liz wife. There was something vaguely familiar about the couple. She had the sense that she should know them, but she couldn't come up with who they might be.

As she took a sip from her Styrofoam cup, she noticed that it was completely dark. She glanced at her watch: 8:00. Richard would be home by now, and she hadn't given a thought to supper preparations. If she was lucky, he'd bring soup from the deli with him. She thought of her dad again. Why did he have to die before he could carry through on his decision? Would he have been able to do that had he lived? Was his pride so wounded by the possibility of someone like Mr. Wallace wanting to make a life with his wife that he could never recover? Was he disappointed in himself for not providing his wife with the kind of life he thought she deserved? So many questions. Liz recognized that she would never know the answers to those questions and would somehow have to find a way to live with them remaining unanswered. She could do that, she decided. She could get used to this forgiveness thing.

The car with the older couple backed out of the stall next to her. From her backed-in parking position, she watched as the gentleman straightened the wheels and pulled away. Arizona license plates, she noticed. Maybe Lainie's neighbors. What was it Jackson had called them? Strays?

CHAPTER 17

Liz welcomed the quiet of Christmas morning after the huge family gathering on the previous evening. The Manley clan, along with Luann's family and other adopted friends, gathered at the family farm. This celebration had always been Liz's favorite of the year. Long ago, it was established that, no matter where they were in the rotation of hosting celebrations, Christmas Eve was always on the farm. No matter what the weather, a huge bonfire was built in the clearing beside the pond, and after a non-traditional dinner of fried catfish, a hay wagon pulled by Richard Sr.'s tractor made as many trips as necessary to deliver carol-singing kids and adults from the house to the bonfire. Years ago, they'd agreed that exchanging gifts was unnecessary and impractical. What mattered most was acknowledging the season, being together, and having fun. Instead of gifts, all who participated in the event slipped some money to Richard Sr. at some point during the evening so that he could purchase a new addition to the manger scene he'd established when Richard and Denise were young. The previous year's donations had provided supplies to build a new open "stable" to house the holy family. On approach, the young Mary and Joseph looked real in the glow of the fire.

Liz turned on the lights of the Christmas tree in her living room and thought of last night's Christmas Eve party. It couldn't have been more perfect: temperatures in the 40s, clear skies littered with stars, tables set up with urns of hot chocolate, dozens of freshly baked cookies and homemade candies, blankets scattered around in the dead winter grass, and people moving from group to group talking and laughing. Such a contrast to her perfect tree with beautifully wrapped presents underneath and her dining room table already set for the evening meal with her best china and gleaming silver. Both good, she decided. So many ways to celebrate.

With only the lights of the Christmas tree to brighten the room, Liz stood in front of two easels. On one, a painting still covered, unrevealed; on the other, the painting from her childhood, the little-girl Liz under the huge oak tree building her moss garden. Later today, Rose, Latisha, and Mr. Retha would come by for the first viewing of the completed painting. Miss Em had accomplished what she set out to do: she'd completed her first painting and had begun sittings with Maria and Maddie.

Liz removed the covering from Latisha's painting and looked at the beautiful little girl seated in the window seat of Miss Em's room, her face transformed in wonder as she read from a book untitled in the painting. Miss Em had discussed with Liz whether to include the title of the book or to leave it to one's imagination. She'd arrived at her own conclusion eventually. "Imagination," she declared. "We'll leave this to the imagination. This child becomes so enrapt in the stories she reads that it shows, not only on her face but in her very posture."

She'd captured that essence of Latisha, Liz thought now. The child's body relaxed yet drawn towards something, her face serene yet energized. Liz looked at the painting of herself. Exactly the same. What a gift to be able to capture the feeling of being enthralled on canvas! No wonder Miss Em was so well-known in the art world. When an untrained eye such as Liz's could see life on a canvas, a true talent was at work.

Liz felt the light touch of Richard's hands on her shoulders. She leaned back into him as he moved his arms around her waist.

"Merry Christmas, little gardener," he whispered in her ear. "You were a beautiful little girl, but you're an even beautifuler woman."

"*Beautifuler* is not a word," Liz said, turning to face him.

"It is for you, Liz. And I'm not talking about just the outside. You are, and always have been, beautiful on the inside and the outside. I'm the luckiest man in the world. There's nothing that could make me happier than what I already have."

"What about that restaurant?" Liz asked. "Have you given up on that?"

"Well, no," he laughed. "But that'll come with time. Right now, I'm happy to make my little grocery store deli the best around and to occasionally cook in my own kitchen. Speaking of which ..."

"Time to get those cinnamon rolls going," Liz agreed. "I'll work on the turkey for tonight's dinner while you mix the dough."

***

Miss Em joined Richard, Liz, and Jackson for their family gift exchange and a late breakfast.

"Miss Liberty agrees, Richard. You make the best cinnamon rolls in the state," Miss Em said as she uncharacteristically pinched off a corner of her pastry and allowed the cat to take it from her fingers. "It's Christmas," she said in response to the looks of amazement from all three Manleys. "One can behave inappropriately on such occasions."

"Where's the camera when we need it?" Jackson said. "If I ever needed to blackmail you, Miss Em, that would be the perfect picture to do it with."

"Speaking of pictures, is Lainie still planning to come for the unveiling of Latisha's painting tonight?" Liz asked.

"Yeah, and for dinner, too," Jackson said. "Her family is having their Christmas dinner at 1:00. We'll be eating all day. What time are we eating here?"

"I told Rose to be here by 4:30. Luann's family is coming too. We'll eat first, then have the official—what do we call it, Miss Em?"

"We'll call it a showing, my dear. And perhaps a presentation, since it will be Latisha's to take home with her. I only hope that the child's great-grandmother can be cognizant enough to recognize her beautiful girl in the painting."

"I hope she can live just to see it," Liz said. "She is so weak. I wasn't sure we'd be able to talk Mr. Retha into coming tonight."

And it was true. The old gentleman was reluctant to leave his wife's bedside. Her hospital bed had been set up in their bedroom, and the man rarely left her side, even when the hospice nurse came to relieve him. Latisha had convinced him to come tonight, with Rose adding a convincing argument. "You need to get out, Daddy. Mama would want you to do this for Latisha and for yourself on Christmas Day."

"Be here at 4:30 sharp, Jackson. We'll do well to keep Mr. Retha here long enough to eat and see the painting. We'll have dinner on the table, ready to go, so eat lightly at Lainie's house."

***

It was a bittersweet evening. The girls—Latisha, Maddie, and Maria—filled the house with their leftover excitement and joy of receiving the perfect gifts under the tree. Rose and Retha, try as they might, could not get rid of the sadness of impending death that surrounded them. Lainie and Jackson's teenage bantering and teasing contributed to the efforts made by Luann, Rob, Richard, and Liz to keep the conversation light, but it was Miss Em who took the situation in hand.

She was in unusually high spirits as she welcomed Mr. Retha. "Sit here beside me," she encouraged. "We are honored guests, and we must behave as such. Rose and Liz have an unfair advantage over me by having had the pleasure of knowing you all these years. I must catch up. I understand that your passion is gardening?"

And from there, she engaged the sad old gentleman in conversation for the remainder of the meal. His features relaxed, and it was evident to everyone that for the length of the meal, at least, he'd forgotten the sadness that waited for him in his home. Seeing that he was taken care of so well gave everyone permission to relax and enjoy their Christmas dinner. Liz marveled at the grace and ease of her dear old friend, at her ability to put a complete stranger at such ease.

"Hey Ma," Jackson said as Liz served cherry pie—baked by Richard—and vanilla ice cream, "save back a piece of this for a midnight snack."

"Jackson!" Lainie scolded in mock admonishment. "Miz. Manley, you have to know this. He arm-wrestled Mr. Parker for the last piece of pecan pie at my house. And he won! And he ate it! Jackson, how can you eat so much?"

"Why do you think we're in the grocery store business?" Richard laughed. "We couldn't feed this boy if we had to pay full price for groceries."

"You said Mr. Parker, Lainie. Is that your neighbor? The family who moved here from Arizona?" asked Liz.

"Yeah, Mom invited them over for Christmas dinner. They don't have any family around here, and they are such nice people. They used to live here a long time ago. It's so sad; they moved away after their son was killed in a car accident. He was just a freshman in college. They moved back here after Mr. Parker retired because they said the people here are so nice, and they thought they would feel closer to their son. They're really nice, aren't they, Jackson?"

"Yeah, Mr. Parker likes to fish and play golf. He promised to teach me ..."

The sound of Jackson's voice faded from Liz's hearing. She could feel the blood rushing through her head, and the room seemed to disappear from her sight. She was vaguely aware of Richard at her elbow, taking charge. She felt the chair being pulled from the table and his strong hands helping her to her feet. She heard his voice without understanding his words but knew instinctively that as he led her to the kitchen, he'd covered for her lapse of consciousness.

In the privacy of the kitchen, he held her in his arms. "It's okay, Liz. Just breathe. If anybody noticed anything, they'll chalk it up to the holidays. Nothing's changed. Nobody knows about any of this."

"But Jackson knows that he likes an old gentleman by the name of Mr. Parker. He knows that they had a son. Steven. My one-night stand." Liz was frozen in place.

"You have to go back in there, Liz. We have to finish this evening on a good note. You can do this. Think of all the people who are counting on you tonight: Rose, Mr. Retha, Latisha, Miss Em."

Miss Em. Simply, the name brought a semblance of peace to Liz. She remembered how the dear woman had immediately engaged

Mr. Retha in conversation, helping him forget that at home, his wife was dying. If she can do that for a person, then I can put on a happy face and get through this evening, she thought. With Richard behind her, she returned to the dining room. He spoke for her.

"We've done about all the damage we can do here. We'll leave the table as it is and head to the living room. And, yes, Jacks, there's pie left for a midnight snack. Onward to the big event!"

Chairs had been placed on either side of the veiled painting, one for Miss Em and one for Latisha. Liz positioned herself behind the easel and gently pulled the covering away. There was perfect quiet and stillness in the room as everyone took in the exquisite painting.

Finally, Mr. Retha spoke. "That's my girl. That's really my girl. Ain't she a picture?"

Rose, for once, was silent. Tears rolled down her cheeks, and she sat shaking her head. Finally, she composed herself. "Thank you, ma'am," she said to Miss Em.

"No, dear Rose, thank you. Thank you for trusting me with your beautiful granddaughter. For giving me a chance to truly live my passion again. I couldn't have painted a more perfect subject than our Latisha."

Liz had neither heard the telephone ring nor had she seen Jackson leave the room to answer it. He came to the door, phone in hand. "Ma, you need to take this. It's Miss Stevens about Miss Willa."

***

Liz hung up the phone. She'd allowed enough time for Rose and her family to arrive home, then called. Rose answered.

163

"She still here, but it won't be much longer. I left Daddy and the nurse with her so I can put Latisha to bed. Thanks be that she is so tired she can't hardly hold her little eyes open. What a day that little girl had. To be the center of attention ..."

"Rose, I'm going to hang up now. You need to take care of Latisha and sit with your daddy. Do you want me to come out and sit with you?"

"We just fine, thank you, Lizbet. I called Brother Jacobson, and he'll be here directly. Daddy will get most comfort from our preacher sitting beside him when Momma draws her last breath."

"Call me."

Liz was consumed by the need to do something—anything to keep her mind from spinning out of control. She knocked gently on Miss Em's door.

"Come in, dear." The woman spoke as if she had been expecting Liz all along.

"Just wanted to see that you'd gotten settled in for the night. Can I do anything for you? Are you simply exhausted?"

"I'm mysteriously energized, Elizabeth. Being surrounded by all these wonderful people, even with impending death surrounding us—perhaps because of that—I feel extremely blessed and," the old woman seemed to search for words, "fulfilled. If only it could be I who were passing tonight instead of that dear man's wife. But who am I to question timing? This is all for a purpose, my dear, these sufferings we endure."

Liz busied herself, pulling back the bed covers on Miss Em's bed, folding back sheets, and fluffing the pillows to perfection.

"And what sufferings are you keeping to yourself just now, dear one? It's apparent that you received a shock tonight with Lainie's information about the—what were their names?—the Parkers?"

"Was it that obvious?" she asked.

"Not obvious at all. The attention was all focused on the teenagers and their joyful play. But I'm a reader of people; you, of all who know me, are aware of that gift. I saw your surprise, I saw Richard's immediate concern, and I deduced that something had transpired that disturbed both of you deeply. Am I correct?"

Liz acknowledged that she was indeed deeply disturbed. "But it's nothing that can be discussed or even fixed," she said sadly. "Some things just are, and there's nothing to do but figure out how to live with them. The Parkers are a family from my past, from something I thought was finished."

"Few things are finished in this life, Elizabeth. Once an event is written in your book of life, it remains there forever. Living fully requires one to accept that fact. A healed memory allows one to go back and reread the recordings of those events and make them count for something in one's present circumstances."

"Easier said than done," Liz said to the fragile woman as she helped her climb into bed.

Miss Em reached for Liz's hand and brought it to her lips. "But possible," she whispered. "We'll get through this, too, Elizabeth. I have a suspicion that you are on the verge of living fully."

CHAPTER 18

Rose insisted on returning to work early in January. "There's too much sadness in that house," she explained. "For Latisha's sake, we got to get things back to normal. Daddy's not 'customed to taking his comfort from me, and we just bump around into each others' sadness. Mama wouldn't want us going on like this. She told me that already."

"You mean before she passed on?" Liz asked. The two women were preparing a tray for "High Tea" in Miss Em's room, their beloved ritual finally restored after weeks of interruption.

"I mean now. My mama's body may be passed on, but her spirit is communing with me every day. You white folks don't know how to listen in the spirit world. Sometimes I feel right sorry for you people."

Over the three weeks that had passed since Christmas day, Liz had learned much about the customs of African Americans in burying their dead. This current declaration about the spirit world came as no surprise after all that had transpired. And in some ways, she agreed with Rose: the raw emotion and strong hope the Walker clan and their friends had expressed over the death of Miss Willa had seemed cleansing, even for Liz. It had, at least for the time being, put the news about the Parker family in the background. When she thought of the repercussions of the news Lainie had broken on Christmas night, Liz simply "put the thought on the shelf of her mind," knowing that eventually it would be necessary to deal with the facts. But not now.

"Yoohoo! Anybody home?" Luann called, followed by, "Miss Liberty, I'm so glad to see you, too!" For some strange reason, Miss

Liberty had taken an intense dislike to Luann and showed it by hissing at her every time Luann showed up.

"She's just trying to tell you to find a more polite way to come into somebody's home," Liz said. "Yoohoo? Have you been introduced to the modern invention of a doorbell?"

"Ring a doorbell? At my sister's home? I don't think so. You and the Miss will just have to come down off your high horses."

Luann took the loaded tray from Rose and set it on the counter. Before the older woman could protest, she'd wrapped her arms around Rose. "Are you sure you should be here this soon, Rose? Don't you need to be with your daddy?"

Rose extricated herself from Luann's hug and attempted to pick up the tray. Luann moved to block her, then turned to pick it up herself. "You're the guest today," she said. "I don't know if it's wise for you to be back at work so soon, but I'm sure glad to see you."

"Law me, if you don't just come in and take over a place," Rose reprimanded. "Lizbet is right about you. We got to teach you some manners, girl."

"Not just yet," Luann countered as they moved down the hallway toward Miss Millie's room. "I have some questions to ask you, and they probably won't fall in the realm of good manners. I want to talk about your mama's services. Is that okay?"

She set the tray on the table that Liz had dragged to its usual tea-time location near Miss Em's chair. Miss Em watched and listened with interest to the conversation that was already in progress.

"Luann!" Liz began to protest.

Rose laughed. "It's fine, Lizbet. Maybe I can teach you white women something about respect for the saints who've passed to their reward in heaven. I was at your mama's funeral if you remember rightly. I mean no disrespect now, but it got so quiet in there I thought I might just have myself a nap."

"Just who were those people who sat on the front rows on either side and kept chiming in?" Luann asked. "And how did they know when to say their 'amens' and their 'come ons' and such? Did they plan that ahead?"

Again, Rose laughed. "Don't you know about the Spirit, Luann? Those brothers and sisters were the Amen Corner, and they were Spirit-led. They were the *encouragers*."

"Didn't sound to me like Brother Jacobson needed any encouragement. He sounded like he knew just what he wanted to say and how he wanted to say it. He almost sang his words. Matter of fact, to me, it sounded like music; he sang the lead, and the Amen Corner was back-up."

"That's what it 'posed to do when the Spirit is leading," Rose said. "Now my mama was a woman who lived like a body's 'posed to live. She didn't have a selfish, mean bone in her sweet self. She didn't have many wants and wishes in this old world, and that's why she earned the best send-off to her final home that could be had. Did you ever see a prettier casket? And Mama looking like a fresh-petalled pink rose laying there in that white satin box? She was even prettier than those long-stemmed pink roses lying there on top.

"And my sweet LaMont. He told me on the phone, 'Mama, I can't be there till January 2. I can't be there to have my say in flowers, dresses, and so forth. But you and Pa and Latish know what Gran liked. You don't worry about the money. You get the very best for her.' My LaMont is a good boy."

"So, is that why you waited so long to have the funeral?" Luann asked. "So LaMont could get here?"

"It takes time, Luann, to do things proper. But, yes, we had to wait till LaMont could get back to shore from his oil rig job and for Mama's sister's boys to get here from Chicago. Those boys didn't do too well for theirselves, and they had to go to their church people to get enough money to come. "

"I never saw so many family members at a funeral, Rose. And I never saw a procession like that, marching in two-by-two while we all sat there and looked on. It reminded me of those scenes in movies of New Orleans funerals; you know where they walk behind that carriage-like hearse down the middle of the street? Were all those people related to you? They filled up half the church!"

Liz had thought at first that Luann was out of line when she began quizzing Rose about the funeral customs that were so different from those of the white South, but as she listened to Rose explain—almost got lost in the relaying of events—she realized that this was another layer of grieving for her friend. Liz and Miss Em served as an audience to this healing conversation between Luann and Rose; two women lost in conversation, one simply seeking to understand the other better.

Isn't that what real relationships are about, Liz wondered. Is that why Luann is so much happier than I am? This thought startled Liz even as it came into her mind: Lu *is* happier than I am. She takes people just as they are and is not afraid to get to know them better. What does she have that I don't have? I want to protect Rose; Lu wants to know her. Is that why Jackson is holding back from me? Is that why I feel isolated so much of the time?

Laughter from the three other women jolted Liz back to the present moment just in time to hear Miss Em say, "I haven't eaten that much food at one time in my entire life. Rose, your friends do know how to cook."

"And I thought we knew how to serve comfort food," Luann said. "Does your church put together a cookbook, Rose? If they do, I need a copy of those recipes."

"Cookbook?" Rose hooted. "That's for you white ladies that don't have natural cookin' instincts. We don't need cookbooks!"

***

Settling back into a routine was both good and bad for Liz. The good part was the normalcy of having regular tea time, having Miss Em back to her painting, having Rose back to running the household and preparing her wonderful meals, and having the freedom to come and go without concern of whether someone was nearby in case Miss Em needed something. The downside was that it left her free to think, which brought her to the point of considering a return to the grocery store.

"Absolutely not, Liz," Richard said when she approached him about relieving Denise of some of the bookkeeping and ordering. "She has her own system. You, better than all people, should know that. How would you have felt if I'd suggested that she come in and relieve you?"

"You're right," Liz agreed, much quicker than she thought she would. Deep down, she really didn't want to return and was secretly grateful that it had been this easy. "It's just that, well, I feel ... *useless.*"

"Useless! What does that mean, useless?" Richard asked incredulously. "Liz, you are caring for an old lady you didn't even really know till six months ago. You have a son graduating from high school and are making all sorts of plans for a grand send-off for him and the entire class. You still supervise the Wednesday night dinners at church. And you feel useless?" Richard's voice had risen with the naming of each activity Liz was involved in.

"Maybe you need to run for mayor."

Liz recognized immediately that if she was going to salvage this rare evening before the fireplace with Richard, she would have to change the tone of the conversation. She forced a laugh. "Mayor, huh? Do you think I could get Miss Gracie's vote?"

"Liz, Liz. You've got to let that go. Miss Gracie's just a ..."

Too late, Liz recognized she'd taken a wrong turn in the conversation. Or maybe—she hated the thought—no matter how she tried to control (she hated the word)—the conversation, what needed to be discussed would be discussed. She recognized that by shelving the events of Christmas night in her own mind, she'd forced Richard to do the same. Feeling very small, she said, "Richard, I am letting that go. But it came at me so fast—first opening up that whole can of worms about Mama and Daddy, then finding out the Parkers have moved back and have already won the heart of my son, then Rose's mama dying, all at holiday time. There's nothing going on to keep my mind off those things."

"Maybe you shouldn't."

"Shouldn't what?" Even as she asked the question, Liz knew the answer.

"Shouldn't keep your mind off those things. Maybe we need to figure out how to deal with the question of Jackson's paternity."

Something about the impassive way Richard spoke the words frightened Liz. She wanted to ask, "What do you mean?" She wanted to leave the room. She wanted to turn the clock back. Instead, she forced herself to sit quietly. Filled with fear, she waited for Richard to speak again.

"Liz," he began, then stopped.

She waited.

Richard sighed deeply. "We've never really talked about this. About how hard this whole thing has been. I'm not saying I wished we'd done things any different because I don't. You and Jackson are the best parts of my life. But that doesn't mean this—and I mean from the very beginning—hasn't hurt like hell."

That single word, *hell,* told Liz that, conversation-wise, they had moved to a place they'd never been before. Richard never uttered a word that could be construed as cursing. Not a single damn had ever passed his lips in her hearing, nor, she suspected, in anyone else's. He didn't need expletives to communicate with other people. He said what he meant, and cliché as it sounded, meant what he said.

All these years, he'd carried the hurt of betrayal and had protected her by keeping it to himself. In that moment, she felt the full burden of what she'd done to him. She felt as though she was suffocating. For the first time since she'd discovered she was pregnant with Jackson, from the time she'd told Richard and had been overcome with both relief and fear as he'd said it didn't matter, he still loved her and wanted to marry her, for the first time ever, she felt the pain he'd carried all those years.

That single word, *hell,* conveyed to her all that he'd been through. All those years of caring what other people thought, all those years of it being about her, her self-centeredness, came crashing down on her. Liz understood that what happened in the next moment could determine the course of her marriage to Richard.

She stood, her body feeling as though it weighed a ton, and moved toward Richard. With every movement, she felt lighter, and as she knelt before him and took his hands in her own, she knew with every part of herself that she owed her good life to this man. Tears blinded her as she told him how sorry she was.

CHAPTER 19

Liz had been devastated when Richard asked for a break in their relationship when she was a senior in high school, and he was a college freshman at Ole Miss. The evening was etched in her mind. After eating supper with his mom and dad, they'd walked down to the pond on that beautiful Saturday in April. She'd picked up one of the fishing poles from the bin near the dock, slipped her feet out of her flip-flops, dangled her toes in the water, and cast her line. Liz had never been interested in fishing, but she enjoyed casting the line with the hope of an occasional nibble. Most of all, she enjoyed the peace she felt in this place.

"Liz," Richard had begun. "There's something I want us to talk about, and if I don't do it right now, I'm afraid I won't do it at all."

The seriousness in Richard's voice frightened her. Liz took her time reeling in the line and securing the hook. Without moving from her seated position, she laid the pole beside her and waited for Richard to begin.

After what seemed an eternity, Richard spoke. "Don't take this wrong, Liz, but I need some time away from ... I need some time to ..."

"Just say it, Richard. You're breaking up with me. You've found somebody at Ole Miss, and we're finished." Blinded by anger, she scrambled to her feet, knocking one of her flip-flops into the water. She turned to run down the dock, but Richard caught her by her shoulders, gripping her tightly.

"Don't," he said. "Don't do this. You have to let me talk to explain what I need from you."

She struggled to be free from him, but he'd put his arms around her tightly and wouldn't let her go.

"Listen to me, Liz. I love you. You've always been the one for me and always will be. I just need some time to concentrate on my studies. School learning doesn't come easy for me, and I need to spend my weekends studying instead of coming back here. It's like I've been playing at school and living for coming back here to be with you on the weekends. If I'm serious about this business degree, I've got to work at it. I know about the practical side of the grocery business, but I want to ..."

"That's an excuse, Richard. I'm not stupid. I know what happens when a good-looking guy goes from a small town to a big university campus. You have your pick of girls much prettier and way more sophisticated than me. I get it. Just be honest with me."

"Stop it, Liz. I've always been honest with you, and I always will. We're not breaking up; I just need a few weeks to concentrate on school."

"But what about prom?"

"Liz, that's the week before finals. Anyway, you'll have more fun with your classmates than you would with me. Surely there's some guy who'd love to have you on loan." Richard tried for a moment of levity. "What about Josh Adams? He's like your brother, and he'd jump at the chance to claim you for his prom date."

"Josh Adams? He's your idea for my consolation prize? Well, Richard, I'm just as capable of finding somebody else as you are. Remember that!" And in a moment of outrage, she tugged off the simple engraved silver promise ring and flung it in the water, grabbed her single orange flip-flop, and ran toward the house.

Liz had refused Richard's phone calls that evening. Too furious even to cry over the breakup, she'd set her mind on the flurry of her senior year activities and the new boy in town: Steven Parker. Steven, newly arrived in Roslyn for his senior year, had accepted the attention showered on him by all the girls (there's nothing like the arrival of a handsome boy in a small town to create a stir among high school girls) but had not encouraged a single one of them. Liz, while she liked him and appreciated his good looks, had kept her distance but had caught him staring at her more than once during English class.

Later, after she and Richard were married, and Jackson was born, Liz wondered why she'd become so enraged rather than acting in her customary way of tears and sadness. She thought of how things might have turned out differently if she'd behaved in her usual "weak" way. But she didn't allow herself to dwell on that; after all, she wouldn't have had Jackson in that case, and she could not imagine *not* having him. Instead, she'd stuffed that thought deep down inside herself, along with all the other disappointments of her life.

What she absolutely could not forget nor forgive was her behavior on prom night. She'd been successful, as she knew she would, in getting a date with Steven Parker for the prom. What she could not understand or explain, even to herself, was her betrayal of her own personal moral code. Liz had never been tempted to drink alcohol. She and Richard, while very affectionate with each other, had agreed from the beginning of their relationship that they would limit their physical intimacy to kissing. That's how she knew beyond a doubt that she was pregnant with Steven's baby and not Richard's. That's how Richard knew, too.

Several members of the in-crowd had, with the help of older friends, arranged to rent rooms at a highway motel in Senatobia for an after-prom party. She and Steven found themselves tagging along. Peer pressure, anger towards Richard for breaking up with her—it would never be known what prompted Liz to sip champagne with the rest of the group on that fateful evening. Her defenses down, she'd betrayed herself and Richard, the only person she'd ever really loved, and had unprotected sex with an almost-stranger in the bathroom of a Holiday Inn Express. In that single event, Liz lost both her virginity and her self-respect.

Afterward, the tears she hadn't shed about Richard flowed. She'd insisted that, alcohol or not, Steven take her home immediately. In the final weeks of school, a time to enjoy and celebrate, she could hardly bear to look in the mirror, nor could she look Steven in the eye. Once, he'd stopped her as she walked out of English class.

"Liz, I'm sorry. I'm not really like that."

She'd never know what Steven Parker was really like. Premature sex had taken care of that. She rushed off without allowing him to finish. She learned later that he'd gone off to college somewhere in Missouri—University of Missouri?—and died in a car accident late in his freshman year. She'd waited on his parents in the grocery store a few times before they moved away, but she never conversed with them. By that time, Jackson had been born, and she carried the weight of the knowledge that they were grandparents he would never know, grandparents who would never know they had a grandson.

Richard had come looking for her the day he returned home for summer vacation. She'd walked out to the front porch to get the mail, and there he sat in the swing. She melted at the sight of him.

"Got any acceptances?" he grinned. "College, I mean. Are you coming to Ole Miss?"

At the time, the lateness of her period hadn't concerned her, and, in her mind, she was college-bound. "If I'm going to keep an eye on you, I guess that's my only choice," she shot back at him.

"Catch!" he called as he threw her flip-flop to her. She caught it and threw it back before she joined him in the swing.

"I have something else," he said as he took her left hand and slid the silver ring on her finger. "Thank goodness the orange flip-flop was there. Otherwise, I'd never have found that tiny thing. They were side by side."

It was that easy. They were back together. They had a week to be worry-free teenagers in love again.

***

With Richard's encouragement, Liz decided to bare her soul and confide in Miss Em about the truth of Jackson's parenthood. In the evening, when Liz recognized the extent of the pain Richard had quietly endured for the entirety of their marriage, they talked until Richard finally said, "Liz, I know you feel better by talking about all of this, but—and please understand me—I don't. Does it hurt? Yes. Do I want to spend the rest of my life thinking about it and talking about it? No.

"But I understand that you do. And I really think you need to. If you want to talk to some—what do they call it?—therapist? psychiatrist? I'll go with you, but not more'n once or twice. We can afford for you to go as many times as you need to, as many times as it takes to get over this. As far as I'm concerned, Jackson is my boy and yours. I meant that when I said it the first time, and I mean it now."

"But what do we do about Jackson knowing? What if he needs to know in the future? What if he finds out from someone else?"

"We've had this discussion, Liz. The only two people who know are *you*"—he paused here for effect and pointed to Liz—"and *me*." The final word was spoken with his index finger pointed back at himself. "*We* are Jackson's parents, and if the time ever comes when he needs to know about his," Richard searched for the right word before continuing, "*biology*, then *we* are the ones to tell him."

It was true. Richard had taken the news of Liz's pregnancy with his usual stoicism. She now recognized that it was this very character trait that had allowed her to minimize, in her own mind, the pain he'd carried as well. Stoicism, she now knew, was not synonymous with coldness or an unfeeling nature. She also recognized that his disinterest in discussing the issue didn't come from a lack of caring.

Liz remembered the Sunday afternoon when they'd announced to Richard's parents their change in plans. Richard had taken full responsibility for the pregnancy and had convinced his parents and Liz that he saw it as a good thing: He could come back and work in the grocery store—his dream in the first place—instead of finishing his degree. Had she not been so consumed with her own guilt and worry Liz would have recognized this for what it was: Richard's protection of her.

Her own mother had been simply resigned. Liz had the feeling at the time that she'd almost expected things to turn out this way. When Luann had called from Georgia for her weekly Saturday conversation, Liz heard her mother say, "Yes, Liz will make a good little mother. She always did love her dolls and make-believe."

So, Richard was right. No one even suspected. And with the reported death of Steven Parker, the only other person who could possibly have any information about Jackson's paternity, there was no chance of anyone ever knowing.

Liz and Richard's conversation had ended with the pledge that, for now, the secret would remain with them and with the professional Liz chose to confide in.

Several nights later, Liz approached Richard again as they were preparing for bed. "I've decided not to see a therapist," she began.

"Really? Why not? You aren't going to tie me to a chair and make me talk about this some more, are you?" Liz loved the way Richard could lighten a heavy subject with a simple turn of phrase.

She swatted at him with a towel and said, "No. I've decided to talk to Miss Em about it."

"You sure you can trust her? She's pretty much of a blabber mouth. Actually, I think that's a good idea: that conversation can happen in our house but without my participation. Besides, she's free."

***

"Your secrets will go to the grave with me, Elizabeth. Soon."

"Miss Em! Don't say that."

"Why not, my dear? It's true. And I don't say that in a morbid way. I'm ready any time, especially after today. I daresay this will be my last trip on this busy highway. While I'm grateful we don't traverse over bumpy, ill-kept roads, I'm not particularly fond of cars dashing past me at warp speed. I'm quite finished with travel that doesn't include lovely, diverse scenery."

The two women were returning from their farthest field trip ever. They had driven to Memphis to meet with Donald Jamerson and make sure all the i's were dotted, and t's were crossed in Miss Em's final wishes. Miss Em had listened to Liz with compassion all the way there, only occasionally making comments and asking for clarification.

On the return trip, they'd talked about the details of Miss Em's will, but only for a short time. The conversation soon turned back to the subject of Jackson.

"So, what would you do, Miss Em?" Liz asked. "Would you ever tell him if he were your son?"

"I'll stick with my standard response, dear. A time for all seasons. You'll know if and when the time comes for Jackson to be made aware of his parentage. One bit of advice I'd give you, however, is that this is not your decision to make alone. When, *if* the time comes for him to know, this must be a joint decision between you and Richard."

Tears formed in Liz's eyes. She reached behind Miss Em's seat for a tissue box. "I think I've learned my lesson," she said. "I've held Richard at a distance from this for our entire marriage. I treated this as though I were the only one suffering. Truth is, he's probably been hurt worse than I have. I didn't trust him; I betrayed him and then stood by while he lied to his parents to protect me. On top of all that, I've pretended all this time that he didn't really want to get his degree from Ole Miss. I've pitied myself for losing out on a degree and have not given any thought to his loss."

"Through all this self-flagellation, there's one thing I haven't heard you say, my dear," Miss Em said.

"What's that?" Liz asked.

"You've said nothing about how the two of you have stood by each other and together have reared a handsome young man, a fine young man poised on the brink of adulthood. That's worth every bit of suffering you've endured, wouldn't you say? There would be no Jackson as we know him without his two wonderful parents."

The two women enjoyed the comfortable silence between them as Liz headed down the off-ramp and onto the narrower highway that led to Roslyn. As they approached the town limits, Miss Em spoke again.

"I have a bit more advice for you, dear," she said. "In my Catholic tradition, we confess to a priest. While we recognize that he has no ability to offer forgiveness to us in himself, we believe that when he gives absolution, he does so as a representative of God. I know that in your Protestant tradition, you don't do that, but I believe you have something very close to a trusted priest—a man of God—in your friend Brother Paul. Let me suggest that, with Richard's blessing, you pay him a visit in the near future. He knows you, he knows your history, and he is a compassionate man. Leave something behind with him as a symbol of letting the past go, and perhaps you can walk away with a sense of freedom."

"What would I leave behind?" Liz asked.

"That would be for you to decide, my dear. The symbol would attach a sacramental quality to the occasion. But you have to choose."

CHAPTER 20

The clock radio on Richard's side of the bed clicked on. Somehow, in setting the clock, Liz had moved the dial just enough to produce loud static rather than soft music or the urging of a DJ to "rise and shine." As unwelcome as either of those would have been at 5:15 on a Sunday morning, both would have been preferred over the jarring sound of static.

"What tha ...? What day is this? Isn't this Sunday?" Richard's questions came rapid-fire in his confused, half-asleep state. He continued as he reached over to turn off the noise. "Who set this alarm? We don't need an alarm on Sunday morning."

"I set it, and we do need it on this particular Sunday morning," Liz said as she stood and stretched. "Get up, lazy bones. We're going on an adventure."

"I'll pass," Richard moaned as he settled back under the covers. "The only adventure I want is in my dreams. I'm taking a raincheck."

"That'll cost you a few bucks then. We have a departing flight in Memphis at 8:45."

"A flight?" Richard sat up. "Why? Where?"

"It's a surprise," Liz called from the bathroom. "You'll know where we're going when we get to our gate. If you'd think a minute, you might figure out why. Do you know what happens this week?"

"Work?" he asked. "And more work? It's not your birthday ... or mine? It's not our anniversary?" The question in Richard's voice gave away his fear that he could have forgotten a special occasion. "It's the middle of February."

"Bingo!" called Liz above the sound of water spraying from the shower. "Valentine's Day. Get moving. Those jet planes don't wait on slow-pokes."

"Liz, what have you done?" Richard asked. "Where are we going? I can't leave like this. "Who's going to mind the store? Literally!"

"Denise and your dad," Liz called, clearly enjoying the moment. "And Jackson after school and evenings. You think they can't do it? Pick up the phone and call. On second thought, don't. They might back out if you wake them at 5:30 on Sunday morning. It's all set, Richard. All you have to do is get dressed and get in the car."

The idea had come to Liz after her talk with Miss Em. She desperately needed to do something to solidify her long overdue recognition of Richard's love and sacrifice all these years. They'd never had a honeymoon, had never even been on a trip that included just the two of them. They'd had family vacations and multiple trips with friends but never had she and Richard, as a couple in love, left Roslyn for the sheer pleasure of being together. This trip was her Valentine to Richard.

The ease with which the plans fell into place caused her to wonder why they'd never done something like this before. She admitted the truth herself: she'd never wanted it to happen. She recalled her vague responses to Richard's occasional urgings that they "get away," just the two of them: it was tax season, her car needed to be replaced, his car needed to be replaced, Jackson had a school program. Her list was endless, and Richard, recognizing that, finally gave up. No more suggestions.

As Liz planned their getaway, she gave considerable thought to her motives in all those refusals. The best she could come up with on her own—and God forbid she drag another fault out to be examined by Miss Em—was that she didn't deserve it. That, and fear that something would happen to Jackson while they were gone. That somehow, she, and she alone was responsible for his well-being and that if she allowed herself to let down her guard, even for a few days, her world would collapse. And she *would* deserve that.

Maybe Richard's right, she thought more than once. Maybe I do need to see a therapist or a professional. Once identified, she recognized her reasoning as irrational. She also recognized that, even though she would carry through on her plan for this trip, twisted thinking still lurked in the back of her mind. Her childhood magical thinking was still with her. Her hope was that in going through with the plan, she'd exorcise those demons. Something like the mantra, *feel the fear and do it anyway.*

And so she'd persisted. Denise and Big Richard had been tickled to be included in the secret planning. "Fish aren't biting anyway," Big Richard had grinned. "Too cold." Accommodations at a ski resort near Denver had been easily acquired, thanks to the timing of her call. The first place she contacted had just received a cancellation. On the other hand, the plane tickets, purchased at such a late date, had cost a fortune. She only paused briefly to consider the expense.

Rose, in typical fashion, just shook her head. "You doing what?" she asked. "Go to some ski place? Don't they have snow in those sorts of places? You want to go where they have snow? Why don't you go south, Lizbet? Smart people go where it's warmer, not colder."

"I'm not asking for your approval, Rose. I'm asking for your help. Can you or can you not be here those four days? That would include Sunday, and I know you don't like to miss church. I don't either, but this is for an especially good cause."

"Course I can, girl. I know how to have church without bein' in church. You go on and make those crazy plans of yours."

When she shared the plan with Luann, her sister threw up her hand for a high-five. "That's the spirit, Sister!" she exclaimed. "We Breedloves are made of good stuff. I knew you had it in you!" And to the question of spending her nights at Liz's house while she and Richard were gone: "Rob is due to play Mr. Mom. He can stop by McDonald's for the girls' breakfast before he drops them off at school. Besides, I'm ready for some solo Miss Em time. I can't wait to have her all to myself."

"Elizabeth, what an exciting, creative idea," Miss Em had said when Liz shared the plans with her. She had beamed with approval. "And not just that, dear," she added. "You're embracing life, not running from it. That's a clear sign of health. You're doing something simply because you want to do it, not because you think it should be done. I hear that in your voice, see it in your face."

"I still have the same worries: Jackson going to college, or not, people finding out about his biological father, him and Lainie, not to mention Miss Gracie and her tale-bearing."

"Of course, the worries are still there, Elizabeth. But you are talking back to them. You're changing the tapes that play in your head. It's a process, dear. How well I know that. I listened repeatedly to the tapes in my head that said, 'It's time to die. Your life is over. Arrange for your own death.' I didn't stop to consider the source of those narratives because I was too dejected. I wanted things to go my own way. I wanted my loneliness to end, even while, at the same time, I didn't admit to myself that I actually was lonely. That's what happens when we spend too much time alone and focus on our misery. We don't acknowledge the truth.

"We forget about a kind, loving God and attempt to take things into our own hands. We try to control things, but even when we do that and forget that He is ultimately in control, He doesn't forget us. Look at the kindness He used to show me how wrong I was. I was making preparations to die, but God had plans for me to spend my last days with the good people of Roslyn. Even in my dejection, He didn't desert me."

Liz looked at her friend with a sad smile, remembering. "I stood by your bed that night in the hospital and prayed, Miss Em. I asked God to let you live so that I could truly get to know you. Even before I really knew you, I knew there was something special about you."

"And I knew the same about you, Elizabeth. I saw you under that big oak tree and I knew that about you, my dear." Miss Em chuckled." Hand me my Bible, please. As I spoke those words, I recalled Jesus saying something very similar to one of His disciples before he became a disciple."

Liz picked up the big Bible, different from her own Bible, but a Bible just the same.

"You might want to keep this for yourself, dear after I'm gone. I'm afraid it resembles a very colorful rainbow where I've marked my favorite words. There's a key for all the colors, so it shouldn't be too much of a mystery. You Protestants are missing out on some excellent verses of Scripture. A good place to start would be the Book of Wisdom, a title that's most definitely not a misnomer."

All the while Miss Em was talking, her fingers were flipping through the thin pages of her Bible. "Ah, here it is in the book of

John," she said and began to read. *"When Jesus saw Nathanael coming he said of him, 'There, truly, is an Israelite in whom there is no deception.' Nathanael asked, 'How do you know me?' Jesus replied, 'Before Phillip came to call you, I saw you under the fig tree.'*

"I don't think we can compare ourselves to Jesus, Elizabeth, and besides, it was under an oak tree, not a fig tree, where I first encountered you." Miss Em laughed as she spoke. "However, even though our circumstances and timelines were very different, we recognized each other in that same way. We were drawn together by a force outside ourselves. I choose to call that force God, and I believe you do, too."

The two women sat in silence, Liz thinking about the words she'd heard, Miss Em, recovering her stamina so that she could continue.

"I have been blessed with a good life, with considerable good fortune, monetarily speaking. My estate, as you already know, is large, and I can think of no better hands to leave it in than yours. It's meant to do good on this earth, and you will use it for such. Oh, I know Donald would have done a wonderful job of managing my wealth. He would have carried out my orders to the best of his ability. But you will think outside the box, as they say. With my blessing, you will have the freedom to invest in people and projects that I don't even know exist. Perhaps because they *don't* exist at this time.

"However, there's one promise I must extract from you, dear. You must promise me that every time you invest in something you do so because you want to, not because you think you should. Your heart will lead you to those places, and you'll know it's the right thing to do because you'll be filled with joy and happiness at the results. Just as you are now in planning your getaway with your wonderful Richard."

***

"Denver, huh?" Richard said as they settled in at the gate to wait for boarding. "Ski country."

Liz couldn't answer. She could only sit and grin at him. The fact that she'd pulled this off without a slip from anyone filled her with happiness that words couldn't express.

"Ski country?" Richard repeated, but this time with a question in his voice. "How did you know?"

"How did I know what?" Liz asked, feigning ignorance.

"How did you know that this is my dream vacation? My idea of a real escape?"

"Remember when you were a senior and I was a junior in school and our church youth group went on that ski trip? Remember how much fun we had? How we said that when we got married we were going to do that at least once a year?" Liz asked.

"Yeah, I remember, but I didn't think you did," Richard said. "I don't mean that in a bad way," he began.

"Richard, I'm going to say just this one thing, and then we're not going to talk about anything remotely downheartening on this entire trip. I've been wrong about a lot of things in our marriage, and I have lots of making up to do."

She put her hand over his mouth as he started to interrupt. "Don't. Let me finish. I have to make some changes, and this is one of the big ones. Jackson, rather than our marriage, has been my focus all these years. You, not I, have been responsible for our marriage being as strong as it is. I plan to do my part from now on out. This trip is my pledge to do that. Just ..." Liz paused to compose herself. "Just be patient with me. I promise to become the wife you deserve."

Richard removed her hand from his mouth with both his hands and clasped it tightly. Looking directly into her eyes he said, "You already are and you always will be. But there's just one other thing. Are you going to keep that other promise?"

Liz was puzzled. "Which other promise?"

"The one about us doing this ski trip thing at least once a year?"

***

Liz checked in twice a day with Rose and Luann. Both chided her each time she called. Rose with, "Nothin' happenin' here that wouldn't be happenin' if you *was* here, Lizbet."

Luann made her feel even less needed at home. "Couldn't you stay at least one more day, Liz? Miss Em and I are having such wonderful conversations." This on Tuesday evening before she and Richard were due to return home late Wednesday. "There's just one thing I'd change," Luann continued.

"What's that?" Liz asked.

"That horrid cat!"

"Miss Liberty? What's she doing besides hissing at you? She's no trouble at all. Are you filling her food bowl before you go to bed?"

"That's just it," Luann said. "I filled it Sunday night and she hadn't touched a bite of food when I looked in on Monday night. I asked Rose and she said 'I ain't touched that cat's food. I feed people, not animals! That's your job.'"

"Ask Rob. He's the vet. He'll know what's up."

"I did. He brought the girls with him on Monday night and looked her over pretty carefully. Says she's just fine. And she acted fine while the girls were here. Just like her old, sweet self. Didn't even hiss at me. In fact, that's the thing that's got me most worried. She's not hissing at me at all. Just spreads herself out in the doorway to Miss Em's room. I have to step over her to get inside. Rose has threatened to put her in the garage."

"I can imagine. Just tell Rose to be careful and not trip over her. Miss Em, too. She's not leaving her room, is she? She's been pretty confined there the past few days. Tell her to let one of you know if she wants to join you in the kitchen. Better yet, put her in her wheelchair."

"We got this, Liz. Later." And Luann hung up.

***

Simultaneously, Liz grabbed the phone, glanced at the clock and looked out at the still-dark sky. At 5:45 in the morning this could only be bad news. "Hello?" she questioned.

"She's gone, Liz," Luann's voice was barely audible.

"Who? Miss Liberty? What happened?"

"No! No! Not Miss Liberty!" Luann's voice was stronger. "It's Miss Em, Liz. She's gone."

CHAPTER 21

The space that just a few short months ago had seemed so elegant and foreign to Liz now felt like a haven to her. Lucinda, Donald Jamerson's receptionist, had offered her condolences to Liz as she walked the somber group back to his spacious corner office.

"I only saw the two of you together that one time," Lucinda was saying, "but it was enough to let me know how much you loved each other. You were her angel, Liz."

"Just the opposite," Liz said. "She was mine."

Lucinda was referring to the trip Liz and Miss Em had made to Memphis just two short weeks ago to finalize details of her *Last Will and Testament*—Miss Em's joking reference to her final wishes. Liz smiled as she remembered the self-deprecating tone that was always in Miss Em's voice when she referred to the business that required so much attention. "A necessary evil, my dear," she said when referring to her fortune. "Not the work that generated my earnings, of course, but the monetary value that's attached to it. We are all so very fortunate to have our team in place to put that in its proper perspective. I'm referring, of course, to you and Donald, two people that I can trust with my life and my money. Money is a wonderful thing when it falls into the proper hands."

The enormity of the role she'd agreed to play began to settle on Liz as the group convened. At Donald Jamerson's request, Richard, Rose, and Luann had accompanied Liz to his office one week after Miss Em had been laid to rest in Queen of Angels cemetery next to her beloved Rudolph. She looked around at the small group seated in comfortable chairs formed in a semi-circle facing a window with a view of the Mississippi River. Her own trusted family; Lucinda, poised to provide any comfort they might need; Donald's secretary

Ms. Ruth (an extremely efficient, almost robot-like lady whose first name Liz didn't know, but found her to be a perfect balance to Lucinda's warmth); and two elderly gentlemen that Liz had met briefly at Miss Em's graveside. Father John had said brief words at the burial and Frederick Johnston ("Any friend of Millie's is a friend of mine," he'd said when they were introduced. "Call me Fred.") was a longtime friend from Miss Em's art world who would act as a liaison in the collection, storage, and distribution of her artwork.

"Thank you all for coming," Donald began. "This won't take long, thanks to the efficiency of our friend who knew exactly what she wanted. We're all here now just to make sure we are aware of how this will be handled. In short, we have a new Miss Em; a much younger version, to be sure, with a different name. Liz is now solely in control of everything Miss Em owned. The rest of us—Frederick, myself, my team—are simply here to guide. Liz makes decisions, we carry them out. At Em's direction, I've made sure everything is in perfect order to proceed in that way. She was here a couple of weeks ago to make sure of that. She knew it wouldn't be long." Uncharacteristically, Donald was overcome with emotion, and the group sat silently as he recovered his poise.

Liz pulled a tissue from her pocket and brushed at the tears that slid uncontrollably down her cheeks. Richard, seated next to her, laid his hand on her leg protectively. The group gave a collective sigh as Donald continued.

"One thing that Em wanted is a bit of a sticky situation for me legally. It has to do with the disposal of her personal property, her home—or I should say *homes*—and her personal effects, furnishings, and so forth. She was adamant about this, so I have no choice but to follow her wishes. She wanted Rose to have the house in Roslyn, to do with as she chooses: live in it, sell it ... that's to be Rose's call."

He turned to address her directly. "Rose, in addition to that, there will be money set aside for Latisha's education. It's set up so that she can choose any school she wishes—with your blessing, and her father's, of course—and she can advance as far as she chooses. The money will be there.

"But back to the properties. This is where the sticky part comes in. Em left specific instructions that you ladies,"—he paused to point to Liz, Luann, and Rose— "are going to have to come up with your own solution for disposing of the furnishings. You can keep them, sell them, divide them, burn them, Em's words, not mine. Liz will oversee and have the final word, but, and on this Em was clear, she trusts the three of you to work it out so that everybody is happy. Seems to me a final test of your friendship and loyalty to each other. No worries; she knew you would pass." Donald had a smile both on his face and in his voice as he spoke those words.

"Anybody have questions up to this point?" he asked.

The room was quiet, everyone in their own way absorbing the words and remembering the unique personality who was only present in spirit. Even Rose had no comment to this astounding news.

"Well," Donald continued. "That leaves one thing for this afternoon, and as Em would say, that requires a field trip. Frederick, Father, this will be familiar to the two of you. Liz, Richard, Rose, Luann, you're about to see another side of your Miss Em. The four of you can ride with me. Frederick and Father, we'll see you there. We're adjourning now to reconvene in Miss Em's Memphis residence."

***

194

Liz had never seen Reserved Rose before. She'd seen Angry Rose, Sad Rose, Disgusted Rose, but never before today had she seen the woman so quiet. She was clearly out of her element, but it was more than that. Liz, while not accustomed to visiting attorney's offices in high rise, high rent buildings, had accepted this as part of a world that, while unfamiliar to her, existed for others. Rose moved as if in a dream. She only balked mildly when Donald Jamerson ushered her into the front seat of his Mercedes, settling herself into the seat and turning her head to stare out the window as they left the parking garage and entered mid-day, downtown traffic.

Most likely Rose *was* in a dream state, Liz thought. She'd just heard words that would bring change to her life. A new home, a college education for her beloved Latisha—things that moments before had not been a consideration. At least Liz had been privy to previous conversations that prepared her for what was ahead. While she hadn't fully comprehended the magnitude of what was before her—still didn't for that matter—she'd had prior warning. Rose had been hit cold.

Liz thought now of the first High Tea the ladies had enjoyed after Rose returned following her mother's death. She thought of the funeral customs that were so unfamiliar and the questions Luann had plied Rose with on that day, thoughts which brought her to remembrance of Miss Em's simple graveside service.

In spite of all Miss Em's hints that her departure was near, Liz had not been prepared for the sudden way she left them. But is anyone ever prepared? If only she'd been there. Immediately Liz could hear Em's voice: "And what could you have done, my dear, when the Angel of Death pays a visit? Neither life nor death is yours to control, Elizabeth."

Seated in the backseat of Donald Jamerson's Mercedes, Liz felt her entire body shudder.

"What?" Richard asked, concerned.

"Nothing," she said. "I'm hearing Miss Em talk in my head."

"Like she's channeling you?" Luann asked.

"You don't believe in that stuff, do you Luann?" Richard asked. Richard, while he loved being around Luann since they'd moved back to Roslyn, didn't fully *get* her.

"No, Richard, she doesn't believe in that *stuff*," Liz replied.

"You never know," Lu said. "Rose believes she can hear her mother's voice. Don't you Rose?"

There was no response from the front seat.

"Well, she does," Luann insisted.

"It's not the same thing," Liz said. "Besides, this isn't the time to discuss it. I'm just thinking about Miss Em's going so suddenly and in my head I can hear her answering back like she would have if she were here. She *lives* in my head." To her dismay, Liz began to cry.

"No, really, I'm okay," she protested as Richard attempted to console her. "I just need to be quiet."

Rose spoke clearly from the front seat. "Some other people been trying to do that this entire ride."

The car fell silent and Liz returned to her thoughts about the graveside service. When Liz had entertained thoughts of Miss Em's funeral, she'd visualized a beautiful spring day, the sun shining brightly and temperature perfect for short sleeves, maybe a light sweater. She'd pictured loads of spring flowers and music to match the singing of angels. In her mind there would be hundreds of people in attendance. All those fantasies had remained in place even after she'd learned of the simple arrangements Miss Em had made: her longtime friend and confidante, Father John, would read Luke 12:13-34, would then say a simple prayer commending her spirit to her final Home, and those few special friends in attendance would leave the cemetery for a late afternoon meal in a nice restaurant as she was laid to rest beside her precious Rudolph. She'd asked for a Mass to be said for her in her parish church, Immaculate Conception in Memphis, following her burial. As for flowers, there was to be a gigantic spring arrangement to cover her casket and to be left on her gravesite afterwards.

Nothing was as Liz pictured it, including the weather. It had been a cold, overcast day, fitting the mood of the small entourage who gathered at the gravesite. In spite of that, Liz had insisted that Richard take her back to Queen of Angels cemetery after the dinner, which was hosted by Donald Jamerson and was an occasion for anecdotes about their dear friend.

When Liz approached the covered grave, the simplicity of the scene overwhelmed her. She'd not noticed earlier that Miss Em's gravestone was already in place. It was, in itself, a work of art, probably designed by Miss Em after Rudolph's death. It was a study in symmetry, a tribute to the man Miss Em had loved completely. Two identical structures resembling conch shells rested on either end of a large base that extended the width of both graves. The "shells" rested on their broader tips and each curved at the same angle towards the other. The base, except for a smooth space in the center, was littered with fragments of shells attached to the granite. In the smooth polished center a perfect conch shell rested above the simple inscription, *Millicent and Rudolph.* In each corner of the stone the dates of their births—Rudolph's date of death was included—were engraved. The effect was profoundly moving.

Liz knelt in the fresh dirt and for the first time since she'd received the phone call in the early morning hours, she allowed herself to grieve deeply as Richard waited quietly. After what seemed an eternity but was in reality less than five minutes, she reached a place of quiet. She remained on her knees and it was in this position that she again "heard" Miss Em's voice in her head. "It's permissible to allow oneself a period of grief, my dear," she heard, "as long as one remembers that there's much to be accomplished and little time, relatively speaking, to *accomplish*. I lost many years to grief, but so have you. It's now time for you to truly live."

She answered out loud, not caring that Richard heard, not caring if he thought she'd lost her mind. "I will, Miss Em. I promise you I will."

Liz knew that the shells were significant and decided as she knelt in the dirt of Miss Em's fresh grave to research what the conch shells symbolized. She had been surprised to learn during the week between the funeral and the meeting in Donald Jamerson's office, that covering graves or outlining their perimeters with seashells was a centuries-old custom with many different meanings. Some believed that shells were a symbol of baptism; others attributed their significance to the house that contained the soul's immortal presence, now emptied. Still others maintained that shells were a symbol of the afterlife. The one that Liz favored was that the shell—particularly the conch shell—was a symbol of wisdom.

***

That Miss Em was a woman of wisdom was clear to all who knew her. That she was a keeper of secrets was slowly being revealed to those she'd chosen for her inner circle in the final months of her life. If Rose had been awed by the events that had occurred in the earlier part of the day, she was in complete shock as the Mercedes parked in front of the huge high rise apartment complex on Madison Avenue. Watching Rose, Liz was reminded of her first visit to Donald Jamerson's office in downtown Memphis, how she and Luann had gawked and stumbled over the curb. How she had fretted over her appearance and worried that she wasn't smart enough to have a conversation with a big city lawyer. She identified with her friend's amazement. They waited on the sidewalk as Father John and Frederick (call me Fred) found a parking spot and joined them, then together they walked to the entry where Donald was greeted by the doorman.

"It's all ready for you, sir," the stately man said. "It was cleaned top to bottom this week and everything is in order. Would you like me to go up with you?"

"That's fine, Adam. You have plenty to do without us bothering you further."

"Just let me get the elevator for you, sir." With this said, he slipped a key card into a slot and the door magically slid open. "Shall I get a key card for Miss Elizabeth, sir?" he asked, making the correct assumption that he was escorting the new owner of the apartment.

"Would you, please?" Donald answered. "Can you have that ready when we come down?"

"Absolutely, sir," he replied. And just like that, Liz was the owner of a luxury apartment on Madison Avenue. Again, the thought came to her, "What have I gotten myself into?"

As they entered the large, elegantly furnished apartment on the top floor, Rose found her voice. "Law me!" she exclaimed. "What you think that ole' Grace Carlson say about you now, Lizbet? You really is Miss Astor!"

Frederick and Father John clearly appreciated the comic relief offered with this remark. As members of a generation who recognized the reference for its true meaning, they were curious as to how one so gracious and unassuming as Liz could be called "Miss Astor."

Liz gave a brief description of the animosity that Miss Grace had expressed towards, not only Liz but Miss Em as well. "She's just a bitter old woman who doesn't think she's gotten what she deserves out of this life," Liz explained. "When Miss Em didn't accept her offer of friendship, if you can call it that, she set out to destroy her with her own made-up versions of who Miss Em was. She was especially concerned about Miss Em's Catholic religion. Living in a town that doesn't even have a Catholic church, this seemed strange, even evil I think, to people like Grace Carlson. She's always lived by the creed, 'If you don't know the truth about something, make it up.'"

Rose, having finally found her voice, had lost interest in Grace Carlson. "So, what kinda people lives in a place such as this?" This question was pointedly addressed to Donald Jamerson.

"Well, the clientele today is much different than it was in Miss Em's day. She and Rudolph rented this apartment in the early 70's when she was in her heyday of painting. There was a period of time when she was highly sought after, not just for her portraits of children, which was her first love, but for painting icons and other religious paintings. She painted for churches and cathedrals all over the country." He turned to Liz.

"You'll have all of that information at your disposal. You might be interested in visiting some of the places where her work is housed."

He turned back to Rose. "To answer your question," he continued, "today this building is filled with up-and-coming attorneys, physicians, NBA basketball players ..."

"You think Michael Jordan might live here?" Rose asked.

Donald laughed. "I'm pretty sure he doesn't live here," he said. "Maybe Chicago? That would make sense with him playing for the Bulls."

Once again, just by being herself, Rose had worked her magic. The mood of the day had lightened considerably.

CHAPTER 22

Liz wasn't prepared for the empty feeling that pervaded her home in the weeks after Miss Em's death. Not only had she been transformed by the presence of the elderly woman during the nine months she'd lived there, but the home itself had been changed. The renovations that had been quickly but efficiently done to accommodate Miss Em now seemed bleak and ill-fitting. Following Miss Em's death Liz avoided the space where her friend had lived out her final days, knowing that at some point she'd have to deal with the personal effects left behind. After the meeting in Donald Jamerson's office and the "messages" from Miss Em herself about getting on with living, Liz decided that her own home was a good place to begin.

February had given way to March and, while winter still hung on, there was a hint of spring in the air. Liz chose a Saturday in mid-March to begin emptying the room of Miss Em's personal belongings. She picked a Saturday because Rose always stayed at home with Latisha on weekends, and Richard and Jackson left early for the grocery store. She wanted plenty of time to process; this was a task that demanded her full attention. Still, it was hard to get started.

As she finished her third cup of coffee, Liz decided she'd make a quick trip to the grocery store to pick up boxes. Boxes are a necessity when one is clearing a space, she reasoned, all the while recognizing her delay tactics. She also recognized that once leaving, she might find other so-called important tasks to complete while she was out and might not return to the job she'd assigned to herself. She picked up her coffee mug and walked down the long hallway to Miss Em's room.

Sometime over the past few weeks Rose had cleaned it from top to bottom. The large bay window sparkled under the sun's bright examination, revealing no smudges. Liz noticed a large pressed down space in the comforter at the foot of the bed and vaguely recollected Miss Liberty brushing against her ankle as she'd entered Miss Em's room—the empty room, she corrected herself.

Where to start? She dragged a small padded rocker near the window, sat down and gazed around the room. The easel, still in place, brought an immediate ache to Liz's chest. Miss Em hadn't completed the painting of Luann's girls. She'd done many sketches but had struggled with how to portray the girls. "Such active, vibrant, young women," she'd said to Liz. "They definitely must be in motion."

As always, the artist had found a way to express the personalities of her subjects on canvas. The incomplete canvas showed a young girl hanging by her knees from a large branch high off the ground. Madison. On the ground below, another child knelt, spade in hand, a packet of seeds on the ground nearby. Maria. Her face was in silhouette and, though incomplete, was easily recognizable as Maria.

Sad, Liz thought, but not really. Luann would treasure the unfinished painting. Liz knew her sister well enough to understand that even though the painting hadn't been completed, the love that had gone into the sketches and the painting itself would be enough of Miss Em to earn a prominent space in Luann's home. It's incompleteness in some way would make it even more of a treasure. As Miss Em would say metaphorically, "A work in progress."

Liz forced herself out of the chair, out of the house, and into her car. Boxes, she reminded herself. She needed boxes.

***

Liz was both pleased and mildly irritated with herself when she discovered on her return that the house was unlocked: irritated because she'd finally convinced her entire family of the necessity of locking up when everyone was away from home and had broken her own rule; pleased because she was carrying a tower of boxes and could barely manage to turn the knob which, out of long habit, she'd tried before dragging out her keys. She set the boxes down in the mudroom and, noticing that the coffee pot was still on, poured herself another cup of coffee for fortification before she began her work.

As she walked down the hallway, Liz paused. She had the distinct feeling that she wasn't alone, that someone was in the house with her. Miss Em's spirit she wondered? She peered in doors as she walked and, seeing nothing out of place, continued towards the bedroom.

The hot coffee sloshed onto her hand and she yelled in pain as she entered the room. Seated in the chair she'd recently moved was a young woman.

"What are you doing here? No, I don't mean it that way ..." Liz deleted the unwelcome tone in her voice and tried again. "You scared me. I didn't expect anyone to be here," she explained.

"I'm sorry, Miz Manley," Lainie said as she stood. "I don't usually walk into houses when nobody's home, but I called out thinking you were in the basement or in the back of the house and when I got to Miss Em's room ..." She put her hands to her face and spoke in a muffled voice. "I miss her so much," she said.

"It's okay, Lainie. Really. I don't mind you being here. You're always welcome in our home." As Liz spoke the words, she realized that she had never made the girl feel as welcome as she'd always felt when she visited Richard's home while they were dating. She'd always held her at a distance. Lainie was too smart and too sensitive a person not to have recognized how Liz truly felt about her.

"Really," she said again and meant it. "I'm glad you're here. I'm just surprised, that's all. How did you get here? There's no car?"

"I rode my bike," Lainie said. "It's such a beautiful day and I don't go to work at the nursing home till afternoon. I was riding by and decided to stop and ... I knew Miss Em was gone, but ..."

"I understand, Lainie. I really do. I'm boxing up some of her things today hoping that helps me understand that she's really gone. I keep looking for her too.

"Look," she said. "Miss Liberty does, too." Liz pointed to the bed where the cat was curled up, oblivious to the conversation around her.

"I thought she was sleeping in here, now there's proof." Liz told Lainie about her experience earlier in the morning. "I'm surprised Rose is allowing it, but I guess she's not willing to close the door. That would be the only way to keep the little Miss out."

"I'd like to help you, Miz Manley. I've got a few hours before I go to the nursing home to do shampoos and manicures. If you'd let me?"

Liz heard the plea in the young woman's voice: *Please accept me. I want us to be friends.* And in hearing the plea, she asked herself a question: What better place to let this girl into her heart than in Miss Em's final home? Her friend was gone, and she had a choice. She could accept all the wisdom Miss Em had tried to plant in her over the past nine months, or she could reject it.

"I'd love your help, Lainie," she said. "I can't tell you how much I've dreaded this job."

***

By noon they'd boxed up all the art supplies, Miss Em's clothes and her personal effects. Lainie had been exceptional at both packing and decision making. At her suggestion, all of Miss Em's toiletries and clothing were packed, labelled and placed in Liz's car to be taken to the nursing home.

"Things just disappear there, Miz Manley," the girl said as they folded and packed. "This one lady, Miss Teeters? She can't keep a hairbrush. She swears her roommate steals them when she's out of the room and plants them in other patients' rooms. We've even tried putting her name on them in red nail polish, but they never turn up. What do you think's happening to them?"

Liz had no idea, but was amazed at the way conversation flowed the entire morning. She learned, also to her amazement, that Lainie had visited Miss Em every Wednesday afternoon during the time she was shopping for and preparing the Wednesday night dinners at church. Liz wondered momentarily if both Rose and Miss Em had kept this from her intentionally, if they'd thought Liz might object, or, more likely, feel threatened by this friendship.

"She helped me so much, Miz Manley," the girl confided in her. "I always knew I wanted to be a nurse, but talking with Miss Em helped me decide what kind of nurse I want to be. I love old people. I don't mean that disrespectfully, not that you're old." Flustered, Lainie stopped momentarily then began again. "You're young, really," she said. "Too young to have a kid going off to college. My dad is 46 and I'm 17. You must have been really young when you had Jackson."

Liz couldn't keep up with her. From nursing to Miss Em to old people in general and then a quick turn and Lainie was into her personal business. She decided to steer the conversation to a safer place.

"Lainie," she said, hands on her hips. "I've had about enough of this *Miz Manley* thing. You're right, I'm not that old. And I answer to *Liz* much quicker than I answer to *Miz Manley*. Do you think you could accommodate me and drop the formality? We'd seem more like ..." she hesitated before committing herself, "... friends."

"I'd love to be your friend, Miz ... Liz," the girl said.

For the third time Liz "heard" Miss Em speak to her. "It's your turn, my dear. You don't think this happened by coincidence, or worse yet, *accident*, do you? No, Elizabeth, this morning took place by design. You and young Lainie need each other to fill the empty space I've left in your lives. What better place for the two of you to connect than in my empty shell of a room?"

***

After Lainie left, Liz wrapped the unfinished canvas in a sheet, folded the easel to fit in her trunk and delivered both to Luann. She rang the familiar doorbell and listened as running footsteps alerted her that a child was on her way to the door. "Come in, Aunt Liz," Maddy welcomed, pushing the old wooden framed screen door open and grabbing Liz by the hand. "Mama made egg salad sandwiches for lunch, my favorite. There's enough for you too. Come on." She dragged Liz to the bright kitchen where bowls of egg salad, cherry tomatoes, and carrot strips sat on a table covered with a bright blue and orange vintage table cloth.

"I'll never figure out how you make a simple meal on a simple table cloth look like a work of art," Liz said to her sister who was pouring juice into blue and yellow coffee mugs for the girls.

"Coffee or juice?" she asked before replying, "It's all in what you choose to love. Grab your own plate. I didn't know you were coming. And while you're at it, would you pop another couple pieces of toast in the toaster. That is if you want your bread toasted. Otherwise ..."

Liz admired the easy way her sister accomplished routine tasks, making them seem like fun. At Luann's house, every day was a party. Her kids were far from perfect; sibling rivalry was often shown between Maria and Maddy, but situations never became full-blown arguments. This, she knew, was due to Luann's no-nonsense manner of handling anything that came her way.

"What brings you here in the middle of a Saturday? No committees to run? No attorneys to confer with?" Luann's light tone removed any hint of sting the words might have conveyed.

"I come bearing gifts," Liz said. "Not gifts from me, and to be precise, it's singular, gift."

"I can't wait," Luann replied. "Can we see now and eat later?"

"Eat your lunch. It can wait. Once you see what I've brought you'll have to do some rearranging, so eat and gain your strength. This is delicious, by the way. Egg salad didn't sound too tempting when Maddy invited me to lunch, but this is great. What do you put in it?"

"It's an old family recipe, and if I tell you I'll have to kill you," Luann quipped.

"We never once had egg salad—sandwiches or otherwise— during our entire growing-up years," Liz argued. "And for the killing part, you don't want to leave two aunt-less, motherless daughters to be raised by a father who treats cats, dogs, and hamsters.

"Anyway," she continued, "this is delicious. Thanks for lunch. Lainie and I were so busy this morning I never once thought about lunch, breakfast either, for that matter."

"Lainie and you? That's a new pairing," Luann said.

"It's time, don't you think?" Liz asked.

"Don't you like Lainie, Aunt Liz?" Maria asked. "I love Lainie. She's the coolest."

"Little pitchers, big ears," Luann cautioned. "Finish up with those sandwiches, girls. I can't wait to see what Aunt Liz brought us."

Later, after they'd arranged and rearranged the living room to find just the perfect spot for the unfinished portrait, Liz, Luann, and the girls sat around the room, trading spots at intervals to view the painting from every angle.

"It really is me hanging from a tree," Maddy said. "How did Miss Em know I liked hanging by my legs from tree limbs?" she asked. "She never ever saw me in a tree."

"She didn't have to see you, Little Goose," her mother said. "She *knew* you. Her imagination told her the rest."

***

Somewhere between drifting off and falling into a deep restful sleep, Liz was roused by "Hey Maw? You asleep?"

"Jackson, what's wrong?" She sat up in bed, placing her hand on Richard's shoulder, ready to wake him.

"Chill, Maw. Nothin's wrong. I just wanted to say thanks. Sorry, I woke you up, but I didn't want to wait till mornin'."

"It's okay, Jacks. But what are you thanking me for?" Liz asked, fully awake now.

"For Lainie. What you did today. She said you acted like you liked her today for the first time ever. She thinks you two can be friends. We'd both like that, Ma ... if you two could be friends."

"Yeah," Liz said softly. "I'd like that too."

"Night now," her son said as he closed the door.

Liz sat for a moment and stared into the dark, then slowly lay back down and pulled the covers up to her chin, looking up at the darkened ceiling.

"Friends, huh?" Richard asked without turning towards her. "You holding out on me, Liz? Want to tell me about it?"

"Go back to sleep," she said, smiling. "It'll wait till tomorrow."

"So, is Lainie gonna be like the daughter we never had?" Richard asked, reaching for her as he turned towards her.

She snuggled close. Richard drifted back to sleep, but Liz lay beside him, wide awake, wondering.

CHAPTER 23

"Which it gonna be, Lizbet?" Rose complained. "This house has got to have either a new vacuum or a new Rose. This cat hair has finally got the best of me."

This, the most recent of Rose's complaints about cat hair, was by far the most serious. Not that Liz hadn't taken her request for a new vacuum seriously, she simply hadn't had time to shop for and purchase the item.

"I'll have a new vacuum here for you by the end of the day," she promised Rose.

"While you're looking for a super powerful machine guaranteed to pick up cat hair, you might as well get another little one I can carry around in my hands and suck up all the hair that ugly orange cat leaves on Miss Em's bed and such. I declare I never thought I'd be cleaning up after a nasty old cat every day. She moves from bed to chair, from chair to bed, like she think she owns that room now Miss Em's gone."

"Squatter's rights, Rose," Liz agreed. "She does own it as long as you don't make good on your hourly threats and close the door while she's out of the room. Which brings me to a suggestion."

Rose set down her bucket of cleaning supplies and turned to face Liz. "You're not about to tell me you're taking in a whole litter of strays? If that be the case, I quit right now!"

"Why would I take in more cats, Rose? One is more than enough. Don't forget how Miss Liberty came to be a part of this family; that was all Jackson's doing.

"No, I think my suggestion will make your work easier. If we move Miss Liberty's litter box into Miss Em's room, that'll limit her coming and going. She won't need to make as many trips down the hall. She stays in there most of the time anyway except to eat or when Latisha, Lu's girls, or Lainie are here. If she didn't have to leave to use her ..."

"You want to put a box of cat poop in Miss Em's room?" The older woman appeared to be outraged. "A fine lady like Miss Em? Where's your sense of decoratin'?"

"You mean my sense of decorum?" Liz asked, barely covering her smile.

"Just your sense, woman," Rose shot back. "Where's your sense?"

"Well," said Liz, "my *sense* tells me that it would be much less work if we limited Miss Liberty's comings and goings, and having her litter box in the same space where she sleeps would make a lot of *sense*. Food and drink too," she added.

"Humph!" Rose muttered as she picked up her bucket and started down the hall, a sure sign that she was beginning to see reason in Liz's decision. For Rose, "humph" indicated that she'd given in, that the plan would be carried out by the end of the day. It also meant she'd never let the matter drop, that every piece of scattered litter or food would be an occasion to remind Liz that the plan she'd devised was not a good one.

The cat had indeed claimed Miss Em's room from the time she guarded the door during the week of the elderly woman's death. The cat that had been so vigorously pursued by Miss Em during the weeks before her fall had allowed herself to be captured after all. Her independent airs had, in fact, been an act. After those first few days in captivity, she'd taken to being a housecat as though she'd been born to it. And Rose, who vehemently denied it, cared for Miss Liberty with a similar passion.

Her attachment to the mother cat and her kittens had become apparent on the day they released the babies to the homes that claimed them. Lainie had come up with the idea of a "Goodbye Kitty" party, an idea that caught on immediately with the children. They'd purchased paper plates, cups, and napkins sporting the popular design "Hello Kitty" and, using a black permanent marker, had changed the "Hello" to "Goodbye." Rose, grumbling and complaining the entire time, had baked and iced cookies—some with blue icing (after all there were two males in the litter) and some with pink—and prepared pink lemonade to be served to the adoptive parents. With Rob's help, Liz had purchased and gift-wrapped basic necessities for the departing kittens: litter boxes, food, water bowls, and brushes. She had been surprised by Rose as they worked to prepare for the party.

"Why you get five of everything, Lizbet? You didn't say nothin' bout that ole mama cat finding a new home."

She saw the relief in Rose's face when she explained that she thought Miss Liberty deserved a new start along with her babies. "I didn't want her to feel left out when her babies were getting all these gifts," she joked to Rose. "You didn't think we'd give her away, did you?" Rose had turned her head and sniffed in answer.

Afterward, as Rose swept crumbs from the kitchen floor and Liz put away the remains of the party, Miss Liberty had ambled into the room. Liz smiled as Rose crooned, "You missin' those babies, Little Mama? Now you just go on there. You take some time for yourself. You sure have earned it."

As Liz shopped now for the perfect supplies that would make Rose happy, she thought of that happy day last summer. So much had happened since then.

Later in the day, Liz presented Rose with, not only a good lightweight Oreck vacuum cleaner, but a hand-held, powerful upholstery vac, and all the cat hair removal paraphernalia she could locate in Target and Walmart. In typical fashion, Rose bemoaned the fact that Liz had spent too much money.

"Now you owe me, Rose," Liz said as Rose was packing up to leave for the day.

"What do I owe you, Lizbet?" the woman asked.

"Tomorrow you're going to visit your new house. "

"Now, Lizbet." Rose started to protest.

"I know. You don't think it's your house. But it is. Whether you ever live in it or not, it's yours. You can sell it, or rent it, you can give it away if that's what you want to do. But, the fact remains, it's yours. The least you can do for Miss Em is to honor her by going to look at it through an owner's eyes."

***

For reasons she couldn't explain, even to herself, Liz wanted Rose's first trip to Miss Em's home—now Rose's property—to not include Luann. It seemed to Liz to be another step in grieving the loss of her dear friend, and she knew that Luann would be hard-pressed to keep from oohing and aahing about the furnishings and accessories that remained. Rose had cleaned the house several times during Miss Em's illness, but this trip would be different: she was now the owner, and as such she would see everything in a different light.

Rose reminded her of this fact. "I don't need to go see that house again. I cleaned every little nook and cranny of that place mor'n once. You think I got memory problems? You think I don't know what that house looks like?"

"It's different now, Rose," Liz said searching her key ring for the back door key. She stopped looking and turned to Rose. "Why am I unlocking the door to your house? You have a key, and that alone makes things different. This is your house, Rose. Unlock your own door."

"Humph!" was the only verbal response she received, as she stepped back and Rose stepped forward, key already in her hand.

Rose entered the house before her and pushed the frame door back, leaving only the screen door to separate them from the cool spring air. "Let's open some windows," Liz suggested. "Air the place out. It's been closed up all winter." She reached behind the small dinette table to open the window and as she did her mind flashed back to the day she'd learned of Miss Em's accident. As clearly as if it were still there, she saw the monogramed notepaper, the envelope with her name on it, the fountain pen, uncapped, lying there, and a surge of emotion overtook her. She covered it by continuing with her task of opening the stubborn window and, with her back still to Rose, said, "You go on and look around the house by yourself, Rose. I'm going to check the cabinets and make sure we've gotten rid of all the food, check drawers, things like that."

Rose didn't argue. She'd been Elizabeth's friend long enough to recognize the overwhelming sadness when it struck, and, while she couldn't quite grasp the private, on-going way her white folk friends worked through grief, she respected Elizabeth's need to be alone.

Liz sat down in a shiny-as-new vinyl and chrome chair, the one Miss Em had most likely sat in the day she was composing her note, and wondered why. Why did she choose this place to sit? Why not sit at the elegant desk in her bedroom? As suddenly as the question had formed, the answer came: exhaustion. Miss Em had truly reached the end of her rope. She had become focused on one thing: dying. That's all she had energy for. Sitting here in the chair now Liz felt it. All of it. The loneliness, the exhaustion, the frustration. She put her elbows on the table and covered her face with her hands. And once again Liz wept for her friend. The cool breeze caught the gauzy white curtain and whipped it against Liz's shoulder. Simultaneously Liz felt a cool hand placed gently on her other shoulder. Rose spoke not a word, but stood by Elizabeth as, once again, she expressed the sadness of her loss.

After a few minutes, Rose pulled out the chair that faced the window and sat down. She drummed her fingers on the cool Formica of the table, a signal that she was about to speak. Liz pulled a tissue from her pocket, mopped her face, and blew her nose. "What?" she asked.

"Miss Em's spirit is freed," Rose began. "She left this place and all the sadness she had here behind. This house was her shell, just like that empty shell on that grave marker. Her body, it's another shell she left behind. And Lizbet, this is what I know. I know if Miss Em was sittin' at this table right now what she'd say. She'd say, 'Move on, *E-lizbet*. Do what you got to do to put all this sadness behind you and move on.' And now this is me talkin'. And I say get on with this bizness of putting those demons from your past to rest. You held on to that stuff too long and here you are adding to it instead of taking away.

She continued, "What promises did you make to Miss Em that you're not keepin'?"

"What do you mean?" Liz asked.

"You know what I mean, girl. Don't give me that 'what-do-you-mean' stuff! You cried on that poor old woman's shoulder over and over, and she was always tellin' you what was best for you. Trouble is, you always come back and ask again, 'cause you don't do what you know to do. So don't go askin' me 'What do you mean?' What I mean is, do what Miss Em told you to do! And the sooner the better."

The two women sat in silence. Through the open window sounds of hope and Spring in the form of bird calls came to them. Finally, Liz spoke.

"You're right, Rose. She did tell me what I needed to do. I've hidden behind all this busyness, but I know what must happen. Can you help me? I want to go away for a while. Just me. I have to put some things to rest. Will you help me out?"

"Now you're makin' some sense. And while you're bein' sensible, let me tell you another thing. I'm not leavin' my house in the country. My daddy's house, that is," she corrected. And Rose laid out her plan for the house she'd inherited from Miss Em.

Along with the house, enough money had been left to Rose for upkeep and any needed renovations to make the house suitable for family living again. In Miss Em fashion, the amount was substantial, far greater than what was needed. But the money was to be used at Rose's discretion, and even could be used for other purposes if Rose desired. It was apparent that Rose had spent long hours considering the dilemma of the house because she'd left nothing to chance. She would remain in the house she'd grown up in, would use some of the money to make repairs on that property, and, short of necessary maintenance, the house in town would be left as it was. After dispersing the items that were to be divided up among Liz, Luann, and Rose, the rest of the furnishings would be left in the house, enough so that the house was habitable. Liz was instructed to find out just how many nights someone would need to sleep in the house to satisfy the insurance people. Rose herself would organize family members, out-of-town guests, and friends to alternate days and nights spent there to satisfy the requirements.

"But how long can we keep this up, Rose," Liz asked after Rose had finished outlining her plan.

"As long as we need to," was the cryptic answer.

"But, then what?" Liz asked. "Will you sell it, rent it? You can't just keep an empty house forever. It'll become run down, overtaken by mice and insects."

Rose hooted at this. "Ain't no mouse livin' in my house!" she declared. "And don't you worry none 'bout what or how long. That'll work its own self out. Now, let's go get that bossy sister of yours and settle these belongin's."

And that was the end of the discussion.

***

What had seemed to be a daunting undertaking turned out to be simple, mainly because of Rose's decision to not use the home as her residence. The only items she wanted for herself were from the kitchen, including the retro chrome and vinyl dinette set that was in perfect condition. She also claimed Miss Em's wheat pattern dishes and her simple stainless flatware. After much discussion and reassurance that she wasn't being piggish, Luann claimed the formal tableware, which included beautiful linen table coverings and napkins, Haviland china, silver—sterling—and crystal. The living room was left intact, except for a lamp that Liz chose for her bedroom. It had the same simple understated elegance that was so Miss Em and would sit on a table beside Liz's favorite bedroom chair.

The women decided to refurnish the bedroom with a new bed and chest and move Miss Em's remaining bedroom furniture to the room she'd occupied in Liz's home. The upholstered chair and writing desk would complete what was begun when they had moved the antique sleigh bed there at the beginning. "I wish we'd thought to do that when she moved in with us," Liz said.

"Good thing you didn't," Rose said. "You'd just be makin' a Miss Em Museum with these belongin's. Nobody wants to live in a museum!"

"You are so right," Luann said. "What would we do without your commonsense, Rose?"

"And what would we do without your big truck and strong back?" Rose asked Luann.

"And without my abundant grocery store boxes?" Liz chimed in. "Lu, how about you drive your "big truck" over to the store and load it up with boxes? I have a pile of newspapers in my trunk. We need to start wrapping and packing. While you're there, ask Richard if he can spare a couple of grocery stockers later this afternoon to load up these big pieces for us."

The day, which had started on a sad note, suddenly acquired a festive tone.

***

Liz slid between crisp clean sheets and snuggled up to Richard. "What a day!" she exclaimed. "But the three of us accomplished

219

what I've been dreading, we sorted all of Miss Em's belongings. Now for the job of figuring out what to do with the house."

"I thought that was for Rose to decide," Richard said.

"If Rose had her way, we'd lock the door and leave it as is." Liz giggled.

"What?" asked Richard, closing his book and placing it on the nightstand. "What's funny about that?"

"Oh, not that. Just Rose. She has such a funny way of saying things. After we unloaded the last boxes today, she said to Luann, 'Now you white folks can breathe easier. You make sure all these neighbors know they won't be looking at my shinin' face every morning, Luann. And on the mornin's they do see me, they can just pretend it's the cleaning woman making her regular appearance.'

"Luann tried to convince her that no one would feel that way, but it didn't work."

"Funny, but true," Richard said. "And sad, really. Rose is right. There are still too many people around Roslyn who look at the color of a person's skin. Do you think that's the reason Rose doesn't want to live in Miss Em's, *her,* house?"

"Not at all," Liz spoke with confidence. "Rose wouldn't let a little thing like prejudice keep her from doing what she wanted to do. She may be the most self-assured person I know." Liz giggled again. "I haven't told you the funny part yet. When Lu tried to tell her that people didn't feel that way, Rose stopped her in mid-sentence. She put both hands up like a traffic cop stopping traffic and said, 'Maybe they do, maybe they don't. But Rose gots to have relief from you white folks every now and then. I gots to have my soul purified every day and I can't do that with folks breathin' down my neck!'"

Richard didn't respond, and in the telling of her story, Liz realized that there was more truth than humor in what Rose had to say. She thought of her own fractured life, how she was constantly concerned with what others said or thought. Of how she had lived her life feeling that she was a bug on a microscope slide being constantly viewed and examined by others. Where, she thought now, did she get her soul "purified?"

Richard reached over and turned out the light on his nightstand and pulled Liz into his arms. They lay in the darkness, in the quiet, and the tears—ever near the surface—began to slide down her cheeks. Richard brushed them from her cheeks and kissed the damp tracks left behind.

"She knows me better than anyone, except maybe you," Liz said. "Better than my mother did, better than Lu, better than I know myself. Next to you, Rose is my best friend."

CHAPTER 24

*Friendship with oneself is all-important
because without it one cannot be friends with
anyone else.*

-Eleanor Roosevelt

After much negotiation with Rose—"You promised, Lizbet"—Liz delayed her time away till summer. A month, she'd decided, possibly July, with no idea as to where she'd go, or what on earth she'd do with an entire month to herself.

"A promise is a promise," she declared to Rose. "A commitment, a commitment. Jackson would never forgive me if I didn't go on the trip to St. Louis with the seniors." Even as she spoke the words, Liz recognized that she was hiding behind her son. He wouldn't give a hoot whether she went or not. He'd have as much fun, maybe more, if she stayed at home. Still. She'd worked hard on the details of this trip. This was her only son, her final opportunity to do something for her *little boy*. He'd be a grown-up college student after this. Besides, she'd missed out on her own senior trip (Where did her class go?), self-punishment because of her rash behavior on prom night. Her mother had only mildly protested, "But I've already paid for it."

Liz did, however, fully embrace the credo "A promise is a promise." She'd made a promise, not only to Rose but to Miss Em as well, that she'd soon pay another visit to Brother Paul. All Miss Em had to go on was Liz's description of the man, but that was enough for her to understand him exactly as Liz knew him to be: *He's a man of God, a compassionate man; leave something with him as a symbol of letting go*—what had Miss Em called it? —A sacrament? No, a *sacramental*. When Liz questioned her about what that might be, the woman had smiled at her and said, "You'll know. It will be something special to you. Give yourself time."

It came to her early one morning as she lay in bed beside Richard, listening to his soft snoring. The ring. The simple silver band with the infinity symbol engraved inside. The ring that Richard had given her the week before he left for college with the solemn promise: *I want to spend the rest of my life with you.* Then he'd joked in his usual way: *To infinity and beyond.* The ring that had as many lives as a cat. She slipped out of bed and turned on the small lamp on her dresser, opened the jewelry box that contained her limited costume jewelry, and began to rummage around. There it was, slightly tarnished from neglect over the years. She rubbed at it vigorously with the tail of her pajama top.

"Shoot!" she exclaimed, louder than she meant to. A black stain marred the yellow pajama top.

"Not me, I hope," Richard said, yawning. "What've I done now?"

"Me, not you. Do you know if silver tarnish will wash out? I've ruined my pj's rubbing on this old ring."

"We have a whole assortment of stain removers in the store. Just come in and read the labels. What old ring are you rubbing on? Are you hoping for a genie to appear and grant your deepest wish?"

"Not exactly," said Liz, "but sort of. It has more meaning than that." Liz sat on the bed, her feet dangling on the floor. She showed Richard the ring and explained to him what she planned to do.

"Whatever floats your boat, Lizzie-girl," Richard said. "Me? I'd go out on Sardis Lake in my daddy's boat, catch me a whole mess of fish, and come back a different man. But you gotta do what you gotta do."

Liz punched him in the arm. "You're making fun."

Richard turned serious. "Not at all. Miss Millie was a wise woman, and those months she spent in our home gave me a different Liz. A better Liz. Anything she told you to do I'm in favor of whether I understand or not." He pulled her to him for a quick kiss before crawling out of bed. "When is this visit to Brother Paul taking place?"

"Since next Sunday is Mother's Day, I decided to give this day trip to myself as a pre-Mother's Day gift. I'm going on Friday. Maybe by Sunday, I'll be the perfect mother. Besides, the year anniversary of the beginning of my saga with Miss Millie is approaching and I need all the fortification I can get."

***

Liz pulled into the lane leading to Brother Paul's little cottage in the pine grove and stopped. She rolled down the windows, closed her eyes, and breathed in the pine-scented air. "I could get used to this," she said aloud, giving way to a longing that she hadn't recognized until this moment. She longed to breathe. Just breathe. With nothing to plan for, nothing to anticipate, nothing to expect. This place seemed almost magical, like ... with a start of recognition, she opened her eyes. Like her little moss gardens. This feeling was exactly the same as the one she'd felt as a child when she collected bits of moss, sticks, colored glass, and flowers, then found a shady spot and allowed the pieces to seemingly arrange themselves.

As she put the car in gear and proceeded down the lane Liz wondered if it was possible for an adult to recapture those long-lost, carefree feelings of childhood. She decided that she'd talk to Brother Paul about that. There was a playful air about him, even in his advanced years he spoke and moved with the unhurried abandon of a child lost in his own enjoyment. Maybe that was something a person could learn.

He was waiting for her. Was she late? Guiltily, she glanced at the car clock. No, just before 10:00. Brother Paul stood just off the small front porch holding something out in his hand. Liz looked again and saw the dog, Master, ambling towards him. The dog's mouth was open, tongue lolling slightly to the side, with an expression on his face that looked like a grin. It wasn't Liz Brother Paul was waiting for; it was Master. *Why do I always think it's about me?*

That's the question Liz started with after they'd poured themselves glasses of iced tea and settled in old sling chairs on the tiny deck off the kitchen.

"I'm going to dive right in," Liz cautioned her friend. "Remember last time when Lu and I were here? We all sat around waiting for the other to start the real conversation? For me, that was because I really didn't know where to start. At least I've learned a little something over the past few months. At least I can form my questions!"

"Questions are an excellent place to start," Brother Paul encouraged. "How can you find answers if you don't ask questions?"

"So," she plunged in. "Here's my big question: Why do I think things are always about me?"

He sat for so long that Liz became uncomfortable. *Did he hear me,* she wondered? *Could he be in the beginning stages of Alzheimer's? Is he shocked at my selfishness and looking for a way to answer my question tactfully?*

Brother Paul interrupted her increasingly alarming thoughts. "I need to hear more, dear," he said softly. "This isn't the Liz I know and love. Explain her to me."

How to explain? It was Liz's turn to think. "Well ..." she started, then stopped. She thought of the day when Rose had returned to work after her mother's death and how Luann had bombarded her with question after question about Willa's funeral. How she'd cautioned her sister to leave Rose alone, but how Rose had seemed to welcome the chance to talk about her grief. She remembered realizing after the fact that it was a good thing. She told Brother Paul the story, including her amazement as she'd witnessed the interaction between her sister and Rose. They were both involved in a conversation that sought only to understand and be understood.

"And at our Christmas dinner," she went on, "Miss Em had never met Rose's dad, Retha. And he was so sad because his wife was dying. You should have seen how she got him talking about his garden and the things he loved. For several minutes I think he actually forgot that he was sad. His face lit up with happiness as the two of them talked."

They sat in silence until Liz broke it with, "I don't know how to do that. I'm always wondering if the other person is in a hurry when, truthfully, *I'm* the one who's in a hurry, or if I have a smudge on my face; really, I wonder if the other person is even listening to me. Worst of all, I'm thinking about what I'm going to say next."

"Are you doing that now?"

"Doing what now? You mean the smudge-on-my-face thing, the wondering-if-you're-listening thing? No, but this is different."

"How, Liz? How is this different?"

It was Liz's turn to sit quietly. Brother Paul didn't seem to be disturbed at all as the minutes ticked by. He waited until she was ready to speak.

"I know you accept me just like I am. I don't have to pretend anything with you because you know me. You loved my parents in spite of the fact that they weren't perfect, and I believe you care about me in that same way. It's quiet here, and you act like you don't have anything else in the whole world to do except talk with me, listen to me. Even if there is a smudge on my face." Liz grinned as she said those last words.

"I want you to think again, Liz. Sit quietly as though you were here all by yourself. Think about times, and people you were with, when you've had those same kinds of interactions. You've had them, my dear, more often than you realize. Recall some of them."

Having given his instructions, Brother Paul stood and quietly walked away, leaving Liz alone. So much stillness, not even the sound of the wind moving the tree branches, not so much as a bird trilling. Just silence and the thoughts in Liz's head. *Richard.* Of course, Richard. She'd had many such times with him. And *Miss Em*; they could have talked forever had it not been for Liz worrying that she would overtire the woman. *Rose.* They almost knew what the other would say before the words came out. But they were family or near family. She thought of how she'd struggled to open up to Luann earlier in the year. Her sister had almost bullied her into conversation. At first, it had been strained, but gradually, she'd opened up. Her mental meandering brought her finally to Lainie. The day they'd cleaned Miss Millie's room they'd chatted like old friends. She remembered the choice she'd consciously made when the young girl offered her help in the daunting task, to let Lainie into her heart. It's a choice, she decided.

I can choose to let people in or keep them out. I decide what I give away of myself and what I don't. She remembered the way she'd described herself—or was it Luann describing her—as a big cake sporting a placard "Take a piece of Liz." She remembered Miss

Em's words: *Look in the mirrors all around you, Elizabeth. They reflect back to you who you really are.*

Liz was so lost in her thoughts that she didn't notice when Brother Paul returned. She looked to her right and there he was, stretched out in his sling chair, fresh glasses of iced tea on the railing. He reached for the dripping glasses and passed one to her without a word.

"I'll need practice," she said, "and coaching. Are you up to coaching me?"

"Always wanted to be a coach," he said. "That was what I wanted to do instead of seminary. Not my mother's choice, as I told you before," he said, smiling at her. He sat quietly for a few seconds before saying, "I'd be honored to teach you what I know. You understand that in teaching you I'll learn also. That's what happens when we become vulnerable to each other."

"I may be hopeless," she said. "There's Grace Carlson, you know, self-delegated leader of the band of town gossips. She hates me with a passion and does everything she can to rile me."

"Grace," he chuckled. "I can tell you a few Grace Carlson stories. I learned early in my tenure in Roslyn to let her talk herself out. The trick is to utter as few words as possible and to keep those as agreeable and positive as one can. She needs something to work with, and if you don't give her anything she runs out of steam pretty fast. She actually began to avoid me after a few months. Moved on to greener pastures."

"You're telling me I play right into her hands? Encourage her to beat me up?"

"Grace isn't your enemy, Liz. Your enemy is self-doubt, your fear of being found lacking. Grace, and I don't mean Grace Carlson here, is your friend."

Liz considered his words. "Yes," she said, "I'm definitely afraid of being found out. That's my main reason for coming today."

"Yes," he said, "about that 'confession' you mentioned on the phone. And leaving something as a sacramental behind? But first, tell me one or two things you heard in your little silent retreat just now on my deck. Then we'll have a bite of lunch before we delve into the heavy business of confession."

"One or two sentences, huh? When I have two or three file cabinets of clutter stored in my mind? I think what I *heard*, as you call it, is that crammed up there with all that junk are some pretty good things to work with. That's one thing I heard."

"Anything else?"

"Yeah. I had an inkling about what could happen when I give myself an entire month away. I just might get rid of a lot of clutter that's stored up there."

"And that you will, Liz. That you will. Seems to me that what you need is time to get acquainted with the real Elizabeth, to get to know her and like her. A couple of very important men had something to say on that subject. The Buddha said it this way, and I'm paraphrasing here. 'You can search the entire universe for someone more worthy of your love than yourself and that person is not to be found.'

"Jesus said something similar. He said, 'Love your neighbor as yourself.' That calls for some thought, Liz. If you think about it, you can only love your neighbor to the degree that you love yourself. If you don't love yourself, then how can you really love your neighbor? I think there are a lot of people out there, your Grace Carlson, for example, who are filled with self-doubt. Instead of admitting their doubt, they compare themselves to others, constantly looking for shortcomings in others to make themselves feel good."

He stopped talking so that his words could soak in, then drove his point home. "You'll know, Liz, when you're living your life from a position of love. It's not exhausting, it doesn't take away but adds to it. I think you experienced that with your Miss Millie. You owe it to yourself, and to her, to always live in that way. You're worthy of love, dear child, just exactly the way you are.

"Now, let's go have that lunch." He stood and offered Liz his hand. "I put together a little tuna salad while you were sitting here inching open those file drawers. I chose something Master can't stand the smell of. He'll leave us alone while we eat. I think the smell of tuna reminds him of his arch enemies, cats.

"And one more thing. Don't go telling Grace Carlson that I'm quoting the Buddha. She'll damn me to hell for sure." His laughter was a testimony to how much he enjoyed his own joke.

***

As Liz started home she noted, for the first time, that the tree-lined lane to the main road was an incline. Though she'd driven up this lane before, she'd not noticed, perhaps because it wasn't a sharp climb, but gradual, one that you wouldn't particularly notice in a car but would definitely feel in your leg muscles on a bicycle. She'd bring her bicycle when she came back this summer, she decided.

Liz looked forward to the drive back to Roslyn. It gave her a chance to reflect on the happenings of the day with Brother Paul. She'd left home at 9:00 that morning and, glancing at the clock,

230

realized it was just after 2:30. She felt, however, that she was returning home after a week-long vacation to a foreign country. The only thing missing was the exhaustion one usually feels after such a vacation, the result of constant motion and sightseeing. Instead, she was exhilarated, reluctant to leave but anticipating her return home.

They'd stayed indoors after lunch. Seated in two comfortable chairs angled towards each other in front of a large bay window that spanned almost the entire wall of the small house they looked out at tall pines. "You're surrounded by trees, here," Liz said. "Down in a little valley, surrounded by trees."

"Don't think we could call this a valley, exactly," laughed Brother Paul. "More of a nest at the bottom of a small incline. But yes, that's the main thing that attracted me to this property. I sometimes imagine myself nestled at the bottom of a small bowl. When I've been away and return home, I savor the feeling of settling down in my little nest. I'll be away for a while this summer and part of the anticipation of my trip is that luxurious drive down my little lane when I return."

"Where are you going?" Liz asked, genuinely interested.

"Let's do what you came here to do first, young lady. We'll talk about my trip before you leave. I think there might be a way we can help each other out in that regard. But now," he asked, "what about this *confession*?"

The difference in her friend's approach was noticeable. More direct. Where he'd listened and gently guided her to silence earlier in the day, he now took charge. She sensed a strength emanating from him that gave her the courage to speak up, to say clearly what she had come here to say.

She took the little silver ring from her pocket and slipped it on her finger. After all these years it still fit perfectly. "I brought this to leave with you," she said. "I'm going to tell you about a huge mistake I made years ago and have carried around with me ever since. Richard is the only other person who knows about it now that Miss Millie is gone, and I promised her I'd share it with you and then leave my sadness behind. That's what the ring represents, my broken promise, my crippling sadness."

She told her story as she looked directly into Brother Paul's eyes, and when she'd finished, she slipped the ring off her finger and handed it to him. He placed it in the palm of his left hand and with his right hand reached for hers. "Put both your hands on top of mine," he instructed as he covered them with his right hand. "You don't need to carry this any longer, Liz. In giving this ring to me for safekeeping, you're handing your guilt and shame over to God. When you leave here today, you'll leave a free woman."

He released her hands, stood, and walked over to the small mantle behind them. He lifted the lid of a large pottery urn, dropped the ring inside, and replaced the lid. Turning to face her he dusted his hands together. "God forgives you. He already had, you know. You just hadn't accepted it. Now you've made a choice. The best choice."

***

It was later than usual when Richard returned home from the store. Liz had called him on her way home and volunteered to prepare dinner rather than have him bring leftovers from the deli, their typical Friday night routine. Jackson always had Friday night plans, usually involving Lainie, but also including a horde of mutual friends. Liz had recently begun to notice that, except for study dates and special occasions, Jackson and Lainie were almost always with other kids: ballgames, bowling, movies, hanging out at someone's house. The Manley home had become a favorite in the last couple of months.

With Miss Millie gone their routine had changed. Jackson felt freer to invite a gang over, and his friends loved coming to his home. Food and drink were plentiful, thanks to the grocery store and Richard's passion for trying new recipes. He could organize a group of teenagers into an assembly line and whip up a half-dozen pizzas in record time. The deadline for commencing such activities, however, was 9:00, and Liz knew the kids had planned on an 8:00 movie and a late snack out afterward.

She looked forward to a quiet evening with Richard and had stopped by the grocery store on her way home to pick up ingredients for his favorite dish, chicken parmesan, one of the few things she could prepare better than he.

Liz had showered and dressed comfortably but stylishly in her favorite dress, a loose-fitting, just-above-the-knee yellow cotton shift. She momentarily regretted not having found time for her ritual beginning-of-summer pedicure, but reminded herself that she was leaving regret, both small and large, behind. She opted to go barefoot and without make-up instead. Richard always loved her simple look.

He didn't fail to notice. "Wow!" he exclaimed. "What's the occasion?"

"Dinner for two at the famed Manley Restaurant," she said, standing on tiptoe to kiss him. She handed him the corkscrew and a bottle of Pinot Noir. "You can do the honors," she invited.

"Whoa! Wine! This *is* a special occasion. Are you going to tell me what this is all about?"

"Over dinner. Take a minute to wash the *eau d'grocerie store* scent off and join me at the dining table."

"The dining table??!!!" she heard him exclaim as he walked away.

***

"A month, huh?"   They'd cleaned the kitchen together. While Richard showered, Liz changed into pj's and was waiting for him in the study, curled up at one end of the giant sofa with a blanket over her feet.

"You can manage things for a month, can't you? Rose will be here, and anything she can't cover, Luann ..."

"Not a two-for-one deal!" Richard protested. "We'll do just fine, Liz. Matter of fact, Rose really won't need to come in as often as she usually does. Jacks and I will be at the store most of the time. And when he's not at the store with me he'll be with his friends. Last free summer and all that, you know."

"I'll let you fight that battle with Rose, but I'm putting my money on her, not you. She won't trust this house to two men."

Over dinner Liz had told Richard about her day in Brother Paul's *nest*, about how her problem of where to go away for several weeks had been solved so easily. She'd been puzzled over how she could help her friend out with his summer trip and had been unable to contain her excitement when he asked her to look after the little house and Master while he was away in July. He was going to Scotland for a month, he told her. His brother had property there and he had a standing invitation to visit when he liked. Always before he'd taken Master with him, but the dog was failing and he was afraid the trip would be too much for him. Liz didn't wait for him to finish before she agreed to the plan, she told Richard now.

"You can drive down for an occasional night and Luann will love bringing the girls down for a weekend or two," she planned with Richard. "And I'm just a few minutes away from the university. I can check out the campus while I'm there. I've already applied for admission."

Richard interrupted her with a laugh and a shake of his head. "You don't stop, do you, kid? You just change directions. But I've got to say, I like this direction. Who would have guessed? A man like me married to a college chick!"

CHAPTER 25

The decision to leave for St. Louis on Sunday afternoon for the Senior Trip had been a difficult one to make. Since the games were of the highest interest to most involved, in the end it was the pre-set schedule of baseball games that determined everything. Time for girls to shop and guys to trail along behind them or hang out at the food court, a chance to relax around the hotel pool, and a brief nod to an educational experience at the Science Center were taken into consideration. But when it came down to it, the Cardinals' schedule determined the travel plans. Most of the men involved in planning wanted to see the Cardinals play both the Chicago Cubs and the Cincinnati Reds, home games played in early June. Even though the kids would have been out of school for more than a week by the time they left, it was decided that the bus would leave at 2:00 on Sunday afternoon, arriving in St. Louis for a good night's sleep and a full day of sightseeing on Monday before the evening game.

Jackson was packed well before Liz was ready to leave. "Just gotta run and say 'bye to Lainie," he called up the stairs to Liz. "See you at the bus."

"Sure," Liz called, smiling to herself and thinking, *Not if you can help it!*

Her car radio was on full blast, a sign that Jackson had recently driven it. A blaring radio was always something he left behind, and more often than not, a half-empty soda can. She adjusted the volume and listened briefly to the half-hour news headlines. "For the first time since 1994, the Democrats control Congress. James Jeffords, a Republican, single-handedly gave power ..."

Who cares? was Liz's reaction. After the recent election debacle that had taken weeks to determine who won the 2000 Presidential election, George W. or Al Gore, Liz rarely listened to newscasts. Politics, a topic that had never been of great interest, rated even less favorably with her in recent months. She switched the dial to hear the Dixie Chicks blasting out the lyrics, "... missing person who nobody missed at all ..." a dreadful song that had spawned a dreadful video. What was the title? Liz wondered, not out of real interest, but out of curiosity about where such a morbid song could have originated. The song ended and the announcer, a female, chirped the answer to her unvoiced first question. "That was the Dixie Chicks singing 'Goodbye Earl.' They were awarded accolades for Best Music Video by the Academy of Country Music featuring the song you just heard. Guys, you might want to take a look at that video and listen to the warning from these gals. Treat your ladies well, or you could end up like Earl."

Yeah, that was it. She remembered an evening a few weeks back; a rare Sunday evening of television viewing. As usual, Liz sat with a magazine in her lap, something to pay attention to as Richard did his channel surfing with the remote. He'd paused briefly to listen to the opening performance of the annual Academy of Country Music Awards show just as Jackson and Lainie returned from youth group.

"Oooo, I love country music. I didn't know you liked it too, Miz ... Liz. Have they announced a female vocalist for the year? Don't you love Lee Ann Womack? She really should ..."

"Take a breath, Lain!" Jackson interrupted.

"You just don't get it, Jackson. This is the biggest night of the year. Can I stay and watch with you? I'll call my mom. She'd let me watch it at home anyway. Mmm ... *Liz*—I'll never get used to calling you that—it would be so much fun to watch with you since I know that you like country music, too. Jackson, you'd watch it with us wouldn't you, since your mom and dad ..."

"Of course, we can watch it together," Liz interrupted. If she could help it, Lainie would never know that the awards show would be the last thing on a list of Sunday night pastimes for her. Would be even further down the list for Richard.

"Call your mom and make sure it's okay if you stay while I pop a giant bowl of popcorn and get us something to drink. If Richard and Jackson get tired of watching, they can find another TV to watch," she finished with a stern look in the direction of the males.

They read her look perfectly. *Don't make one peep of protest*, it clearly stated.

She returned to the study to find Lainie alone. "They already left, Miz uh Liz. I guess men just don't understand our kind of music."

Liz turned with a smile and took a bowl of popcorn downstairs to the family room. "Get your own drinks, you two," she called as she headed back up the stairs. "And don't bother us. We're listening to *our kind of music*."

"I just don't get it," the young girl lamented after watching the 'Goodby Earl' video. "Do you know anybody like that? I sure don't. Why do people want to hurt each other? And why do people *sing* about it? I mean, the Dixie Chicks are cool and all that, but I just don't get *singing* about beating somebody up and killing people. And then, it's like, it's not enough to *sing* about it; they have to make a video and make you *see* it.

"Oooo, I do hope Lee Ann wins!"

Liz had just enough time to think, *Lee Ann who?* before Lainie was off again with her stream of words.

"Don't you just love 'I Hope You Dance,' Liz? I did it! Did you notice? I called you Liz without the Mmmm first! Don't you?"

She'd never once thought of herself as aging before this moment. Liz simply could not keep up with the conversation, one-sided as it had become. She didn't need to do anything more than listen, a good thing, because it took every bit of her concentration just to do that.

The chirpy female deejay broke into Liz's thoughts. "And now for a kinder, gentler reminder of life," she said, "it's Lee Ann Womack singing 'I Hope You Dance.'"

Lee Ann had indeed won Female Vocalist of the Year. Liz agreed with Lainie: it was an excellent song, a reminder to embrace the good in life. Liz decided right then and there that she would buy the CD. No, she'd buy two. One for her and one for Lainie. If the girl already had it, which she probably did, she could give it away.

But for now, the Senior Trip. To say she was excited about it would be a stretch. She was, however, looking forward to seeing the long-laid plans come to fruition. Being around all that youthful energy would be contagious—she hoped she could keep up with their conversations—and they were a good bunch of kids. She'd known most of them to some degree their entire lives. Many of them would go on to college; some would stay behind and get married too quickly. She hoped none of them turned out like poor Wanda of Dixie Chicks fame. Wanda, the poor girl who'd "looked all around and all she found was Earl." Thank God it hadn't been that way for her. Thank God for Richard.

Lainie had posed an interesting question on the night of the music awards. "Do you know anybody like that?" she'd asked, referring to poor Wanda. Liz thought of the girls she knew in Jackson's class and couldn't think of a single one. Rosemary Picken's mother came to mind, a pretty, fidgety woman who could never look Liz in the eye when she came through the check-out line at the store. All those years she'd been in a perfect place to pay attention to what might be going on in other people's lives and she'd never once given it a thought. At seventeen, Lainie was so much farther ahead of her when it came to interaction with people.

Liz's thoughts drifted to the young girl, positive thoughts that nudged out her constant worries about Jackson and Lainie spending so much time together. She thought about Lainie's love for the old people in Roslyn's nursing home. She really was a remarkable young lady, with a definite plan for her future in geriatric care. She had confided in Liz that she wanted to be the person who *revolutionized*—Lainie's word—nursing homes. "You're my inspiration, Liz. I loved the way you took care of Miss Em. Why can't nursing homes be more like real homes? With made-up families like we were with Miss Em."

It had taken only seconds for Liz to interpret what Lainie meant: Rose, Miss Em, Luann, the children. A funny, but accurate, description of their afternoon tea times.

As she pulled into the parking lot it occurred to her that she wished Lainie was coming along. Only seniors were allowed, a rule that she wholeheartedly endorsed. Goodness knows they'd have their hands full even with that.

***

Without knowing how it could happen, Liz had hoped to have some time alone in St. Louis with Jackson. She wanted to walk down to the Gateway Arch. She wanted to see if she could locate the exact spot where she'd picnicked all those years ago with her parents and Luann. All the kids had turned in signed permission slips from their parents entitling them to a couple hours' freedom once they arrived at Busch Stadium on Monday evening. The

240

agreement was that they would hang out in groups of three or more. This arrangement worked for all involved giving the kids a break from the chaperones and vice versa.

She was surprised that Jackson agreed so readily to spend the time with her. "Sure, Mom," he said. "I can spare an hour for you. Besides, I'm getting a little tired of being around so many people 24/7."

"24/7?" Liz asked. "What does that mean?"

"Get with the times, Ma," he grinned. "You know: 24 hours in a day, 7 days in a week."

"Makes perfect sense once you explain," Liz agreed.

Once the bus had parked and Liz and other chaperones were assured that everyone was grouped properly, she and Jackson set off towards the Gateway Arch. The streets were busy with pre-game pedestrians and vehicles hoping to park as near the stadium as possible. Mother and son concentrated on crossing streets safely, a task that kept conversation minimal until they reached the broad expanse of green lawn leading to the Arch.

Liz caught Jackson's arm and tugged, causing him to stop. "Wait," she said. "I need to look for a minute."

"Yeah," he responded. "It's pretty awesome, isn't it?" He lifted his head, bending his neck back to look at the graceful, silver metal structure slicing through the cloudless blue sky. "Wonder how it just stands there?"

Liz laughed out loud. "That's exactly the question I asked my daddy the first time I saw it," Liz said.

"What'd he say?"

"I don't remember, Jacks," she replied. "But what I do remember are the picnics we had here when we came to games."

"You came here for baseball games when you were a kid?" he asked.

"More than once. I don't remember how many times, but I know it was more than once. My daddy loved the Cardinals. He loved to bring our family here for weekends. We'd leave home early on Saturday morning, find a cheap motel outside of St. Louis, then drive into town and spend the rest of the day here."

"Why didn't we ever do that? You and Dad and me? Man! That would have been fun." There was an absence of accusation in Jackson's voice. He simply wanted to know why.

Liz answered him in the same spirit. "I can't tell you why, Jackson. I don't really know myself. It had to do with how ..." Liz struggled now for the right words, wondering if she'd made a mistake bringing him here. She started again. "I was always so preoccupied with doing the right thing. Keeping the grocery store running, building our house, church work. It never seemed that important, and both your dad and I were always so busy. Now I know that it might have been among the most important things we could have done. Because this is the place I wanted to bring you to tell you about my dad. It's a place he loved, a place where our family had some of our best times."

"So that's why I love baseball so much, huh? Because of a grandpa I never knew? Like I love fishing so much because of Grandpa Richard? Is it in my genes or something?"

Liz smiled. "Could have something to do with it," she replied. "Or maybe you got it from your dad. He was a crackerjack second baseman in his day."

"So where did I get this urge to take up golf?" he asked. "Did I tell you Mr. Parker is going to teach me and Lainie to play golf this summer? Yeah, I told you ..."

Breathe, Liz reminded herself. Just breathe. She closed her eyes and drew a long breath. She opened them, and replied, "You'll make an awesome golfer, son."

***

Sunday night had been a breeze for the chaperones. The kids were exhausted from the bus ride and had settled down in their rooms by midnight. Whether they were asleep or not was of no concern; the guys were all on the third floor and the girls on the fourth. The adults shared rooms near the elevators and staircases and left the doors cracked until they'd made the last rounds and found everyone sound asleep. Breakfast was served in the lobby beginning at 6:30 the next morning and the adults who had the late-night watch were given an extra couple hours sleep.

Not so on Monday night. They had been forewarned by parents from previous senior trips: beware the second night! The kids were pumped after the Cardinals' 5-2 win over Cincinnati. Even after a stern lecture from John Graves before the students left the bus, it took the efforts of the entire dozen chaperones to herd them like cattle into the Hampton Inn, shushing them every step of the way. The women chaperones learned on Tuesday morning that three of the men had slept in the hallway of the third floor; that was the only way to keep the guys where they belonged. They reasoned that if the guys were contained, the girls would stay put, too.

The women had different sorts of problems to deal with. Sometime between the seventh-inning stretch and the end of the game, Mindy Wintchell and Matt Graves broke up. Matt took the break-up in stride; after all, he'd had his eye on Shelley Adams since April and was waiting for the right opportunity to break it off with Mindy. Mindy was inconsolable and had to be led from the game to the bus by her two best friends. She sobbed the entire way to the motel. Loudly. It seemed that if she were to be miserable, then everyone else would be miserable. She emerged on Tuesday morning, subdued but puffy-faced.

"I'm not going to the game," she announced. "I'll stay here and sit by the pool."

"We travel as a group, Mindy," Alicia Winston, one of the chaperones, reminded her. "No one stays behind. You can sit with me on the bus and at the game as well, but you can't stay here."

The conversation continued, but in the end, Alicia convinced her that she would go. Just in time for another outbreak of female hysteria.

"I got my period!" echoed down the hall as Liz opened the door of the room she shared with Marcia Graves. She closed the door, turned around, and leaned her back against it. "You want to take this one?"

"I'll pass," said Marcia. "I'm in the doghouse with all the girls, with the exception of Shelly Adams and her crew. Remember, I'm Matt's mother. The girls will all be united against our entire family for a week or two. At least until Mindy finds another guy."

All was well until the group began boarding the bus, and two girls discovered they were wearing identical blouses. Neither wanted to be seen in said blouse so both girls were sent to their rooms to change.

"Five minutes," John ordered. "Go. Hurry! We'll leave without you." Everyone except the relieved, running girls knew it was a bluff.

Liz was grateful to sink into her aisle seat in the stadium. She didn't even object to the frequent need to swing her legs to the side as yet another teenager, both hands laden with food—hotdogs, nachos, giant sodas—worked his or her way past her. On perhaps the twentieth interruption and the game had not even begun, Liz glanced to the section on her left and down several rows. *That girl looks just like ... it can't be ... but it is Lainie! What's she doing here? How did she get here?* The thoughts tumbled through her brain like rocks released in a landslide.

A man was leaning towards Lainie, separated from him by a woman. Liz felt an electric current race through her body. The Parkers. Lainie was here with the Parkers. Liz watched in shock as the man stood and Lainie turned to the woman on her left, a woman dressed in a bright red Cardinal's jacket and matching ball cap. Yes, it was Lainie, the Parkers, and the last person on Earth Liz expected to see at a St. Louis Cardinals' stadium. Grace Carlson. How had this happened?

Mr. Parker and Grace Carlson leaned towards each other, apparently so they could better hear what the other had to say. After a few exchanges, he turned away and started up the steps towards an exit, a path that would take him within inches of Liz. She turned her face in the opposite direction and closed her eyes.

What to do? First, breathe, she reminded herself. Breathe and consider options. She could stay in her seat and pretend they weren't here. She could trade seats with someone and move herself out of the line of vision. Thoughts were swirling around so quickly in her head that she felt as though she were in the middle of a stinging desert sandstorm. She felt betrayed, embarrassed, angry.

It was as if the words were spoken aloud: "You are not your feelings, Elizabeth. You may feel all those things and more, but you have a rational mind. You can make a decision. You can choose what you do with this situation." The words were spoken clearly in her head in the voice of her dear friend.

"You're right, Miss Em. I do have a choice. Give me a minute here and I'll do my best to make you proud."

Rationally Liz recognized that only seconds had passed. Rationally she knew that Miss Em wasn't here and that the voice she'd heard came from her own thoughts. But in those few seconds, she gained the courage to do what she knew she had to do.

"Mrs. Parker, Lainie, Miss Gracie," she began, forcing what she hoped resembled a real smile to her lips. "You're the last people on earth I expected to see here today." True words.

"Miz ... Liz!" Lainie jumped from her seat, reached across Mrs. Parker, and grabbed Liz. "Where are you sitting? Where are ...?" The girl turned her attention away from Liz and scanned the crowd. "Oh, look. There's everybody. Hey, Charlie," she called. She was almost dancing with excitement as she waved and called out the names of her friends in the senior class.

Mrs. Parker stood and extended her hand. "I'm Sarah Parker," she introduced herself. "I feel like I already know you. Your son and Lainie here are almost like our children, well, grandchildren," she finished with a laugh. "They're much too young, actually we're much too old, for them to be our children. I like the sound of the words "too young" much better than saying we're too old," she said with a trill of laughter.

Lainie interrupted, "And you saw Miss Gracie, didn't you Liz? Miss Gracie is the reason for us being here. She's always wanted to see a Cardinals game. How old did you say you are, Miss Gracie? Seventy-nine? Can you believe it? She's always just loved the Cardinals and finally, she gets to see a real live game."

Up to this point, the old woman had remained seated, staring straight ahead as though the empty diamond in front of her held her captive. Liz, however, recognized the disdain in the rigidity of her shoulders and the unflinching set of her jaw. Taking a deep breath, she addressed the woman with as much kindness mixed with honesty as she could muster. "You are amazing, Miss Gracie. I don't know anyone who can move mountains like you can. Maybe you'll be just the good luck charm the Cardinals need to win today."

Miss Gracie sniffed, but before she could make another sound Lainie spoke up.

"We're their best cheerleaders, aren't we Miss Gracie?"

Then, just in time, the crowd was invited to stand for the National Anthem. Liz smiled and moved out of the way to allow Mr. Parker, one hand holding a cardboard tray of hotdogs and chips and the other balancing four paper cups of soft drinks, to return to his seat.

***

Liz made it through the game and the dinner out at a restaurant. She even managed to forget the foursome seated in front and to the left of her as she cheered a losing Cardinals team on. But she asked Jackson to sit with her on the return trip to the hotel.

247

"Yeah," he admitted, he did know it was going to happen. But, "No," he didn't know their seats were going to be so close.

"Lainie didn't either," he said. "Nobody knew where our seats were going to be, so how could they choose seats near us on purpose?

"Why do you care so much, Ma?" he asked. "She wanted to do something nice for a little old lady and the Parkers wanted to help her. I know you don't like Miss Gracie and all that, but she's like a different person when Lainie is around. They make each other laugh. It's kinda cool to see them together, like Father Time and the New Year's baby hangin' out together."

Put that way, Liz had nothing to object to. "But why did you keep it from me?" she asked.

Jackson took his cap off and ran his fingers through his hair, a gesture that was so like Richard Liz could only stare.

"We were going to tell you about it after," he said. "We thought that in a place the size of Busch Stadium, there wasn't a chance in a million you'd see each other."

"Chance in a million, huh? When the entire stadium has a seating capacity of 50,000?"

"Who's countin', Ma?" He turned to her and grinned, his teeth flashing white in the darkness of the bus. "We counted on you. We knew you'd be okay with it in the end. Just didn't want you obsessin' about it the entire trip."

It was Liz's turn to grin. "Who, me? Obsess?"

CHAPTER 26

June sped by and the date for Liz's departure for her month away was looming, along with an increasing uneasiness about her decision to go. She had a crate in the corner of her bedroom to which she added daily: books she'd intended to read forever but never quite gotten around to, a small CD player along with a few favorite CDs, and pads for writing. She even tucked in little notebooks that contained scribbles from past years. The crate had become so full that she recognized the need to either stop collecting, begin culling through what was already there, or buy another crate.

To add to her worries, it seemed that everyone knew about her planned escape. She'd only shared her plan with those who needed to know, Richard, Jackson, Rose, Luann, but somehow everyone she saw brought it up. Next time, she reminded herself, I'll tell them to keep their mouths shut. Even as she thought the words, she wondered *Will there be a next time?*

Denise, Richard's sister, was the first to exclaim over her disappearance. "But who's going to bring the potato salad to Fourth of July, Liz? And who's going to keep the kids occupied? Just kidding, kiddo. But we'll miss you. This will be the first time you've missed the Fourth since ..."

"Yeah," Liz interrupted, "since before Richard and I were married. I'll also miss our anniversary, our eighteenth. Can you believe we've been married that long? This year marks a halfway point for me. I've been married exactly half of my life!" For the first time in her life, Liz felt pleasure in bringing the first and second halves of her life together. She imagined Miss Em smiling in the background, "You're integrating, dear. You're accepting life as a whole, not compartmentalizing."

Spooky how she imagined her departed friend's voice. Maybe she'd hung around Rose too long.

Rose. The dear woman reminded her every day. "Six more days and you'll be outta here. Five more days and I'll get me some peace and quiet." And so on. The countdown was at three.

Liz didn't hear Rose come in that Thursday morning, but she did hear the sound of water rushing into the tub of the washing machine. She called down, "Sorry! I forgot to start the first load. Thanks."

She neither expected nor received a reply, but she imagined—correctly—Rose ambling back to the kitchen mumbling under her breath *What this family do without Rose? Not enough sense to come in outta the rain!* Or something to that effect.

When Liz appeared in the kitchen some minutes later Rose had disappeared. She looked around for Rose's telltale red plastic cup filled with *co'cola* but didn't see it. Yep, there it was still in its spot in the front row in the cabinet where glasses were kept. Unusual, since that was almost always the first task of Rose's day. Liz opened the ice bin and placed exactly 8 cubes of ice, the required number, into the twelve-ounce cup to which she began pouring the contents of Rose's favorite drink, Dr. Pepper. The woman refused to call it by its correct name, even though she knew the difference between Coke and Dr. Pepper. It was always *co'cola*, no matter what the brand or flavor. She left the drink to settle, again following Rose's exact regimen. *No mor'n half. Don't like watered-down co'cola.* Liz pulled a paper towel from the roll, tore it in half, wadded it to a tight ball, and stuffed it in the opening left by the tab. "Cain't let none of the fizz escape," she said aloud.

"If you got nothin' better to do than make fun of an old black lady you can just get out of my kitchen."

"Three more days, Rose. You can put up with me for three more days, can't you?"

"Think you're smart, don't you, Miz Astor." (Rose loved adopting the name Grace Carlson had bestowed on Liz some months ago.) Years of practice had given each of them an understanding of the implied meaning in all conversations. Liz knew without being told that Rose noticed she'd been preempted in counting down the days till her departure.

"But I got big news," the older woman went on. "I got my house rented out."

"You what?!!!" Liz set the coffee pot back on the warmer without having added any coffee to her cup. "When? Who?"

"Now you just hold on to your kitty cats, Missy. The way I understand things, this is my house to do with as I choose. And I choose to rent it out for a spell."

"I know, Rose. I'm sorry. You're right, I overreacted." Liz picked up the coffee pot once again, filled her cup, and moved to the table. "Let's sit down while you tell me about it."

Rose hadn't set out to rent her house, but in the way of small towns word had gotten out that the house was empty most of the time. In record time almost everyone knew the full story. Miss Millie had left it to Rose but Rose had chosen to stay with her Daddy in the country. Her solution had been, with help from the Manleys, to keep it occupied the required number of days so that insurance wouldn't lapse. The plan had proved easier to hatch than to sustain. Rose, although she was burdened by the necessity of caring for the place, had spoken not a word. She'd been taken by surprise when Mr. and Mrs. Parker appeared in the little lane of her daddy's home. They stood in the yard beside the Parkers' big silver Mercury Marquis as they told her what they had in mind.

"The Whites—no I don't mean the white folks—that's their name," Rose chortled at her joke. "Miz White, she's Miz Parker's younger sister, and her husband want to come down South and give us a look-see. They want to keep their house up North—Michigan? Minnesota? One of those M states—while they check out to see if they want to come down here permanent like. That's why they don't want to buy, just rent."

"You won't sell Miss Em's house, will you Rose?" She felt the loss by saying the words.

"Now, Lizbet, hold on to them kitty cats again! Nobody's talkin' about sellin' nothin'. I said rent and that's what I aim to do."

It was settled. But not in Liz's heart. It seemed that no matter where she turned, the Parkers were right there in front of her. She knew that, sooner or later, she'd have to face them head-on.

***

On the Saturday before Liz was to leave—July 1 fell on a Sunday and Liz had determined to begin her time away at the very beginning of the month—she was surprised by a phone call from Lainie asking if she and her mom could stop by.

"We both have something to give you to make your trip more fun," Lainie explained. At least, there was a simple explanation as to how Lainie had found out she was going away. Jackson.

Over the years Liz had gleaned bits of information about Lainie and her family, some through stories Jackson told about her and some from the small-town rumor mill. She knew for a fact that

252

Lainie had entered Roslyn Elementary in third grade. She remembered Jackson's excitement when he was in fourth grade as he talked about "that girl named Lainie."

"She's the best kickball player in the entire school, Mom," he told her the first week of school. "I felt a little sorry for her standin' over by the little kids' slide and asked her if she wanted to be on my team 'cause we needed two more to even out the teams and she said yes. Boy, am I glad she said yes. She's the best."

"That's great, Jackson," she had replied. And it *was* great until the kids matured into teenagers and thought about things other than kickball.

From Jackson, and from Lainie herself, Liz had learned that her parents' divorce was the reason she and her mother Cindy had relocated to Roslyn. Much of the rest Liz learned from Luann; her sister knew how to ferret out the truth from the rumor mill in Roslyn and she was the only person Liz trusted to present a fair assessment. From Luann, she learned that Lainie's dad was a trial lawyer who began his practice on the Gulf Coast but had relocated to Jackson to be closer to his daughter after the divorce. Cindy Claiborne, a nurse who'd practiced her profession only a couple of years before marrying the up-and-coming attorney, found a job as far away from her previous life as a socialite attorney's wife as possible. She'd never enjoyed the role but didn't find a way to extricate herself from a bad situation until she became aware that Jonathan, her husband, had become involved with one of the paralegals in his firm. He eventually married the woman, and Lainie now shared her dad with another sister and a brother.

What Liz would learn later about Cindy was that she'd shed her role and her bitterness simultaneously, vowing that her daughter would be tainted by neither. Liz saw Cindy only occasionally around town. She shopped in their grocery store but, to Liz's knowledge, participated in little other than school activities that included her daughter and her work as Nursing Director of Roslyn's nursing home. She was polite, even friendly, but seemed content to be her own, and her daughter's, best friend. While she supported Lainie's church activities, she chose not to attend, a choice that, in Luann's words, "Gave the old cows around town plenty of fodder to chew on."

Liz was watering the hanging ferns on her front porch when the two pulled into her driveway. She set the watering can down and walked out to meet them.

"Come in," she invited. "I need to wash my hands and get us something to drink. We'll sit on the back deck; it's shaded this time of day."

"Oooo, I just love your back deck, Liz," Lainie crooned. "Mom, you'll love it, too. Doesn't matter what time of year it is, you can look for miles, well ..." she hesitated, "maybe *yards*," she decided, "and see some kind of wildflowers. Except in winter time," she finished, "but it's still pretty even then."

"How about acres?" Liz asked. She spoke to Cindy. "We have six acres surrounding the house. We like our space."

"I hear you," Cindy agreed. "I have to make do with a privacy fence and shrubbery. Works for me, though."

The three women stood, tea glasses in hand, and looked at the beautiful landscape surrounding them, Liz remembering the June days from just a year past when she'd surveyed the same scene from Miss Em's bedroom; the girl and her mother momentarily lost in their own thoughts.

As usual, Lainie broke the silence. "We came to bring you something, Liz. And we have news of our own." She turned to her mom. "Which first, Mom?" she asked.

"Oh, the gifts, by all means," her mother exclaimed. She handed Liz a simple brown bag, pink and green tissue paper dressing up its plainness.

"I didn't put mine in a bag," Lainie said as she passed a small book to Liz.

"I didn't know there was a book by the same name as the song," Liz said. She held the book up so that Cindy could see. "We watched the CMA awards show together, and Lainie and I agree that we both love the song, same title as the book, 'I Hope You Dance.'"

"I completely forgot until now," she continued as she stood. "I have something for you," Liz handed the book to Cindy. "Isn't that a precious little girl," she commented about the smiling blond girl on the cover.

"Precious," agreed Cindy. "I have a picture of you that looks just like this little girl," she said to Lainie. "You were five when it was taken. Your blond hair had that same wispy look."

Until she was reminded by Lainie's gift, Liz had forgotten the two CDs, one tucked into her stash to go with her tomorrow and the other, waiting on the kitchen counter until she saw Lainie again. She returned and handed the CD to the girl. "I bought one for both of us," she said. "You probably already have your own copy by now, but you can give this one to a friend."

Lainie, forever honest, said, "Yeah, I have one at home. I'm glad you bought yourself one because the CD in the book only has the title song on it. Thanks, Liz. I'll find somebody who loves Leann as much as we do to give the extra one to."

"My gift is a book too," Cindy said, calling Liz's attention to the gift beside her chair. "One of my favorites that I read at the beginning of every summer. I hope you like it as much as I do."

***

Liz sat on a deck. A different deck, but one with a view just as beautiful as what she'd left behind. The air here seemed crisper, cleaner, more scented. Pine-scented, to be accurate. She placed the book on the floor beside her chair and propped her feet on the railing surrounding the deck. She had completed four days in Brother Paul's little house and had felt no desire, as she'd feared, to do anything different than what she was doing right now. She'd taken no bike rides; short walks sufficed. She hadn't needed anything from town; she ate when she was hungry and slept when she was tired. Surprisingly, she had done very little writing up to now, something she had been so sure that she would do.

Another surprise to her was how much she wanted to sleep. Twelve hours plus at night, going to bed when it was fully dark, and waking up to the light. Within twenty-four hours she'd adjusted to the strange sounds of a strange place, had even forgotten to lock the back door when she came in from the deck last night. She was a little horror-struck when she'd discovered that this morning, but was also pleased with herself. As she opened the blinds to the morning sun after discovering her safety lapse, she decided that this would be the last time she touched them. Why open and close blinds every day? Here she was in the middle of a pine forest, shielded from the view of every human creature, so why not open up to the darkness of night and the light of day? Her sense of freedom was growing stronger every day.

She picked up the paperback Cindy had given her and remembered her words, "I hope you like it as much as I do." Liz had never heard of the book, *Gift from the Sea*, by Anne Morrow Lindbergh. She glanced now at the copyright date: 1955. It could have been written yesterday, written just for Liz. Every word spoke to her. Liz recognized that something beyond her understanding was happening here. As she read, she not only soaked up the words of the famous pilot's wife, but she realized that by sharing this book Cindy was offering something of herself.

How is it that this book, written so long ago by someone far removed from here, said many of the same things she'd heard over and over from her old friends, Miss Em first and then Brother Paul? Liz reread the author's words. Mrs. Lindbergh's hope to "achieve a state of inner spiritual grace from which I could function and give as I was meant to in the eye of God" resonated with Liz. Until last year she'd never considered the word *grace* except in the context of Grace Carlson, but now it seemed to pop up everywhere. She reread Socrates' quote: "May the outward and inward man be at one." I'm getting there, she decided. Slowly, but I'm moving in that direction. That'll have to do for now.

She looked upward, past the tall pines and into the sky above filled with clouds. Looks like rain, she considered. Oh, well. Who cares if I get wet? I'm going for a bike ride.

***

As planned, Richard showed up in time for a late dinner on Saturday. Main Street Groceries had never been open on Sunday. Even with the change in habits in recent years making Sunday a day of shopping rather than a day of rest, the Manley family refused to give in to the trend. Big Richard summed it up in one terse sentence: "Let 'em go to Walmart."

By Saturday Liz was ready for company, but only for Richard's company. She had so many things to talk about with him, nothing of real importance, but, then again, things of Major Importance. On Friday she'd begun to write in her journal and on the first page she'd written the words Things of Major Importance, then underlined the words for further emphasis. First on the list was *I love being here alone.*

Liz considered her list as she sliced tomatoes to go with the simple mac and cheese dinner and tiny fried perch—full of minuscule bones—she'd prepared for the two of them. Would Richard understand? Would he be threatened by her new-found freedom, by her immersion in solitude? She wondered if he would notice a difference in her.

Any fears she had were immediately laid to rest. When she heard the approach of the car, the crunch of gravel under the weight of Richard's Jeep Cherokee, Liz quickly rinsed her hands, set the plate of tomatoes on the table, and hurried outside to the tiny front porch.

"Come on, Master; time for a potty break and meeting a new friend. No barking! Tail-wagging is an appropriate greeting, and feel free to lick his shoes, too. That smell you'll notice is a cat." With the absence of human companionship, Liz quickly developed a habit of ongoing conversation with the dog. One-sided except for an occasional whine, tail-thump, or quick bark.

Liz remained seated on the single step as Richard parked the Jeep and stepped out of the vehicle. He hesitated before closing the door, looking full circle at the now darkening forest. After closing the door, he walked quickly towards her, the dog eying him warily. It seemed that Master couldn't decide whether to protect Liz or chase the strange human away. Liz called to him and he moved, reluctantly, in her direction, obviously determined to keep himself between the two humans, ready to go against his basic nature and attack if necessary.

Liz stood as Richard approached. He reached for her hands and, clasping them loosely, stood staring at her face. Neither of them spoke, and the dog sat back on his haunches, apparently satisfied that no harm would come to his new temporary mistress.

"I get it now," Richard said, nodding his head. "I see why you wanted to come here. It's perfectly quiet, and beautiful." Liz tried to recall if she'd ever heard him say the word *beautiful*. Pretty, fine, nice, hunky-dory, those were descriptors Richard commonly used, but she'd never heard the word *beautiful* come from this man's lips.

As if almost embarrassed at having spoken the word, Richard reverted. "Purt near perfect," he quipped, "except for one thing. Where does a man fish around here?"

"Or woman. There's a pond in the back, beyond the trees. Come see the evidence. But first, what does a lady have to do to be kissed by her prince?"

***

Darkness had fully fallen by the time they'd finished the simple dinner, washed the dishes, and tidied the kitchen, the only light coming from the candles on the table and the old oil lamp in the small living room. Liz lit several large candles—she'd had the foresight to bring several along with her—and joined Richard on the small deck. The soft chirps of crickets and the occasional trill of a bird that had delayed his bedtime were the only sounds. It felt natural to sit with Richard in the darkness and study the stars, so visible in the absence of artificial light.

"So, you aren't scared out here all alone?" Richard asked after a time. "You don't need your big, strong husband with his twenty-two to protect you from the bad guys?"

Liz recognized that Richard's light-hearted question was an invitation to talk about her past week. She knew him well enough to understand that he would accept as much or as little as she wanted to share. She could respond with a light-hearted answer or she could take the conversation to a deeper level. She opted for the latter.

"I've figured out already that my fears aren't so much about other people," she said. "Miss Em tried to get me to pay attention to what was inside instead of paying so much attention to what other people thought. Brother Paul did the same. I know you can't understand, Richard, why that was so hard for me because it comes so easy for you. I'd have never guessed in a million years that what needed to happen for me to *feel* peace was to spend time with just myself."

Liz laughed. "Rose describes what I feel here better than anybody. Remember how she sometimes says, 'It's so noisy in here I can't hear myself think!' That's exactly how my brain has been for years. For the first time ever, at least since I was a little girl, I can hear myself think. The noise has stopped. And, can you believe it? I like my thoughts! I'm even writing them down."

He reached over and took her hand. "You're right, Liz. I didn't understand, but I didn't need to understand to love you. I've always loved you and I always will, but I think I like this new Liz, this girl who rides her bicycle in the rain and catches her own fish." He squeezed her hand tightly before releasing it.

"So, enough about me. What's going on at home?" she asked.

"Home? Where's that? Oh, you mean what's Jackson been up to?"

"And Lainie, and Rose, and Lu?" She recognized the dig.

"You'd be proud of your boy, Liz. He's set to take twelve hours up at the junior college. He worked out a schedule so that all his classes are on Tuesdays and Thursdays with one online class. Said he's afraid to overdo his first semester. Wants to spend some time in the store and have a little left over for his friends. Sounds like a good plan to me."

Liz, while not exactly pleased with the arrangement, accepted Jackson's decision to commute to the junior college in Senatobia. "It's a beginning," she agreed.

"And Lainie," Richard continued. "That girl is just buzzing with excitement about her trip to New York City with her mom. Not supposed to happen for weeks but you'd think she's leaving tomorrow. It's all she can talk about. I forget what they're going for, but it must be important if the kid will miss a week of school."

"I'd forgotten about the trip. Lainie told me about it when she brought her mom over last Saturday. It's some kind of Geriatric Health Professionals convention. That's what Lainie plans to train for in college; first get her RN and then go on to *revolutionize* nursing homes in America.

"I know," she responded to Richard's laughter. "But that's what she says she's going to do, and I wouldn't be surprised to see her accomplish it."

"Is it my imagination, or are you not so worried about the Jackson/Lainie romance?" Richard asked. "Seems to me you actually like the girl now, like you don't think she's out to steal your son away from you."

"*Our* son, Richard," she corrected him. "And you're right. It's funny, but I rarely think of her as Jackson's girlfriend any longer. She's become *my* friend. I think her mom, Cindy, and I can be friends too."

CHAPTER 27

The house was empty when Liz returned from Brother Paul's place around noon on Saturday, three days short of a full month. No one expected her. She hadn't intended to surprise or deceive anyone, she'd simply needed to return home to silence, and her best chance of doing so was to return on a day when Richard and Jackson were at the store and Rose didn't come. In truth, Liz had been reluctant to shortchange herself three days, but as she considered her options, a return to a quiet house won out over the extra time. Her biggest hurdle was the care of Master. What to do with the dog? Kenneling him was not an option; he was too old to learn new ways. Instead, she made a trip to Brother Paul's neighbors who usually kept an eye on things while he was away. They were familiar with Master, he was content with them, and they were pleased to be responsible for his care until the dog's owner returned home.

Arriving home, Liz unloaded the car, piling her bags and crates in the laundry room temporarily, and gave herself a welcome-back tour of home. She moved from one empty room to another, touching the surface of the big trestle table in the kitchen, adjusting a window blind to allow more light to flood the bedroom, shifting the soap bottle from the right side of the sink to the left in Richard's and her bathroom. Home is such a simple word, but so full of meaning as to bring multiple sensations to one just by its utterance.

Liz returned downstairs and drifted into the seldom-used living room, a space dominated by Miss Em's painting. She sat on the floor in front of the easel to look at it. Sitting there, she recognized that for the first time ever she fully identified with the child in the painting. The child of *before*. Before her parents drifted apart. Before her daddy retreated to his nightly rituals of drinking. Before her impulsive, life-changing behavior. Before she withdrew into herself.

Not that much different from your father, the voice in her head said. Miss Em! Would the dear woman ever leave her alone? Followed immediately by the thought, *I hope not*. She spoke aloud to the empty room, "I really do forgive you, Daddy. And I forgive myself. I'm going to live the rest of my life the same way this little Before Girl lived hers. That's a promise."

The phone rang, and from long habit, she stood to go answer it, then stopped herself. A ringing phone no longer determined her behavior. She heard the answering machine's directive to "please leave a message," then silence. Not so important after all, the caller had apparently decided.

She spent the rest of the day returning her belongings to their proper places. When she had put everything away except the crate containing the books and writing materials, she headed down the hallway to the part of the house where Miss Em had lived. Miss Liberty, true to her independent nature, was curled up on the foot of the sleigh bed that had been so recently occupied by Miss Em. The cat continued her morning nap, undisturbed by Liz's return home. Liz stepped into the small room across the hall from Miss Em's room, now emptied of various paraphernalia related to her deceased friend's care. Only a desk, a small TV, and a couple of chairs remained. She looked around the room, plans for her own private space unfolding in her mind. Bookshelves here, file cabinet there, Miss Em's recently moved desk suitable for a desktop computer. She'd remove the chairs and replace them with the chair that had been in Miss Em's bedroom at her old house. She retrieved the crate with her books and writing materials and plopped it down in the middle of the floor of her reclaimed space. "The perfect room for a college freshman to study and write," she announced to the silence.

Like Jackson, she had limited herself to a few class hours. Unlike Jackson, she'd enrolled at the University of Mississippi. It took her until the third week of her retreat to visit the campus and take care of her final enrollment as a student. She had no idea whether she wanted to pursue a degree or simply dabble in classes that suited her. "To be determined," she said now, just as she'd told her adviser.

***

Liz knew it wouldn't take long for the Manley household to fall back into its old routine, but she was determined to delay said routine as long as she could. She didn't go to church on Sunday and gave direct orders to Richard and Jackson: "Don't breathe to a soul that I'm at home. Not even Luann, especially not Luann!"

She loved her sister and had come to lean on her in the past year, in fact. But Luann was like Lainie in many ways. She always had something going and was invariably trying to pull her sister into her projects. She'd driven down to spend a Saturday with Liz at Brother Paul's house. Liz had counted on a day of conversation, of sharing the quiet space with her sister, maybe even an hour or so on the banks of the pond. Instead, Luann had begun immediately voicing her own plans for the day. "We're in antique country here," she said. "I know two perfect places that are just brimming with finds and there's this other place I've been dying to check out."

They spent the entire day rummaging through flea markets and antique stores. At the end of the day, Luann was thrilled with her purchases: an antique rocker—doesn't need a thing except a little cleaning and an old faded soft pillow to complete it—and a small chest that looked beyond repair. Like their parents, Luann found great excitement in bringing old pieces of furniture back to life.

"Did you buy anything, Liz?" she asked as they finished the day at a favorite tea room in Oxford. "Oh, yeah! You found that blue crockery piece—that pitcher. Perfect," she said in reply to her own question.

On the other hand, Lainie and her mom, Cindy, had stopped by on Sunday afternoon as they returned from Winona, the little town to the south where they met Lainie's dad to make the exchange before and after her visits with him. Cindy had called early on Sunday morning to see if Liz was still open to a short visit, an idea discussed the Saturday afternoon before Liz left. She was pleased that Cindy had remembered, pleased at the prospect of sharing this space with the woman she barely knew but with whom she already sensed a bond.

"You have a gift for providing decks with a view," her new friend had complimented as they relaxed after an early supper of tuna sandwiches, —*keeps Master away from the table*, Liz quoted Brother Paul—fresh fruit and iced tea. Lainie, never one for sitting for long periods of time and tired from spending a large portion of her afternoon on the highway, headed towards the little pond, fishing pole and a small can of worms she'd dug herself in hand.

Liz was looking forward to the conversation with Cindy and was secretly delighted at the girl's choice. "Lainie reminds me so much of my sister," Liz began. "Luann was here yesterday and we were on the go from the time she arrived till the time she left. She exhausts me with her chatter and activity. We are complete opposites. I don't understand how this whole gene thing works."

"Nor do I," Cindy replied. "I think Lainie got her 'active' gene from her dad. The girl never stops till she falls into bed at night. And then she sleeps like a log. Doesn't move. Next morning, she pops out of bed at the first glimmer of sunlight to do it all over again. She's been like this from the time she was a year or so old. She gave up the two-naps-a-day routine, narrowed it down to one two-hour nap right in the middle of the day. The great thing was she was asleep by 7:00 in the evening. Such an easy baby. Once we had her though, things changed in my marriage. I realized all I wanted was a family and a home. I wanted more children, but as time went on, I was glad I'd only brought Lainie into the world. Looking back, I see that my marriage to Jonathan was doomed from the beginning.

"Don't get me wrong," she said with a wave of her hand. "I'm not blaming Jonathan for the failure of our marriage. He needed more from a wife than a stay-at-home mom. Funny thing, after the divorce, I gave up my position as a stay-at-home anything. But I think the trade-off has worked. Bringing myself and Lainie to Roslyn has been so good for both of us."

Liz was amazed at the flood of words that came from Cindy, wondering if perhaps it was the pine trees themselves that gave a person the ease with which to think and talk honestly. Being closed in by the trees felt somewhat like being surrounded by a cocoon. Relaxed by the feeling of safety, she thought briefly of sharing with Cindy the struggle she'd had with early motherhood but decided that now wasn't the time. This was Cindy's turn to open up and her chance to listen.

The women talked non-stop until Cindy suddenly jumped from her chair. "My goodness," she exclaimed. "It's almost dark. Where is that girl?" she asked. As if by magic, Lainie appeared in the opening,

"Where's your catch, young lady? I was counting on those fish you caught for lunch tomorrow," Liz called.

"Catch and release," the girl yelled back. "I can't bear to put those poor little guys on a string."

"That's my girl," smiled Cindy as Lainie disappeared again into the small shed where outdoor equipment was stored.

Liz sat on her own deck now, warmed by the early morning July sun, and thought of the conversation with Cindy. She's my first real girlfriend ever, she realized. *I'm 36 years old and I've never had an honest-to-goodness female friend in my entire life.* There had been playmates, school friends, and neighborhood children with whom she'd played, but never a real honest-to-goodness-share-anything-with friend her own age. Rose, yes, but Rose was more like a mother, a mother who knew her inside and out. How easy this is, she thought. Natural. Nothing forced, but a simple matter of opening up, sharing, and listening.

She had listened as Cindy talked about life with Lainie, how she had to constantly find a balance between releasing her and keeping her safe. She talked of the friendship Lainie had forged with Miss Millie, bicycling to the Manley home at times when she knew she would find the old woman alone; how the friendship had taught her daughter so much, and how Lainie had begun to question her about her own faith. "Do you believe in God?" Lainie had asked her mother after a particularly in-depth conversation with Miss Em about such matters. Cindy told Liz how Lainie had struggled with the decision to befriend Grace Carlson, how she'd learned from town gossip—and from the old bat herself—how Grace had maligned Miss Millie for years. She talked about her daughter's friendship with the Parkers next door and how that had helped her to make her choice.

She'd finished with, "I really don't know what makes the child tick, but I like hearing her tick, watching her tick. I'm not embarrassed to say that my daughter is the most amazing person I've ever known."

It was after this that Cindy talked of their approaching trip to New York City. "From the time I first mentioned it, she asked if she could go with me. She wouldn't let up, even convinced her dad to buy her plane ticket, without my knowledge I might add. How could I say no?" Cindy had expressed her concern about the times when she'd be involved in conference workshops and Lainie would have free time, legitimate concerns about an almost 18-year-old on her own in a city the size of New York. She trusted her daughter, but not other people so much.

But, once again, Lainie was taking things into her own hands, investigating via the internet the safest places to stay, the best ways to get around, and workshops from the conference she could be included in. Mother and daughter had agreed that they would each have an itinerary—put together by Lainie—of exactly where each would be at any given time. "She's on the brink of adulthood, responsible and mature beyond her years. I've done my best with her and this is a test for both of us. A real test of letting go. Maybe more for me than for her because I don't know what I'll do when she's gone."

Liz interrupted her reverie to walk around to the garage. She found her outdoor broom and returned to the deck, where she swept vigorously, thinking all the while. *We can learn from each other, Cindy and I.* As she swept, another thought came to her: *We haven't talked about the book she gave me at all.* Propping the broom against the railing, Liz went inside and picked up the phone. "Cindy," she greeted the other woman. "Yeah, I came back a couple of days early. Wanted to have some time alone at home before the entire town of Roslyn knew I was back. Don't tell Lainie," she laughed, realizing there was no need to voice the suggestion. She continued, "Let's have dinner together some evening this week. Your convenience. We haven't talked about the book you gave me. There's so much in it to talk over with a friend who's read it, too."

***

Rose repositioned the calendar she'd just returned to its hook above the kitchen phone. "Ain't no place in Mississippi looks that colorful," she commented as she stepped back to observe the brightly colored meadow that announced August in some other part of the world. "They sure are getting more rain in that place than we do here. Daddy's garden looks like somebody set a torch to it, 'cept for his corn and them fall string beans he planted. He's out there every morning dragging that hosiery from one place to another."

Hosiery. Liz briefly entertained a mental picture of the old man stringing pantyhose from one cornstalk to another. "Don't you mean *hose*, Rose?" she corrected. Each of them refused to give in to the other in their ongoing game. Liz sometimes suspected that Rose misspoke intentionally, checking to see if she would take the bait or not. Invariably, Liz did.

"I say what I mean and I mean what I say, Lizbet," Rose said, reclaiming the conversation. "My daddy's garden 'bout burned up. May be a good thing. He's gettin' too far up in years to spend time out in the hot sun like this. And I'm gettin' there, too. I got no time to be cannin' and freezin' and puttin' up for winter. Especially since we got a perfectly good grocery store in town that transports fresh vegetables and fruits from all over the country for any time of the year."

"There's an attitude that's been a long time coming. I never thought I'd hear you say such a thing, Rose. Aren't you the lady who harvests the last turnip, who picks the green tomatoes and stores them in newspapers before the first frost? You're going to switch over just like that to trucked-in produce?"

"A body just has so much time in the day," Rose said. "Runnin' Latisha to this lesson and that, checkin' on my property ..."

"Ah, I get it. You're switching from canning to real estate," Liz teased the woman. "Really, now Rose, since you have your house rented, I don't see that it will occupy much of your time."

"Now there's a difference 'tween you and me. Some of us just take the day as it come to us and don't go around pushin', plottin', and plannin' every minute of our time. Some of us just let things happen as they happen."

"Give me time, Rose. I'm a slow learner. But really, your rented house is none of my business. Still, I just can't help but worry about how it's going to turn out."

Rose ignored Liz for some moments before saying, "That's a impermanent arrangement," enunciating each word carefully.

The clipped words sounded strange coming from Rose, causing Liz to momentarily question whether *impermanent* was really a word. She suspected her friend was directly quoting the couple from the North who had temporarily rented the home Rose had inherited from Miss Em.

The house, she knew, was both a blessing and a burden to Rose, as was her own new obligation as administrator of Miss Em's legacy. She had enough to concentrate on without taking on Rose's obligation. She poured herself another cup of coffee, picked up her day planner and cell phone and left Rose to whatever tasks she'd assigned to herself for the day.

Liz sat at her desk in her newly claimed office. She'd changed nothing so far, but still she thought of it as hers. The crate she'd placed in the middle of the floor remained in the same spot. Perhaps she'd have time to shop this afternoon for bookshelves. She located Luann's number in her phone and waited for her sister to pick up.

"What's up, Liz?" her sister greeted. Then, "Hold on." Liz listened as her sister instructed the girls. "Go on without me. Maddie, you can move for me."

She returned to the conversation with Liz. "We have a hot game of Sorry going on here. Thanks for the rescue. What do you need?"

Liz told her about her project. "Shoot yeah. I can go with you. Do you think the girls can hang out at your house with Rose? I'll lay down the law and supply the table games. How about 1:00? We can spend a few minutes looking the room situation over, talk about paint color and other decorating necessities. You probably need a rug on the floor. Does that room have a ...?"

"Take it easy, Martha," Liz interrupted. "We're looking for bookcases, not an entire remodel."

Luann hated being compared to Martha Stewart, claiming "She does those things just to show off to the world. I do them because I love it."

Liz disconnected and turned to her day planner. The big thing looming on her calendar was the trip to Chicago. She was terrified about the upcoming exhibition of Miss Em's work at the Art Institute, the opening of which was set for late September. While she had no distinct duties connected with the showing, she was expected to be there for opening night, associating with people connected to the art world. People, she feared, who were very different from her. On the one hand, she didn't get Rose's concern about caring for her property in Roslyn; on the other she understood perfectly. The two responsibilities—hers to Miss Em's art and Rose's to the house—were equally daunting to the two women. Her empathy for Rose helped somehow as she faced her newest task. If she can do it, so can I, she comforted herself, scrolling down her address book and touching the number to connect her with Donald Jamerson. He and his wife, along with Luann, would hold her hand through the entire affair.

How different her world had become, she mused, after completing her conversation with the Memphis attorney. She entertained a mental picture of Grace Carlson. *Hobnobbing with the rich and famous, are you, young lady. Think you're* ... Liz interrupted her own thoughts. I have to stop that, she corrected herself. I will begin thinking kinder thoughts about Grace. If only for Lainie's sake, I can change that bad habit. I've given Grace way too much control over my thoughts, she concluded.

One more phone call to make. She glanced at the time on her cell. 10:30. Was this a good time to call Cindy at the nursing home? It wasn't necessary, but since she was organizing her calendar for September it seemed a good idea to go ahead and take care of this now. Only three more weeks till orientation began at Ole Miss, and once that happened, she would barely have time to breathe.

"Hi Cindy," she responded to the other woman's greeting. "Is this a good time? I won't keep you but a minute, but I'm in the middle of looking ahead to September, a busy month for me with school and all, and I wanted to run something by you."

"You probably know that Jackson and Lainie are already making plans for your departure to New York next month. Their plan is for him to drive the two of you to Memphis on the Saturday you're set to leave."

Liz laughed at her friend's reply. "It's hard to tell which of them comes up with these ideas. Doesn't matter. We can exercise our prerogative as mothers to tweak their little schemes. That's what I wanted to ask you about. Jackson can find his way around most places, but he's never driven to the Memphis airport. I know I sound like a hovering mother, but it's not just that. I'd really enjoy going along for the ride. You and I could sit in the back seat and visit. Do you mind if I come along?" Even as she had the conversation, Liz was examining her motives. No, Jackson hadn't ever navigated the

Memphis airport. Was he capable of doing so? Absolutely. Liz admitted to herself as she spoke the words to Cindy that her real motive in tagging along was to spend time with her new friend. She looked forward to knowing her better and this was a perfect opportunity.

It was decided. Their flight departed on Saturday, September 8, at 2:00 in the afternoon. Cindy wanted to have Sunday to sightsee and acclimate to New York City with Lainie before her conference began on Monday morning. Jackson and Liz would drive them up Saturday morning, have lunch with them, then see them off at the airport.

CHAPTER 28

With the exception of a hamper perpetually filled with Jackson's dirty clothes and Rose's constant complaint— "Git these nasty books off my island; no tellin' what kind of germs crawlin' around in these pages!"—one wouldn't realize that the youngest member of the Manley household lived there any longer. Among classes, work, and time spent with Lainie and friends, Jackson was never at home. He ate on the run either at the deli, the student union, or at a fast-food restaurant. While she wondered how he found the time to study, Liz had determined to leave him alone. She knew he would hear her questions as subtle nagging, as indeed they would be, so she kept them to herself. Besides, it was all she could do to keep up with the two classes in which she was enrolled. The trips to and from the university alone took a huge chunk out of her day and she spent several hours on campus after her classes to acclimate to the library, hours in which she completely lost track of time.

Liz was pleased on a late Wednesday afternoon shortly after classes had begun when Jackson stopped by to change clothes before heading to youth group and an evening with friends. Intentionally she approached him as she would a friend, or perhaps her sister with an invitation, "Got time to sit for a few minutes to compare notes on our classes? Who'd have guessed that we'd be college freshmen together? Maybe you can give me a few pointers on college lingo. Keep them from thinking I'm an old fuddy-duddy."

Jackson patted her on the head. "That's one you won't be sayin', Ma, *fuddy-duddy*. Be sure not to say *fuddy-duddy*, that is just sooo not tight. But still, Ma, you da bomb and chillin' wid you is just what I want to do. So ... waasssuup?"

"On second thought, maybe not. Not sure those pointers will benefit me," Liz reconsidered. "I'll probably say just as little as possible and maybe get by with that."

"Aiight, Mom. Good plan," Jackson ruffled his mom's hair with one hand and opened the refrigerator door with the other. "Hey man, anything good to eat in here?"

Still her boy in so many ways. But there was so much she didn't know about her son. Listening to the constant youthful chatter on campus was a reminder to her of the gap, not so much in years as in experience and interests, that separated her from the teenagers she now interacted with. And her son was one of them, the only difference being location of campus. She'd heard enough of the slang thrown around on campus to realize that Jackson was editing, giving her the cleaned-up version of lingo that he was exposed to daily. She could only hope and pray that they had done their job well. From all she saw, which wasn't much these days, they had.

"Nah, it's simple stuff. Like we did in senior English," he responded to her question about Freshman English.

"It's been a long time since I had Senior English," Liz said. "We do lots of writing in my class. I don't remember doing that when I was in high school."

"Things changed, then, 'cause we did," he replied. "Lain and I traded off. I helped her with math and science and she helped me with the writing stuff. She's good," he finished, "like you."

"How do you know whether I'm good or not?" she asked.

"Don't really, but if you like it, you must be good. People don't usually like what they're not good at."

Simple commonsense. *Richard sense.* Her boy was so much like his dad.

"I miss seeing Lainie, since your schedule has changed," Liz said. "How's her year going?"

"Only been in school a couple of weeks, but you know her. She always has a good time. Good thing she got chemistry behind her last year. With me helpin' she pulled an A. Don't think I'd have the time to help her this year like I did last."

"What about next year?" Liz asked, and immediately realized that this question crossed the line. "I mean, do you think she can handle the science part of her nursing classes?"

Jackson's pause before answering told her that he'd noticed the lapse, that the "what-about-next-year question" could be just as easily interpreted as "where's-your-relationship-going." But as his mother had done, he diverted that discussion with, "She's got it now. She won't have any trouble in college."

With that simple reply he changed the subject. "Hey, Ma, glad you're going up to Memphis with us next Saturday. Tight!" He grinned at her. "Get it?" he asked. "Tight. You *could* use that word instead of *cool*. But only occasionally and in the right crowd."

"Won't even try. To me *tight* will always mean *best friend*, as in 'we're really tight' or on the negative side, *slightly intoxicated.* Don't see how you get *cool* out of that. Speaking of tight, how's the Lainie/Grace Carlson friendship coming along?"

Jackson pushed his chair from the table and stood, draining the last drop of milk from his glass before rinsing it and leaving it in the kitchen sink. He turned to his mom, ran his hand through his hair, much longer than Liz's now, and grinned broadly. "Strange," he said, then broke into laughter. "I think Lainie must have some kind of magic in her. Would you believe she's got the entire youth group organized to clean up around that woman's house and then paint it for her? Her 'long-range plan'—that's what she calls it—is to convince Miss Gracie to sell her house and move into the assisted living part of the nursing home. She's talked her daddy into coming up here from Jackson and helping Miss Gracie 'get her affairs in order.' In case you're wondering, those are Lainie's words too, not mine."

***

Lainie's words. Friends and family counted the days, days that stretched to a week. The count continued. The entire town of Roslyn held its collective breath waiting for word about Lainie. Enough facts were given to know that she was among the missing. Still, they waited, knowing that the only words they would ever have from her again would be those they remembered or those she'd valued enough to put on paper.

As quickly as she could book a flight to New York City Liz went to be with Cindy. She arrived on Wednesday, September 19, around noon. Lainie's body still had not been recovered.

Cindy met her in the lobby of the hotel. They hugged briefly and except for minimal details—*Jonathan, Lainie's dad, arrived last night and was able to book a room here, too; you'll stay with me, but we need to check you in*—they exchanged few words. It became apparent to Liz that Cindy was in shock. White-faced, with robot-like movements, she took care of details, even insisting that they have lunch. "You must be famished," she declared, ever the nurse. "Let's get you something to eat."

They located a deli near the hotel, just off Times Square. Once seated, Cindy seemed to have forgotten why they were there, so Liz ordered cups of soup and an iced tea for each of them.

"I shouldn't have let her go," Cindy began, then stopped, her eyes skipping from one brightly colored painting on the walls to the next. The colors seemed almost obscene in light of the events of the past few days.

Liz struggled for words. "You couldn't know," she said. From phone calls with Jonathan, Liz had pieced together the events that had placed Lainie in harm's way on the day of the attacks on the World Trade Center. After a good night's sleep on Saturday night, Lainie and Cindy cashed in their prepaid vouchers on Sunday for their 72-hour pass on Grayline's tour buses. Lainie had done all the research from home and, with her mother's permission, had purchased tickets, with upgrades which included night tours as well, for their first three days in NYC. On Monday, after Cindy had completed her conference obligations, they resumed their touring and continued into the evening. After much coaxing, Cindy reluctantly agreed to allow Lainie to go alone on Tuesday morning.

"She had the bus tour thing down to perfection, much better than I. Besides, she had her cell phone and I thought that would be enough. How could I be so naïve?" Cindy lamented.

An unsmiling middle-aged man sporting tattoos and an earring in each ear placed a bowl of steaming chowder in front of each of them. Neither woman made a move to eat, and Liz sensed that Cindy's story could only be told on her own terms. Questions and prodding were not appropriate with such monumental grief. She sat quietly and sipped her tea.

"We were on the upper deck on Monday night, and she couldn't get the right angle of the Twin Towers. I think that's what gave her the idea of returning on her own. She said then, 'Could I come back tomorrow, Mom, while you're at the conference?' There wasn't anything she was interested in at the conference till late Tuesday afternoon, so she'd decided to do as much sightseeing as possible during that time. That's why we had the tickets for the first three days. We were going to see an evening performance of *Lion King* on Wednesday before flying out Thursday morning."

Cindy unfolded her napkin, placed it in her lap, and picked up her spoon. She stirred the soup before removing the spoon and placing it on her plate. She sighed deeply and looked at Liz.

"I'm not making any sense," she said. "I can't seem to keep my train of thought. I want to get up and walk out of here, but I have no idea where I'd go or what I'd do. I've called the numbers they have set up for people like me ..." She paused here and shook her head. "People like me," she repeated. "What on earth does that mean?"

"Anyway," she continued, "I've called the numbers so many times and they are very patient with me, but they have nothing to tell me."

"I thought she'd forgotten," Cindy said and for a moment Liz didn't recognize that she was still talking about Lainie. Cindy offered a small, sad smile.

"She never gives up," she said. "She started in on me Monday night at dinner. Had her plans all made. 'I can take a taxi down early tomorrow,' she said. 'Then I can catch the tour bus back from the Trade Center and ride all the way back to Times Square, just in time to meet you for lunch and go to the afternoon session of the conference.'"

"When Lainie hatched a plan, it always seemed to make sense," she finished.

Liz recognized the past tense—hatched, seemed—juxtaposed against the earlier *never-gives-up* and felt the torment that her friend was experiencing, the agonizing fear of the unknown: will they find her, and in what condition will they find her?

"I shouldn't have listened to her. I shouldn't have let her go," she said again.

Liz thought of a conversation she'd had months ago with Miss Em about letting Jackson go. Different contexts of letting go, to be sure, but letting go just the same. She remembered what Miss Em had said about her own son, Rudy, and his choice to go away to college. Miss Em had said something to the effect that he might be with her still had he made different choices, but the wise old woman left Liz with the clear impression that she would have done nothing to influence his choice, even knowing that she would lose him at a young age. Not the same, but still.

"We can never know the outcome of a single choice, Cindy. We can make the choice to live freely, and that's what Lainie always did. She's a free, fearless girl, and nothing will ever change that. Even a tragedy like this. We'll get through this together, whatever *this* is. We have to, for Lainie's sake. It's what she would want."

***

This turned out to be an early Monday morning call requesting that Lainie's parents visit a makeshift morgue. When her body was found in the rubble of the collapsed North Tower, her cell phone was clutched in her right hand, her hot pink backpack still draped over her back. She was one of only two 18-year-old victims of the 9/11 World Trade Center attack.

As Lainie would have instructed, Cindy, Jonathan, and Liz returned to Roslyn to plan a Celebration of Life for her.

281

Two weeks after the attack, school was canceled so that the entire town could pack into the gymnasium to honor the girl who'd influenced so many, young and old. They filled the gym, standing room only, ignoring the discomfort of sweaty bodies in the September heat and fire code warnings posted around the building.

Charles Collison, the Baptist minister, began with a prayer, asking for comfort for all victims of the tragedy and giving thanks for the privilege of knowing someone with a zest for life like Lainie. He followed the prayer by reading from the third chapter of Ecclesiastes, ending with verse 14: *"I know that whatever God does endures forever; nothing can be added to it, nor anything taken from it; God has done this so that all should stand in awe of Him."*

As was his custom after reading from the Bible, Brother Collison paused. In the brief time his pause took, Liz felt her pulse quicken, and a firm "No!" resound in her brain. The sound was so clear to her that for a second, she wondered if she'd shouted it aloud and looked around to see if anyone had reacted. *He can't tell us that God did this to Lainie, that God caused the horrible deaths of all those innocent people.* Busy as she was with her own thoughts, she almost missed Brother Collison's tribute as he talked of Lainie's gift of bringing out the best in all she knew, of her love of dancing and music, and her way of rallying people around her to accomplish a task. "We can all stand in awe of God today," he told the mourners, "because anyone who knew Lainie had a perfect opportunity to see God at work. *'Nothing can be added to her, nor anything taken from her,'* he paraphrased the Scripture. We all have our memories of her and can best honor her by sharing them with each other. He continued by quoting William Blake, " *'... he who kisses the joy as it flies lives in Eternity's sunrise.'* She taught all who would learn how to *kiss the joy as it flies*," he said.

Brother Collison ended with a quote from C. S. Lewis and an admonition to heed the wise writer's words: *" '... when pain is to be born, a little courage helps more than much knowledge, a little human sympathy more than much courage, and the least tincture of the love of God more than all.'"*

After a brief silence, the opening bars of Beethoven's "Ode to Joy" were recognized by many in the audience. As they watched, wondering what was about to happen, two young dancers dressed in leotards and flowing, gauzy, rainbow-hued skirts appeared from behind walls of flowers. Maria and Maddie twirled and skipped across the makeshift stage, a tribute to the beautiful teenager with whom they had spent so much time. As the song crescendoed to the end, the girls stepped to either side of the stage and directed the attention of viewers to center stage. All watched in awed silence as a cloud of monarch butterflies swarmed from behind the wall of flowers. Some perched on the multi-colored flowers, many floated towards the ceiling, while others drifted to the open windows. One settled among the huge arrangement of wildflowers that rested on Lainie's silvery-blue casket. The music ended, and after what seemed like minutes of silence, those in attendance began murmuring, their sounds and words of awe filling the gymnasium. *Breathtaking, amazing, aaahhhh* voiced the reaction of some, while others sat in silence, tears streaming down their faces at the sheer beauty.

Everyone waited as Latisha slipped from her position behind a small screen, her task as butterfly-releaser complete. Beaming, she made her way to the second row and sat beside her grandmother.

Two large projection screens had been suspended from the ceiling of the gymnasium, and a photo of a smiling Lainie, taken only weeks before her death, appeared on the screen. The mourners sat briefly in silence before the video, accompanied by a recording of "I Hope You Dance" by Lee Ann Womack. Jonathan and Cindy had spent hours going through albums to put together this final tribute to the daughter they'd loved for too few years. The words of the song and the smiles of the girl from birth to the end of her life encouraged all to do just what she had done her entire life: dance. The video ended as it had begun, with a close-up of Lainie's smiling face. Liz listened to her own voice read her tribute to the girl whom she had once thought of as her nemesis. She'd recorded it days earlier because she knew her limitations. She could never stand before the crowd of people paying tribute to Lainie and utter a word without breaking down. Tears flowed down her cheeks as she listened to her own words:

Hostile to her charms

I resisted.

She waited—

Not passively.

Armed with a smile

And a kind word

She took captives elsewhere

Each conquest thriving under her spell;

Until the day

Transported by her two-wheeled chariot,

She broke into my world of grief

By pouring out her own.

No locked-up cages, no sealed-off rooms

No grudges to carry like heavy stones;

Only love, life, dancing.

Always—

Dancing.

***

The time-honored Southern custom of lining up behind a hearse and driving slowly in a procession complete with police escort was one Cindy insisted on ignoring. "This is private," she said. "Placing my daughter in the ground ..." Cindy couldn't complete the sentence, but her point was taken.

She'd also insisted that her daughter be buried in Roslyn. Jonathan pushed back, arguing that there was no family here, that their families, *both* their families, lived near Meridian. "They even have cemetery plots for us," he offered as he made his final push.

Cindy maintained that Roslyn was the girl's home, that she herself had made it such, and that since she—Cindy—intended to stay here permanently, her daughter would stay here as well. Reluctantly, Jonathan and those family members who were supporting his argument gave in.

The huge crowd attending the celebration of Lainie's life was given simple words of dismissal. "Private interment will be at a later time," Brother Collison announced, "with only family and close friends in attendance." The "later time" was at dusk on the same evening. Liz was surprised to see Grace Carlson in the group of fifty or so mourners and was about to comment to Luann, "Who invited her? Bet she just invited herself," but stopped herself from saying the unkind words just in time. She knew, deep down, that Lainie would have wanted the old woman here, that, in her own way, Grace Carlson was just as important to the girl as anyone else. In that moment, Liz recognized something else: She'd never have a warm, fuzzy feeling for Grace; they'd never be friends. In spite of that, she determined again to stop entertaining negative, malicious thoughts about her.

The simple service was short, just a few words committing Lainie to God and ending with a prayer, "... in the name of the Father, the Son, and the Holy Spirit. Amen." Even so, crickets were beginning to chirp, and birds were singing their final goodnight songs as each mourner added a single wildflower to the already brimming bouquet on top of Lainie's casket as a final goodbye.

Liz and Richard held on to Jackson's arms, one on each side of him, as he stood—eyes closed, jaw clenched to hold back the tears—clutching a daisy he couldn't seem to release. Richard bent, then Liz, and placed their flowers on the bouquet. After a moment, Jackson did the same, but not before holding it briefly to his lips as he allowed the tears to stream down his face.

The small crowd dispersed in silence. As the Manley family walked away from the gravesite, Liz saw two people waiting near their car. In the approaching darkness, she didn't realize it was Mr. and Mrs. Parker until they were within a few feet of them. Mrs. Parker stepped towards Jackson and wrapped her arms around him. Liz was taken aback and inexplicably pleased to see how he readily received her grandmotherly embrace. Momentarily, the thought flitted through her head: *she* is *his grandmother.*

Mr. Parker placed his hand on Jackson's shoulder and said, "Don't forget about us, son. You won't have a reason ..." His voice broke, and he took a moment to compose himself before beginning again. "You won't be coming our way as often as you have, but Sarah will still be baking those chocolate chip cookies just as often."

"And we need your expert driving skills on the golf cart," Sarah Parker added.

Her own grief diminished briefly as Liz recognized the loss that this old couple had experienced. Twice. First, their son, Stephen, then Lainie, a girl who was more a granddaughter than a neighbor. Two young people were snatched from them before either had a chance to prove what kind of adults they would become.

She walked around the car to get in the backseat behind Richard. As they opened the doors, they exchanged a look. Brief though it was, there was no doubt about their identical thoughts. It was time to introduce their son to his biological grandparents.

CHAPTER 29

What does one do after such horrific tragedy, such raw, excruciating emotion? Cindy took a week off work, a week she later confided to Liz that she'd have rather spent alone than with her parents. "I couldn't deal with my own grief," she told her new confidante, "How on earth did they think they were any help by being with me, their hearts as broken as mine. But, if I'm honest," she continued, "just the act of taking care of them helped, kept my mind occupied."

Richard, having closed the grocery store on the day of the funeral, returned to work. Jackson and his grandpa headed for Sardis Lake and a day of fishing. Jackson had briefly considered a golf game with the Parkers—he and Lainie had followed through on their commitment to learn the game from the older couple—but couldn't face being with them without her. A fishing trip with his grandpa was a reminder of happier, more carefree days.

Liz didn't remind him that it was a class day for him. It took every ounce of energy to take care of her own business. She and Luann were to fly to Chicago on Thursday for the Friday night opening of Miss Em's exhibition. Thankfully, it was a small affair, organized as a memorial tribute. When Liz got the call late in April from Fred Johnston, head of the team responsible for the management of Miss Em's collection, she immediately called Luann.

"Put this date on your calendar," she ordered her sister. "You have to come along and hold my hand, make sure I don't put my proverbial foot in my mouth."

Luann, of course, was thrilled. "You are paying?" she said, a question in her voice but not in her mind.

Had Liz known—but who could know? —of the devastation the entire nation would face in September, she wouldn't have entertained the idea of mixing with art experts in Chicago. Even as she considered backing out, she heard not one voice, but two—they were double-teaming her, Miss Em and Lainie—speaking clearly in her head: *'You must go on, my dear!'* and *'Don't even think about backing out, Liz!'*

***

The trip turned out to be a good thing for both Liz and Luann. For brief moments, each of them forgot the painful past two weeks. One such moment for Liz was when she and her sister stood in front of the painting of Latisha, on loan to the museum for the duration of the exhibition. To see the beautiful child who ran in and out of their ordinary home on a regular basis in the elegant setting of the Art Institute was surreal. But there was Latisha for all the world to see, lost in her book.

"I wish we could bring her to see it," Liz said as she stood at the rear of a large crowd gathered around Miss Em's final completed work of art.

"So, what's stopping you?" her sister asked.

They looked at each other and nodded. Thanksgiving vacation, they decided, was a perfect opportunity to bring all three kids. They were out of school at noon on Wednesday, allowing them to drive part way, complete the trip on Thanksgiving Day, and be ready to visit the exhibit on Friday. A girl trip.

"Do you think Rose would come?" Lu asked, to which Liz replied, "We'll make her."

Surprisingly, there was no resistance from Rose. On Monday morning, Liz was sitting at the table waiting for her. She'd removed Rose's large calendar from the back of the pantry door, pen in hand and coffee cup nearby.

"Do not turn the television on, Rose. I've had it up to here with so-called news shows constantly regurgitating the same old crap. You can do whatever you like when I'm not here, but I'm not listening to it anymore. I saw it first hand, and that was more than enough for me."

Liz's outburst surprised both of them, and she made an attempt to soften her words. "I'm sorry, Rose ..." she began.

"Nothin' to be sorry 'bout, Lizbet. We all got to get through this in our own way, but we got to be gentle with other people's way of gettin' through it, too." She set her purse on the table, the very act of breaking her own hard and fast rule indicating her distraction. She shrugged out of her light jacket and hung it on the back of a chair before removing her red plastic cup from the cabinet, going to the freezer, counting out eight ice cubes, and pouring her *co'cola* from the Dr. Pepper Can she'd picked up in the garage before she came inside.

Liz sat silently, the only sounds in the room made by Rose's movements and the fizzing soda as it settled in the glass. Rose pulled out a chair and sat across from Liz. They looked across the table at each other, acknowledging in their solemnity the deep grief each of them carried. Liz placed her arms on the table, cradle-fashion, and laid her head there as Rose sipped her drink.

They sat this way for several minutes before Liz sat up and pushed the calendar toward the woman she'd thought incapable of change. She told her of the planned trip.

"Just got to see that my daddy be cared for," was Rose's acknowledgment that she was in.

***

On a Thursday after class early in October, Liz stopped by Brother Paul's house before returning home. She'd discovered a pie shop in Oxford and decided, spur of the moment, to pick up a blueberry pie and drop it off as a surprise. As she stopped in front of the small house, she hesitated. She'd never just dropped in on him and realized, too late, that she probably should have called first. The front door was open as usual, only the screen door separating indoors from out. She called out, "Brother Paul! Master! Are you in there?" only to be met with silence. She opened the screen door and stepped inside the small living area. Still no sign of life inside. She walked into the kitchen, set the pie on the table, and continued to the back door. His car was parked around back, so she knew he couldn't have gone far unless a friend had picked him up. In that case, she considered, he would have at least closed his front door.

She stepped outside and called again, louder this time. Was that a bark? Yes, definitely a bark. She recognized the sound as coming from the faithful old dog. The only path she knew of was the path to the pond, so she followed it into the pine woods, stopped, and called again. Master returned her greeting, and this time she heard Brother Paul yell, "We're over here," from a direction just to the east of the pond. "Wait there," he called, "We'll come and get you."

She waited till she heard panting and the rustle of pine straw underfoot, and then suddenly, the man and his dog were right in front of her.

"Where did you come from?" she asked. "Your voices sounded like they were to my left. Were you at the pond?"

"We were not," her friend said. "I see you didn't discover my secret garden when you were here during the month of July. Follow me, I think it's time to introduce you to my treasure."

Liz followed the two of them, Master taking the lead, down the path that led to the pond for several yards until, one at a time, they disappeared. She stopped, bewildered, until Brother Paul appeared again, laughing. "It's a bit like a maze in here," he said as he took her elbow. "An intentional maze to be discovered by those not faint of heart." He led her around a low-growing stand of pine trees and made an immediate sharp right that opened up to a narrow trail strewn with the ever-present pine straw. Liz was delighted at the secrecy and the anticipation of what might come next.

The dog ran ahead of them now, out of sight for a moment, running back to urge them on. It was as if Master was just as excited to show her the hidden place as she was excited to see it. Liz heard the trickle of water before they stepped into the clearing. The woods were transformed before her eyes into a beautiful garden the size of a small room. The "room" was bordered on three sides by tall pines and on the eastern side by a small stream. Everything was natural: the "floor" was moss, ferns, lichens, small pine seedlings, and other plants that Liz couldn't name but recognized as woodland species. They were strategically placed at intervals in the "room." Even pieces of rotting wood were put to use, packed with humus, and planted with varying shades of green.

"Have a seat, my dear," Brother Paul invited, indicating tree stumps made smooth by human hands, his own, no doubt.

"I haven't finished taking this in," she said, declining his offer. "This is amazing! How did you create this?"

"I created nothing, Liz. God did. I simply took what He generously gave me and arranged it to my, and obviously your, liking. Perhaps, in a sense, I did *create* this, as you said, but only by using what already existed."

"The variety!" she exclaimed. "And the moss underfoot." Liz could only speak in phrases as she took in the beauty of the small space.

"It all began with the moss," he said. "Master and I were tromping around in the woods one day, following the spring—it empties into the pond, you know—when I came across this space completely covered in thick, luxurious moss. Our project started slowly. To create the room-like effect, I needed help in clearing a few trees. The stump you're sitting on is what's left of a large pine, as are the other three *stools*."

"I felt somewhat like the boy in Shel Silverstien's *The Giving Tree* as I watched the sawyers haul out the trunks, but the end result lessened my guilt." He sat on the stump next to Liz, directing her attention to the focal point of the space. Nestled in a corner facing the stream were three crosses, the center one more prominent than the two flanking it. All three had been crafted from pine branches, tied together with vine. The entire area was built up with rocks of varying sizes, shapes, and colors.

Words weren't necessary. The three of them rested, Liz and Brother Paul on their stumps, Master stretched out beneath them, his head resting on Liz's feet. She lost track of time only to be made aware again by a wet tongue licking her feet. She smiled at the dog before turning to her friend.

"Thank you, Brother Paul," she said.

"I have something to ask in return," he said. "Could we drop the 'Brother'?" We're friends now, you know. I'm no longer just your ex-pastor. My friends call me Paul."

Liz considered a moment before answering, "I'll try, but it won't be easy. I think I'm about to find out just how hard it was for Lainie to call me Liz." And, smiling, she told him about Lainie's struggle with calling her Liz, realizing as she talked that there were many Lainie stories to be told in the future.

***

The unspoken agreement that Richard and Liz made with each other following Lainie's graveside service remained unaddressed for weeks. Neither wanted to open the conversation that would lead to a final choice about how to handle the issue that had been between them for their entire marriage. Both would have preferred to ignore the situation, but their integrity demanded otherwise.

It came up quite by accident on a Saturday evening early in November, surprisingly introduced by Jackson. Even more surprising because he mentioned both the Parkers and Lainie in the same sentence. While it was apparent that his thoughts were never far away from the girl, he'd been unable to talk about her with his parents. He'd even avoided his friends, choosing to spend his time at school, in the store, fishing with his Grandpa, and, his newest pastime, going with Mr. Parker to oversee the construction of a small cabin on property the couple owned near the lake.

They were having a rare supper together when Jackson made an even rarer announcement: he was meeting some of the guys later in the evening just to hang out.

As usual, Richard attempted to keep the conversation light. "You got more energy than I have, boy. All I want to do is stretch out in front of the TV. Been a long week."

That simple declaration broke a conversational dam in Jackson, and he began, for some reason known only to him, to talk about Mr.

Parker's building project. "He may be an old man," he volunteered, "maybe in his seventies? But he works as hard as any of the hired men on his construction crew."

The conversation was focused on the cabin for some minutes before Jackson said, again out of the blue, "Lainie called them Gramps and Gram, and she got me started doing the same thing. You don't think Grandma and Grandpa would mind, do you? I think it makes them feel good to be called that. You knew about their son who was killed? He was their only child. And then Lainie ..."

"That's a lot for people to deal with," Richard filled in as Jackson's voice drifted to silence.

"No, son, I don't think your grandparents would mind at all," he addressed Jackson's original question. "Think they'd be proud of you instead."

Liz barely made it out of the room and down the hall to her study, her new haven, before the tears flowed. "It's time," she breathed with the tiny amount of air she could suck into her lungs.

When Liz returned to the kitchen several minutes later, Jackson had left, and Richard was rinsing dishes and stacking them in the dishwasher. He turned off the tap, dried his hands, and took her in his arms. "It's time to do this," he echoed her thoughts. "Let's figure out just how and when."

They agreed to tell Jackson on the Saturday evening before Thanksgiving. Liz suggested, and Richard agreed, that it would be good for him to have some space, sometimes without her around, to absorb the news. He could occupy himself with school and work the first two days of the week of Thanksgiving, the "girls" would leave on their Chicago trip Wednesday at noon, and Richard and Jackson could have the next five days on their own.

Together, they decided that the best way to break the shocking news to the Parkers would be following a meal hosted at the Manley home. Liz would invite them for dinner on the Sunday night following their Saturday night announcement to Jackson, pending, of course, his reaction. Both Richard and Liz thought he would want to include the Parkers in this unsettling news but acknowledged the small chance that he would react negatively.

The act of making the decision gave Liz a small amount of relief. It was really going to happen. She was anxious about the fallout, how Jackson would take it, how the Parkers would react. She'd offered to make enchiladas for dinner, a favorite of Jackson, and had gotten assurance that he'd be home for the evening. As their prepared but uncooked dinner waited in the refrigerator, she sat in the room where Miss Em had lived the last months of her life and practiced her newly acquired habit of writing notes to Miss Em in her journal.

Dear Em, she penned, *I did what you told me. Richard and I made the decision together. I'm scared that Jackson will be angry, maybe will even hate me, but I feel good that Richard and I are doing this together. He's always been my anchor, and I know that even if I lose Jackson, it will be a temporary loss. He can't blame his dad for this, and I know that eventually, Richard will bring him back to me. Besides that, this is the right thing to do, and I think the timing has declared itself. Like you always told me, "To everything, there is a season ..." We'll hope this is a season to embrace. For me, it is; it's a season to embrace whatever comes with a choice that I'm making, along with Richard, with my eyes wide open. Thank you for always being there for me. Liz*

***

The enchiladas were a hit. Jackson downed three, along with chips, salsa and queso. He pushed back his chair, stood, and stretched. "Man. That's the best meal I've had in weeks," he said. "Thanks, Ma! You don't cook very often, but you still got it! Tight!" he grinned.

"How 'bout you get that stretch out and sit back down Jacks," Richard said. "Your mom and I want to talk to you about something."

Without an eye blink or a quiver in his voice, Richard told his son the entire story, starting with the break-up. Liz sat quietly through his telling, feeling stronger with each word that came from her husband's mouth. She kept her eyes on Richard the entire time, mesmerized as though by an old story he was telling that had been told many times, one she'd grown to embrace if not fully love. Jackson listened with the same intensity, having no need to ask questions. His father covered every detail, anticipating in advance any sticking point that might arise and addressing it directly. He finished with, "Since the time your mother told me she was carrying you in her body, I've been your father. I chose you when your mother agreed to marry me. You always have been and always will be my son."

Liz released her breath into the space that was created by the silence. She didn't realize she'd been holding it till the moment she let it go. The three of them sat at the table, enchilada sauce drying on the blue plates. Jackson absently touched crumbs of chips that littered the table around his plate, rubbing his thumb against the captured pieces that clung to his fingertips to drop them onto his plate. "Wow," he finally said. "Wow."

"So that's why you wanted me to stay home tonight. To tell me this. I was afraid you were going to tell me something like you were selling the store or you were getting a divorce.

"What?!" he said to their astonished looks. "Parents keep those things from their kids till the last minute.

"So, do the Parkers know?" he continued after a pause. "They don't, do they? Sure, they don't. Are we going to tell them?" he asked, and then, barely missing a beat, "Oh ... that's why you invited them over tomorrow night."

"Only if you agree. We can cancel supper tomorrow night." Liz spoke for the first time. "Your dad and I agreed to tell you, now we all have to be in agreement before this goes any further. What do you want to do?"

"Ma, they really *are* my gramps and gram. Why shouldn't they know?"

He excused himself from the table. He was halfway downstairs when he returned and poked his head in the kitchen. "Hey, Dad," he said, "you ever think about being a politician or a lawyer? Maybe a salesman?"

"I *am* a salesman, son," his dad answered. "I've sold food to people my entire life."

Liz and Richard had wiped the last countertop and put the cooled leftover dish of enchiladas in the fridge when Jackson reappeared with the announcement that he was going to find the guys and hang with them.

He ruffled Liz's hair and pulled her to him with one hand before kissing the top of her head. "Ma, there's something you've been wrong about for a long time. It's about Lainie and me. We weren't that kind of, you know, couple," he said. He hesitated, stuck both hands in his jeans' pockets, leaned against the kitchen counter, and continued. "We wanted to be, tried to be, but it just never happened.

It was more like she was my little sister, my best friend. She said one time she'd rather I'd give her the last bite of my ice cream cone than a kiss any day. She loved that last little tip of the cone, especially if there was a little melted ice cream in it. She always said the funniest things."

He left his parents then, both of them shiny-eyed with unshed tears.

***

Tears were shed on the following night. Plenty of tears. But when the evening was over, Liz felt as though a boulder had been lifted from her shoulders, Richard felt a pride in his son he'd never known before, and Jackson had an additional set of grandparents—real, not just adopted—and the Parkers made rightful claim to their only grandson.

CHAPTER 30

To everything there is a season ...

On a gloomy Saturday in late February, days after the anniversary of Miss Em's death, Liz, feeling the need for female companionship with someone other than her sister or Rose, called Cindy. The two agreed that it was a good afternoon for a late lunch by the fire. Liz was to stop by the deli and pick up whatever looked good to her and be at Cindy's house by 2:00.

The experience of finding the right degree of support for someone in such deep grief had been a learn-as-you-go journey for Liz. Cindy, a self-declared loner, was a kind and patient teacher. Liz checked with her often by phone, but winter had been especially harsh. Liz had been busy with school, Cindy with work, and so, with the exception of occasional Saturday afternoon stop-bys, the women had spent little time together.

Liz was anticipating a quiet conversational lunch with Cindy as she navigated the grocery store aisles. She heard Miss Gracie's voice before she saw her. In the short space of time it took her to walk the distance to the deli and stand beside the woman, Liz had found the *grace* to treat her with dignity.

"Anna," she greeted the harassed attendant, "what is it that Miss Gracie has ordered? Go ahead and get that ready for her. And how about adding a couple of those oatmeal cookies and a carton of vegetable soup? That'll make a nice supper for her tonight." As she talked, Liz pulled a twenty from her wallet and laid it on the counter. "You keep the change, Anna. That'll make a nice tip for you." She smiled at both of them.

"Flashing some of the Millicent Stich money around, are you?" Miss Gracie snapped. It was as if she could only operate in one mode with Liz: destruction.

"Yes, Miss Gracie," she responded gently, "I am. Miss Millie was so generous with my family and in ways far more valuable than money. I love sharing what she gave to us."

"And now, while Anna fills your order, I'm going over to produce and pick out some nice fruit for you. I know you like grapes and oranges. What about a couple of bananas and a few apples?" she added.

The old woman was dumbfounded, at a complete loss for words.

Liz allowed seconds to pass before she continued, "I'll just pick out what looks good and be back in a few minutes." As soon as she was out of Grace Carlson's sight and hearing, she raised both hands, fists clenched. As she brought them down, she bent over slightly. "Yes!" she said and burst out laughing.

Liz completed her self-assigned project. When she returned to the deli, she took charge of arranging the newly acquired food in Miss Gracie's two-wheeled canvas cart and pulled it to the front door of the grocery store, the speechless old woman following meekly behind her.

As she turned the cart over to the old woman on the sidewalk, Liz said, "I'm so glad to hear your good news, Miss Gracie. You'll love your new home with friends in the next room or just down the hallway. And you'll never have to worry about food again. Every meal will be waiting in the dining hall." Before Miss Gracie could form a response, the door was closing behind Liz as she disappeared into the store.

She returned to the deli and a grateful Anna. "How'd you do that, Liz? And, by the way, thanks for the tip. It's way too much, especially when I don't ever get tips anyway."

"You earned it, Anna. All of us who love Miss Gracie earn our keep with her. And, yes, I said *love*. That's my new mantra where Grace is concerned. A wise woman told me once to look in the mirrors held up by the people who loved me if I wanted to see who I really was. Some of the best advice I ever had. That's what I'm trying to do with Grace. Someone, probably more than one person, taught her too well that she wasn't worth much. She really is, you know; all of us are."

Liz was exhilarated as she pulled into the driveway of Cindy's small home. She knew that the next time she saw Grace Carlson, she'd have a repeat performance, but instead of dread, the thought filled her with anticipation. How many ways could she stop the woman in her tracks? How long before Grace realized she couldn't get to Liz any longer? How long before she would see a change in the bitter old woman? Maybe. But that wasn't what mattered now. Liz knew *she* was changing, and that's what was really important.

Cindy, dressed in an oversized Ole Miss sweatshirt and baggy sweatpants, opened the door for Liz. "Grocery delivery," Liz greeted.

"Have you invited other guests?" Cindy asked, noting that Liz held two full bags in her arms.

"Thought you could use some fresh fruits and veggies," Liz said as she set the bags on the counter. "Besides, I didn't know what you might be in the mood for, and since it's the end of the lunch rush, I brought some cartons of soup and stuff that you can freeze. And it's all guilt-free—for me, that is. I loaded Grace Carlson up, too." Liz told Cindy about the woman's ingrained habit of badgering clerks for free food.

"Lainie used to talk about how that got to you," Cindy said. Liz was surprised to hear her bring up her daughter voluntarily. She'd intentionally told the story about Grace to give her friend the option of taking the conversation in whatever direction she wanted. Apparently, Cindy *wanted* to talk about her daughter.

"Yeah, I'm sorry about the way I used to berate that old woman."

The conversation then centered around warming the food, storing the food, and agreeing on a spot to consume the food. They chose to eat in front of the fire, balancing bowls of steaming soup on trays on their laps. "Delicious," Cindy complimented after her first bite of soup. "You're lucky to have a man who can cook."

"And that's just the beginning of his talents," Liz agreed. "Jackson asked him recently if he'd ever considered being a lawyer or maybe a politician."

"Jackson," Cindy repeated. "A chip off the block. I don't know how I'd have survived these past few months if it hadn't been for Jackson. He, Charles, and Sarah—my neighbors? The Parkers? — have saved my life. You, too, Liz. You've been a Godsend. It's hard to explain, but they've formed a family unit around me, something I couldn't escape from. I had the option of escaping from you temporarily; thank you for that—for understanding my need for space." Cindy stopped and threw her hands in the air as if to say she knew she was making no sense.

"You don't owe me an explanation, Cindy," Liz said, "and strangely, I *do* understand. I could never explain to anyone how my relationship with Miss Em changed me. Some things can't be understood or explained, Cindy; they can only be felt. I'm so glad

Jackson has been a comfort to you. I've wondered and worried about him. He rarely speaks of our tragedy at home, and that's concerned me. Thank you for telling me this."

"It's not been six months, Liz, and I feel so raw, like every nerve in my body is exposed. But I get up every morning and go to work like a robot, and every evening, I come home and wrap myself in Lainie's old sweats." She pulled at the baggy shirt to illustrate. "I haven't changed a thing in her room," she finished.

Liz remembered finding Lainie in Miss Millie's room months ago. She was reminded of the poem she wrote as a tribute to the girl and the beginning of their true relationship. "Things always circle back around," she said to Cindy. "When you're ready, let me help you. But don't rush it. You'll know when it's time.

"Speaking of rooms," Liz intentionally changed the subject. "I have a room I'd like you to see when the weather gets warmer. It's tucked away in the pine woods behind the house where I stayed last summer. It's like a secret garden, but I've come to think of it simply as The Room. I'd like you to meet my friend Paul, too, who owns the property."

"You're not trying to fix me up, are you?" Cindy asked. "That's the last thing I need."

Liz laughed out loud. "Not unless you're interested in connecting with an eighty-year-old man," Liz explained to Cindy who Paul was and how and why she and Luann had reconnected with him after many years.

"He helped restore me to sanity," she told Cindy after she shared with her the story of her parents' troubled marriage and her own loneliness as she grew up. "I'm not sure what I'd call him. Certainly, a friend, maybe something like a spiritual advisor? He is so wise, much like Miss Em, but in a different way. You didn't have the chance to meet her, but I'd like to introduce you to Paul."

"I've always shied away from religion," Cindy told her. "Lainie asked but didn't push. I know she wanted me to go to church with her, but that didn't fit me. One of my biggest regrets is that I didn't fully answer her question when she asked me if I believed in God. I know she wanted to talk to me about religion, and I wouldn't let her."

The women sat in pensive silence, Liz waiting as her friend decided how far to take their conversation.

"I do, you know," she continued. "Believe in God. I'm just not sure He believes in me."

Liz stood and took the tray from her friend's lap. "He does," she said with a smile. "I've only recently realized that for myself. I've gone to church my entire life and been religious—whatever that means—since I was a kid, but it's only been in the past few months that I've known how to receive love. And I've found out that it's true, what they told me in Vacation Bible School all those years ago: God *is* love. I just never knew how to receive it. Miss Em taught me how."

"So, back to this place you call The Room," Cindy said as she followed Liz to the kitchen. "I'm interested. And if part of the bargain is to meet your Paul, I'll accept that part, too."

The two women spent the rest of the afternoon lost in easy conversation, both of them realizing, but not acknowledging to the other, that they'd turned a small corner. The grief was there and would be forever, but there was life to be lived. To deny this and remain locked in that grief would be to dishonor Lainie, a girl who *caught the joy as it flew*.

***

Liz thought of the William Blake poem as she sat in the office of her instructor. She'd signed up for two classes for Spring Semester, both of them three-hour classes requiring her to attend on Monday, Wednesday, and Friday. With special permission from the English department head, she'd chosen two classes on short story; one in which she read and responded to short stories and the other in which she would write her own, the second one a 300-level class. She explained to the department head that she wasn't convinced she wanted to pursue a degree, that she was limited in time, but that she really wanted to write. It helped that her professor from her first semester English class had highly praised her work and put in a good word on her behalf.

"This is somewhat irregular, Mrs. Manley," the department head told her, "But in some cases we do make exceptions. My instincts and the pieces of yours that I've read tell me that you are a talented writer." He'd recommended that she simultaneously broaden her reading as she honed the craft of writing, a plan that appealed to Liz.

After class one day, her short story writing instructor asked her to stop by her office to discuss Liz's recently completed writing assignment, a character study of someone she knew or had known in the past.

"Your subject seems to have possessed the quality the French refer to as *joie de vivre*," she told Liz.

"I'm not familiar with the term," Liz said. "Unfortunately, I'm limited in foreign languages. I took Spanish in high school, but even that's all lost now."

"It's a term that refers to the ability to take life as it comes, to feel and express joy, *joie*, in everything, in every moment."

Liz thought for a moment. "She did have that quality when I really got to know her. But she had great sadness in her life as well."

"I understand the true meaning of the phrase to reflect exactly that," the young instructor continued. "There are some who use a more superficial meaning. You can find people who interpret the phrase in different ways, different depths," she continued. "For example, Maslow and Rogers believed it was a by-product of self-discovery, of knowing one's self."

"That would definitely describe Miss Em," Liz said, "But there was much more to her than that. She knew herself—and other people—well, but it was as if her suffering taught her something that the rest of us didn't know."

"That describes exactly how I think of the term," the professor said. "In fact, my personal writing project is a story about that very thing. I'm writing a piece of fiction told from the point of view of Job's wife. Are you familiar with the story of Job in the Bible?"

At Liz's nod, she continued. "Everyone focuses on Job, but I've never seen much about how his wife rebounded from the tragedies that destroyed her entire way of life. Have you ever thought how difficult it must have been for her to conceive after losing all her children? After losing everything? I can't imagine the courage it took to start over!

"But enough about me and my work. We're here to talk about your character study. You've captured the *joie de vivre* quality extremely well in your piece. I'm encouraging you to pursue this. You mentioned in your explanation the reason for choosing to write about Miss Em. I recall reading that she had lived with you for a time, that she was a well-known artist who'd lived her final years in seclusion. Would that, by any chance, be Millicent LaBelle?"

"It is ... was ... is," said Liz, blushing at her struggle to find the correct verb tense in the presence of her writing teacher. "My family cared for her in the remaining months of her life."

"Fascinating," said the woman. "Have you considered writing about the experience? There are many ways you could approach the story: memoir, biography, or even fiction. It seems to be a story that demands to be told."

Liz agreed. It was a story begging to be told, but for her, a story that would never end.

"Tell me more about yourself," she invited the young instructor, much as Miss Em might have done. "How did you get so interested in writing?"

Liz listened as the young woman shared a little of her own story of suffering and perseverance. Later, as she left her instructor's office feeling that she'd found a new friend, Liz reflected on the conversation, trying to determine the precise moment when she recognized her instructor's pain and made the decision to hold up a mirror for her.

***

Liz's spring semester classes consumed her. Her renewed interest in reading and her new passion for writing kept her busy. Rose, for one, was happy to see her occupied. It suited Rose well to be in charge of running the Manley household without interference from Liz.

"Go on back to that study and find yourself somethin' to do," she'd say when Liz emerged and offered to fold a load of clothes or empty the dishwasher.

Rose's duties had diminished greatly, both at her home and the Manley home. Retha had finally given up his vegetable garden, limiting his puttering in the yard to maintaining the flower gardens that were a memorial to his late wife and a few tomato and pepper plants. Liz had hired someone to care for both Rose's yard and their own. While everyone, including Richard, insisted that it was a ridiculous idea, they had come to appreciate the reduction of time spent on home maintenance.

Liz even entertained the idea of bringing help in to lighten Rose's workload, but only briefly. The woman hooted. "That'll be the day I'm outta here," she warned. "You bring somebody else in here to be in my way, and I'll be gone before the door closes on her behind."

The entire family seemed to have settled into a routine. Liz sat on the deck enjoying the warm May sun. Her classes were finished for the semester, and there was nothing she had to accomplish. She recognized the sound of a car engine out front. Jackson, home from school, his semester ended also. She heard the car door slam, the murmur of voices, his and Rose's, and then silence again. She had dozed briefly and was awakened by the sound of the French doors opening behind her. Jackson sat down in the chair nearest her. It was rare for him to seek her out these days. Not that he avoided her, but both were busy with their lives. They'd not spoken of the weekend in November again. The only detectable difference was an air of maturity that came from her son. He had seemingly become a man overnight, and whether the change was due to the loss of Lainie or to the news of his parentage, Liz gave little thought. She focused on interacting with her son as a young man rather than a teenage boy.

"You awake?" he asked.

"Yeah. The warm sun knocked me out. I haven't had a chance to do this in ... ever?" she finished. Liz raised up from the chaise and turned to face her son. "How did finals go?"

"Good, at least I think good. Got to have C's at least to transfer," he baited her.

"Transfer? You're thinking about transferring?" she asked.

"Not thinkin' about it. I did it," he said. "We're going to be coeds, Ma. On the same campus. What'd'ya think about that?"

"You're going to the university?" Liz asked. "What made you…? Why did you change your mind?"

"I don't know. Just figured that if Dad and I are going to be business partners, one of us needs to have a little book learnin' on the subject. Dad thinks it will make a difference. We've been talkin' about how we can change our focus to keep up with the times. You know, outsmart Walmart. We both figured I'd just as well quit foolin' around with junior college and get on with it."

"Hey, Ma, sorry I bothered you. Stretch out there and finish your nap. I'm headed to the store." He thumped her gently on top of her head and left before she could say a word.

***

"Richard!" Liz held his shoulder and shook him gently. "Richard!" she said again, louder. "Wake up."

"Liz," he moaned. "Not again! What time is it?"

"I don't know…" she turned and looked at the clock behind her. "2:36. Time isn't important, Richard. I want to talk to you about something I've been thinking about the past few months."

"If you've been thinking about it for months, can't it wait at least till morning?" he groaned. "Never mind," he sighed. "I'm awake now. What is it?" He turned to her.

"I think we should have a baby," she said, laying her hand in the space between his neck and his shoulder.

Silence.

"Richard, did you hear me?" she asked.

"I heard something like 'we should have a baby,' but I'm not sure if it's a dream I'm having or maybe somebody turned up the downstairs TV extra loud."

"It's me, Richard, and I'm not joking. I've given this a lot of thought. I'm perfectly healthy, but I'm pushing towards forty, so our time is limited. I've been on the pill way too many years. So, I thought we could get pregnant and then afterward do something permanent to keep it from happening again."

"You mean me do something permanent, or you do something permanent?" he asked.

"We can decide that later after I'm pregnant."

"Whoa, now!" he cautioned. "This is moving way too fast. The *baby* isn't even started, and you're already talking like it's a done deal. Have you thought about Jackson's reaction?"

"I have, and this is what I think about that. Jackson is an adult or almost an adult. He won't be with us in this house forever. This is our decision to make together."

The room was very quiet. Richard rolled over on his back and placed the back of his arm across his forehead. Liz could see in the dim light that his eyes were focused on the ceiling. She waited until he spoke.

"Are you sure, Liz? Do you want to do this again? It was so hard for you with Jackson."

"Shhh." She touched his lips with her finger. "We wouldn't be doing anything 'again,'" she said as she raised herself up on her elbow and bent over him. "We've never done this together, at least not from the very beginning. I want to have *your* baby, Richard. I know Jackson is yours, but ..."

"Stop explaining, Liz. You talk too much. Give me a few days to think about it, but while you're still on the pill, we just as well take advantage of it." He pulled her to him and kissed her with a passion that far surpassed sharing the tip of an ice cream cone.

***

Emily Grace Manley was born on February 11, 2003, days before the second anniversary of the death of Miss Em. Her big brother never let his mother forget that she'd named his sister after her biggest thorn in the flesh, a comment that Liz always responded to with the same comeback: "There's more to grace than Grace Carlson."

Everyone called her Emmie, and as she grew older, her name was shortened simply to *Em*. At times, she seemed bewildered as to who her mother was, who her brothers and sisters were, who *her family* was. She was surrounded by people who loved her. Rose summed it up best, "She's God's child. Nobody gonna ever own this baby."

It took a while for Miss Liberty to adjust to Em's arrival. Truth be told, she never did. Nor did she ever know exactly what precipitated her move across town to Cindy's house. Once she adjusted, she was as happy as ever, maybe even happier. Cindy complained much less than Rose when it came time to clean the litter box.

Liz never once buried herself under the bedcovers. She did, on occasion, hide out in her office or drive down to spend an afternoon in The Room. She savored every minute she spent with her daughter and often thought of how it would have pleased Miss Em to be a part of their changed household.

One sunny morning, Em followed her mother into the living room, stopping in front of the painting of Liz under the large oak tree.

"Who dat?" the child questioned.

"That's me," Liz told her. "That's your mother." She picked the child up so she could see the painting better.

Em giggled. "You *big,* Mommy! Who dat *little* girl?" she asked again.

"It's me, Em, the real me. I just grew up to be bigger. Someday, I'll tell you all about it."

EPILOGUE

G.K. Chesterton once wrote, "If there is a story, there is a storyteller." In the case of the story you just read, it took me considerable time to decide that I was the storyteller. I first began thinking of writing Miss Em's story when I sat in my writing instructor's office that cold February day back in 2002. The problem was exactly as she stated: how did I approach it? I first tried to write Em's biography. I had access to all her information, and this seemed the most straightforward way to tell her story. It seemed flat somehow, lifeless. I attempted fiction, changing locations, changing names, changing vocations; that didn't seem authentic. It occurred to me one day as I sat at my computer, in my made-over-by-Luann office, struggling to put these events on paper in a meaningful way, that the story was mine to tell, and the most authentic way to tell it was by telling the truth as it had happened to me.

I, Elizabeth Manley, wrote the story. Writing the story in the third person gave me the distance I needed to tell it accurately. It's a story that doesn't belong to me alone but to all the people—including Grace Carlson—who live in it. Each of them, given the chance, would tell it differently, would perhaps be kinder to some and less kind to others in their telling of events that actually occurred. I told my truth as I understood it, which is all any of us can do in the end. The story is true, and I apologize to anyone in advance who might be offended by anything I've written.

I chose this little place to write my "confession" because it's here where I completed the journey to that space inside myself, the place where the real me resided. Miss Em helped me start the journey, and Brother Paul (I still think of him by that name) guided me the rest of the way. I bought this place from him a few years ago when he made the decision to move to a California retirement community to be near his niece and nephews. Every time Luann makes a trip to the cottage, I extract a brand-new promise from her that she won't touch a thing here. Paul took a few books and mementos with him but otherwise left it exactly as it was when he lived here. Of all the things he left behind, next to The Room, I've loved his books most of all. C. S. Lewis, Thomas Merton, Thomas A. Kempis, along with more contemporary writers like Thomas Keating and James Finley. My journey continues. We still talk frequently on the phone, and I've flown out to see him once. At ninety, he still finds much to enjoy in life.

We'll return to Roslyn at the end of the week so Em can be there for the first day of fourth grade. She loves this place as much as I do and spends much of her day in The Room, adding to its beauty, reading her favorite book, sketching on one of her many tablets, or just sitting quietly. She has an abundance of my genes, or maybe she just learned from her surroundings. Who will ever figure out the argument of heredity versus environment?

Jackson is a strong case for the environmental side of the argument. Except for appearance—his Parker grandparents see Stephen in him. But everybody else who knows him says he's a dead-ringer for me. As far as his character and interests go, he is his dad's son. They eat, sleep, and breathe grocery store. In a good way. Jackson's three years at the university have paid off; he's a business whiz who found a way, along with his dad, to compete with Walmart. They're opening their fifth Main Street Foods store on the Mississippi coast in September.

They found a way to combine Richard's dream of a restaurant and a thriving grocery business under one roof. They sell top-quality produce, meat, bulk items, and anything a person needs to prepare food at home at competitive prices. The deli is still in operation, and Richard has added frozen entrees to his offerings that are soon to be available in larger chains under the label Main Street Deli. He also has a sit-down restaurant that's open evenings. They keep Luann busy—the gods be thanked for that—designing the restaurant and deli spaces.

My pair of intelligent, entrepreneurial men have also developed a training program for young people who are interested in the grocery and/or restaurant business. They give young people who don't have the desire or finances to go to college a chance to learn management skills that will serve them in many places of business, in addition to the restaurant and grocery businesses. They tell anyone who will listen that the managerial staff in all five stores came straight through the Roslyn store, and each one is prepared to replicate the model they've learned.

You might wonder how a little town of two thousand people can support this. So did Jackson until he understood the principle of knowing your market, your demographics. Roslyn sits just off Interstate 55, an hour away from Memphis, less than that from Sardis Lake, Grenada Lake, and the University of Mississippi. On weekends of home football games at Ole Miss, it's all-hands-on-deck for all three sections of the store. Southerners love their tailgate parties. I think it was Richard who proposed the opening of their second store in Oxford, the store from which Jackson works. It's the top-grossing store of the five.

After 9/11, President Bush encouraged all Americans to "get out there and spend." In Roslyn, we interpreted that to mean "spend on others" or, to put it another way, to *invest* in others. The loss of Lainie, a young woman so filled with hope and life, spurred us to act in ways to fight the apathy that sometimes follows disaster. It's paid off for us in many ways.

Lainie once said that she would revolutionize nursing homes, and with her mother's determination and her Joie de Vivre Memorial Fund, she's making that happen. Cindy built a model program at Roslyn's Assisted Living and Full Care Nursing Home, one that brings people in from all over the United States. Like my boys, she uses the talent we have right here in Roslyn by bringing young people from the high school in for training programs. She has presented the program several years in a row at the National Geriatrics Convention in New York City, always a bittersweet occasion for her. We've contributed some of Miss Em's money to the program and plan to expand it in the near future.

Cindy can tell you the exact number of youths who've used scholarship money from the fund to complete their education in some form of health care related to geriatrics. Her goal from the beginning was to plant in the minds of as many kids as possible the love that Lainie had for old people, to help them see that they still have something to offer even as their bodies—and, in some cases, their minds—are letting them down. Through these kids, she offers them a renewed interest in life with beauty enhancements, games, gardening projects, crafts, music, and, yes, dancing. There's nothing more delightful to watch than a seventeen-year-old Roslyn football player gently leading an eighty-year-old woman in a waltz. I can't help it; tears glide down my cheeks every time I witness this scene. I had to leave the room once during a Friday evening "dance" when the captain of the football team took Miss Gracie in his arms.

We never became friends, but we did reach an uneasy truce. Every time I approached her, I made sure I was armed with a gift of food and a smile. I never really knew her entire story, only the one offered by the grapevine. When she died several years ago, her sons didn't come back for her funeral. Cindy heard from both of them; one lived in Seattle and the other somewhere in the southeast, seemingly as far from each other as they could get and still be in the conterminous United States. They made no claim on her considerable estate—Joe Howard was right about that—a good thing since she had left the entire amount to Lainie's memorial fund. I've often wondered what made her so bitter. It wasn't a lack of money. Miss Gracie's life proved the adage that money doesn't make you happy. Maybe my next story will be about her, a story that will be entirely fiction simply because she wouldn't allow anyone to know the real person locked away behind all that grumpiness. I know there was good in her because Lainie managed to tap into it.

The girls, Maria, Maddie, and Latisha, are Em's heroes. She admires them in the same way they used to look up to Lainie. One of the things I love most about growing older is watching that cycle. All three girls are in college now: Maria at Ole Miss, Maddie at her parents' Alma Mater, Auburn, and Latisha forging new ground at Yale. She will pursue a law degree.

And Rose. What can I say about Rose? She still comes to the house, not to work, but to make sure we're taking care of things properly. Her daddy, Retha, left us when Em was three. She's still in the house her parents built and says she'll only leave it feet first. I've tried to convince her to move to an assisted living apartment, but she has a quick retort to that. Something to the effect of, "Now Liz, why you want me goin' up on that hill with all them old people?" Em supports her in that decision. She loves spending weekends with Rose and tells us that she'd "lots rather go to Rose's church than ours." She tells us that their music is way better than what we have at the First Baptist Church in Roslyn. From what I've experienced in occasional visits and at funerals, I'm inclined to agree.

Rose's son, LaMont, returned to Roslyn several years ago when Retha was in poor health. Rose and Latisha were thrilled beyond words, although Latisha chose to stay with her grandmother rather than move in with LaMont and his wife, Callie. It was the only home she'd ever known, and she couldn't bring herself to leave. LaMont started as Head of Maintenance at the nursing home, but in a couple of years, he had trained his replacement and opened his own business. He's now relocated to Oxford, where he owns a cleaning service that does both residential and commercial cleaning in the entire lakes area. In true Roslyn style, he recruits from the local schools and trains—one might say *clones*—workers who take pride in what they have to offer. His grandpa's blood runs thick in him. His cleaning trucks and vans sport a sign that says ***Walker Cleaning Service – We Clean It Like We Own It.*** He, as did I, thought his grandpa owned the Roslyn school buildings when he was a kid.

Jackson and Lili bought Miss Em's house from Rose, and though they've done several remodels, they've enhanced rather than taken away from the symmetrical design of the house. It's beautiful, inside and out, as is Lili. The university was good for Jackson in many ways, not the least of which was giving him his charming wife. She came to Oxford from Hong Kong, and the first time I saw them together, I knew they were in love. Seeing them together made me realize how narrowly I'd viewed the world before Miss Em turned me around. How could I have mistaken what Lainie and Jackson shared for romantic love? Lili, a philosophy major, loves her home. Living there has turned her into a Miss Em fan. She's currently working on an art book complete with text about the religious art Miss Em painted for Catholic churches all over the country. She and I have visited all of them together over the past couple of years. Her studio is in the front room to the right of the porch, the room with a view of the large oak tree.

I hear my daughter and her dog, Mistress, romping in the backyard. They're alerting me to the fact that my writing time is almost over. Earlier today, as I sat collecting my thoughts, I looked at the tiny mantle flanking the gas fireplace. A memory stirred as my eyes rested on the tall pottery urn on the left side. I walked over, picked it up, and looked inside. Staring up at me was the silver promise ring, dulled again after all those years without human touch. I picked it up and—wiser now—found an old dish towel to rub it back to a bright shine. I'll give it to my daughter when she comes inside. I'll tell her about the time her daddy and I promised to love each other forever. The rest of the story she can read when she's older.

-Elizabeth Manley

Author's Note

The next time you drive down an interstate highway and see a large green sign announcing the name of a town you've never heard of, perhaps you should take the scenic route and drive through said town. Instead of grumbling as you get caught by all three red lights on the main drag, use your time to look around, to think about the people who choose to live in Podunk, USA, rather than, say, New York City or Chicago or San Francisco. Think of their stories, their secrets, their contributions to humankind. Maybe a Miss Em lives there, or maybe a family who's sold groceries to their community for four generations. You can be assured that the town has a Miss Gracie. But if we're honest, we have to confess there's a little bit of Miss Gracie in all of us. We have to embrace her, too. As the Desiderata instructs us, *"Speak your truth quietly and clearly; and listen to others, even the dull and ignorant. They, too, have their story."*

About the Author

Linda Harper is the new voice in today's literary world who brings a fresh and unique perspective. Through her work, Linda wants to inspire readers to pay attention to life's seemingly ordinary things that hold a world of extraordinary beauty. Her debut novel "Under the Fig Tree" is Linda's first attempt in this journey, that has proven to be a promising start.

She drew inspiration from the Southern landscape, etched in Linda's mind thanks to her childhood experiences in small town Mississippi. Linda now resides in Ozark, Missouri with her husband Phillip and is determined to write more stories that encourage readers to dive into life's simpler joys and mysteries.

www.ingramcontent.com/pod-product-compliance
Lightning Source LLC
Chambersburg PA
CBHW051946150726
47999CB00004B/1271